GAMBIT

This edition published by Regnery Fiction in 2018. Originally published by Forge in 2008.

Cataloging-in-Publication Data on file with the Library of Congress

ISBN 978-1-62157-781-2
eISBN 978-1-62157-851-2

Published in the United States by
Regnery Fiction
An Imprint of Regnery Publishing
A Division of Salem Media Group
300 New Jersey Ave NW
Washington, DC 20001
www.Regnery.com

Manufactured in the United States of America

10 9 8 7 6 5 4 3 2 1

Books are available in quantity for promotional or premium use. For information on discounts and terms, please visit our website: www.Regnery.com.

GAMBIT

BY

KARNA SMALL BODMAN

REGNERY
FICTION

ACKNOWLEDGMENTS

Welcome to the new and revised international thriller, *Gambit*, the sequel to my first novel, *Checkmate*. In this story, the country is once again facing a national security crisis with enormous and frightening consequences. And, once again, the White House turns to Dr. Cameron Talbot for answers.

Continuing to be inspired by programs first announced by President Ronald Reagan, "Cammy" rushes to update systems and technologies to today's standards, while Col. Hunt Daniels of the White House National Security Council staff searches for the culprits.

In researching this scenario I am indebted to contacts at Northrop Grumman, the Airline Pilots Association, Aerospace Industries Association as well as members of the military and the United States Secret Service for their assistance.

I also want to thank the staff of Regnery Publishing for giving me the opportunity to update and edit the original story of *Gambit* and make it available to fans of political and international intrigue everywhere.

I hope you will enjoy the four stories, Checkmate, Gambit, *Final Finesse* and *Castle Bravo*, along with my new thriller, *Trust but Verify*.

"Gambit" – *n*. In chess, an opening in which a player sacrifices a piece to gain a favorable position.

CHARACTERS
IN CHECKMATE

THE PRINCIPALS

Lt. Col. Hunt Daniels, Special Assistant to the President for Arms Control and Strategic Defense

Jayson Keller, Vice President of the United States

Dr. Cameron Talbot, Senior Project Director, Bandaq Technologies

WHITE HOUSE STAFF

Claudio Del Sarto, Special Assistant to the President for Central and South American Affairs

Austin Gage, National Security Advisor

Stockton Sloan, Deputy National Security Advisor

MEMBERS OF THE CABINET

William Ignatius, Secretary of Defense

Trenton LaSalle, Secretary of Transportation

Franklin Thorne, Secretary of the Department of Homeland Security

BANDAQ TECHNOLOGIES STAFF

Stan Bollinger, Chairman and Chief Executive Officer

Melanie Duvall, Vice President of Corporate Communications

Sarah McIntyre, Staff Scientist

OTHERS

Lt. Col. Pete Feldman, Old friend of Hunt Daniels

Nettar Kooner, Chairman and Chief Executive Officer of Sterling Dynamics

Derek Winters, Senator from Vermont

CHINESE NATIONALS

Wen Hu, M.I.T. Scientist

Zhang Li, Army General

Colonel Tsao, General's aide

Wai Yongping, San Francisco agent

PROLOGUE

Clear blue skies. Clear blue water. Not a harbinger of things to come. Captain Doug Purcell strolled on board Enterprise Air Flight 155 and glanced over at the three flight attendants preparing the cabin.

"Hey, Sandy. Glad to see you on board. Feeling okay about this?"

The young woman looked up, forcing an unsteady smile. "After those other two crashes, I can't say I'm excited about any of this. But . . ." she raised her outstretched hands and shrugged, ". . . guess we have to keep up a good front. I'll tell you one thing though, we don't have any children on board this flight."

"Doesn't surprise me. I wouldn't let my kids fly these days. Hell, I wouldn't let my wife or anybody else in my family fly, but we're not supposed to say that publicly, of course."

Doug moved into the cockpit, hung up his jacket, stowed his kit bag to the left of his seat, checked his headset and the flash light, emergency manuals and in-route charts and began to run through a few of his own check lists on his side. He checked his oxygen mask and smoke goggle and tuned the Nav receiver to the appropriate frequency for the departure procedure from the airport.

"Finished the walk-around, flight plans are fully loaded and the ATIS says the weather and NOTAMS are good to go," the first officer said as he slid into the right hand seat. "We've got good winds. Guess that's better than an ill wind," he muttered.

"I just have to figure the odds," Doug said.

"The odds?"

"Well, yeah. Thousands of flights. Two explosions, or whatever the hell happened."

"Sounds like Flight 800 all over again. I never really believed the explanation on that one, did you?"

"Not sure. But that was a long time ago. They've fixed the fuel tanks, so these latest crashes don't make a lot of sense. Nothing showed up on any radar . . . anywhere."

"I know. That's what makes it so weird. Anyway, guess we'd better get hustling here. I can't wait to get to Chicago. My wife's planning some sort of birthday bash for the twins this weekend."

"Sounds good. I need to get home too. I promised Lorri I'd get to our daughter's final soccer match. Her team's in first place." He looked over his shoulder and saw the last of their sixty-two passengers stowing their luggage and settling down. "Don't have a full flight this time, but I can't say that I blame them."

"Look, everybody's up in arms about those two crashes. NTSB doesn't have a clue, and we're getting cancellations right and left. This run from Logan to O'Hare used to be packed."

"I know. At least we've got a few risk-takers. And speaking of our passengers . . ." he closed the door, turned on the seat belt sign and cued Sandy to make her announcement.

The first officer then read off the check list and Doug began the routine. Hydraulic pumps-High, Pressurization-Set, Fuel pumps-On. They quickly went through the two dozen items, got on the intercom to the ground crew and heard, "Captain. We're all cleared. We've pulled the chocks. All doors are closed. We're ready for pushback."

Doug contacted ground control and was issued his taxi instructions, "Enterprise one-five-five, taxi to runway four right, via Alpha to Bravo. Wind is zero-five at twelve."

He then switched to tower frequency and said, "Enterprise one-five-five ready for take-off."

"Roger, Enterprise one-five-five. Cleared to take off runway four."

"Enterprise one-five-five cleared to go," Doug responded as he taxied to the runway. Once in position, he turned the transponder and exterior lights on, put his hand on the throttles and advanced the power toward the takeoff setting. As he accelerated down the runway, the co-captain called out, "Eighty knots." Then, "V-one . . . rotate."

"Positive rate, gear up."

He heard the radio call from the tower, "Enterprise one-five-five contact departure control on one-one-nine-point-four-five."

"Roger. Switching to departure. Good day." Doug turned to his co-captain, "Flaps up."

The co-pilot took the flap handle and moved it to the up position and then, as commanded, began the after take off check list as the aircraft began the initial climb to its cruising altitude.

In the main cabin, Sandy sat in her jump seat, gazing out at the morning sun as its rays peaked through a few wispy clouds on the horizon. "Sure is a gorgeous day," she said to the attendant next to her.

"Sure is. By the way, is that a new ring on your finger?"

Sandy held out her left hand and stared at the solitaire diamond in the simple Tiffany setting. "Yes. He gave it to me on our last stop-over in Chicago. We were having dinner at the Drake Hotel. That's where he usually stays when he's on his business trips. Anyway, right in the middle of the Cappuccino, he pulls out the little blue box and voila. Can you believe it?"

The other woman sighed. "You are so lucky. I have to admit I'm envious. Is he going to meet you when we land?"

Sandy hesitated. "You mean *if* we land?"

"Oh c'mon, kiddo. How long have we all been flying? So there were a couple of accidents. They happen. We know that. Relax. This is a pretty short hop. We'll be there in no time and you and Mr. Right can go back to the Drake and . . . make plans."

Captain Purcell checked his watch. Eight AM. *An on-time takeoff*, he mused as they headed east into the sun. He thought about the water below and pictured a weekend on their small powerboat docked at Belmont Harbor. If his daughter's soccer team ended up winning the championship, maybe they could take a couple of the girls out for a spin to celebrate. He began to bank left and head toward Chicago when suddenly he felt the plane shudder. "What the hell was that?" he shouted to the co-captain.

"Jesus. What's happening? Look! Fire indication on the left engine."

The plane began to bank harder to the left. The chime sounded four times. Doug pushed the button and heard Sandy screaming. "We have an explosion . . . a fire . . . passengers injured . . . wait . . . oh my God!"

Sandy's left hand was pressed against her forehead, the diamond creating a jagged prism of light as the sun reflected through the shaking windows. She continued on the intercom, her voice now coming in sobs, "Loss of cabin pressure . . . masks are down . . . the cabin is filling with fog . . . wind noise . . . pandemonium . . . can't help them now."

Doug heard the screams of sixty-two souls as he realized a hole had been blown in the wing root and fuel was pouring out. The shouts from the cabin continued. "We've been hit. We're all going to die! Help me. Help me. Please." Plaintive cries were mixed with screams of terror as Sandy's voice was heard over the din. "Captain. It's total chaos."

The master caution light was on. They were losing hydraulic pressure fast. "Holy shit. What the hell?" the co-pilot yelled. "We're losing control."

Doug shouted, "Full right rudder. Pull up. Pull up. Raise the nose." He called out to Departure Control, "Mayday! Mayday! Mayday! Enterprise one-five-five is declaring an emergency. We've been hit. We've lost control."

"What do you mean you've been hit?" the departure controller exclaimed. He turned to his supervisor. "No other aircraft in the area."

The supervisor stared wide-eyed at the radar panel. He saw nothing but Enterprise Air plummeting down. "Good God! Oh my God! Enterprise one-five-five. Departure . . . over . . . Enterprise one-five-five?" No response.

Doug struggled as fire burned through the main spar, then the left wing buckled and collapsed. The plane began to roll and spiral downward. He gripped the throttles with white knuckles. There was nothing he could do. A picture of his wife, her long brown hair flying in the breeze flashed through his mind. He closed his eyes and whispered, "Lorri . . . I love you!"

CHAPTER ONE

THE WHITE HOUSE

The VH-60N helicopter dubbed Marine One hovered over the helipad on the South Lawn of the White House. The impressive craft with two-hundred square feet of interior space housed a large cabin, lavatory, along with the latest communications equipment and missile defense systems. With seating for fourteen passengers, it was, in fact, a flying Oval Office.

When the pilot landed, a fold-down stairway was extended. In his new chopper, the president of the United States never had to duck down when making photogenic arrivals.

He gave a subtle sign to the pilot who nodded imperceptibly. It was the signal to keep the five flared rotor blades turning, thus drowning out the shouts of the gaggle of newsmen straining behind a rope rail at the Diplomatic Entrance to the White House.

"Mr. President . . . Mr. President . . ."

"Who shot down our planes?"

"Was it al Qaeda?"

"Were they missiles? Nothing on radar . . ."

"Did you feel safe flying today? Air Force One has systems. But what about Americans on planes with no protection?"

The president pointed to the rotors, cupped his ear in an *I can't hear you* gesture and hurried through the doors to the Diplomatic Reception Room. He walked past the painted murals on the curved blue walls and hurried into the hallway where his chief of staff was rushing to meet him.

"Is she here?"

"Yes, sir. She's in the Oval along with the vice president and Austin Gage."

"Good. Let's get the hell over there."

Dr. Cameron Talbot jumped up from the plush white couch as the president entered the room. She pushed a strand of strawberry blond hair back behind her headband and straightened the skirt of her navy blue uit.

Vice President Jayson Keller was standing near the white fireplace next to the national security advisor, Austin Gage. They had greeted her when she arrived and asked her to sit down for a few moments while they went over their notes. She had met Austin Gage some months ago and saw that the erudite advisor was clad in his trademark pin striped suit.

This was her first encounter with Keller, the charismatic second-in-command, and she could see why many had dubbed it the kangaroo ticket during the election. More strength in the hind legs. The VP exuded a kind of confidence most politicians had to practice constantly to stay in the game.

The president nodded to the two men but walked directly to Dr. Talbot and extended his hand. "Thank you for coming over on such short notice. Sorry I was a bit delayed on this trip. Our pilots are taking all sorts of circuitous routes these days. Please sit down. We need to talk."

He set his briefcase on the polished mahogany desk and pulled up a green striped side chair. The two others sat on the couch across from Dr. Talbot and opened their leather notebooks.

"Now then," the president began, "We all know the country's in an uproar over these plane crashes. Damn terrorists, or whoever they are, have pulled off a hat trick, and the market's down five-hundred points in the last three days. The Airline Pilots' Association is clamoring for new systems to protect our airliners, and nobody seems to know, yet, what's bringing down the planes." He turned to his NSC advisor. "Austin, anything new from your people?"

"Nothing yet, sir. No group has claimed responsibility. We've been coordinating with Janis over at FBI, with our best CIA people, Interpol, the British, the Israelis, we're even drilling the Russians because so many of their SA-7 Strela shoulder-fired missiles are floating around just waiting for some militant to pick them up. We had one report about how easy it is to get missiles from a former Red army base in Kutaisi, Georgia."

"Why is it easy at that place?" the president asked impatiently.

"First of all, there are no lights at night. They turn off the electricity from midnight until dawn, so it's pretty simple to move around undetected. Second, those places are guarded by soldiers who earn about fifty bucks a month. They're so poor, they can't even afford boots. They wear slippers. So some terrorist comes along and gives the guy a thousand dollars and bingo, you've got an instant fire sale."

"But who says it's one of their rockets?" the president pressed. "The FAA is telling us that in each one of these three crashes, nothing, absolutely nothing showed up on radar and nobody reported seeing anything in the sky. No planes. No missiles. Nothing."

"If I may, Mr. President."

"Go ahead, Jay."

The vice president shifted in his seat and leaned forward. "I know that at Logan they said they didn't see anything, but when that plane took off, it was first heading east, right into the sun. So it would be pretty hard to see anything from the Tower at that angle." He shook his head and added, "I admit the radar part is really puzzling though."

The president turned to Dr. Talbot. "As I'm sure you know, our Department of Homeland Security has got contracts out with a couple of defense contractors to adapt military defense technology to our commercial fleet."

She nodded and said, "Yes, Mr. President. I know about the contracts. Oh, and you can call me Cammy."

"Yes, Cammy. I remember. Last time you were in this office, you were here because you had invented a new technology for a defense against cruise missiles. It was an incredible feat, and we're all in your debt for your work on that project."

Austin Gage interjected, "You probably prevented another war between India and Pakistan when you deployed your system and took control of that weapon aimed at New Delhi."

Cammy saw a ray of sunshine glinting off of a picture frame behind the president's desk and reflected on her last meeting in this historic room. She had been with Hunt Daniels, a member of the National Security Council staff who had worked with her on Q-3 as her technology was called. He had helped her get funding from Congress, protected her when a foreign agent had tried to kill her, and finally made love to her in a way no other man had ever done. She had fallen for him. Hard. And now? Now he was overseas somewhere. On some sort of secret mission, she imagined. He hadn't told her, hadn't called her, hadn't seen her in months.

"Dr. Talbot? Or rather, Cammy? Are you all right?" the president asked as he scrutinized her serious expression.

She looked up, flustered. "Oh, I'm sorry. I was just thinking about our previous meeting, Mr. President. But now, how . . . I mean . . . what can I do for you now . . . sir?"

The president exchanged a glance with Jay Keller and explained. "About these crashes. Nobody thinks they were mere accidents. Everybody here believes they are part of a calculated plan by a very sophisticated terrorist organization. We don't know which one, but damn it, we're going to find out, and we'd better find out fast."

The vice president nodded his agreement. "Here's the situation. As the president said, we have contracts out to try and put military technology on our planes. There are several systems out there. Military jets have sensors that can tell when they've been targeted. They can send out flares or chaff so the missile might go after the decoys. But the jet still takes evasive action. A jumbo jet filled with hundreds of passengers can't exactly fly in loops and you can't have a bunch of decoys or flares landing on our cities and towns. It's different in a war zone. Now we need something else.

"There are different kinds of jammers they're also working on but the systems have to be serviced every 300 or 400 hours. We can't take our planes out of service all the time. That's just not practical. And besides, they're talking about at least two million per plane, and we've got something like sixty-eight hundred planes flying in this country."

The president picked up the discussion. "Another company is working on a system that would put a network of sensors all around airports so that when they detect some heat-seeking device, they can use a high-powered microwave beam to confuse the missile and send it off course. But that costs about $25 million per airport, and we've got a hell of a lot of airports, to say nothing about the ones overseas."

"And speaking of numbers," Austin inerjected, "there are at least half a million missiles of various kinds, many shoulder-fired models, that could be used to bring down a plane. Or a helicopter. We thought we were lucky when we hadn't been hit in the last 30 years. Did you know that over forty aircraft in other parts of the world have been hit by some sort of missile since the 70's?"

"I knew there had been a lot of attacks," Cammy said. "When I was doing my research I read about the Israeli jet in Kenya that was almost brought down years ago, so yes, sir, I'm well aware of the threat. In fact, I've been working on a new laser technique . . ."

"Precisely why you're here," the president said. "We know that your company, Bandaq Technologies, has been on the leading edge of several defensive systems, and we wanted to enlist your help, right now, in this fight to protect air travel. We can't go on like this. We've *got* to have a new system. It must be fast, reliable and more economical than what we have now because what we've got now is useless."

The NSC advisor interrupted. "I don't know that I'd go quite that far, Mr. President. It isn't that it's useless, it's just that it's taking too long and well, I admit it's too expensive. Our major airlines are all in financial trouble."

"Financial trouble?" Jay asked. "That's the understatement of the day. They're trying to save two million dollars a year not giving out pretzels, and you think they're going to pop for a new defensive system?"

"I know. You're right about that," Austin said. "But last I heard, the secretary at Homeland Security was pushing for another appropriation so they can pour more R&D money into those contractors to speed up the process."

"We'll let DHS handle the contractors. If they come up with something, fine. But meanwhile, I want a special project, and I think Dr. Talbot is the one to head it up. How about it, Cammy? Can you work with us on this?"

Cammy sat back, her mind racing. Yes, she had been working on a new scheme. She had been collaborating with a former colleague at M.I.T. who was one of the smartest guys in the research arena. But this was big. This was huge. The whole country was being held hostage by a terrorist trifecta, and now the president of the United States was turning to her to save not only the airline industry, but the whole economy. She was stunned.

"Well, Dr. Talbot? Can you tell us more about your new laser and if you think you can speed up the process?" the president asked directly.

Cammy took a deep breath and began. "You see, Mr. President, it's true that I'm working on a new laser. I have a researcher at M.I.T., and we've been exchanging ideas about a whole new concept."

"Go on."

"We had planned to pitch it to the Pentagon, but it might have commercial applications. It's an idea we've been working on for months now."

"Can you put it on a commercial jet?" The vice president asked, staring at her intently.

"I don't know. I mean, I'm not sure, yet."

"How long will it take to find out?" Austin asked.

"If we had a crash project? Uh, sorry, wrong term."

The president shook his head and shrugged. "Look, we're all rattled right now. The entire country is looking to us for answers, for solutions to this mess. I know this is a tall order, but after I saw what you did with your last missile defense system, I feel you're the right person to work on this one."

"But that was different, sir. That was a defense against guided missiles. I just had to figure out the frequency the terrorists were using to communicate with the missile, use that same frequency, go in, scramble their signal and redirect the missile away from the target. It was a completely different problem."

"I realize that. But from what we know about your new research, we want you to try. Will you do that?" the president implored.

Cammy took a deep breath and gave the only answer she could give, "Of course, Mr. President. I'll do everything I can. I just don't know how long . . ."

"We don't have much time. The press is hammering me on these attacks, and I don't see any recovery coming in the market as long as the threat is out there."

"Have you thought about shutting down the airlines like we did after 9/11?" Cammy asked.

"Not yet. If we shut down our airline transportation system, you're looking at a loss of at least fifteen billion dollars a week or more in revenue and cost to our entire economy. No, we can't do that. Not yet anyway."

He turned to Austin. "I want your staff to work every angle you can on the whole terrorism question. I want telephone and internet surveillance by NSA stepped up, and quite frankly I don't give a damn if lawsuits are filed this time. We've *got* to find these bastards." The NSC advisor made some notes.

The president then focused on Jay Keller. "And I want you to coordinate the new missile defense projects. Work with Dr. Talbot here and pull in anybody you think could be useful. Got that?"

"Why don't we bring back Hunt Daniels?" Austin asked.

Cammy jolted upright. Just hearing his name again almost brought tears to her eyes.

"Good idea," the president said. "He should be about finished with that project in South Korea, right?"

The NSC advisor nodded and said, "Yes, we can get him back. And now that you mention it, he worked with Dr. Talbot before. So let's give these two another try. Is that all right with you, Cammy?"

What could she say? She could hardly admit that she'd fallen in love with a man who might have dumped her. Her personal problems paled in comparison to the terrorism threats facing the country. She looked up at the president's expectant gaze and simply said, "I'll try."

CHAPTER TWO

ROCKVILLE, MARYLAND

Cammy stared into the iris recognition box to the right of the entry to her office and heard the click in the biometric device. She pushed through the double doors and headed down the well-lit hallway, her navy blue heels clicking on the tile floor.

She stopped at a door with a name plate that read VICE PRESIDENT OF CORPORATE COMMUNICATIONS and stepped inside. "Hey Mel, got a minute?"

Melanie Duvall looked up from a desk littered with copies of *Air Force Times*, *Jane's Fighting Ships*, and stacks of press releases. She smiled at her friend. "Sure. What's up?"

Cammy saw four boxes at the edge of the desk that read IN, OUT, LATER, MAYBE NEVER and burst out laughing. "So what's this? A new filing system?"

"Why not? Even with everything supposedly online, this place still produces so much paper, I had to get organized. Hey, what's with the fancy suit?"

"Just got back from the White House."

"The White House?" Mel answered, raising her eyebrows. "What's happening? Another new project to save the world?"

"Basically, yes," Cammy said. "You know that new laser system I've been researching with Wen Hu?"

"That smart guy at M.I.T.?"

"Yes, that one. Well, the president has asked me to speed up the process and see if we can apply it to commercial airliners."

"Wow! Because of all the crashes?"

"Exactly. But I don't know if I can do it," Cammy said.

"Well, if anybody can do it, you can. Have you told Bollinger yet?"

"Not yet. I'm heading to his office now. You work with him more than I do, how do you think he'll react?"

"You know, ever since he went from CFO to CEO he's become even more of a tyrant. All he talks about is profit and loss and his precious bottom line. I always wondered why the board picked an accountant to head up a big company like this."

"I know what you mean. I've always figured that an accountant was somebody who didn't have enough personality to become an economist," Cammy said with a wry smile.

"That about says it. Ever notice how he always has that constantly affronted look? Like whatever you're about to say will be disregarded, so why bother?"

"That's what I'm afraid of. On the other hand, this is a project requested by the president. So how could he possibly object?"

"I don't know, but he'll probably think of something. By the way, I was going to call you later to see if you want to go running with me tonight? Weather's decent, and we could hit the canal. What do you think?"

"Tonight? I thought you had your karate class."

"I usually do," Mel said. "My Sensei got the flu or something, so he cancelled this week. I need the exercise, so why don't you take a break and come along?"

Cammy checked her watch. It was already late afternoon and she wanted to talk to her boss and then spend some FaceTime with Wen Hu to see how they could advance their work on the laser. On the other hand, she'd been working long hours all week and would like to do the run. "Sure, let's go for it. Tell you what, when I get finished here and back to our building, I'll buzz your apartment, and maybe we can head out around seven. Okay?"

"Sounds like a plan."

Cammy closed the door and took the elevator up to the executive suites. She stopped at the secretary's desk and asked, "Is Mr. Bollinger available? I've got something important."

The woman picked up her phone and buzzed the boss. "Excuse me, sir, but Dr. Talbot is here. Can you spare a moment?" She paused and then nodded to Cammy to go right in.

The short, wiry CEO motioned Cammy to a maroon leather chair in front of his massive walnut desk. "What's up, Doctor? You don't venture to this floor very often."

Cammy sat down, crossed her legs and began. "I just came back from a meeting at the White House with the president, the vice president and the national security advisor."

Stan looked at her, his dark eyes showing more emotion than usual. "The White House? I didn't know you were going over there."

"Yes, well, it was a quick call. They asked me to come over for an emergency meeting, and I wanted to tell you about it right away."

"What did they want?"

"It all has to do with the plane crashes. They want me to scale up my new laser program and see if it can be adapted for use on commercial airliners as a defense against these types of attacks."

Bollinger rubbed his chin and thought for a moment. "You say he wants to see if your laser can be put on our fleet of airplanes?"

"That's right."

He stood up from his desk and started pacing across the room. After a few strides, he turned to face her and exclaimed, "No way! Your division is no where near operational status. I hope you didn't tell them you could do it."

"I said I would try," she answered defiantly.

"Jesus Christ! That laser idea of yours is never going to work on a large plane. I only let you spend your time on it because . . . well . . . you had one success with that Q-3 project, and I figured I owed you a little freedom. But this time, I have a sense it'll never work. And if the press finds out we're supposed to be applying some new technology to save lives and it doesn't work, our name will be mud in the entire defense industry."

"But Stan . . ."

"No buts. This could be a fucking disaster! Look what's happened to Sterling Dynamics."

"What do you mean?"

"You know that Sterling has one of those DHS contracts to try and put a shield around airports for just this sort of defense, and their systems aren't working worth a damn. At least not yet anyway. And every time there's a story about how it's taking them forever to get the damn thing to function, their stock price takes a hit. I don't need that kind of trouble."

"But the president asked . . ."

Stan walked over to the large picture window and stared out at a bank of trees that had been planted to block his view of the employee parking lot. "I don't like this. I don't like this at all. Three planes have been shot down. Market's going to hell. Nobody wants to fly anywhere, and the president thinks you're going to save his ass? Give me a break."

Cammy shifted uncomfortably in her chair and posed a question. "So you're telling me to defy the president of the United States and not help when I *might* be able make a difference here? You've got to be kidding."

He turned around to face her again and skewered her with a piercing gaze. "I'm never kidding. Or haven't you noticed?" He sat down at his desk, leaned back in his leather desk chair and thought for a long moment. Finally, he shook his head and gave an audible sigh. "As I said, I don't like this. It's going to be a boondoggle, I'm pretty sure of that. In fact, the only decent part of this equation is that we could bill the administration for time and materials to re-tool that crazy idea of yours." He paused again and pursed his lips into his familiar frown. "What a mess!"

Cammy matched his stare, keeping eye contact. She didn't look away. She wasn't going to be intimidated by this short-sighted little man who never seemed to have an original thought. All he ever did was to demand projections, cost estimates and constant reviews. Yet, here she was, a scientist with nothing but new ideas.

After she had left the White House, she had analyzed her work on the laser and begun to get excited about the possibilities of bringing a new version on line to help the president. Not just the president, but the entire country.

As she sat still and kept her head raised in anticipation of her boss's next comment, Cammy felt more emboldened than ever. If he wouldn't let her pursue this, she'd figure out a way to do it somewhere else.

As if reading her mind, the CEO leaned forward and asked her a question. "You really think this laser is going to work, don't you?"

Cammy slowly nodded her head. "Look, Stan, I know you have other priorities. But right now, the country doesn't. This project could be the most important thing we've developed since . . . well, since Q-3."

"Okay, I'll give you Q-3. It worked. I still don't think this thing's going to pan out, but I'll give you a couple of weeks. And if it doesn't, I'm pulling the plug. I can't afford to keep your whole department heading down some blind alley. Do you understand me?"

"Perfectly," Cammy replied.

"One more thing," Stan said as Cammy was about to stand up, "For heaven's sake, keep it out of the press. Tell Melanie to shut up about it. If that thing doesn't work, I don't want Sterling or any of our stockholders finding out that we have some fiasco on our hands. Got that?"

"Yes, sir. I most certainly do."

Back in the lab, Cammy reviewed her latest set of notes on the laser project. She hoped her friend and fellow scientist would be available. She desperately needed to talk to him, see if she could persuade him to devote more time to their collaboration, and hopefully figure out a way to double-time their experiments.

She had met him when she was working on her Ph.D. at M.I.T. They had been in the same class. When she opted for a job with Bandaq, he accepted an offer to stay in Cambridge to teach and continue his research. They had worked on a couple of projects together, and now she needed his advice and expertise more than ever. She set up her computer, keyed in his number and after a few rings saw his image on the screen.

"Dr. Wen Hu here."

"Hello, Doctor, it's Cammy."

"Yes, Cammy, I saw the ID. How are you today?"

"Quite frankly, I'm in a bit of a jam here."

"I seem to have some troubles of my own. Do you remember we talked about my attending that symposium at the University of Chicago?"

"Yes, but then you said you changed your plans at the last minute because of some work you needed to do."

"That is correct. But do you remember when that conference was?"

"Wait a minute. Uh, it's going on this week, isn't it?"

"Quite so. The plane that was shot down at Logan Airport? I was originally scheduled to be on board."

"Oh no," she exclaimed. "Thank God you changed your plans."

"Yes, indeed. But I find it to be a rather strange coincidence."

"What do you mean?"

"I'll tell you in a minute. But first tell me your situation."

"I was called into a meeting at the White House this morning," Cammy said. "And this must stay just between us, okay?"

"Most certainly. But the White House. I'm impressed. What was the subject?"

"It's about our project. They keep track of our R&D, so they know about my work on a new laser. Now they want me to see if I can speed up the research and try and apply the technology to our commercial planes as a new protection device."

"Because of the recent attacks, of course."

"Yes. Everyone is so up in arms about the crashes, they're trying everything. Or maybe I should say, they'll try anything."

"I see what you mean," he replied. "I've had a few new ideas about our project. Let me make a suggestion. Could you come up here so we could work together for a day?"

"Sure, why not? When would be a good time?"

"The sooner the better. Maybe tomorrow."

"Let me check." Cammy brought up another screen to check her calendar, saw that there was a staff meeting and a luncheon briefing by their internal control officer, but she figured she could miss both of those. "Yes, I could do that. It's just that I don't want to . . ."

"Fly," he finished her sentence. "I completely understand. I know the train ride is quite long, but we can be in touch if need be while you're on the train and then when you get here, we'd still have several hours to work together. Could you do that?"

"Yes. I'll make a reservation on the Acela. But wait a minute, tell me more about that cancelled flight."

There was a long pause. Wen Hu then said in a halting voice, "It's rather difficult. I'm worried that my research, our research, may be compromised."

"Compromised? How is that possible?"

"I have been contacted several times by agents of my country asking me to come back to China and work there. They know I have no desire to go back to Beijing. I want to stay in America and do my work here. But they are most insistent. Rather ironic, isn't it?"

"Ironic?" Cammy asked.

"Yes. The government there is insisting that people like me, ones who came on a legal H-1b work visa, go back, but when the American immigration officials try to repatriate the thousands who come here illegally, China refuses to take them."

"Yes, I've heard about that. Guess they're trying to pick and choose."

"I suppose you are right. Then again, while China won't take back forty or fifty thousand people who fled the country for a better life, they are insisting that the ones who came here for religious reasons must return."

"Our government wouldn't force those people to go back."

"I know. So I guess it is a bit of a standoff. Now in my case, they have been exerting enormous pressure. They make new threats all the time."

"But if you say no, they can't force you to go back," Cammy protested.

"They obviously think they can. You see, they are very interested in my work. They want it for their own defense projects. They don't want me to get the patents. They want them."

"Okay, so they're competitive. Just say no."

"It's a bit more complicated than the old Nancy Reagan program, if I may be so bold. You see, they have been making threats about my family back in China. They're saying that if I don't return, they will either see that my family is never allowed to emigrate or that I may not be allowed to continue my research."

"But that's awful. I mean, here we are working on a new technique that might be able to save lives when a bunch of crazy terrorists are shooting down our planes, and who knows? Their planes might be next. Why in the world would they be so nasty as to want to take your technology or harm your family? Competition is one thing, but we've been cooperating with China on all sorts of projects and trade deals. Why get so difficult?"

"I'm afraid you don't understand the Chinese mind. We, I mean China, ruled the world as they knew it for a thousand years, and they are determined to be pre-eminent once again. They see America and its strength in technology as just a short detour on their road to domination again, and anything they can get their hands on at this point is fair game to them. As for the trade deals, certainly they trade with America. But look who still has the big trade deficit."

"I see your point. Look, I don't want you to be in any kind of danger. That's just not right. But wait! You don't think this has anything to do with your being scheduled on the flight do you? How would they have known your itinerary?"

"They probably saw the notice of the Chicago symposium, and they speculated about which flight I would take. On the other hand, even though I've got a great firewall, maybe they've hacked into my computer. I do change all my passwords frequently though."

"This is crazy. If they want your . . . our . . . technology, they wouldn't try to kill you and take dozens of other people with you when the plane went down. This is just too preposterous," Cammy said.

"Yes, I agree it is a crazy thought. I am probably being overly paranoid."

"Well, with all that's going on, I can certainly understand your concern. Then again, I don't always believe in coincidences. But this is almost too weird to contemplate. Now let me ask you something. Do you still want to work with me on the laser?"

"Yes, I do. I will not capitulate to their demands. Please come up here tomorrow and let's see what we can do for your White House. I shall be waiting."

CHAPTER THREE

THE WHITE HOUSE

The cameramen in the back of the East Room of the White House jockeyed for position and adjusted their tripods as members of the press corps grabbed seats and shuffled their notes. A buzz of conversation bounced off the white walls and polished wooden floor. The gold drapery was the only adornment in place to mute the noise.

The room had been set up quickly for this impromptu news conference, and everyone was anxious for it to begin. The print reporters were close to their evening deadlines, and the TV correspondents needed time to grab the shortest logical sound bite from the president, add their own voice-over explanation and do their live stand-ups on the North lawn for the next top-of-the-hour cable news headlines.

The cameras began to roll, filming a long shot of the president coming down the impressive hallway with its deep red carpet, stepping up to his podium with the presidential seal affixed to the front and a set of American flags behind. He pulled out what looked like a short announcement.

"Ladies and Gentleman," the president began. "The United States airline system has suffered three major attacks in the last week. We are well aware of the effect of these senseless terrorist acts on our transportation systems, our stock market and the well- being of the American people, but especially on the families of those who have lost their lives. I am here to reassure you that I have deployed every resource at my disposal to locate and disarm the group responsible for so much loss of innocent life. Make no mistake. We *will* find these cowards and they *will* be prosecuted!

"At this time, our Department of Homeland Security is working with several of our top defense contractors to speed up the process of applying existing military defensive technology to our fleet of commercial airliners. We are examining a number of systems, not only American made, but we are also working with allies such as Israel which has developed what they call "Flight Guard," a device which uses an advanced radar-based missile warning system to detect shoulder-launched missiles that may be fired at their airplanes. Their technology, called "Dark Flare" diverts a missile away from its target and is not visible to the naked eye as it operates only in the infrared section of the spectrum. Therefore, it will not harm any passengers who may be on board.

"I want to assure the American people that our best scientists are working night and day to perfect a variety of missile defense systems, and we will deploy them as soon as we possibly can.

"Finally, in order to ensure a heightened stage of alert on the part of all local, state and federal employees, especially those working or stationed near our nation's airports, the Department of Homeland Security has raised the threat level from orange to red. Now I'll be glad to take your questions."

In the second row, the reporter from USA Today leaned over and whispered to the anchor from CNN, "Orange to red? This administration is so confused, I'm surprised he didn't raise it to plaid!"

"Mr. President?" A voice called out from the front row.

"Yes. Alan."

"Mr. President. You're saying that you want to put military systems on commercial airplanes to protect against shoulder-fired missiles. But the FAA has announced that no such missiles have been detected on any radar in any of the three crashes. Maybe they were fuel tank explosions. How can you be so sure they were missile attacks?"

"Obviously, this is all under investigation. A team from the National Transportation Safety Board is in the process of raising Enterprise flight one-fifty-five right now. As soon as that wreckage is available, our best people will be examining it along with the other two planes, and we will announce the results as soon as we have them. But meanwhile, I feel it only prudent to take every step necessary to protect our airliners.

"One other point that I meant to make at the outset. I have asked the vice president to head up a team working on these new technologies, and my national security advisor will coordinate the search for the terrorist group that may be responsible for these heinous acts." The president looked down at his watch and then glanced over at his press secretary who took the cue.

"The president is on a very tight schedule. Just one more question please," the press aide called out.

The president pointed to a young woman in the back. "Yes, Carmelita."

"Mr. President. If you're turning the issues of technology and terrorism over to the vice president and NSC advisor, does this mean that you're going to continue with your usual schedule and concentrate on issues you outlined last week such as countering Russian moves to encourage their proxies in the Balkans in an effort to redraw those borders, releasing more animals from the endangered species list and planning the upcoming visit of the president of Mongolia?"

A collective groan rose from the press corps as the president looked exasperated. "I want to assure the American people that I will first focus on this new threat to our lives and to our economy, but yes, my staff will continue to pursue other issues that are important for our wellbeing and that of our allies. Now if you will excuse me, I have another meeting to attend."

"So the ole man is abdicating, huh?" a reporter from the *New York Times* muttered to his colleague in the next seat. "Sure looks like he's turning over the reins in anticipation of the upcoming election. Makes him look awfully weak though."

"Yeah, but we all know he wants Keller to succeed him. Maybe he's a bit craftier than we thought."

"That would be a refreshing change. Let's get outta here so we can file something."

"What's your headline?"

"Out of this? Beats the hell outta me."

"Yeah, this guy is known for his ASTRO performances."

"Right. Always Stating The Really Obvious!"

CHAPTER FOUR

GEORGETOWN

Deep green leaves provided a heavy canopy over the trail along the edge of the Canal in Rock Creek Park. An early summer evening usually drew several runners to the winding path as a balmy breeze offered temporary relief to over-zealous athletes. Cammy wore khaki shorts and a white tee shirt while Melanie, with her jet black hair tied in a ponytail, ran in multi-colored warm-ups that matched the color of her hazel eyes.

"Glad you suggested this," Cammy said as they jogged past a picnic table where a young couple sipped lemonade and kept an eye on two youngsters tossing a Frisbee nearby. There were a few groups of runners far ahead of them and one lone jogger quite far behind. For this next stretch, they seemed to have the path all to themselves. "I've been so slammed with this new laser project, I've been cutting back on my work-outs."

"You'd never know it. You're still thin as a rail. Of course, all I ever see you eat in the cafeteria these days is a salad," Melanie observed.

"Hey, I had a BLT today. But now that I think about it, I eat the same food all the time."

"What do you mean?"

"Well, a BLT has bacon, lettuce, tomato, toast and maybe some mayo dressing, right?"

"Right."

"Then on days when I have a salad, I have lettuce, tomato, bacon bits, croutons . . . that's toast . . . and some sort of dressing. See? Same food. Kinda boring, huh?"

"Well, on that subject, I'm still collecting those silly recipes, you know," Mel said.

"You mean for that restaurant you fantasize about owning some day?"

"Yep. Wanna hear the latest from my don't-ever-serve-this-file?"

"Sure."

"Well, in *Southern Living Magazine* I found Pickled Okra Ham Rolls and Tomato Chutney Cheesecake."

"Who eats that stuff?" Cammy asked with a grin.

"Southerners, I guess. And how about this from the *Wall Street Journal* of all places? They wrote about some restaurant in Denver that serves nachos with Prickly Pear Cactus sauce."

Cammy laughed through her panting breaths and said, "That reminds me of what a congressman told me about the difference between a cactus and a caucus."

"Yeah? What's what?"

"A caucus has the pricks inside."

"Not bad," Melanie giggled as she slowed down and stopped to tie her shoe. When she leaned down, she looked around and noticed that the single jogger was gaining on them. She quickly stood up and said, "You mentioned a congressman, and that reminds me, I wanted to tell you about my big date last night."

Cammy jogged in place until Melanie started again. "With Winters? That senator from Vermont? So does he drive a Subaru hybrid, eat granola and have a weekend place at Stowe?"

Mel laughed again. "Well, some of that. He actually does drive a hybrid."

"And I'll bet he takes the tax deduction too."

"Sure. Doesn't everybody?"

"Most everybody," Cammy admitted. "But that guy seems to spend all his time ranting and raving over proposed tax cuts. He always wants to raise taxes, have the government spend more of our money on Lord knows what, and I just read that he wants to hold hearings on this whole airline disaster. How can you be interested in that guy anyway?"

"Killer smile!" Mel answered. "He's a real SNAG, you know."

"You mean a Sensitive New-Age Guy?" Cammy snickered. "C'mon, Mel. He's a senator, a man who discusses issues all day long. But they're usually his issues, certainly not yours."

"I have to admit we argue about most everything, but how can I explain the magnetism? Sometimes I think I'm in love with him."

"You're not in love with him, Mel. You're in love with the way he makes you feel."

Mel tossed her head, her ponytail flapping in the breeze. "But you thought you were in love with Hunt."

Cammy picked up the pace and muttered. "That was different. At least I *thought* it was different. At the time."

"Sorry, I shouldn't have brought it up."

"No, that's okay. It's just that in that meeting this morning, they said they were bringing him back from wherever he was, and so we may be working together again."

"But Cam, that's great. Maybe you can work things out. I mean, he'll be here and . . ."

"No way," Cammy said firmly. "After all we went through, you'd think he would have the decency to say good bye and at least tell me where he was going. Or call. Or something. No! I'm not going through that again. I spent enough nights crying over that man. Now it's time to concentrate on something far more important than a botched love affair."

"Well, I just thought . . ." Mel's comment trailed off when she glanced back and saw that the lone jogger who had been behind them their entire run was still there, but now he was getting closer.

There were usually a few more people around, but now that evening shadows deepened over the trail, the others had evidently finished their runs and headed home. Except for the guy a little bit back, they were very much alone.

She turned back to Cammy. "Look, I didn't mean to open up old wounds. But when it comes to Derek Winters, you can't fault me for having fun with him once in a while. And going out with a senator has been fun. About his opinions, though, he told me he was really undone by that last accident, or whatever it was. Seems there was a group of students from Vermont on board, heading to an environmental conference or something. Now he's vowing to get to the bottom of those crashes if he has to bring down the whole administration to do it."

"Sounds like he's starting his campaign for the presidency rather early, wouldn't you say?" Cammy observed.

"I guess. He'll probably run against Jay Keller."

"Well, I trust you won't tell him anything about my project. Stan wants to keep this thing under wraps in case it doesn't work."

"Don't worry. Say, it's getting kinda late. Think we should go back?"

Cammy slowed down, and they both turned around to see the lone jogger suddenly run right up to them. He was wearing black running shorts, a black tee shirt and had a cap pulled way down over most of his face.

As Cammy and Melanie tried to jog past him, he reached out, pushed Melanie to one side and grabbed Cammy's arm. She started to struggle and was stunned to see the man snap open a knife and hold it to her throat. "Dr. Talbot, you're coming with me."

"I'm not . . . let me go . . . who are you anyway?" she stammered as she strained against the man's tightening grip.

"It doesn't matter who I am. It's who *you* are that matters. If you're smart, you'll come along."

"I'm not going anywhere with you . . . you . . ." she tried to wrench away but the knife grazed the side of her neck and she cried out.

Off to the side, Melanie had been thrown to her knees. Now, she stood up, raised her hands to a boxer-like stance, her knees were slightly bent, about a shoulder-width apart. She lifted her right knee to waist high and pivoted on her left foot with her left heel pointing at the attacker. She thrust out her right leg, leading with the outer edge of her foot to cut him down at the back of his knee.

He was thrown off balance, leaned backwards and lost his grip on Cammy as the knife skittered away. She pulled away as Mel shouted, "Run!" But Cammy stood there transfixed by the scene. No way would she leave Melanie alone to deal with this brute.

Who was this guy? What did he want? Why was he coming after her? She had no weapon. She frantically looked around for a rock, a branch, something. She had that dreadful sense of panic she had felt several months ago when she was the target of a terrorist who was trying to steal her Q-3 technology and ship it overseas

The man had tried to run her car off the road and had actually killed a young man who had been working for her at Bandaq. Back then, Hunt Daniels had arranged FBI protection for her. He had even taken her into his home for a while. She had been terrified then. Now she was terrified again as she watched in stunned silence as her best friend was engaged in a life and death struggle with this . . . this what?

Melanie then sprang up and crashed her right elbow into the bridge of the man's nose. He screamed in pain, fell down and clutched his face with one hand as blood poured out of his nostrils. But he still was able to grab Cammy's left ankle. He yanked her down. She broke the fall with her hands and looked up just Melanie was getting into a new position.

Mel's last move looked like a soccer player shooting a penalty kick as she smashed her foot into his groin, and he doubled over in agony.

"C'mon. C'mon. Whoever he is, he won't be down for long," Mel ordered.

Cammy scrambled to her feet. She and Mel took off and with adrenaline coursing through them both, they made it back to the car in minutes, never stopping to look back.

They jumped into Cammy's Audi A4, locked the doors and roared out of the parking area. She was driving as fast as she could and hardly noticed bits of blood dropping onto her tee shirt. "Damn. The man actually cut my neck," she said, pressing one hand to her throat.

Mel reached for her purse on the floor, found a Kleenex and held it to Cammy's wound. "Too bad he got you there. You don't want a scar on your neck."

"Who cares about a scar on my neck?"

"Well, it's a place that shows. Besides, your neck is so long, it would make Nefertiti jealous." Mel dabbed at the blood and added, "Just trying to change the subject to calm you down, that's all."

It was only after they were safely back on the Rockwood Parkway that Cammy took a deep breath and said, "I'll be okay. But my God, Mel, you were incredible!"

"Better than pepper spray, huh?" Melanie said with a hint of bravado.

"You bet. Your Sensei would be proud."

"I guess. He's been telling us every week that women have to learn to defend themselves."

"Well, he's right. But who in the world was that guy? I've never seen him before in my life, but he knew my name," Cammy said, her breath finally evening out as she made the turn onto Massachusetts Avenue.

"I have no idea. Then again, you were all over the newspapers a couple of months ago when you pulled off that trick with Q-3. Maybe it had something to do with that. And we'd better call the police."

"Which police? This city is so mixed up. The Park police have the sidewalks and parks. The Metro police have the streets. The Secret Service has the White House grounds. Embassy security is all over town."

"Yeah, but where is one of them when you need 'em?"

"Who knows? I guess we could make a report to the Georgetown force, but what are they going to do? The guy, whoever he is, will be long gone. There weren't any other witnesses. I doubt if I'd recognize him again since he had that stocking cap thing pulled down a ways. Did you get a good look at him?"

"No. I was too busy figuring out which vital part to hit."

"Trouble is, the police in D.C. are so busy with murders and break-ins, they're hardly going to get excited about an attempted . . ." she turned to Mel, "just what was that anyway? An attempted kidnapping or what?"

"I don't know but it sure was weird. Guy had been following us the whole way. He certainly knew who you were and was bent on taking you somewhere. But where?"

"And why?" Cammy asked, a forlorn expression covering her face.

CHAPTER FIVE

THE WHITE HOUSE

The vice president stepped out of his black limousine and headed to the basement entrance of the White House on West Executive Avenue, the driveway between the West Wing and the Old Executive Office Building. A sign indicated that the large Empire building erected in the late 1800's to house the State, War and Navy Departments was officially named the Eisenhower Building, but everyone still called it the OEOB.

Jayson Keller had a spacious ceremonial office there on the second floor, but he spent most of his time at another smaller office on the first floor of the West Wing. His first meeting today was in the Situation Room.

He walked under the awning, opened the door to a small vestibule and nodded to the secret service agent sitting at a desk just inside. He turned right into a reception area with a beige carpet, a sofa and several wing back chairs covered in a dark cherry chenille fabric.

The clock on the wall next to the door to the Situation Room complex read seven AM. Another agent sitting to the side punched in the key code so the vice president could push through the heavy door and head in to his meeting. He dropped his cell into the protective bin where everyone had to leave their devices when entering a secure facility and strode into the conference room where he took his place at the head of the long mahogany table.

The NSC advisor was already seated to his right, talking animatedly to Trenton LaSalle, the secretary of transportation. Trent's parents had emigrated from Jamaica and settled in New York. He had worked hard growing up, been awarded a scholarship to NYU and got his first job with a railroad. He spent his entire career there, finally working up to the position of CEO of the company. When he became active in politics the president tapped him for his Cabinet. On this day, the secretary looked agitated as he shuffled his notes and looked over at the vice president. "Good morning, Jay."

"Morning Trent. I see you've brought your briefing papers."

"Always. We've got a lot on our plate today."

"We'll get to that in a minute." The vice president checked his watch and asked, "Where are Thorne and the SecDef?"

"DHS just called to say that the secretary is on his way. As for Iggy, I think he just stopped to pick up a cup of coffee. He'll be here in a minute."

As if on cue, William Ignatius, the secretary of defense, bustled into the room carrying a mug in one hand and a bulging briefcase in the other. The stocky man still bore a military demeanor even though he had retired from the Marine Corps twelve years before. No active member of the military could serve as secretary of defense. You had to be out at least seven years because it was a long-standing tradition that the military is run by a civilian appointee unless Congress voted a pass as they did when General Mattis was tapped to head up DOD. He settled into a brown leather chair on the far side of the conference table. "Traffic from the Pentagon's a bitch this morning. Sorry to hold you up."

"No problem. We're just waiting for Franklin Thorne." A moment later, the door opened again, and a haggard looking man came through, buttoning his jacket on the way. Jay watched as the secretary of the

Department of Homeland Security took a seat next to Iggy and mopped his brow with a handkerchief. The man's face looked perpetually sad, with jowls hanging down like a basset hound. He looked lonely in his suit. It hung on his body and gave the image of a man with the weight of the world on his shoulders instead of on his slight frame.

"All right, gentlemen, we'd better get started. Oh, and Austin, thanks for pushing your staff meeting back to seven-thirty. I need you here, and I thought we'd better get an early start. We'll try to keep it brief. As you all heard in the president's news conference, he's asked Austin here to coordinate the search for the terrorist group or groups responsible for the latest attacks on our airplanes. And he's asked me to get a team in place to try and speed up every line of technology we have in the works so that we can deploy a defensive system on our commercial fleet as soon as possible.

"We all recognize the gravity of the situation," he continued. "The market was down at the close yesterday, and God knows how it will open this morning. So let's get a status report."

He turned to the man with the coffee colored complexion. Trent, why don't you start. Bring us up to speed on the transportation situation."

"It's bad! Not only have all the airlines had massive cancellations, but three of them are saying that if this goes on for another month or, God forbid, if there's another attack of some kind, they're talking chapter eleven.

"The pilots are screaming. First it was the fuel tank situation. We thought we had that under control. Then it was the hardened cockpit doors. Then they wanted guns in the cockpits and more air marshals. Now they want a missile defense system. But then so does everybody.

"And one more thing, the Air Traffic Controllers Union just held a meeting, and they're talking about a possible strike if we don't do something drastic."

"A strike?" Jay exclaimed. "They can't do that."

"They did it before. Well, we all know that. Even though they had signed an agreement not to strike, they went out anyway even when the president at the time offered them an eleven percent raise."

"What did they want then? Wasn't it some outrageous number as I recall?" Iggy asked.

"Yes. Back then, they demanded a one-hundred percent raise. And when they walked, well we all know that President Reagan fired them. But that was then. Now, we've got much bigger problems."

"Why would they walk now?" Thorne asked.

"They're demanding safety systems, just like the pilots. And they want that dome system." He turned to the DHS secretary. "You know, the contract that calls for the fancy radar to be set up around all the airports to detect missiles when they're fired."

Franklin Thorne interrupted. "Well, I for one agree with them. I don't mean the strike thing. I mean, I agree that we should be moving faster on that new radar. In fact, I wanted to get your support for an emergency appropriation for both of the contractors who are working on new defensive systems."

"But Frank, remember, nobody saw anything when those planes went down. Nothing showed up on radar, so why would we want to go ahead and spend more millions, money we don't have right now, on some new-fangled radar system when we don't have a clue that it'll solve our problem?" Jay asked.

"I thought I heard the president clearly say that my department is working to speed up the process of finding new technologies to protect our planes and that's exactly what I'm trying to do," Secretary Thorne replied. "In fact, I've got meetings scheduled up on the Hill later this morning with the heads of several committees. We've *got* to get another appropriation. I trust I can tell them that you all agree . . . with the president, I mean." He cast his glance around the table but none of the other men made eye contact with him.

"Look, Frank, you do your best on those contracts," the vice president said. "The president also indicated that we were talking to our allies and looking at various ways to protect the country. And let me interject at this point that Austin and I met with the president and a very special scientist yesterday. I'm sure you all remember Dr. Cameron Talbot." They all nodded.

"The president has tasked Dr. Talbot to work on her own defensive system as well. She has a new laser technique that just might work on our planes. We don't know yet, but she may be on to something. She's on our team. And by the way, that's not for public consumption. We don't want her name or her research to make the news." The vice president glanced around the table and everyone murmured their agreement. "So Frank," Jay concluded. "You handle your two companies, we'll handle the rest."

"But you can't count on that thirty-something woman to come up with a brand new technology in a short period of time. That's nonsense. Our two companies have been working on their systems for years," Frank countered.

"That's the whole point," Jay said. "They're taking too long and spending too much money as it is, and what have we got for our investment? Zip. Zilch. So far anyway."

"But?" Frank sputtered.

"I said you can handle them. For a while longer, that is." He scanned the room again and said, "By the way, where's the secretary of state? I thought he would be back here by now."

Austin answered, "He's still in Minsk."

"Belarus?" the vice president asked. "Why is that trip taking so long?"

"Moscow's trying to cut off their gas again, and he's trying to tie up some trade issue while he's there."

"Well, see if you can get his ass back here. Seems like he's always out of town when we need him. Last week he was at that conference on investing in Wales."

"Why? Are we running out of them again," Thorne asked with a frown.

"Not the mammals, the country, for God's sake."

"Sorry," the older man said, looking down at his papers again.

The vice president was trying to keep his temper in check. It seemed that every time they had a crisis, the head of DHS turned out to be part of the problem rather than part of the solution. He had been trying to sell the idea of an additional appropriation all over town like a regular Willy Lohman. And he was just about as successful.

The president had once said the head of DHS was a thorn in his side. At first Jay had laughed at the use of his name, but now he understood why everyone always seemed exasperated with the little weasel. The trouble was, the president could hardly fire the guy in the midst of this crisis. No, in this situation, they'd have to put up a good front and all work together.

"Now then, Austin, what do we have on the terrorist groups? Anything yet?" Jay asked.

"We've tasked NSA to increase their surveillance. As for the CIA, I dare say most of their seventeen thousand employees are working on this problem in one way or another. They have a possible lead in South America. I don't have anything firm on that yet, but I'm bringing Hunt Daniels back to put a terrorism task force together and analyze what we've got. Our agents are fanning out throughout the Middle East, the Philippines, Indonesia, Pakistan, Russia as well as Venezuela and Central America. Remember, there are tons of missiles in Nicaragua left over from when the Soviets armed the Sandinistas. So there might be a connection there."

"All right. Keep focusing on the groups and the weapons. And, Iggy, see if your people can prod those defense contractors to get their asses in gear on adapting those military technologies and work with Frank on the timetable."

Jay then looked over at the secretary of transportation. "And Trent, I want you to ride herd on the FAA and NTSB to get results from those crash sites. We need a thorough analysis, and I mean right now." Trenton nodded. The vice president continued, "And do you think you can tamp down the controllers for a while?"

"I'll do my best, sir."

"Good. Finally, I hear the senator from Vermont is about to call for hearings on the crash investigations and everything else we're doing," Jay said. "As if we needed that kind of distraction."

"Yeah. It'll probably be a group grope in terms of looking for some-body to take the fall for all of this." Iggy remarked. "It sounds like your likely opponent wants to turn this crisis into a political circus."

"And if I fall off my high horse," Jay said with a wry look, "I'm sure the senator will have a camera crew on hand to record the moment."

"They won't need any prodding," Iggy said. "The press always shoots the wounded."

CHAPTER SIX

SEOUL, SOUTH KOREA

Lieutenant Colonel Hunt Daniels cradled a large cup of coffee in his hands as his guest sipped tea and looked nervously around the comfortably appointed living room. They were meeting in the private residence of the U.S. ambassador to South Korea, a house built in the traditional Korean style that stretched outward in long, clean lines but had a roofline that curved up at the sides.

It was rare to hold a private meeting in a place usually reserved for diplomatic dinner parties and family gatherings. But Hunt had pressed the ambassador to invite this important scientist to a place where he could feel absolutely safe. And safety was a top priority right now.

"Don't worry, sir, everyone in this household has been cleared by our security forces. You can relax here."

The older gentleman took another sip of his tea and settled back in his chair. He glanced over at the interpreter who nodded reassuringly. "I am sure you are right, Col. Daniels. It's just that I fear for my life, for my family, for all of us who have managed to escape from Pyongyang."

"We understand completely. And let me assure you that we will do everything in our power to maintain a safe place for you to live, and to work. For as you have said before, you want to continue your work on nuclear research for the benefit of mankind. Not the north."

"What I meant was," the gentleman reiterated, "I am willing to help this government in exchange for a promise of safety and a promise that they will work to disarm the maniac who rules my home. I have no wish to work on weapons systems that may be trained on innocent people. Ours especially have suffered enough. They are weak and starving while the government is strong and eating well. They made us work in the tunnels built deep into the ground where their weapons are stored. Yes, they fed us to keep us going, but the rest have nothing. In fact, they lowered the height limit for soldiers to four feet eleven inches. The people are so malnourished, they cannot grow."

"We know," Hunt said, his deep blue eyes focused on his guest. "But what's important now is for us to learn as much as we can about their systems, their continued miniaturizing nuclear warheads as well as new missile delivery systems and who is buying them."

"You have seen their tests of the Taepodongs as well as others," the man replied. "Now there is so much more. I never thought I would get out. When the South Korean agents put me on that raft and floated me down the river to safety, it was a miracle. But I came with nothing on my back, only what's in my head."

Hunt leaned his six foot two inch frame forward and said, "That's exactly what we're interested in. We know that North Korea has helped both Pakistan and Iran with missile technology, but we also need to know what they are exchanging with China and other countries. We have now had three attacks in the United States, attacks on our commercial airplanes. Hundreds of innocent people have been killed, and in addition to my work here to investigate nuclear proliferation, I've been asked to follow every lead to discover who might be responsible for these crimes. Any help, any thoughts you may have about ground-to-air or even air-to-air missiles would be most helpful."

"I understand your concern. My work was focused on nuclear warheads, but I do know that some of my colleagues were exchanging other technology with China and Russia."

"What kind of technology?"

"Some of it involved smaller missiles, I believe. But I have no details. On my nuclear issues, it was work I was forced to do, and now I must atone for my contribution to their madness," he said lowering eyes.

Hunt motioned to a steward to pour some more tea and then said reassuringly, "We understand the pressures you were under. We know about the threats, the intimidation. But now you are free, and we're going to do everything we can to keep it that way."

"Will you stay here and help me, Col. Daniels?" the scientist implored.

"I'm afraid I'm being recalled to the United States to work on our own problems."

"The airline attacks?"

"Yes. But I've been working with our staff here as well as the president's staff at the Blue House to ensure your safety. They have set up a safe house for you in the Itaewon shopping district. It is a busy area. Not a place where anyone would look to find a famous nuclear scientist. You will blend in well and be surrounded by people who care about you. So do not worry."

Hunt reached in his pocket and pulled out a small cell phone. "Here. We want you to keep this."

The man inspected the device. "Can I keep in touch with you this way?"

"Yes. We have this number, and here is a list of contacts. Someone will come to you if you need anything. And when it is time for another meeting, they will call you on this phone."

The scientist stared at the small cell. "Very good., This is good. I just hope their agents cannot listen in."

"Don't worry. I doubt if they can."

They finished their discussion and Hunt ushered the scientist out to a waiting car. He handed him a satchel filled with new clothes, shoes and toiletries. The gentleman unzipped the top, glanced inside and a broad smile covered his face. "I thank you, Col. Daniels. I will wait for a call to meet with your successor. And I wish you a safe flight back home to America."

"Do you think that guy can really help us out?" the ambassador asked Hunt as they sat down to dinner a few hours later.

"Oh yeah. That was quite a coup when those South Korean agents spirited him out of Pyongyang. I'll bet that slimy dictator is pretty pissed off right about now."

"I'm sure you're right. And this man seems especially bright. I really liked him. He's smart, brave, dedicated. Don't see too many of those coming south these days."

"Not for lack of trying, though."

"Yes, of course." The ambassador finished his salad and the steward removed the plate from the right and served a large plate of lamb and rice pilaf from the left.

"We're sorry you have to go back to D.C.," he said. "You've been invaluable to us here, interviewing this scientist and working with others who have escaped that regime. The trouble is, I fear for all of them here. The North Koreans who have been able to get away are usually followed by others who are bent on taking them back, or killing them instead. And not only Koreans, I've been quite worried about people on my staff and people like you. Word gets around about who's working on what in this city, and that's why I assigned that guard to stay with you 24/7."

"I know. I appreciate the body guard." Hunt took a bite of his lamb and then checked his watch. "I think we've been able to accomplish quite a lot these past several weeks. We had a meeting with the defense minister's top guys this morning to analyze the latest intelligence on the threat of FOB's from a number of different countries."

"You mean Fractional Orbital Bombardment?"

"Yes. Then we talked about multiple independently targeted re-entry vehicles in the nose of a war-head. You know, if there are fifteen in there, they go out in all different directions," Hunt said.

The ambassador picked up his glass of wine and said with a wry smile, "You mean, MARVing their MIRVs?"

Hunt chuckled. "Well, yes. I'd laugh about it if all of this new stuff weren't so damned dangerous."

"I know. You're right. But back to our new scientist, since you're leaving in the morning, how about checking in, see if he's settling in all right. What do you think?"

"Good idea." Hunt pulled out his cell phone, flipped it open and dialed a number.

After several rings, a gruff voice answered. "You think you can steal our scientists?" the menacing voice announced. "You're wrong. We've taken him back where he belongs and people like you will pay."

CHAPTER SEVEN

SAN FRANCISCO

A teenager with chunks of dark hair spiking up haphazardly just above his forehead signed for the two large packages and handed the pen back to the delivery man. He brought the boxes inside where two other men were lounging on a faded divan, picking at a plate of sushi and watching a soccer match on TV.

"Got the latest," he announced.

"Open 'em up and see if they're any better than the last ones," the older man ordered. "And while you're up, get me another can of Jolt."

The young man quickly complied, handing over the caffeine laden drink and started to open one of the boxes. He slashed the tape, pushed aside the packing materials and lifted out a long metal case. It occurred to him that it could have carried a couple of fishing rods rather than this particular cargo. Perhaps that's what the delivery people thought when they transported these things.

He opened the case and examined the long rods inside. "These look better," he said, quickly fitting two pieces together.

"Just make sure you can put those other heads on 'em while you're playing around," the boss commanded. "And when you're sure they're compatible, split everything up and ship them out. Just like the order says."

"Got it. But how do we know the others are going to do things right next time?"

"We don't know," the older man said. "Those idiots already screwed up one operation in D.C. and another one at Logan. Let's just hope Boston got the message."

"Boston was pretty good with the last plane, even if the right people weren't on board," the young man countered.

"Yeah, but this new problem takes a little more imagination. It's not a point-and-shoot deal any more. This time it's gonna take more brains."

"Are you sure they should be targeting one of our own again?" the teenager asked.

"Shut up, you fool. You know he's a traitor."

"But . . ."

The older man turned away from the TV set, pulled a small .22 from his pocket and aimed it at the young man. "I said shut up! Anyone wants to question our mission here answers to me. You got that?"

"I only wondered . . . I mean, as I've said before, I don't think. . . ."

"You think too much." A single shot hit the young man in the chest. He staggered and grabbed the edge of the table, sending the metal case and all its parts crashing to the floor.

"Little bastard never did fit with our program. We're all part of a big plan here. We all agreed to help our country regain what is ours. Always has been ours. Nobody said it would be easy. But we agreed. And besides, they're paying us a ton to do things right. I think that little shit has been in *this* country too long to understand what's important." He reached for the can, took a long pull and turned to the other man on the couch. "Get up and get rid of that sorry excuse for a countryman. We've got work to do."

CHAPTER EIGHT

THE WHITE HOUSE

"Hunt, welcome back," Austin Gage said, motioning to a small round table with four chairs off to the side in his expansive West Wing corner office. Rather than reserving the Situation Room for small sensitive meetings, the NSC advisor's office was a good venue. It was right down the hall from the Oval Office and sported special glass windows that precluded any eavesdropping microwaves from snooping embassies with a direct line of sight to the building.

"The vice president is going to join us," Austin said. "He wants to hear about your time in South Korea, and then we've got a whole list of things to cover. I trust you had a good flight back?"

Hunt was tired. He had been away for almost two months on a number of secret missions to try and negotiate safeguards for older nuclear weapons while he also investigated newer systems that seemed to be proliferating at the speed of a NASCAR race.

He had been in remote places where he was never certain which were the good guys or bad guys. He had been shot at, nearly run over twice and finally had ended up being the hand-holder for that defector from North Korea. At least he had felt relatively safe in South Korea, even though it turned out he couldn't protect that poor scientist. The ambassador had sent several of our agents to search for him. No luck with that operation. Either they must have quickly returned him north, or they simply eliminated him. What a tragic waste of a good man.

Yesterday, Hunt had flown in a military plane from Seoul to Hawaii and then onto Andrews Air Force Base. As soon as they landed he had gone into his office in the OEOB to be greeted by stacks of memos and a safe filled with classified documents. He had scanned the latest ones about the terrorist attacks, but was far from feeling up-to-speed on anything.

He had been relieved to hit the sack in his own home in Georgetown last night, not even caring if the maid hadn't remembered to restock the cupboard with his favorite brand of coffee. At least he'd gotten a few good hours of shut-eye and then the best shower he'd had since leaving town. He always marveled at the water pressure in Washington. A lot of things were screwed up in this city, but a good shower wasn't one of them.

He ran his hand through his sandy blond hair and responded, "I'm fine, sir. Just need a little time to decompress and get through the latest intel, I guess."

He turned to see Jayson Keller stroll in, clad in a tailored grey suit and crisp white shirt with a red-striped tie. The man was a couple of inches shorter than Hunt, but his muscular build made him appear to be the most powerful man in the room. Hunt stood up to greet the vice president.

"Morning, sir."

"Good to see you again, colonel."

The three men sat down at the round table and opened their leather notebooks. Each one had several pages of notes, and Austin began the meeting. "Hunt, give us a quick run-down of the situation in South Korea and whether you saw anything at all that could be connected to these airline attacks."

Hunt told them about the defection of the North Korean scientist who had been debriefed, but later captured, and how the government in Pyongyang was getting more brazen by the hour. He went on to summarize what he had learned about North Korea's ballistic missile capabilities, and said he heard they may have been exchanging new technology for smaller missiles from other countries such as Iran.

"With respect to their constant saber-rattling, or rather missile-rattling," Hunt said, we know the Chinese keep objecting to our deployment of various missile defense system in South Korea and Japan. But I'd like to put a Decision Directive together recommending that DOD assign several of our Navy cruisers and destroyers to the area. Many of those ships are equipped with the Aegis missile defense system. They could patrol the Sea of Japan . . ."

"And what? Try to shoot down the next missile North Korea decides to test? Austin asked, raising his eyebrows.

"Precisely," Hunt answered.

"And what if we miss? It would be a humiliation and further embolden that crazy dictator."

"First, we wouldn't announce our intentions in advance," Hunt countered. "Second, if we miss, of course the world would know we sent up an interceptor. But our commanders could simply say we are testing some new systems to see how close we could come. And third, if we destroy it, North Korea would have to reassess their entire program and all the money they are spending on missiles that won't be able to hit anybody. Or at least we'd be sowing tremendous doubt into their calculus."

"It's true their economy is so dismal and their people are completely impoverished, except for the chosen ones who live and work in the capital for the government," Austin said. "I heard that they're now practically drafting dwarfs to serve in the military. As for their being the ones who are messing around with our commercial airplanes, what would be the point?"

"Remember what the Lilliputians did to Gulliver?" The vice president muttered.

Hunt shook his head. "Yeah, but still. I couldn't pick up any intel connecting North Korea to those attacks. Besides, they'd have to know that if we ever figured out they were responsible, we'd flatten their capital."

"True," Austin said. "And when you talk about a motive, I finally have the manifests here from the three planes that were downed. We've been going over these lists to see if there might be specific people who were the targets."

"Anything obvious?" Hunt asked.

"A couple of interesting possibilities. The Spanish ambassador was on the first plane with several of his ministers. They were going to some festival, I believe."

"That could be al Qaeda," Jay Keller suggested. "Remember what they did with those trains in Madrid some years ago?"

"Yes. We've been looking at that. In fact, I had our director of European Affairs give me a paper on that whole history." Austin pulled out a memo and pointed to a particular paragraph. "Interesting history if you'll recall. Remember how that Muslim Army came across the Strait of Gibraltar from Northern Africa back in the 8th century? They fought a huge fight against the King of Spain. After a few battles, the Moors were running the place, from the coast to the Pyrenees until they were kicked out in the late 1400's."

"I know they ran things for over seven centuries," Jay observed. "In fact, they're the ones who actually brought a decent civilization to Europe. They had kept the writings from the Greek philosophers and from the Roman and Egyptian civilizations too. They had libraries and marble balconies when London was a village full of mud huts."

"That's the thing," Austin said, "The Moors really had it all going. Commerce, culture, agriculture. But of course, it was too good to last. They ended up like what we see in the Middle East today with Arab groups breaking up into different factions, fighting amongst themselves. And then when the Christians finally got their act together, they were able to drive the Moors out of Spain in 1492,"

"Same year Columbus discovered America," Hunt interjected.

"Yes, but it turned into a huge conflagration with Christians killing what was left of the Muslims and the Jews too or sending them into exile."

"And so, to follow your point," Jay said, "the Muslims have been furious for seven hundred years and are trying to push the borders back to their heyday. And since we always get in the way, we're a good target."

"Makes sense to me," Hunt said. "Of course, that's been our analysis of their mission ever since 9/11, or even before that. It's just that up to now, they've always managed to take credit for their biggest attacks, and I don't think we've had anybody own up to these things, have we?"

"No," Jay said. "Not a one. Seems like we're looking for a Moriarty here rather than some crazed jihadists."

"Well, we've got to keep digging on that connection. But there are other possibilities we have to consider," Austin said. He pulled another memo out of his stack. "As long as we're focusing on the Spanish, I suppose we should check out ETA. They used to set up all kinds of explosives at airports, so it might follow their M.O. Except for the fact that they declared a permanent cease-fire back in 2006."

"Right," Jay said. "Then the Spanish government started a whole round of talks about the future of the Basque region. Haven't heard much about it lately, though."

"Maybe some of the factions held off," Hunt said. "I don't remember any of them actually disarming."

"We'd better check out our sources on that group again, though it seems awfully far-fetched. Besides, I don't see where they would get the right kind of missiles. Let me check these manifests again." The NSC advisor perused one sheet and handed the others to Jay and Hunt.

"I don't see Spanish types on the second plane," Hunt said, "although there are a couple of names here we could look at again."

"No," the vice president said, shaking his head. "This doesn't feel right at all. I think we've got a much bigger agenda on our hands here. What about the South Americans? Venezuela has imploded and signed another new pact with a couple of the other socialist regimes down there. And they're doing absolutely nothing to stem the flow of drugs into this country. Do you see any connection with the drug cartels?"

Hunt answered. "Our guys are watching the Norte Valle Cartel. They've sent something like five-hundred tons of cocaine up here through Mexico in the last ten years or so. And that's gotta be worth . . . what? Ten billion anyway. Then again, I don't see the connection. We're their best customer. Why irritate us any more than they already have?"

"Their leaders are on our 'Most Wanted List.' Maybe that's enough to set them off," Jay suggested.

"That doesn't seem right either," Austin said. He reached over to the telephone on a side table and buzzed his secretary. "Lucy, could you send in some coffee? We may be a while longer here. Thanks."

"Okay. The Russians," Hunt said. "When I was over there trying to negotiate those proliferation agreements, I heard about all sorts of missile systems that they've got stashed away in Georgia, the Stans. You name it, they've got it, and we all know their Army guys love to make a buck on the side so they'll sell anything to anybody. And as for their latest variety, remember that contract they signed to sell a couple million dollars worth of S-300PMU1 surface-to-air missiles to Vietnam? How about that connection?"

"The Russians? I wonder," Jay said. "The FBI has been working on that problem for years. Remember the men who tried to smuggle a Russian shoulder-fired missile into New Jersey a while back? He was an arms dealer with some sort of scheme to sell missiles from Russia to people he thought were terrorists right here in America. But they were federal agents. Talk about a sting for stingers!"

"Yes, but that was just one dealer trying to make a buck. Again, motive, gentlemen," Austin intoned. "We have no motive. But I think we should follow-up on all of these ideas, just to be sure. Meanwhile, Hunt, since you've been away, you probably haven't heard that we're trying to fast-track a number of the technology contracts that DHS has out now."

"The ones where they're trying to put military defensive systems on civilian planes or around airports?"

"Yes, those and one other track."

"What's the other one?"

The vice president intervened. "While Austin here is focusing on the terrorist angle, the president has asked me to concentrate on those contractors but also to work with Dr. Cameron Talbot because she has a new laser technology that just might be adaptable."

"Cammy?" Hunt said, snapping his head up at the mere mention of her name.

"Yes. I heard you had worked with her before on that India-Pakistan situation. She was pretty spectacular with that near-disaster in Delhi."

"Hunt was there too, you know," the NSC advisor said.

"Oh yes, that's right. Good work on that one."

"Thank you, sir," Hunt said, his mind reeling. So now he was going to work with her again. But would she even speak to him after his long absence? He knew he should have figured out a way to let her know what he was doing. But it was a top secret mission. He had been instructed not to tell anyone where he was going, who he was meeting with or how long he'd be gone. Sure he should have figured out something. Some way to say that he really cared about her. Some way to ask her to wait until he got back and maybe they could take up where they'd left off. That is if he ever got back.

On the other hand, the last time he'd been through a major affair, he'd married the woman, and it had been a disaster. His wife hadn't taken to the military life at all and ended up leaving him for some investment banker in New York who actually came home for dinner. So even though he thought the world of Cammy, he had held back, figuring that if he got home, alive, he'd wait and see how he felt and take it from there.

Now he'd have to try and sort it out at the same time he was trying to figure out who the hell was killing all of these innocent Americans.

CHAPTER NINE

EN ROUTE TO BOSTON

ammy showed her ticket to the gate attendant in the cavernous Union Station and hurried through the doors to Track Eighteen, the early morning Acela bound for Boston. Hundreds of other travelers who were also avoiding air travel scurried by her, some pulling small carry-ons, most juggling briefcases, newspapers and tall Styrofoam cups of coffee. At least they hadn't banned those from trains. Yet.

Cammy not only didn't want to get on an airliner right now after the three crashes, she'd developed a terrible fear of flying ever since he father had been killed when his Air Force jet went down. She still had occasional nightmares about his plane exploding in the air, with horrible images of her father struggling to eject but having no time to escape the inferno.

Every time she had been faced with a long trip, she had tried to figure out a way to drive or take the train. The one exception had been her travel to India when she had taken her Q-3 missile defense system over seas to protect New Delhi when they feared a terrorist attack. That assignment had been on a military jet. At least she had been surrounded by her staff.

She'd always felt that a commercial flight was such a lonesome experience. First, she had to relinquish any semblance of control over her life, and she hated that. Then, if anything did happen, she would be surrounded by other passengers who were strangers with no reason to care about her safety. No, it was a bad scene any way she pictured it.

She hurried on board the second car of the train and pushed her way down the aisle. She spotted a porter and asked where the "Quiet Car" was. She always tried to get a seat in that one because passengers weren't allowed to talk on their cell phones, and you could actually get some work done on the ride. If she had to use her phone, it was easy to simply walk back to another location and place a call. By the time she found the right car though, she saw that it was already filled.

She kept on walking forward. When she got to an available one, she took a seat by the window, hung her beige blazer over the back, pulled down the tray table and lifted her laptop out of her briefcase. Just then an overweight man in a seersucker suit wedged himself into the seat next to her. She quickly jammed the arm rest down between them and hoped he wasn't the chatty type.

The conductor made his announcement about the stops coming up at BWI, Wilmington, Philadelphia, New York and Boston. He then told everybody to have their tickets out. If they didn't have a ticket for train number twenty-two-seventy-one, they'd better get off. She pulled her ticket out, knowing that she was in the right place.

As the train pulled away from the station, she began to mentally review the routines she wanted to check with Wan Hu. After the first hour she saw that her seat-mate was dialing a number on his cell phone. It was only seven o'clock in the morning and this guy was already calling somebody?

He started talking loudly about the meeting he was going to have in New York. Just great. That meant she'd be sitting next to this bozo for the next two hours. She tried to ignore him but he kept talking as if the other party were way down the hall. The conversation went on for at least fifteen minutes and Cammy couldn't concentrate on a single thought.

When he finally ended the call, she reached down to her briefcase and pulled out a paperback book she'd brought along. She opened it to the first chapter and began reading aloud. By the time she got through the first paragraph, the hefty one nudged her and said in an irritated tone, "Do you have to read out loud and make so much noise?"

"Not any more than you had to talk so loudly on your cell phone . . . sir."

He glared at her and turned back to his copy of *Sports Illustrated*. She finally shut her book.

When they arrived in Boston, Cammy stood in the taxi line and gave the driver an address in Cambridge. They headed north over a bridge at the Charles River, crossed Memorial Drive, and went another quarter mile to Kendall Square. She got out and entered a grey stone building, part of the large M.I.T. complex.

It was good to be back. Cammy had graduated from Stanford at the top of her class and then studied for two years at M.I.T. She often wondered whether she should have stayed here and spent her time simply researching missile defense systems rather than going to work for Bandaq Technologies.

She had never been exposed to the business world. She had been raised on military bases since her father had been an Air Force pilot. She remembered how her father told her that several years before she was born, he had been watching television with him at home one night when President Reagan announced something called his *Strategic Defense Initiative*. It sounded exciting to her at the time. It was a program where he asked scientists to figure out how to knock down incoming missiles that might threaten the whole country. She had told her father she wanted to grow up to be a scientist and knock down the missiles. Of course, she was only nine at the time.

When she was a teenager, she had been completely devastated when a Sidewinder missile miss-fired causing her father's plane to crash. She had always blamed the manufacturer of that missile, Sterling Dynamics, even though an investigation hadn't really proved anything. So she had gladly signed up when she had a job offer from Bandaq, a company that was a direct competitor of Sterling's.

As she looked back on it, she knew that she was not only trying to live up to her childhood dream of saving the world from errant missiles, but trying to exact some sort of revenge from Sterling for her father's death.

She had made some major inroads when she was able to implement her first big invention, the Q-3 system which targeted cruise missiles and send them off course. That trumped anything Sterling had in their pipeline. But they were still in business. Big business. And they had snagged one of the DHS contracts to protect the airports. Maybe she could review the bidding, set up a new cross-rough, and trump whatever Sterling was touting. Perhaps this time, she'd finally win the hand.

She walked down the hall to the door with Dr. Wen Hu's name on it, knocked and went inside. The young Chinese man jumped up from his desk and extended his hand. "Dr. Talbot, Cammy, so good to see you in person after all of our work at long distance. Here, let me take your jacket."

He motioned to a table next to his desk. "You can put your bag over there. But first sit down and talk to me. You've had a long journey. We have much to discuss. I took the liberty of bringing in lunch for us both. I have it here in my refrigerator. As I recall, you prefer bacon, lettuce and tomato. I have that along with a fruit salad and some brownies. Will that be all right?"

She laughed softly. "You remember well, my friend. And yes, it's great to be with you again too. I have some notes I made on the train, and I need your advice on the new laser feature we've been working on. For a while there I was having problems." She smiled and explained, "There were times I have to admit I felt my mind was a blank slate, and I could never find the chalk."

"I know that feeling. Sometimes it's like the Sunday crossword in the *New York Times*. You think you've got almost all the words in the right rows, but in the end nothing works right."

"You've got it. But here, let me show you my latest iteration. As I explained before, the president is totally focused on finding a new technology to protect our planes. The trouble is, nothing was ever picked up on radar at any of the crash sites. So in a way, I'm worried that we're working on something old to defeat something new. Something we can't even see."

"I too know about the radar. And I have a new idea. I didn't want to discuss it over the phone or even on email because as I told you, I am worried about my communications being compromised."

"I know you said that. Have those agents been back?"

"Yes. Well, not in person this time, but I had a call last night warning me to start packing for a return trip to Beijing."

"What did you say?"

"I hung up on them."

"Have you told anybody else about the threats?"

"Who can I tell?"

Cammy thought for a moment. I have some ideas. As soon as I get back to Washington, I'm going to talk to the vice president."

"The vice president of the United States?" he asked in an awed tone.

"Yes. I'll be working with him on this project. I'm sure he'll want to set up some sort of protection for you. Don't worry. We'll think of something. Now, back to your new ideas."

Wen Hu went to his drawer and pulled out some papers. "Here. I have some information from a colleague in China. We keep in touch."

"Wait a minute. If you think their agents are monitoring you, what do you use? One of the one-time anonymous accounts?" she asked.

"Sometimes we use Anonymizer.com or Findnet.com. And sometimes he just sends one of his studies to my PO Box. It's amazing how old-fashioned mail gets by the agents. His last study was intriguing. It was about a new imaging seeker that can differentiate between certain kinds of targets. Between different kinds of airplanes for example. It uses a high-resolution camera that decides what kind of object it is, on a CCD array, a charged coupled device. It takes a picture of the plane, tracks it on a screen and follows it. So it only goes after the plane, not any chaff or decoys."

"Incredible!" Cammy exclaimed. "But even if they had such a system, our radar would pick up a missile it had on board unless. . . ." She thought for a long moment and said, "Do you think there's any possibility that China is working on some kind of new stealth technology?"

"That I do not know. All I can do is speculate."

"Well, think about this. What if they have some sort of a stealth missile, and they put this new camera on it to track the planes? They could conceivably program it to go after a particular kind of plane, shoot the missile which follows the right image and destroys the plane, without any radar detection at all."

Cammy sat still, her mind racing to envelope the new concept. Yes. Yes. It was a bit far-fetched. A bit futuristic, with kind of a sci-fi element to it. But yes, they just might be on to something. She quickly ran through the basic elements of their laser experiments and thought about a new approach.

"What about dumping the idea of a single laser aimed at a target and instead, we develop a three hundred sixty degree cone by taking several lasers that fire rapidly on low power. I mean, if a missile has a camera feature, maybe we could blind it and interrupt its journey. We intercept its guidance features, and later when it opens its eyes again, so to speak, the plane has now moved out of its field of regard. So it can no longer engage. It would be too late."

Wen Hu's eyes grew wide with excitement. He grabbed a tablet and began making calculations. Cammy reached for another one and also began jotting down notes. They worked together for the next several hours, interrupting their exchanges only when it was time to eat their sandwiches.

"I have a modification," Wen Hu announced. "Perhaps we could add a pulse modulation. This could handle any counter-measure that a missile may have built into it."

"And a pulse laser could work with our computer program to have that CLIRCM capability," she said.

"Yes. Closed loop infra-red counter measure."

Cammy jumped up and hugged the man. He looked completely startled. She said, "This is so exciting. This could be it. This could really be the solution. That is if we've actually figured out the problem. At least it's a start. A really good start." she said, her face glowing.

Wen Hu took her by the shoulders and looked into her eyes. "I always said I would enjoy working with a genius!"

She laughed out loud and reached over to grab her shoulder bag. "Tell you what. We need more work to perfect this thing, but what say we take a quick break to celebrate?"

"I'm sorry I don't drink, you know."

"I don't mean champagne or wine or anything. How about coffee or ice cream or something?"

"Good idea. There is a Starbucks about a block down, right around the corner. They opened it the year after you left here. Do you want me to go?"

"No, I'd like a short walk. Write down everything we just said, give me ten minutes, and I'll be right back with a mocha smoothie or something else equally sinful." She shoved her notes into her purse and left the building. She was happy. Buoyant. What a day.

After so many months working on the laser, weeks of missing Hunt, days of tragic news about the crashes, now, finally, she felt she just might be on the right track.

She couldn't wait to get back to the White House and tell Jayson Keller about their new ideas. She didn't know how Stan Bollinger would react. He'd probably complain about the cost of setting up new tests. She mused that her boss was the type who kept expanding his bandwidth of bitching. Or was it that he was narrowing his bandwidth of approval?

At this point, she couldn't care less. How in the world could the man object when it might mean a major increase in their defense contracts to say nothing of possibly saving thousands of lives in the future?

She almost skipped along the sidewalk and then spied the big Starbucks logo with the "Help Wanted" sign in the window. She went inside
and stood at the back of a long line. She checked the board to decide
which drinks to order, looked at her watch and saw that she still had
another two hours before she'd have to head to the station for the long
ride back to Washington. The line wasn't moving very fast. She watched
the clerk behind the counter who didn't seem to understand a couple of
the orders. She stood there for several more minutes and thought to
herself, *why do I always get the trainee?*

Fifteen minutes later, armed with two Java Chip Frappuccino's, she
headed back to the lab. She had been thinking of a few more variations
on their idea and couldn't wait to get back to her friend. She was walking
quickly now and had just reached the small walkway leading to his building when suddenly, she heard a loud explosion.

The blast shattered windows, sending shards of glass and concrete
out into the street. The force knocked her down, along with several other
students who had gathered on the sidewalk. Screams were heard inside
the building as people started streaming out the front door, some covered
with blood, others holding a hand to their mouths, or limping on
injured knees.

Cammy couldn't believe the sight. She scrambled back onto her feet,
the Frappuccino's rolling away creating a foamy mess on the nearby
grass. She ran to help a woman who had tiny pieces of glass embedded
in her arm. People came racing toward the scene. Students on bicycles
rode up, drivers slammed on their brakes, and a few hellish moments
later, sirens could be heard in the distance.

She moved toward the door. More people were trying to get out.
They were bunched up at the opening, coughing as smoke billowed
through the small set of doors. She saw fire down the hall and grabbed
a student who had just run out of the building, holding his hands over
his face. "Can you tell me . . . where . . . what happened? What was it
. . . do you know?"

The student stumbled. She reached for his arm to guide him to the safety of the street. "Please. Can you tell me what it was? I mean, where did it happen? Do you have any idea?"

The young boy blew his nose, his eyes still watering as he tried to talk. He muttered in a strained whisper. "It was the lab. The lab of Dr. Wen Hu."

CHAPTER TEN

WASHINGTON, D.C.

The two men meeting in the private Abraham Lincoln suite in the historic Willard Hotel couldn't have looked more different. Stan Bollinger, CEO of Bandaq Technologies, was a short, wiry, somewhat reclusive accountant, elevated to the top position by impressing the board with his cost-cutting and dedication to building shareholder value for their stockholders. He hardly ever stood still, his nervous energy obvious as he paced around the room examining paintings of old Washington landscapes.

Dr. Nettar Kooner was tall, outgoing and almost ebullient in his better moments. He had emigrated from India to work for Sterling Dynamics. Now, as its chairman and CEO, he relied on hand-picked teams of young highly-educated men brought over from New Delhi's top schools along with a bevy of Washington insiders to advise him on every aspect of their product lines, contracts with the Pentagon, sales to favored allies, relations with Congress and the general state of the economy.

The Willard seemed like the perfect place for Kooner's company to maintain an account since the term "lobbyist" was coined by General Ulysses S. Grant right there in the foyer. Kooner wasn't only trying to gain favoritism with Congress, he was always looking for a new patent, a new opportunity, or a new deal. And it was a possible deal he had come to investigate during this secret luncheon meeting with one of his key competitors.

As Kooner welcomed his guest into the spacious living room area with its off-white walls, deep blue and gold carpet and dark blue drapery, he remarked, "After all these years trying to wrest contracts away from your outfit, I guess it's high time we got together to see if we could somehow pool our resources and gain an advantage when it comes to dwindling tax dollars."

Bollinger stopped and sat down on the sofa in the massive suite reserved for the occasion. He reflected that this was an apt setting for their discussions, a place on Pennsylvania Avenue half way between the White House and Capitol Hill, where Presidents Lincoln, Grant, Coolidge and Harding, among others, had stayed, and where any number of high level conferences had been held over the years. He recalled that Lincoln had agreed to meet with members of the so-called Peace Conference back in 1860 in a futile effort to avoid the Civil War. He wondered if this meeting would be more successful.

"You're right," Stan said. "I've been thinking a lot about things we could do together rather than competing all the time. For one thing, I'm sure you're ramping up your R&D on that DHS contract for the airports."

"Indeed. We're getting pressure not only from Franklin Thorne, who calls almost hourly, it seems, but the vice president is now riding herd on our contract as well."

"I've been reading about that. On the other hand, you have your other line of ground-based missile defense systems that you've been selling to Taiwan and other countries, I believe."

"Yes, we're in the process of shipping our latest systems over to Taipei for initial testing, though they performed flawlessly here in our test areas."

"So I've heard," Stan said. "And you know about our Q-3 system which was developed to take control of cruise missiles."

"Who doesn't? Ever since that Dr. Talbot of yours pulled off the trick in New Delhi, my country has been in your debt. Her Q-3 system must have turned into quite a cash cow for you boys," Kooner remarked. "Then again, our ballistic missile defense platforms might turn out at least to be cash calves," he said with a laugh.

"And on that subject," Stan observed, "it occurs to me that if we were able to work out some sort of merger agreement, we could combine our missile defense systems and be able to offer package deals to any number of countries concerned about ballistic as well as cruise missile threats."

"A very interesting idea," Kooner said. "Then we'd both have some skin in the game." A knock on the door prompted him to get up and usher in a waiter pushing a large cart laden with dishes of lobster bisque, medallions of veal in a mushroom and Marsala wine sauce and a bottle of Nuits-Saint-Georges. "I don't usually drink at lunch," Kooner remarked as he motioned to the waiter to open the wine and pour him a sample, "but under the circumstances, I thought we could relax a bit while we talk."

He watched as the waiter began to set up their lunch in the dining area, complete with a table that could comfortably seat eight. Kooner added, "I thought about ordering corned beef and cabbage because I heard that's what Abe Lincoln had here for his lunch right after he was sworn in as president, but I figured the veal might be more tender."

"Good thinking," Bollinger replied.

The waiter lit the gold chandelier, laid a crisp white linen cloth over the large table, quickly set out the two place settings, napkins, goblets and glasses of ice water and proceeded to ladle the soup into wide bowls. A single rose in a narrow crystal vase was placed next to the sterling silver salt and pepper shakers, along with cream and sugar and a silver carafe of steaming hot coffee.

He kept the main course in the warming oven in the cart, placed a bill on the table, which Kooner quickly initialed after adding a twenty-five percent tip, which would all go onto his corporate account. The waiter then discretely left the room.

"Now then," Kooner suggested, "won't you join me?"

Bollinger sat down in one of the Hepplewhite chairs and put a napkin on his lap. "So as I was saying, if we combined Q-3 with your latest ground systems, we could offer quite a package deal to a number of countries, if we can get the export licenses, of course."

"I think we can manage that. My boys are on top of those little details. And quite frankly, I'd like to get my hands on Dr. Talbot's invention. By the way, what's your computer genius up to lately?" he asked as he poured the wine for his guest.

"She's working on some other programs. I can't go into the details just yet, but the lady does keep busy."

He could hardly tell Nettar Kooner about Cammy's latest laser idea. He still thought it was a complete fiasco, and he had no intention of letting Kooner know about any of their weak spots. In fact, if he were going to negotiate favorable terms for this merger or acquisition or whatever it turned out to be, he'd like to find some weak spots in Sterling's business plan. Then he could drive the price down a bit.

"Back on your DHS contract," Stan said, "this whole put-a-dome-over-the-airport idea is rather clever, but even if you could get enough money out of that department to deploy your system throughout the United States, what about airports overseas? Terrorists just might decide to shoot down our planes, or anybody's planes from foreign locations and many of those are almost advertising for easy access. Take Bangkok, for example. It's so simple to get near enough to shoot down a place, it's amazing. They have a golf course within the airport grounds. All you have to do is text in a request to play golf, show an ID, and you're inside."

Kooner finished his soup and reached into the little oven for his plate of veal. "You have a point there. Right now we have to concentrate on American airports, of course, and the way we figure it, if we can get an additional appropriation out of DHS, we can add several more personnel to the dome project, get it up and running and start deploying within a few weeks."

"Additional appropriation? How the hell are you going to pull that off with the deficits they're running right now?"

"In this atmosphere with those three crashes, I figure Congress will be willing to write checks for just about anything."

"Write checks? There have been so many requests for add-ons, earmarks and God knows what, so much fighting going on it's like the Donner party up there."

Kooner chuckled, "Don't worry, Stan, I've got it wired. Now, getting back to your Dr. Talbot, I figure you gave her a big promotion when she pulled off that Q-3 deal, right?"

Stan paused, thinking about his difficult relationship with the brash young scientist. He had given her a bonus and let her play around in her lab for a while, but he was afraid she was more of a one-trick pony than real executive material. So, so instead of a major promotion, he had given her a nice bonus and upped her title a bit.

Just that morning he was trying to figure out a way to fire the woman, but for now, until the merger was complete, he wanted to be sure that Kooner didn't hire her away in case she actually came up with something that worked. "Quite frankly, I'm not sure if she'll ever have the same level of success," Stan said. "I did give her a better title though. From project director to senior project director."

Kooner laughed. "That's all? That's like appointing someone to the job of press spokesman for the CIA."

Stan shrugged. "It's just that she's probably best working alone in her lab. Not being promoted to a higher position. I just haven't seen the potential in her, or any of our other women, to take to top jobs, if you know what I mean."

"How can you say that women don't have executive skills? What about Mary Barra, who's been CEO of General Motors? Ginnie Romatty of IBM? Indra Nooryi at Pepsico? You even have a woman heading up a defense contractor, Lockheed Martin's Marilyn Hewson."

Bollinger seemed momentarily taken aback and wanted to change the subject. "Yes, I take your point. Perhaps we just don't have enough of the right kind of females on our staff. However, we have other teams that are on the cutting edge of a new system for Navy helos. It's similar but even better than what they've got on the new Sikorsky."

"You mean the ones they're using for Marine One?"

"Yes. Ours is going to be next generation critical."

"You sure about that?" Kooner asked.

"Absolutely. You can take it to the Federal Reserve."

They continued their negotiations for the next two hours, agreeing that no one, not their boards, their employees or their shareholders should learn one detail about their meeting or possible joint action. If they did, they'd figure out pretty quickly that with a merger of this magnitude, they'd have to down-size, get rid of comparable job descriptions and any number of people would be out of a job. And fast.

CHAPTER ELEVEN

THE WHITE HOUSE

D ozens of tourists pressed against the wrought iron fence surrounding the fifty-five thousand square foot White House, many holding small cameras between the balustrades to capture the flowers, fountains and action at the North Portico.

As Cammy presented her driver's license to the guard at the Northwest Gate, she wondered if she'd ever develop an absence of awe about this place. As he checked his log, handed her a security pass and instructed her to walk through the metal detector, she doubted she ever would.

She took the walkway to the entrance to the West Wing where a uniformed guard turned, opened the door and said, "Good morning, ma'am."

Inside the reception area she again checked in. An aide to the NSC advisor escorted her down the hall, then left to the door of the Roosevelt Room where Austin Gage and the vice president were standing in front of the white fireplace, a visage of Teddy Roosevelt looking down over their shoulders. They both walked over, shook her hand and invited her to take a seat at the long oval conference table surrounded by brown leather chairs, decorated with brass trim tacks around the edges.

She hadn't been in this room before. Her previous trips had been to the Oval Office. She got her bearings and figured out that another door across the room must lead out to the hallway directly in front of the president's office. She wondered if he would be joining their meeting.

After her horrible experience in Cambridge watching the police and firemen rushing to the scene of the blast and carrying out the body of her colleague, We Hu, she had escaped the chaos, not wanting to reveal anything about her collaboration on the laser.

It was a secret project, and there was nothing she could to do help at that point. Besides, she was scared. She had hopped into a nearby taxi, taken the train back to Washington and had several hours to try and figure out what to do next.

Now she was in the quiet comfort of the West Wing. At least she felt safe here. She glanced over and saw four flags in brass stands lined up along one side wall. A wide cherry wood cabinet stood at the end of the room, while an arrangement of light rose upholstered furniture, a camel back couch and two side chairs offered a comfortable spot off to the side for a more intimate gathering. But since they all had a lot of notes to review, she figured they'd stay at the big table.

She was anxious to hear about the progress of the other defense contractors. Had they done any more testing or could they be moving ahead so quickly that she'd be aced out of this competition to equip the airlines? Just as she was taking her seat and putting her notes together, the door opened and Hunt Daniels walked in.

Cammy caught her breath and tried not to stare at the handsome man with the square jaw, sandy hair, chiseled features and deep blue eyes. When he saw her sitting there, he stopped in mid-stride and looked like he was forcing a smile.

Damn him, she thought, as he slid into a chair across from her and uttered a greeting to Jayson Keller and his boss, Austin Gage. Then his eyes met hers again and he said, "Good morning, Dr. Talbot. Good to see you again."

I'll bet. The man has to come in here looking like an advertisement for Brooks Brothers, straight-lined grin, and he thinks I'm just going to sit here and act like nothing ever happened between us. Well, I can play that game as well as he can.

She reached up, absently straightened her head-band and replied, "Yes, you too . . . colonel."

Jay Keller was eyeing Cammy and sensed there was something wrong. He glanced over at Hunt and saw him shift uncomfortably in his seat. There was a certain tension in the room. It was palpable. What was it with these two? He'd heard they had worked together before, but now their expressions mirrored the Hatfields and McCoys. Interesting.

At the same time, he appraised Cammy again. She certainly was attractive with high cheek bones, a slim figure and great legs. He couldn't help noticing them when she had walked gracefully into the room. He wondered what she was really like. Was she always so serious? Did she have a sense of humor? Did she ever relax and laugh once in a while?

He tried to picture the no-nonsense scientist at a football game or sunbathing on the prow of his sailboat. Now that was a pleasant image. After all, he was single, his wife had died two months before the last election. While he had been heartbroken at the time, he realized much later that their ticket had benefited enormously from a big sympathy factor. Then again, he had done everything in his power to save her, but when the brain aneurysm had hit so suddenly, it was the one time in his life that he felt truly powerless.

Austin Gage cleared his throat and began the meeting, forcing Jay out of his reverie. "We have some results from the FAA and NTSB on those crashes I want to show you. They've raised the wreckage from the Logan flight and compared it to what was left of the other two planes. Here, we have some video." He pointed to a multimedia center and a member of his staff who had quietly slipped into the room started the DVD.

Images of part of an airplane filled the screen. As the camera panned across, Cammy saw where something, obviously a projectile of some sort, had torn through the wing and fuselage. Parts of mangled and charred seats filled the frame, along with what she feared were body parts. It all made her cringe. As the picture moved to a close-up of the jagged opening, Cammy started to speak.

"It had to be a missile."

"Yes, I think so," Austin said, looking closely at the carnage. "But what kind? That's the big question. And if it really was a missile, why didn't our radar systems detect it? Not once, but three times?"

"Are we certain it couldn't have been an interior explosion of some sort?" Hunt asked.

"No, that doesn't look right," Cammy said defiantly challenging his idea.

He looked over at her and repeated his question, "How can you be so sure it wasn't a device that exploded on board the plane, Dr Talbot? That would explain the lack of radar detection, you know."

Antagonistic bastard, she thought. *Not a diplomatic bone in his body.* "There could be other explanations for the lack of radar sightings, colonel."

"Like what? Give us your best SWAG," Hunt said.

She paused and I glanced from Hunt to Austin and Jay, who had puzzled looks. "My best Scientific Wild-Ass Guess?" Cammy said, emphasizing the next to the last words. "I lived on an Air Force Base, colonel. I recognize military jargon."

The vice president chuckled and stared at her expectantly. Should she mention her theory about a new type of missile? It was only a theory, she had no proof, and this was a group that appreciated facts, not crazy propositions. On the other hand, Hunt was challenging her, so why not come up with a new hypothesis. "I have an idea that it was a missile with stealth capability."

"You've gotta be kidding," Hunt said. "We know all of the countries with stealth technology. Russia, India, France, Israel, China. There are lots of them, but they're not spending their money on stealth missiles. It's going for planes. Besides, of all the countries with that capability, what motive would any of them have for shooting down innocent Americans?"

"I'm not sure," Cammy said. "But I intend to do some more research on the concept because I think it's a valid one."

"The lady may have a point here," the vice president said, quickly coming to her defense. "What do you think, Austin?"

"She may be right. But as Hunt said, in all of our meetings so far, we haven't been able to come up with a single, logical motive for these attacks."

"Except for al Qaeda," Hunt said.

"Right. Except for al Qaeda or one of their off-shoots," Austin said. "Then again, we have absolutely no evidence that their groups are operating at anywhere near that level of sophistication."

"We're still working on all of that, though," Hunt interjected.

"Now, about our own technology for the airlines," Austin continued. "What do we hear from DHS?"

Jay pulled a sheaf of notes from his folder and read off some numbers. "Thorne says that if he can get an extra fifty million for the test phase, he believes both of those companies will be able to gear up and be good to go within a matter of months."

"We may not have months," Austin said.

"And Congress may not pop for the fifty million, although at the Pentagon they spill more than that over coffee," Jay answered with a slight wave of his hand. He then turned to Cammy, "How are you coming with your laser project, Dr. Talbot?"

Should she say that she and Wen Hu had developed a new plan for a pulse laser even though it was only in the initial stage at this point? She didn't want to say anything about the photo concept for a missile. That was too far out. She had to do a lot more checking on that one. But she could certainly explain her three hundred sixty degree laser idea. She wondered if they would give her time to set up her own tests. Or would

Hunt Daniels find a way to knock her down again? She kept trying to ignore him, even though she felt a frisson of electricity every time she glanced at him across the table. She decided to forge ahead.

"Right now, I'm working on a new concept. It involves a pulse laser that I believe could be effective against any number of search-and-destroy devices. Stealthy or not."

"Why would yours work when the other contractors are having such a tough time?" Hunt asked.

There he goes again. Damn it. Can't he ever accept the fact that I may have some new ideas here? She went on to describe her work with Wen Hu and her trip to Cambridge, the threats on his life, his original reservation on the doomed plane at Logan and finally, she described the explosion at his lab.

Hunt listened intently to her explanations and realized he was holding his breath when she got to the part about the explosion. "I did see the report of an explosion in Cambridge, but I had no idea . . ."

"Yes, we all heard that news, Austin said. I didn't realize that's where *you* were. My God!"

As the others were lamenting the blast, Hunt lamented to himself that it was hard being in the same room with the woman, a woman he had taken into his home for a week when she was being threatened, a woman he had protected, a woman he had made love to, not just in Washington, but over in India when they had worked together to protect New Delhi from a terrorist attack. How could he ever forget those magical nights they had spent at the hotel overlooking the Taj Mahal when the crisis was finally over? She had been magnificent.

On the other hand, there was a time back then when she had been rather maddening as well, accusing him of collaborating with Sterling Dynamics at one point, not trusting his judgment. It had really irritated him at the time, but when she had apologized and taken him to bed, well, what the hell?

Then he was sent away, and he couldn't tell her anything. Now he was back and any thoughts he had about rekindling the whole affair were being doused by Miss High and Mighty over there. Every time he had opened his mouth, she had countered him. She must have been royally pissed when he hadn't called. How the hell was he supposed to crack through that damn shell of hers anyway? And even if he could, did he want to?

Then again, when she described the fireball at the lab, the people running out with blood on their clothes, women crying, men coughing and how her friend and fellow scientist had been blown to smithereens, his stomach tightened at the thought that if she had gone back in with her Starbucks' drinks, or whatever she said they were, she would have been killed too. No, he couldn't bear that thought. He lifted his head up and tried to make eye contact, but she was looking at Jayson Keller with what seemed like a rather intense stare. What now?

The vice president listened to the whole story. He was aghast. It certainly sounded to him like this Dr. Hu had been targeted. Murdered. And Cammy could have been a victim as well. As he listened, though, and watched her face, he realized that he wished he had been there with her in Cambridge. Been there to comfort her when she had been through such a traumatic experience.

He suddenly realized that this was the first time he had paid this much attention to another woman since his wife died. He'd been so focused on his job and world events, he never allowed himself the luxury of thinking about female companionship. Not until now anyway. He wondered what his next move should be.

He tore his eyes away from the pretty scientist and began to watch Hunt Daniels and saw that the colonel was mesmerized by the woman as well. *This could get interesting. But only if Daniels stays in town,* he thought. *Maybe I can do something about that.*

CHAPTER TWELVE

WASHINGTON, D.C.

"I can't believe you talked me into this!" Cammy muttered to Melanie as she got out of her car, handed it over to the valet and shoved the claim chit into her evening bag. She took hold of her long black silk skirt and walked up the steps of the Andrew Mellon Hall on Constitution Avenue. Her strappy high heels were already bothering her. She hadn't worn them in ages and wasn't too pleased about having to walk around in them all night.

"This is a command performance, Cam," Melanie said, pulling the door open and heading for a long receiving table. "Bollinger decided we had to take a table at this shindig. You know, keep up the corporate presence routine, especially since there'll be so many muckety-mucks at this one."

They checked in, found their table assignments and moved into the reception area, a room with forty foot ceilings decorated with bronze frescoes. "You know how I feel about these balls and stand-arounds,"

Cammy said, eyeing the men in black tie and women in the latest that Versace or Chanel had to offer. "At least I guess this one is for a good cause, Heart Association or something?"

"Yep. It should be better than the usual organ balls."

"Organ balls?"

"You know, Heart Ball, Kidney Ball. They even had an Eye Ball last year."

Cammy started to laugh in spite of her rather somber mood. She had spent the day briefing Stan Bollinger on her last meeting at the White House, her collaboration with Wen Hu just before the explosion, and her ideas about a pulse laser. He said he didn't think it would work, but he had finally agreed to have their engineers retune her original laser experiments and to arrange for some field tests. He hadn't sounded too happy about it, though.

"By the way," Cammy said, "I assume Bollinger will be here hosting the table, right?"

"Oh sure. He's bringing his wife."

"I've never met her. Have you?"

"Only saw her once. I don't think he takes her out much, but we'll see what she's like when we sit down. Hey, I didn't tell you that I think that's a neat outfit. Is that your grandmother's jewelry?"

Cammy fingered the ruby necklace and moved her hair to show off the earrings she had inherited. "Yes. I love these pieces. I don't get a chance to wear them very often."

"Well, this is the perfect place." Mel turned to accept a glass of champagne offered by a waiter carrying a silver tray laden with a variety of beverages. Cammy selected a glass of white wine and began to scan the room.

"Hey look. Isn't that Congressman Davis Metcher over there? I wonder who that woman . . . or rather . . . girl is that he's got this time?"

Melanie giggled and inclined her head toward a stunning redhead holding on to the paunchy lawmaker's arm. "She looks like she could be his daughter. I think he likes the ones still using Clearasil. And speaking of dates, thanks for bailing me out tonight. When Derek couldn't make it, you were really nice to come with me."

Cammy sighed and said, "After Cambridge, tension at the office, pressure from the White House and the general hysteria around this town, I guess I should be glad for a night out. It's just that I've been feeling so slammed, it's sometimes hard to relax."

They mingled around the room, chatting with a few friends they spotted interspersed with the heavy hitters. After another round of cocktails and passed hors d'oeuvres, a waiter began moving through the crowd hitting a little metallic triangle. "That's our cue to find our table," Melanie said. "But I'll bet it takes these folks a good half hour to go to their seats. In this town it's all about who you can see and be seen with rather than the food or the speeches."

"I guess. Ever notice how there are little circles around some people at these things?"

"Sure. The larger the circle, the more impressive the resume. The important people stand still. The climbers float around the room, trying to attract the attention of the stationary ones. Kind of reminds me of sharks circling their prey. Of course, once you get a chance to shake hands with some guest of honor type, he's usually looking over your shoulder to see if there's someone more important he should be talking to."

"Exactly. Actually, I don't think there's anybody here I have to talk to, so why don't we find our table?"

Melanie eyed her friend and replied, "Guess Hunt wouldn't be at one of these things, would he?"

Cammy jerked her head around and furrowed her brow. "Not on your life. He hates these things. Besides, even if he were here, I'm not sure I'd want to talk to him."

"Still shutting him out, huh?"

"It's not a question of shutting him out. I don't think he wants back in. At that last meeting, all he did was argue."

"Give it time," Mel suggested.

When they sat down on gold Louis XVI ballroom chairs and checked the small menus done in calligraphy and propped up at each place, Melanie started to laugh.

"What's so funny?" Cammy asked, setting her wine glass down next to three other goblets of varying sizes.

"It says here that the main course will be a fillet of beef, and I was just thinking that that's a heck of a lot better than the nutty recipes I pulled out of the paper today."

"What have you got this time?"

"There's this restaurant in Denver that's serving Tamal al huitlacoche."

"What in the world is that?" Cammy asked.

"Steamed corn tamales with corn fungus."

"Oh, for Lord's sake!"

Several other guests arrived at the table, walked around and introduced themselves. One was Congresswoman Betty Barton of California who remembered Cammy from the time she had testified before their committee several months ago. Cammy was surprised that the woman even recalled her name, given the number of issues those people had to contend with. Cammy then saw Stan Bollinger walk up with a very thin older woman on his arm. She appeared to be scowling about something.

"Is that Stan's wife?" Cammy whispered.

"I guess so," Mel said. "Looks kind of like a cross between a gargoyle and a Grant Wood painting, don't you think?"

Cammy grinned and nodded her head. "No wonder he's always in such a bad mood."

Before the dinner got underway, everyone stood up as an honor guard made up of young military representatives of the various services marched in, carrying flags. They stopped in front of the head table and lowered all but the American flag which was carried high and erect. Then the orchestra struck up the national anthem. Everyone put their hand over their heart and sang along. When the music ended, the flag bearers made a professional exit from the ballroom.

Next came the invocation by a Bishop. He referred to the tragedies in the skies, prayed for the souls of those lost to the senseless attacks and then segued into a general thank you to everyone for supporting a good cause tonight.

They all sat down again and waited patiently. Bollinger's wife, acting as hostess at their table, finally picked up her fork, the signal that everyone else at the table could begin eating.

Cammy wasn't very hungry. She sort of picked at the small grilled scallop on a nest of what looked like dandelion leaves with a smattering of mandarin orange slices served as a first course. She leaned over and heard Melanie talking with the man on her right saying something about a catch and release program. Cammy said, "Catch and release? That's what they do in California where I grew up."

The man glanced over at Cammy with a quizzical look. "They have fly fishing in California?"

"Oh," Cammy replied. "Sorry, I thought you were talking about illegal immigrants."

Melanie laughed and said, "This man's from Wyoming. He was just explaining how they have the best salmon and trout fishing out there, but you can't keep anything you catch. You have to release them."

They finished their salads, and the waiters then served the beef fillet along with a few pieces of red potato and a small bundle of asparagus spears tied with a slice of pimento.

Melanie was still engrossed in her conversation, and the man to Cammy's left was talking to someone else, so she picked up the program and saw a list of honorees and corporate sponsors. At the top of the list was Jayson Keller. She hadn't realized that the vice president would be here. She turned around in her seat since the head table was behind her. There he was, sitting in the middle, looking rather attractive in his black tie and gleaming white dress shirt.

She had to admit the man had an interesting aura about him. She wondered why he was here. Then she read a paragraph at the bottom of the page indicating that the vice president's late wife had served as the

chairman of this ball in prior years so it was only natural that he continued to support the cause.

During the break between dinner and dessert, the orchestra began
to play a familiar Gershwin song. A few moments later, Cammy heard
a voice over her shoulder, "Do you have a spot on your dance card
for me?"

She whirled around and saw the smiling face of Jayson Keller. All
conversation at her table stopped as nine other pairs of eyes focused on
the vice president's choice of dance partners.

Across the room, the reporter for the Style Section of the *Washington
Post* strained to get a closer look and tripped over a tripod set up by the
Washington Life photographer. Melanie sat still, enraptured by the
proximity of so much power.

Jay held her chair as Cammy got up from the table. He took her arm,
leading her to the dance floor as other guests parted to let them through.
He took her in his arms, and she easily followed his lead. "I must say
you're looking lovely tonight, Dr. Talbot."

"Thank you, sir," she replied evenly.

"Please. It's Jay. I saw you sitting over there and thought it would be
nice to talk to you about something other than stealth missiles," he said
with a smile.

"I know all of us have been preoccupied with the crashes. I haven't
been able to think of anything else. Though I guess it's all right to take
a break once in a while to support a good cause."

"Absolutely. Even though the market is going to hell in a hand-bas-
ket, and we've got every single one of our sixteen intelligence agencies
working overtime on this problem, we still have to look like we're carrying on. We can't let the bastards totally run our lives."

"I know you're right. But on your investigations, I was curious. Have
you come up with any new leads about the terrorists, or whoever
they are?"

"We do have one situation we're checking out in South America."

"South America?" she questioned.

"Yes. I know it sounds odd, but our station chief in Brasilia has a line on an aerospace company down there that's already put a missile defense system on their new planes. He's got a notion that they may be trying to create a market for their aircraft by saying they're safer."

"But they wouldn't shoot down innocent people just to sell some airplanes, would they?" Cammy asked in an astonished tone.

"We don't know. But we've sent Col. Daniels and Claudia Del Sarto down there to find out."

At the mention of Hunt's name, Cammy had stiffened and missed a step. "Oh, sorry," she said, averting her gaze. Recovering quickly, she asked, "Who's Claudia Del Sarto?" She wanted to know, but she was trying not to sound too interested.

"She an NSC specialist on South America. Bright gal. Raised down there. I heard her father headed up operations in a couple of those countries for one of our oil companies. So she went with Hunt as an investigator and interpreter."

"Oh," Cammy said, wishing she weren't so curious about Hunt's traveling companion.

The vice president noticed her reaction immediately. He had brought up Hunt's name on purpose. He was a pretty good judge of character, and this woman's response made it rather clear that something had happened involving the Lt. Col., though he had no idea what it was.

When she had asked about Claudia he had been tempted to tell Cammy that the woman was an extremely attractive brunette who spoke four languages. But he couldn't quite work that into the conversation.

As for Cammy's relationship with Hunt, he wondered if it was ongoing or a thing of the past. He was curious, but he was more interested in developing a relationship of his own than finding out about some previous affair, if that's what it was. He had never had to compete with another man for a woman's affections before. It was a new revelation.

Jay held Cammy closer and caught the faint scent of vanilla in her hair. At this point he wished they weren't in such a pubic place with everyone staring, including reporters, members of Congress, and various cave-dwellers, as the old-line Washingtonians were called.

He'd like to spirit her off on his sailboat for a private cruise, even though he knew that wherever he went, his Secret Service detail would be shadowing them. He'd have to think about that.

The song ended and Jay escorted Cammy back to her table. "Thank you very much, Dr. Talbot," giving her a slight bow for the benefit of the onlookers. Then he added in an undertone, "If anything comes up in your work on the laser or anything else where I can help, you'll call me, won't you?"

She gave a slight nod, smiled and slid back onto her chair.

CHAPTER THIRTEEN

STERLING, VIRGINIA

N ettar Kooner hung up the phone. Another call from the Department of Homeland Security! Another demand that they fast-track their technology. Another confrontation with that usually obsequious little secretary, a man Kooner usually had in his expansive back pocket. After promising that they were moving at full speed on the airport project, he now wanted to concentrate on his other contract. The one where he was certain of a built-in profit, if only they could advance that timetable as well. With a sense of irritation, he reached for his telephone again.

He dialed an internal extension and barked into the phone, "Can you get down here ASAP? Yes, it's about that system for Taiwan." He slammed the phone down once more and sifted through some contracts on his desk.

The government in Taipei was pressing for delivery of several complete missile defense systems. He had made some initial shipments, but a few key elements hadn't hit their port yet. He mentally calculated how long they would take to arrive, how long it would take for their payments to be wired and how long it would be until his board of directors was so pleased with this deal that they'd grant him another set of stock options.

He heard a quick knock on the door, and then his chief of staff, as he liked to call the man, stepped inside the spacious office with sleek black leather couches and Eames chairs surrounding a low glass coffee table.

His number two ignored the couches and took his usual seat in an arm chair across from Kooner's desk. "Yes, sir. You needed to see me?"

"Damn right. I want to know the status of our agreement with that facility in China that's making our chips for the ballistic defense system."

The chief of staff leaned forward, his eyes guarded. "I'm concerned about that situation, Nettar."

"I know," Kooner snapped. "You made that clear when I negotiated the deal in the first place."

"It's just that outsourcing those chips to that Chinese manufacturer could run afoul of ITAR."

"You think I don't know that too?"

"Yes, but then why . . ."

"Why do I want a second round of their chips? Isn't that rather obvious? We are saving a ton of money by having them made over there. You're well aware of our bottom line on that project. We had to find ways to cut our costs. And letting them do what they do best, make those chips, seemed like the best way to get the line out on time and on budget."

"But if we get caught violating Section 38 of the Arms Export Control Act . . ." his chief speculated with a worried look.

"I've read the regs. I know the International Traffic in Arms Regulations as well as you do. They may be there on paper somewhere, but since when does the American State Department have the time or the balls to try and enforce that piece of crap? And don't tell me there aren't tons of other companies doing the same thing."

The other man shook his head and replied. "I don't want to rain on your parade, boss . . ."

"Then don't," Kooner declared. "We all know that ever since we had those chips made overseas, the whole system has performed flawlessly. Right here, not only in the Atlantic but also in our Pacific test ranges."

"I know, sir, but . . ."

"No buts, damn it. Just re-order the chips and put a rush on them. We've got to get that system up and running in Taiwan fast. Those folks are petrified that some of the rumors about China hardening their position toward them might pan out one day and they're all running scared. And with some eight hundred Chinese missiles of various kinds pointing at them, I can hardly say I blame them. And that's to say nothing about the crazy North Koreans who are mucking around in the same part of the world. So get about it."

Kooner swiveled his chair around and added, "And if you can't keep those chips coming in, I'll find somebody who can."

CHAPTER FOURTEEN

OVERSEAS

The general chairing a meeting of his most trusted aides quickly read the story he had just printed out from his computer and announced, "The American Dow Jones Average is down a thousand points so far. And with only three attacks on three airplanes. Think what will happen when our people strike again."

They were gathered around a small folding table at one end of a large hangar. Morning light filtered through a few high windows, but two metal goose neck lamps provided most of the illumination for the gathering. A colonel spoke up. "Yes, but it is unfortunate that we had to kill hundreds of innocent people just to get the Americans distracted"

"Shut up, you fool. Over three-thousand innocent people died on 9/11. What's a few hundred when it comes to our grand scheme? Look at America now. Not only is their market way down, they can't focus on any other issue. Not domestic policy. Not foreign policy. Not trade policy. Nothing, because all anybody in their media wants to talk about is the safety of their airplanes, the pilots' demands and the specter of a strike by their air traffic controllers. Everybody knows that Congress and their feckless president concentrate on whatever the media concentrates on. No, we have them exactly where we want them."

"Speaking of the media," another officer interjected, "it's being reported that the president has appointed his national security advisor and his vice president to handle the investigation of the airliner attacks and figure out their next steps."

"Yes, I know. These are crafty men." He turned to the aide on his right. "If we don't stop that man, Keller, soon, make a note to start siphoning contributions to his likely opponent in their upcoming presidential race. That Senator Winters. We can't have a hard-liner like Keller in the White House for another four years."

The aide looked puzzled and asked, "How do we get around their laws against foreign contributions?"

"Were you asleep every time we did this in the past?" the general barked. "We have ways. Many ways. Just get it done and done right."

He turned back to the colonel. "Now then, we have to concentrate on our own upcoming military exercises which will camouflage our real plans. Be sure we have enough amphibious craft available for a final assault if we need them, and contact our trusted friends at the missile sites to be ready to launch."

The colonel made several notes. "And as for those two Americans," the general continued, "the ones who are trying to foil our plans, I suggest we craft another of our special messages."

"You mean to eliminate the crafty ones?"

The general stroked his goatee and flicked a speck of dust off the row of medals across his chest. "Precisely."

CHAPTER FIFTEEN

THE WHITE HOUSE

Austin Gage walked into the Oval Office to join the vice president and the director of national intelligence for their usual early morning briefing. The president came around his desk and joined the others on the two couches and high back chairs in the middle of the room.

"So gentlemen, where are we on the investigation?"

The DNI pulled out his summary. "First of all, Mr. President, we believe the missiles that struck our airplanes could have been made in Pakistan, China, Egypt or the old Soviet Union. Or, of course, right here in America. We're not sure why they didn't show up on radar. They may have been modified. Right now we're focusing on places we know have thousands of shoulder-fired missiles. Ones that should have been rounded up or destroyed, but which are still floating around, available to the highest bidder."

"Who are your most likely candidates?" The president asked.

"At this point we're focusing on three places. First, in the Middle East, we know that during Saddam Hussein's time, he accumulated some

5,000 of the things. Only about one-third of them have been recovered, even with our troops searching the country. Trouble is, they don't weigh much. They're less than six feet long."

"They could fit in a golf bag," Jay observed.

The intelligence director continued his report. "In Russia, the defense minister of the Ukraine has now admitted that several hundred decommissioned surface-to-air missiles are unaccounted for. They could have been destroyed, but no records were kept. He was probably referring to S-75 air defense missiles. We call them SA-2's. And they were sold to any number of countries."

"But those are pretty old. Isn't that the same type of missile that brought down Francis Gary Power's U-2 spy plane over fifty years ago?" the president asked.

"You're right about that. And since these recent attacks are so mysterious, we doubt that the Russian missiles were used, unless, as I said, they've been modified in recent years. So we're continuing to check their updated versions. And as you've asked many times, where's their motive? Our agents in Moscow and the other major cities are scouring their sources."

"And what's your third concentration?"

"Nicaragua," the DNI replied. "We figure they've got about two-thousand SA-7's and even later models kicking around. The president of Nicaragua says he will destroy them. But nobody gives that much credence."

"What about missiles with stealth technology?" The vice president asked.

"We haven't been able to pinpoint any new research programs with stealth. At least not yet," the DNI replied. "And as for terrorist groups who might have such weapons, we're still searching and trying to analyze which ones could have that level of sophistication. It's tough right now, but we're on it. Also, NSA has increased their wiretaps and internet surveillance as you ordered, Mr. President."

"Anything new?"

"Not yet. If the group responsible is clever enough to have some sort of weapon our radar can't see, you can be sure they've also figured out clever ways to communicate. But we have some new programs in place that are analyzing thousands of messages a second. So we'll keep you posted."

"We've sent Col. Daniels down to South America with a small team to check on that aerospace company, you know," Jay ventured.

"Yes, I'm anxious to hear if they uncover any links," Austin said.

"Meanwhile, we're working with Dr Talbot on a new laser approach for the airlines," the president said. "The other systems in the pipeline would be so damned expensive, I can't see our airlines being able to afford them, even if they work."

"You're right," Jay interjected. "At last count, for the sixty-eight hundred aircraft we have flying right now, the cost could be anywhere from ten to forty billion. On the other hand if Cammy's, uh, Dr. Talbot's system proves out, it might be more economically feasible."

"Yes, that looks like the one bright spot in this whole bleak scenario," the DNI said.

The NSC advisor checked his watch, got up and announced, "Sorry, Mr. President, speaking of bleak scenarios, as I mentioned earlier, I'm going to have to leave to catch a plane."

"Yes, I know. Your daughter. Damn shame. I hear that reports of her accident have already hit the wires," the president said. "It was a drunk driver, wasn't it?"

"Yes, sir, it was. Happened two nights ago when she was biking home from the library there at Duke. The idiot lost control of his car. Now she's in the hospital. At first we thought she'd come through all right. My wife flew down yesterday to stay with her. But then she took a turn for the worse. She's in surgery, so I'm taking the first flight out of Dulles. At least the planes are still flying. Some of them anyway."

"We could have arranged a special flight, Austin," Jay said.

"I know, but this is personal, not official business. Besides, we agreed in that Cabinet meeting that we'd all try to fly commercial, try to offer some assurances . . ." His voice trailed off.

"Go on. Get out of here," the president said with a wave of his hand, "and keep us posted on how she's doing, will you?"

"Of course, Mr. President." He gathered up his papers and hurried out of the Oval Office through a side door.

After the others had gone, the president continued his busy schedule, endeavoring to keep up a good front in the face of another day of falling stock prices. The director of Asian Affairs came in to brief him on the latest developments in Ulan Bator and he took a phone call from the head of the EPA who was concerned about the extension of the Endangered Species Act.

"What's the matter with that one," the president asked.

"There's a provision about alligators."

"Why? They've been killing dogs, even people in Florida for God's sake. Get them off the list and tell 'em to make more belts," he said and hung up the phone.

He shuffled some more papers until his press secretary and chief of staff came in to report that the networks were all showing video of the wreckages of the downed airplanes along with interviews in airports with nervous travelers, shaky flight attendants and pilots who were discussing how they might go out on strike in sympathy with the controllers if they decided to walk. The president told his spokesman to try and hold the fort until they had more information.

The press secretary went back to his office to conduct the first briefing of the day while the chief of staff stayed to go over a list of new problems.

"In addition to your preparations for the visit of the president of Mongolia, we've got a problem up at the UN. They're planning to name Zimbabwe to head up their Human Rights Council. Our ambassador may want a word with you on that one."

The president gave a slight groan as his aide leafed through a number of scheduling requests. "Let's see, we need to add a couple quicker things today."

"As if we didn't have enough on our plate," the president said, "my wife says we should try to show up at that panda celebration at the zoo this afternoon. Says it would be a nice gesture toward China. What do you think?"

His aide chuckled and replied, "It might be more entertaining than the reception for the Nut Growers Association."

"Are we still banning pistachios from Iran?"

"What else are we going to ban?"

"Good point," the president agreed. "And on trade issues, what's this problem with Belarus I keep hearing about?"

"Last I heard they wanted to be sure we'd let them export musk ox."

"I doubt it would give much competition to the cattle boys. Go ahead and let them. What else have you got there?"

"The most important project, in addition to our transportation disasters, involves the new tax bill. The joint committee on taxation just came out with a new estimate that your proposed tax cut would cost the government over two-hundred and eighty billion dollars in one year alone."

"It would *cost* the government? Bullshit! It would *cost* the American people two-hundred and eighty billion. They're the ones paying the bill. The government doesn't own *all* their money. Not yet, anyway. Those guys on the Hill need a new vocabulary. And get some decent economists who use dynamic econometric models instead of the static ones those idiots use to give us some new estimates. At least then we'll get numbers that include how the *behavior* of taxpayers changes when we lower their rates, like creating more jobs and expanding the economy. Well, you know the drill"

"I'm on it, sir. By the way, we've got a few congressional types coming over to meet with the economic team this afternoon. Maybe you could stop in, make a few remarks."

The president nodded.

The door burst open and the press secretary rushed in, his face ashen. "Sorry, Mr. President. There's been another crash."

"Oh no!" the president blurted as he jumped up from his chair. "Where? When?"

"Just now out near Dulles."

"That close? What plane? How many people?"

"It was just leaving, bound for Raleigh-Durham."

"Oh my God!" the president exclaimed, "Austin Gage was on board!"

CHAPTER SIXTEEN

BRASILIA

"This place looks like a set for a sci-fi flick," Hunt said, gazing out the window of the embassy car transporting him and NSC staffer, Claudia Del Sarto, from the airport to the National Congress building."

"When they built this capital back in the 60's, they wanted to be on the cutting edge," Claudia explained, turning to point to a building that looked like a flying saucer with a crown on the top. "See that one? It's the Nossa Senhora Aparecida."

"The what?" Hunt said, staring at the strange round structure.

"It's their metropolitan cathedral. Pretty impressive, don't you think?"

"Impressive? I guess. Everything is so sleek and modern . . . . and strange. Who designed this place anyway?"

"They literally carved the city out of the jungle. The master plan was called Plano Pilot. It was put together by a guy named Luci Costa. Then a lot of the buildings were designed by Oscar Niemeyer, the architect who also worked on the United Nations building."

"Same guy?"

"Yes. He was a Communist, you know."

"You're joking!" Hunt said, as he gazed at the wide boulevards. "Where are the sidewalks? Doesn't anybody walk in this town?"

"They can't. Not in most places anyway. Look over there at those apartment buildings."

"Pretty stark, I'd say."

"Very. Brazilians love to enjoy the outdoors, the good weather. And in Rio they have a lot of balconies everywhere so they can sit outside."

"But there aren't any balconies or outside doors that I can see on those buildings," Hunt said.

"The word that went around is that Niemeyer was afraid that people would hang their laundry over their balconies. He thought that would make his buildings look shabby, so he wouldn't let them put doors or balconies on them."

"And this was a champion of the people?" Hunt said with a laugh.

"After a while he was more or less booted out because of his communist connections."

"Yeah? Then where'd he go?"

"He moved to France and designed the Communist Party headquarters over there."

"Amazing. Well, he sure did a wild job with this place. Why in the world did they put their capital here in the middle of the jungle anyway?"

"They were trying to develop the interior of Brazil back then. Get people to move out of Rio and Sao Paulo, places like that."

"Did they want to move?"

"Of course not. In the beginning, all of the bureaucrats were given extra pay to live here, and they still hopped a flight back to Rio every weekend. That's what my family did when we were posted here for a while," she laughed, swinging her straight brown hair back off her shoulder."

"I can see why. After living with the beaches, the carnivals and all the rest, coming to this place must have been total culture shock. Even if it was their own culture, so to speak."

"Wait until you see this place at night," she ventured.

"Why?"

"A lot of the streets have sodium lights."

Hunt chuckled. "So you end up looking all yellow?"

"Remind me to wear extra make-up," she quipped.

"So did you like growing up here? Here and in Rio, I mean?" Hunt asked.

"Sure. It was pretty exotic compared to the states. But I think I liked Argentina even better."

"Why?"

"The men," she said, flashing her violet eyes.

"The men?"

"Sure. The way they dance. The way they act. The way they treat a woman."

"Before they marry you though," Hunt added.

"Well, there is that, yes. They're a pretty complicated bunch, though."

"Complicated?"

"You know the old description of an Argentine?"

"No, what?"

"That they're really Italians who speak Spanish and want to be British, but act French."

Hunt burst out laughing. "So why didn't you stay down here?"

"Reality got the best of me, I guess. Besides, deep down inside, I love America too much to stay away for long."

Hunt glanced over at the attractive woman and wondered about her personal life. He'd only known her a few months since she had joined the NSC staff. He knew she was smart as hell and spoke a bunch of languages. Then again it was obvious that she was single and had a great bod. But he'd decided a long time ago never to mess around with the staff. Too dangerous. Too much trouble. No, he kept the pretty ones at arms length.

Besides, he still felt conflicted over Cammy. A picture of her with wisps of strawberry blond hair framing her face flashed through his mind. He thought about how he might call her when he got back to D.C., ask her for lunch or a drink or something. He could try to explain why he hadn't been able to contact her before, see if she believed him this time.

Trouble was, it would probably sound like a pretty lame excuse. She couldn't know how dangerous his mission had been. How he had that awful sense that he might never get back, that he might be a target of one of the groups he was investigating for selling nuclear material on the black market. It was too critical to their bottom line as well as their survival to let some guy like him nose around and try to put them out of business.

He knew the risks. That was one of the reasons he hadn't wanted to get too involved. He didn't want to ask her to wait for him like some soldier in a sappy movie, going off to war and asking his best girl to sit by the mailbox for a bunch of months. He'd seen those movies and didn't always like the endings.

Their driver pulled up in front of two tall sleek buildings that looked like a pair of Washington Monuments cut off at the top. They were flanked by two saucer-shaped structures. One facing up. One down.

"That thing over there looks like an upside-down bathtub," Hunt said, grabbing his briefcase and getting out of the car."

"I don't think modern art is exactly your thing, colonel," Claudia said, sliding her long legs out of the other door.

"You've got that one right."

They began a series of meetings with key lawmakers, men suggested by their ambassador as being quite plugged in to Brazil's aerospace industry. Men who could brief them about Brazil's major players as well as their products and profits. They spent hours asking about the formerly state-owned company that had been privatized and was now touting a new missile defense system that had been added to their latest models at great expense.

They were told that the CEO, while ambitious and a bit devious at times, was mostly a straight-up guy who was marketing his planes aggressively, but could never be accused of shady dealings or contacts with terrorists.

They continued their discussions with the director of Brazil's transportation system, the head of their drug enforcement operation, and they finally retired to the American embassy for a secret meeting with the station chief, otherwise known as the CIA's man in Brazil, Chase Osborn.

"So how did you come up with this theory about the aerospace company?" Hunt asked the agent.

"When the first two planes were shot down, we had a contact in Sao Paulo who said he thought it rather strange that the company was suddenly advertising the hell out of their onboard missile defense system. It all seemed just too timely. Too pat. So we started to check them out."

"What did you find?" Claudia pressed.

"We found out that some time back, their CEO had made contact with the Russians, inquiring about their Tor-M1 air defense systems," Chase said.

"The ones the Russians sold to Tehran a few years ago?"

"Yep. Same ones."

"But that's a completely different type of system."

"We know that. But it put this guy on our radar."

"At least you can see things on your screen," Hunt said with a shake of his head.

"Yeah. We know about the no-radar-detection problem with the plane crashes. Anyway, we kept an eye on this guy, trying to figure out where he was getting his new anti-missile system for his planes because if he was playing around with Russia, or even with Iran, we wanted to know about it."

"And?" Claudia said, raising her dark eyebrows.

"Turns out that he paid a military contractor to adapt some of their stuff to fit on his planes," the station chief explained. "Thing sends out some chaff to confuse a heat-seeking missile. But it's a pretty basic version, if you ask me. Nothing dramatic or top secret. Nothing that we couldn't do, except I don't think we'd want to bother, because first, he spent a ton of money on that modification. And second, from what we know about those attacks, his system wouldn't have prevented them anyway. At least we don't think so."

"So we're back to square one," Hunt said, raking a hand through his hair.

"Afraid so, colonel," Chase said.

A hard knock on the door interrupted their conversation. An aide burst in waving a print-out. "We just got word. There's been another crash in the States."

"Jesus Christ!" Hunt blurted. "Where?"

"Dulles Airport."

"Oh my God!" Claudia said, holding her hand to her mouth.

"How many people on board?" the station chief asked.

The aide read through the advisory. "Uh . . . let me see . . . oh no!"

"What?" they said in unison.

"It says here that there were fifty-three people on board, including the crew. But one of those killed was Austin Gage, the national security advisor."

Hunt closed his eyes and swore. Everyone was silent for a moment, the aide gripping the page and standing mute. Hunt finally took a deep breath. "The bastards! The God damned bloody bastards! Austin Gage was one of the finest men I've ever known. He dedicated his life to our country, to his family, to everything we admire and try to be. God damn it. We've *got* to find these guys and nail their asses to the cross." His face was red, the muscles of his neck straining as he raised his voice. "I mean it. This *cannot* and *will not* go on," he thundered to his stunned audience.

Claudia put her hand on his arm, a gesture meant to calm him down. It was futile. Hunt got up from his chair and pulled out his encrypted cell phone. He dialed a number and waited, his face contorted in fury. "Stock? I just heard. What the hell . . ."

"Hunt," the deputy national security advisor answered, "I was just about to call you. Tragic situation here."

"God damned tragic. What the hell was Austin doing on that plane anyway?"

"He was on his way to Raleigh-Durham to see his daughter. She had been in an accident. She's in the hospital."

"Oh Christ! Daughter's in the hospital, Austin's in the morgue. Where is his wife?"

"We're getting a hold of her right now," Stockton Sloan explained. "The president is convening an emergency cabinet meeting within the hour. All hell is breaking loose around this place."

"In contrast to this place."

"What do you mean?"

"Seems that we've run into a dead end down here. I need to get back."

"I agree. We could use you up here. How soon can you leave?"

"Claudia and I will catch the next plane back. At least the international flights haven't been targeted."

"Not yet."

Hunt checked his watch and motioned to Claudia who nodded and rushed to his side. "I'll get our people here to reserve space. If there's anything leaving soon, we'll head straight to the airport which would put us in D.C. in ten to twelve hours. I'll call you when we land."

"You do that."

"Uh, Stock?"

"Yes?"

"Does this mean you're the new national security advisor?"

There was a slight pause. "Not sure about that."

"Why not? You're the deputy for God's sake."

"There may be some things other than succession at play here."

CHAPTER SEVENTEEN

THE WHITE HOUSE

A bank of grey clouds cut off the sun that usually streamed through the triple windows behind the president's desk in the Oval Office. A rumble of thunder could be heard in the distance and the president muttered, "Just what we need right now, a damn thunderstorm in the middle of an arrival ceremony, along with all the other disasters around here."

"Quite right, sir. We may only have a few minutes before the rain starts, and the president of Mongolia's entourage is lining up at the Dip Entrance. By the way," he added, "your state gift is out there too."

"State gift? What is it this time?"

"A pair of yaks!"

"Yaks? On the South Lawn? What do they think this is? Noah's Ark?"

"I have to admit the press corps is having a field day out there."

"Christ Almighty! Whatever happened to crystal bowls and hand towels?"

"Maybe they took a cue from the Chinese when they gave us the pandas. At least the live ones go to the Zoo, the children come look, and next thing you know everybody knows where their country is."

"I suppose. So now what? I go out there, shake hands with the president and go pet some yaks?" the president scoffed.

"Could be worse," the chief of staff observed.

"How?"

"Remember years ago when that guy from India brought a baby elephant, and they had it all decked out in some heavy jeweled blanket or something? That was in August. It was a hundred degrees and the little thing died."

The president looked up from his schedule and rolled his eyes. "Well, I hope these animals are in better health. Guess we'd better get outside and get it over with. We need to refocus on the Dulles crash, not some guy whose people live in yurts." He glanced over his shoulder at the windows. "Storm's moving in. All we need now is some yak to be struck by lightening."

The president, chief of staff and assorted secret service agents went outside, walked down the colonnade next to the Rose Garden, moved inside the main building, down a long hall and turned right into the Diplomatic Reception Room.

Stepping outside again, they could see the line of black limousines off to the left, dozens of reporters and photographers on the right, and a large group of well-dressed guests sitting on rows of white garden chairs.

"Where'd we get the audience?" the president asked as he headed toward the lead limo.

"We couldn't find enough Mongolians, so some of those are staff from the OEOB," his aide muttered.

"Good thinking."

The president went through the arrival ceremony, made his brief welcoming remarks, gave the president of Mongolia a chance to make his statement and then stood back while the man talked on, through a state department interpreter, for a full fifteen minutes. "I didn't know we had that much to discuss," the president whispered to his aide.

"We don't, but it's his one moment in the sun, uh, so to speak," the aide said under his breath. Just then a crack of thunder drowned out the Mongolian's last line. The yaks bolted from their handlers and started to run toward the back lawn. The reporters started to laugh, the photographers jerked their cameras around to record the scene as six secret service agents fanned out to try and trap the frightened animals.

The aide leaned over and muttered to the president, "I can just imagine the HPS on this one."

"Headline, picture, story?" the president answered. "I don't even want to speculate!" He turned and said, "Let's get out of here," motioning to the official party to head inside just as rain started to pelt the guests who now looked flustered, obviously wondering where they should go.

A staffer from the office of public liaison shouted, "Follow me," and the bedraggled group rushed in after the president and headed to the wash rooms down the hall to try and dry their hair and clothes.

The president led his guest, along with his seven assistants, back to the West Wing and into the Roosevelt Room where he explained they would have a briefing session with the assistant secretary of state for Asian Affairs and the head of the NSC's Economic Affairs section. The president said he would continue their meeting later in the day and slipped out the side door.

"Glad that's over," he said, brushing a few drops from his navy blue suit and straightening his tie. He walked across the hall and into the Cabinet Room resplendent with a new red wool rug with gold stars and a border of olive branches.

He moved to the far side of the large oval conference table with a leather inset top, set on a series of pedestals and took his seat on the Queen Anne-style leather armchair in the middle, right in front of two flags set in stands against the sandstone walls. Six gold eagle-form sconces lit the impressive room along with three hanging bronze lights with tassel finials.

The rest of the cabinet and a smattering of aides stood up to greet him and then sat down again after he did. Instead of having his secretary of state sitting on one side and the secretary of defense on the other, the president had Vice President Jayson Keller sitting to his right as the secretary of state would not be back in town until later that evening. Besides, the president had a special announcement to make. He cleared his throat and began the meeting.

"Ladies and Gentlemen. Thank you for coming over on such short notice. You all have heard the tragic news about Austin Gage and the other innocent people shot out of the sky this morning at Dulles Airport." Everyone nodded soberly. "And since we are engaged in this new war on terror, a war that has once again come to our shores, we need to move ahead with all speed to search for the perpetrators of these heinous crimes while we also analyze the best way to protect our commercial airlines and keep our transportation system moving." They all nodded once more.

"And so, I am breaking ground somewhat and announcing the appointment of Vice President Jayson Keller to take on the additional role as my national security advisor." A murmur swept through the room as several cabinet members looked over at Stockton Sloan, the deputy national security advisor who sat stoically in one of the chairs along the wall with the other aides.

"I realize this is an unusual move. However, I've made it for several reasons. First, I had already asked Jay to focus on one part of our challenge—to select the best of our technologies to protect the airliners. And, as you know, I had asked Austin to concentrate on the search for the terrorist group responsible for these crimes. Jay and Austin have been working closely together. Therefore, Jay is completely up-to-speed on all of our efforts.

"Second, I wanted to move quickly to replace Austin and since this is a White House staff position, and not subject to Senate confirmation, I knew I could move ahead with great speed. As I said, Jay is on top of these issues, so he can make a seamless transition.

"As for Stockton Sloan," the president turned and motioned to the blond-haired former military officer with short platinum hair and wire-rimmed glasses. "He will continue in his role as deputy national security advisor. I am very pleased to have him on our team."

What the president didn't disclose is that he had cut a deal with Jayson Keller to appoint Sloan to be his secretary of state after the election when, they both hoped, Jayson would be sworn in as the next president of the United States.

"One more point on this new assignment for the vice president. While some of you are obviously surprised that the man will be wearing two hats from now on, this is not entirely without precedent. You all may recall that Henry Kissinger served as both national security advisor and secretary of state for a good two years, if memory serves.

"Now then, we have several other subjects we need to cover today," the president said. "I decided to bring you all together because we need to maintain a concerted effort and united front when it comes to solving this most difficult situation."

He turned to his director of national intelligence. "I know you've been doing daily briefings on the terrorist search, but can you give us all an update?"

The DNI checked his notes and said in a serious tone, "Mr. President, I want to assure you that we have deployed every agent we have available to key locations around the world. We are working closely with teams of FBI agents in this country, pooling our resources in our search for the culprits." At this last statement, several aides exchanged glances, knowing full well that if the two agencies were in fact pooling all of their information and resources, it would be unique.

The DNI continued. "NSA is utilizing advanced surveillance programs, as we've discussed, and may be giving us new leads any day now."

"Does this mean we're infringing on the rights of law-abiding citizens?" the secretary of the interior asked.

"We're going to be hit with a new wave of lawsuits, you can be sure of that," the secretary of HHS said.

The intelligence director shot them both a withering stare. "Under the circumstances, I think we'd all agree that in these extraordinary times, extraordinary measures are needed."

At that point, the room erupted in noisy confrontation. "But, Mr. President," the EPA secretary implored, "We can't spy on Americans again . . ."

"Who says we're spying? We're evaluating patterns," the secretary of defense declared.

"Do we have court-ordered . . . ?"

"What about subpoenas?"

"We changed the FISA rules once."

"But the Patriot Act was amended."

The president pounded the table. "God damn it. This is *not* how we run cabinet meetings!" He took a deep breath and glowered at his colleagues. "While I do value your input, let's remember, *I* run these meetings. And *I* have made the decision to give NSA the tools it needs to find these bastards who are shooting our planes out of the sky. If we have to ruffle some feathers in the process, I'd rather do that than let these terrorists shoot down the whole flock, so to speak. Now then, let's hear what else the DNI has to say."

"Thank you, Mr. President. As I said, we have agents working round the clock, around the world to find these people. However, let me caution you that the CIA is still in a rebuilding mode. Ever since our ranks were reduced by twenty-three percent some years ago, we feel we've been playing catch-up ball in this war on terror. You'll recall that at one point, back then, there were more FBI agents in New York City than we had CIA agents working overseas. Since then, we have engaged in crash recruitment programs, and I'm glad to say we have no dearth of candidates."

The president shook his head in resignation and turned to William Ignatius, his secretary of defense. "Iggy, you sent over a report about Russia's TOR anti-aircraft missiles and how they've been selling them to Iran. What's your take on the possibility that they've updated those weapons so that they could have been used in these attacks?"

The secretary of defense explained how his department had been working closely with their defense counterparts in Moscow on all of these transfer-of-technology issues and said that they'd had some success in slowing down the sales. He went on to say that even if Russian missiles had been used, what would be their motive in shooting down our planes? And by the same token, what would be Iran's motive? Even though Iran remained a huge problem for the United States, they and every other country that might be on our target list, would have to know that as soon as we discovered who was directing the attacks, we would immediately annihilate that country in retaliation.

"People talk about 'proportional response,' Mr. President," Iggy said, "But in this country, that wouldn't even be a consideration."

"What do you mean?" the deputy secretary of state, who was sitting in for his absent boss, asked in an alarmed tone.

"What I mean," Iggy said, staring intently at the Harvard-trained diplomat, "is that this is America. Sure, we sit back and play the benevolent buddy when we give foreign aid to a hundred and fifty-four countries, send millions of dollars worth of medicine to Africa and Lord knows where else, and our people give more in charitable donations than anybody else on the planet. But when we're hit like we were at Pearl Harbor, we don't just go and bomb some shipyard in Japan, no sirree, we got into WWII full steam, and when they kept attacking, in order to put an end to it, we didn't just send over a few more ships, we dropped two atom bombs on the bastards and leveled the place.

"And as for 9/11, we didn't shoot down a couple of planes, we moved into Afghanistan and saw to it that that they installed a whole new government. I admit that a few years ago under a completely different administration, we took a step back and just tried diplomacy. But now, we're back on track. In this country, there *will be* no such thing as proportional response. Right, Mister President?"

The president nodded solemnly, reached over and patted Iggy on the shoulder as the rest of the cabinet sat stock still.

The secretary of transportation, Trenton LaSalle then gave his report, indicating that the air traffic controllers were about to take a vote on whether to go on strike, the Airline Pilots Association was demanding new technology to protect the planes within the month or they would stage a sit-down, and a number of the airlines had cancelled at least fifty percent of their flights.

Even though the last attack occurred at Dulles, he summarized their surveys of all airports near water, Logan, LaGuardia, Kennedy, Reagan, Los Angeles as well as others, on the assumption that terrorists could take aim from a boat and quickly get away. He assured the group that special measures were being taken by the Coast Guard and Harbor Patrols in all of our waterways. And he closed by saying they were trying to delay any strike actions for as long as possible.

Next the United States Trade Representative raised the issue of China, saying she had been asked to analyze a possible motive on their part. She emphasized that China was begging for more trade and less tariffs, and she pointed out that some years back they had ordered eighty Boeing 737's to the tune of over five-billion dollars and had said they might be in the market for twenty-six hundred more planes over the next twenty years. So why would they want to bring down our airline industry?

There was a pause in the proceedings as everyone pondered her statement. Finally, the president checked his watch, gathered his notes and stood up. "It's time to wrap this up. I've got another meeting, and I know you all have to get back to your agencies and get us some answers. Either we find these groups and bring them to justice, or our economy will be in the tank and the American people will . . . justifiably . . . throw us all out of office. So get about it and report back to me as soon as you learn anything."

Everyone stood up as the president walked to the door, his chief of staff in tow. "So what do you think, sir?" the aide muttered as he held the door open.

"What to I think?" the president echoed. "I think we're absolutely nowhere!"

CHAPTER EIGHTEEN

ROCKVILLE, MARYLAND

"A re you sure you know where we're going?" Cammy asked as she steered her Audi A4 off I-270 and headed down an unfamiliar road.

Melanie flicked on the interior light and double checked her map. "I think so. We stay on this road for another four or five miles then there should be a turn-off."

Rain was coming down in torrents, and Cammy turned her windshield wipers to a higher setting. "How did you hear about this place, anyway?"

"I read an article about all of the little puppies and kittens at this shelter, and it just broke my heart. So I called, and they said I could have any one I wanted. They usually charge a fee to adopt an animal, but they're waiving all of that to encourage people to come and adopt right now."

Cammy strained to find a landmark or road sign. Then she checked her rear view mirror. "Amazing that anybody else is on this road tonight.

There's a car back there. Been with us the whole way. It sure doesn't look like there are many houses out here."

"Maybe they're going to the shelter too," Melanie ventured.

"Maybe." With no street lights, Cammy was having trouble navigating. When she spotted a sign coming up on the right, she said. "Quick, read that."

Melanie peered out and read the words, "Adopt a Highway, Litter Control."

"Big help," Cammy muttered.

"Hey, don't worry. We'll get there. Should be just a few more miles," Melanie said, trying to sound cheery. "It was really nice of you to come along and help me pick out a kitten tonight. I know you're doing nothing but concentrating on your work these days."

"Concentrating is right," Cammy said. "On this new laser. I'm wondering, where is David Copperfield when I need him?"

Melanie giggled. "By the way, anything new from Hunt? I mean, since that meeting and all?"

Cammy signed. "Nope. Not a word. Remember the vice president told me they'd sent him down to South America with Claudia Del Sarto."

"Who's Claudia Del Sarto?"

"That's what I wondered, so I googled her."

"Really? What did you find out?"

"Well, first of all, she's gorgeous."

"Oh, no!"

"Second, she joined the NSC staff a few months ago, and she speaks four languages."

"Oh geez! So they're down in South America together?" Melanie said, "I wonder for how long?"

"Beats me. Official business and all of that, I suppose." She turned to her friend and added, "But that's fine with me. I'm putting that guy out of my mind," Cammy said defiantly.

"That easy, huh?"

"Okay, so a memory is a hard thing to delete. But I'm trying." She looked at her mirrors again and saw that the one car was still trailing them. She tried to shake off a brooding sense of vulnerability, remembering her friend's quick rescue the last time she had been threatened. She thought again about her previous stalker. It had been the most horrible experience of her life. It had been an awful nightmare, and she couldn't help but look over her shoulder all the time.

"Shouldn't there be a turn-off here somewhere?" Cammy asked.

"I think so," Melanie replied. "Sure wish this rain would let up. It just keeps coming down."

"Like our 401K plans," Cammy said.

"Yeah. Those and the entire economy right now."

"Every time I pick up the *Wall Street Journal* and see all those articles about the airlines being near bankruptcy and the pilots refusing to fly and FedEx and UPS not being able to make their deliveries, except locally with trucks or even drones . . . I mean, what a mess!" She checked her gas gauge. "At least the price of gas isn't going up."

"Course not. Nobody's buying fuel for the planes." Melanie looked up ahead and saw a street sign. "There it is. Next corner, turn right."

"Thank God!" Cammy said. As she made the turn, she saw that the car behind them continued down the main road. "Finally," Cammy said as she let out her breath. She spotted the animal shelter up ahead, pulled in, grabbed an umbrella from the back seat and both women raced inside.

They were greeted by a young woman in jeans, a T-shirt and leather sandals who led them into a room filled with small cages. Melanie pointed to the girl's shoes and murmured to Cammy, "Did I tell you I went shopping for some sandals over lunch yesterday? I saw some kind of like hers only fancier, and they wanted four-hundred bucks for them."

Cammy replied, "Talk about slipper shock,"

Melanie laughed and then pointed to one of the cages. "Oh, look at those cute little things."

The girl stopped and said, "Yes, they just came in the other day. A whole litter. Those kittens are ready for adoption if you want one. Take your pick."

Melanie and Cammy reached in, picked up a few of the kittens, stroked their tiny heads and debated which one to take home. "How about this one? I could call him Domino," Mel said, pointing to a black and white kitten that was now purring contently in her arms.

"Sure," the girl said. "Take him." She turned to Cammy, "You sure you don't want one too?"

"Wish I could. They're really cute, but I keep such late hours, and I'm in and out. I don't think it would be fair to have one right now."

"That's okay. We're going to run another ad in the paper this weekend. Maybe some other folks will come around."

Melanie took the kitten, wrote a check as a donation to the shelter, thanked the woman for the small bag of cat food to get started, and they ran back to the car. As they drove home, Cammy saw the kitten nuzzle up to her friend's face, and she reflected on the unconditional love that an animal could show to a human being.

Would she ever find unconditional love? From anybody? Certainly not from Hunt Daniels. She had thought . . . she had dreamed . . . that he might be the one. After a string of disastrous love affairs, she thought she might have finally found the right man. The timing would have been good too. How much longer was she going to slave away in her lab for a jerk like Stan Bollinger, even if she did want to continue to work on defense projects? After all, her body was telling her to take a break. She could always go back to her projects or maybe work part time in the future.

She shook her head, trying to clear away the mental images of Hunt, the tall man with the warm embrace and the tender smile. No, she couldn't think about a biological clock right now. It was the technological clock that she had to race against.

She had been having a lot of problems with her new laser idea, and she didn't know how much more time it would take to perfect it, fit it into a special pod that would be attached to some test plane and see if, once again, she had figured out a way to save lives. As she drove through the storm, she said a silent prayer that somehow, some way, she'd figure it out before it was too late.

CHAPTER NINETEEN

NORTH OF GUANGZHOU, CHINA

"Have you seen this message from Wai Yongping?" the colonel said, waving a piece of paper at his aide.

"From our San Francisco contact?"

"Yes. He reports that he needs extra money to pay off his agents in Washington."

"For the last plane?" the younger man asked.

"Yes, for that and also for the new recruit who is watching that scientist."

"Ah yes, the one we failed to eliminate in Cambridge when she was working with the traitor."

"Yes, that one. He says that they are just waiting for the right moment."

"She is but a gnat on our screen here, I believe."

"Quite so, but an irritant nevertheless." Colonel Tsao folded the report and shoved it in the pocket of his uniform. "Right now I am more concerned with the military exercises and the general's grand plan."

"In all of our meetings, General Li keeps talking about the problems in the countryside, the nine-hundred protests so far this year, the polluted drinking water, the bad air."

"Of course there's bad air when over a thousand cars are bought every single day."

"But not by the farmers," the younger man countered. "And all the general seems to think about are the farmers."

"Perhaps you would think about them too if you had come from the countryside," Colonel Tsao suggested. "After all, his parents died of starvation before any aid arrived in their village. All of his people work in the fields while the children of the Central Committee go to rock concerts in the Great Hall of the People."

"Yes, it is quite ironic that back in the 70's, if you even listened to rock and roll, you could end up in jail. Now you listen and you just end up deaf. The trouble is, I don't see how the general's grand plan is going to change the difference between rich and poor in our country. When just one percent of our people control sixty percent of our country's wealth, they're not going to use it to help the farmers, they're going to spend it at Saks, Louis Vuitton or Prada in the Bund District of Shanghai."

The colonel shrugged. "True. However, I believe that the general's plan does have an upside when it comes to economics."

"What do you mean?

"When we finally take over Taiwan, think of all the assets we will then control."

"That is if we control them and not the Central Committee."

"Ah yes, another challenge for another day."

CHAPTER TWENTY

BETHESDA, MARYLAND

Cammy checked the meager contents of her refrigerator and pulled out some lettuce, a tomato and what was left of a small roast chicken. She sliced off a few pieces and put them in a salad bowl with the other ingredients, added a little crumbled blue cheese, some oil and vinegar and tossed it all together.

Maybe she should have taken Melanie up on her invitation to have dinner at her apartment when they got back from their foray to that shelter, but Cammy had decided she should get home, check her email and try to do some more work in the few hours she had left that evening.

She was glad she and Mel lived in the same apartment building. It was nice to have a good friend so near by. And with Mel's parents being French and her innate talent in the kitchen, it made for some nice dinner parties, when she had the time to enjoy them.

She thought about the little sign in Melanie's kitchen. It was a quote from some Duchess that read, "If you accept an invitation to dinner, you have an obligation to at least be amusing." The trouble was, Cammy hadn't felt amused by much of anything lately, what with the threats facing the country, her problems at the office and her continuing melancholy over Hunt Daniels. The man who never called.

Cammy glanced at the telephone on the side table next to the beige chenille couches in her living room. An oriental rug covered the hardwood floor. A few antiques, a painting of the Golden Gate Bridge over her fireplace and a pair of ficus trees in large moss green pots in the corners completed the scene. As she stared at the phone, she willed it to ring and then felt foolish. *I'm acting like a teenager wishing the football star would call to invite me to the junior prom*, she thought. *Grow up!*

Her kitchen was usually light and airy, but as Cammy sat down at the round breakfast table by the window she could see the storm still raging outside. She was used to living alone although tonight, with the wind and rain beating against her building, she suddenly felt rather lonely so she reached for the remote, flicked on the small kitchen TV set and tuned it to Fox News just to keep her company.

She saw one of their regular commentators analyzing the appointment of the vice president to the additional post of national security advisor. She was momentarily taken aback when they flashed a rather attractive photo of Jayson Keller on the screen.

She had heard about the crash at Dulles that had killed Austin Gage. She had been horrified at the news. She had met with the NSC advisor several times and really liked the man. He was generally an all business, no nonsense type, and yet he had a very personable side to him that warmed to people on his staff. He wasn't one of those martinets who sucks up to his superiors and degrades those at lower levels. She would truly miss the man. She made a mental note to be sure to attend his funeral, whenever it was.

She stared at the TV. While everyone knew about today's crash, this was the first she'd heard about the emergency cabinet meeting and the president's announcement.

"Is it your judgment that Vice President Keller will do a better job locating the terrorists than Austin Gage?" the newscaster asked.

"It's hard to tell at this point. The White House isn't saying much," replied the analyst.

"Yes, their press secretary is trying to paint this as just a logical transition, but how logical is it to put so much on Keller's plate right now?"

"Exactly right. As if he didn't have enough to worry about, Senator Winters is calling hearings on the airline crash situation. And with his presidential ambitions out there for all to see, this could be quite a noisy forum."

Her cell rang. She picked it up while putting the TV on mute. At first she wondered whether Hunt had finally decided to get in touch. "Cameron Talbot," she said.

"Cammy? This is Jayson."

She hesitated and then realized that it was the vice president of the United States calling himself. No staff putting through his calls. How unique. "Yes, sir. How are you? I was just watching a program about your new appointment. Congratulations . . . I guess. I was so sorry to hear about Austin Gage. I mean, to lose him and all of those other passengers. It's just so awful. Do you have any details on this one?"

"Not yet. I'm afraid it's a repeat of the other attacks. Nothing on radar, just a sudden attack. The pilot only had a few moments to shout a Mayday."

"My God! But what does this mean for you, if I may ask?"

"You can ask me anything you want. And by the way, I'm sorry to bother you at home. After everything that's happened today, I just wanted to check in."

"Oh, that's okay. I'm just finishing a late dinner."

"Been working late too, huh?"

"Sort of. But what can I do for you, sir?"

He chuckled. "You can stop calling me 'sir' for one thing," Jayson said.

"All right."

"Look, I'm sure you're swamped with your work and all, but I just wanted to see if there might be anything new on your project. Anything at all?" he asked, sounding hopeful.

Cammy paused and thought about all the simulations that weren't working in her lab and all the trouble Bollinger was giving her at the office. Here she was talking to the second most powerful man in the nation, maybe in the world, a man who had so much to worry about as he was searching for terrorists, she didn't want to bother him with her own issues. Then again, she had to be honest with the man. "Right now we've got a few glitches," she admitted, "but I'm trying to fix them."

"Glitches?"

"Let me put it this way. You know how sometimes you're looking for the magic bullet and all you come up with is blanks?"

The vice president gave a short laugh. "Yes, I seem to be doing that a lot these days." He certainly enjoyed talking to this bright woman, even if it was about a deadly subject. He wanted to keep the conversation going, but it was getting late, and he still had a stack of briefing papers to go through.

"Say, Cammy, since I'm sure we both have pretty busy schedules, do you think there might be an evening when we could continue our discussions? Maybe over dinner?"

He was asking her for a date? Cammy wound the telephone cord around her finger and tried to think of a good response. Sure it would be interesting to have dinner with him. Who wouldn't want to have dinner with the vice president of the United States? But after she had danced with him at that charity dinner, she had been hounded with questions.

Reporters had tried to get through to her to find out if she and the VP were "an item," but all the calls had been routed to Melanie's office, and Mel hadn't said a word. Not to the press anyway.

Did she want this kind of attention? Did she need it? Then again, if they could do it discretely, why not have dinner and talk about her work? After all, she was trying desperately to come up with a system that could neutralize these deadly missiles. And he certainly had been acting like a champion for her cause.

"Uh, I guess we could do that some time. It's just that with your . . ."

"You mean the secret service protection, the press scrutiny, and the general live-life-in-the-spotlight-routine I have going here?" he said with a laugh.

"Well, yes. It's just that after the other night, I was kind of inundated . . ."

"Figures. Look, I'm sorry about that. I just saw you there and wanted to," he hesitated, "to touch base."

"I understand. When the press came after me, I didn't answer the phone or any of the emails or texts."

"That's about all you can do. Now about dinner. What say we pick an evening, you can drive over to the Naval Observatory and we'll get the steward to rustle up something casual. You know where my place is, right?"

"Who doesn't?" she said.

"How about tomorrow?"

"That soon? I don't know if I'll have . . ."

"Don't worry. We'll just talk through the work you've done so far and see if I can offer any help. I have a rather long day, so say around eight?"

"Sure, eight's good. See you then."

She hung clicked off and stared at the cell for a full minute. Dinner with the vice president, and at his home? Now that was a unique invitation. She bet that any other single woman in town would trade her soul for a date like that.

Was it a date? No, of course not. It was business. All business. And as for trading her soul, she hadn't done that since she'd fallen madly in love with Hunt Daniels, and look where that got her. Not exactly a pact with the devil, although there were times she really did feel like Mephistopheles. On the other hand, Jayson Keller wasn't asking for any Faustian bargain. It was only dinner.

CHAPTER TWENTY-ONE

CAPITOL HILL

"The meeting will please come to order," Senator Derek Winters intoned as he banged his gavel, trying to gain some semblance of order in the noisy hearing room. Banks of television cameras crowded the back and sides of the room while reporters jostled for a clear view in the cramped space they had been allotted.

The members of the Senate Intelligence Committee were seated on either side of the chairman. They continued to compare notes with staff who juggled papers, whispered suggested questions and kept watch from a row of chairs right behind them.

The senator from Vermont sat several inches taller than his colleagues. His six foot four inch frame was clad in a gray suit, light blue shirt and blue and red Hermes tie. Perfect shades for television. He never wore ties with small stripes because he didn't want to create his own test pattern. His press secretary had even patted some clear powder on his nose and forehead before he walked in to ensure that his time on camera wouldn't be marred by a reflective shine.

The senator tapped his gavel another three times and the conversations finally dwindled down. He made his opening statement, looking directly into the cameras where he emphasized the gravity of the situation facing the nation's airline industry. He reminded the audience that they would be hearing from the heads of the FAA, the NTSB, DOT, DHS and DOD in an effort to learn why the administration had been so lax in their efforts to protect air travel throughout the United States, why the president and his staff had not yet figured out who was shooting down our planes, if in fact someone was, and why we should have any faith in the investigations underway or the technology under development to solve the problem.

"But first, I would like to introduce a special witness we have with us today," the senator said. "Mrs. Lorri Pucell is the widow of Captain Doug Purcell, the brave pilot of Enterprise Air Flight One-fifty-five which went down just outside of Logan Airport in Boston."

Senator Winters looked down at the witness table where an attractive woman dressed in a black suit with a single strand of pearls at her neck, sat quietly. Her long brown hair the color of the mahogany framed her lovely, but sad face.

"Oh boy, leave it to Winters to lead with a heart-breaker," the correspondent for MSNBC whispered to his cameraman, who had snagged a position at the side of the room to get a good angle on the witnesses.

"Got a two-fer there. She's not only sympathetic, she's striking!"

"Yeah, zoom in."

"And so," the chairman continued, "I want to welcome you, Mrs. Purcell. Please tell us what you've been told about the crash that killed your husband and so many other innocent Americans."

The widow read an opening statement prepared in advance by Winter's legislative aide. He had met with Lorri Purcell the previous day to work out the language since the senator didn't want to leave anything to chance.

She told the story about how she had received the dreadful phone call from the president of Enterprise Air and how, much later, she had been contacted by a representative of the NTSB when they had raised the wreckage of the plane. That man had told her that they had analyzed the recordings in the black box and Doug's last words were "Lorri, I love you."

When she uttered the phrase, her eyes glistened and a single tear fell down her cheek. There was utter silence in the room as the senator let the impact of the statement echo in the large paneled chamber.

Melanie continued to watch the proceedings on her office TV set while trying to write a press release at the same time about Bandaq's latest research for Sikorsky Sea King Helicopters. She saw that Derek Winters looked elegant in his gray suit and blue shirt. She had suggested the color combination, and she was glad he had taken her advice. The trouble was, his appearance was the only thing that pleased her that morning.

She almost yelled at the set when he started raking Secretary Ignatius over the coals about the possibility of military exercises being conducted too near our commercial aircraft and insinuating that perhaps the Air Force had shot off missiles that had downed our planes by mistake.

Then she was outraged when she saw her lover take on the entire FBI for not finding the terrorists yet, if that's who was shooting down the planes. It had only been a few weeks, so how was the administration supposed to figure out where a missile came from when it had no return address?

When Franklin Thorne testified about the DHS contracts, she had to admit that he didn't make a very good case for the two defense contractors who had yet to test their defensive systems for airplanes and airports. And yet, he kept hammering away about how they needed more money. She hoped the senators wouldn't cave in to that one because she sensed that Cammy would come up with something better. At least she fervently hoped so.

When they finally broke for lunch, Melanie switched off the set, grabbed her purse and went down the hall to Cammy's lab. "Hey there, got time for a break?"

Cammy looked up from her computer simulations and pushed a few strands of hair out of her eyes. She glanced at her watch and replied,

"Why not. I've been working on all of this since seven this morning. May as well get some lunch."

As they took the elevator down to the company cafeteria, Mel asked, "Did you catch any of the hearings?"

"Oh, that's right, they started today. No, I was concentrating on my computer screen, not the TV screen. I'm going crazy trying to enhance the pulse feature. I'm also trying to research an idea that Wen Hu had about how the missiles could have been guided."

"Really? You haven't mentioned that. Do you really think you've figured it out?"

"I'll tell you in a minute."

They walked into the cafeteria where Melanie handed Cammy a tray and pushed her own along the metal track. She picked up a tuna sandwich, a small bowl of fruit and a glass of iced tea as Cammy reached for her favorite salad and yogurt. After paying the cashier, they took a table off to the side of the large dining hall.

"Now, about a new missile," Cammy said, putting her plate on the table and setting her tray aside. "Wen had been corresponding with a guy back in Beijing who told him about some new kind of high resolution camera they're developing, and we talked about the possibility that they could put something like that on a missile. It takes certain kinds of photos, gets a bead on the plane so to speak, and then is able to follow it and take it down."

"Wow! Could that really work?"

"I've been scouring all sorts of sources. I think I've finally got a line on it. Yes."

"But China? Why would they want to shoot down our planes? I mean, what's the point?"

"I'm not sure about a motive. Everybody at the White House is focused on motive too. In fact, I went up to talk to Bollinger this morning. I told him my theory. He said I was nuts." Cammy took a bite of her salad and waved her fork. "Well, he always says I'm nuts. And you know what else he said about it?"

"What?"

"He said, 'you couldn't sell that idea on eBay'."

"Sounds just like him," Mel muttered. "That guy really is pretty judgmental."

"Judgmental?" Cammy echoed. "He's just to the right of Saint Peter."

"So what are you gonna do?"

"I'm not sure. Right now I feel kind of like Paul Revere and nobody's paying attention to my lantern."

Melanie rolled her eyes. "Look, Cam, you just may be on to something here. What about Hunt? Isn't he working the whole intelligence-terrorist angle now?"

Cammy shook her head. "I can't go to him. We're not even on speaking terms any more. Besides, he's probably still in South America with that gorgeous woman."

"Still no word, huh? That seems so sad to me. I mean, after all you went through and everything he said. Back then, I mean."

"Yeah, well, I keep remembering some of my dad's advice."

"What was that?"

"Don't just listen to what someone says, watch what he does."

Melanie paused and said, "I see what you mean. Okay, so what about Jayson Keller? I'll bet he'd listen to you."

"Now that you mention it, I'm having dinner with him tonight."

"You're what?" Mel exclaimed, almost knocking over her iced tea. She steadied the glass and stared at her friend. "When? Where? How did this happen? C'mon. Tell all," she demanded.

"He called me last night. He wants to get together and go over my research."

"Go over your research, my eye!" Melanie chided. "He wants to go over your bod."

Cammy gave her friend a sideways glance. "Oh, I'm not so sure about that. Man could obviously have any woman he wanted. Why me?"

"Look in the mirror, my friend. Of course, maybe he's only attracted to your mind," she said with a wry smile.

Cammy finished her yogurt and idly sifted through her thoughts. "I don't know. But I figure that dinner can't hurt. I'm going over to his place tonight."

"His place? You mean to the Naval Observatory?"

"MmmHmm. That way, we don't have to contend with nosy press people."

"I like it. And speaking of dinner dates, I've got one with Derek tomorrow night," Mel said.

"You're really still hooked on that guy?"

"Well, after watching his performance at those hearings, I have to say I'm having some second thoughts," she admitted.

"Why, what did he do?"

"Let's just say that it's obvious he loves the cameras. He's using these crashes to make himself the lead story on every network out there, and I'm afraid he's getting a really early start on the presidential campaign."

"He does sound like the kind of guy who believes his own press releases. But how does that make him any different from all the other senators on the Hill?" Cammy asked.

"I suppose you've got a point there. I just hate to see him use this whole terrorist thing to tear down the administration. I mean, wouldn't you think they'd try to work together to figure out who's attacking us?" Mel asked plaintively.

"Not in this life, my dear. Anyway, let me know how it goes tomorrow."

"I will. Oh, about tomorrow. I do have a quick favor to ask."

"Sure, what?"

"Well, I mean," Melanie hesitated."

"Go on, what is it?"

"After dinner, I might. I mean I may stay. Well, you know. At his place."

"Okay. You don't have to explain," Cammy said.

"I know. What I mean is, since I may not be going home, could you do me a favor and go up and feed little Domino for me tomorrow night?"

"The kitten?" Cammy asked. "Sure, no problem." She looked over Melanie's shoulder at the large clock on the back wall. "Look, I've got to get back to work. And Mel, I just may talk to Jayson about the whole China thing. I know it's far-fetched, but we know somebody is master-minding these awful attacks, and I've just got this feeling that something terribly weird, something really strange and diabolical is going on."

CHAPTER TWENTY-TWO

WASHINGTON, D.C.

The sky was the color of pewter as Cammy drove down Massachusetts Avenue that evening. The rain had tapered off, but there was still the occasional drizzle. It was a cool evening so she had donned her light trench coat over a black skirt and light blue silk sweater that matched her eyes.

She had finally begun to take Melanie's advice about adding a bit of color to her wardrobe. She had a closet full of taupe, beige, white and ecru. Mel had told her that she always looked like an egret and should branch out a bit. She was hoping that this outfit would be appropriate for a casual dinner, even if it was with the second most powerful man in the country.

She pulled up to the guard gate at the entrance to the vice president's residence at One Observatory Circle. She showed her driver's license to the agent who motioned for her to drive on up to the house. She knew that this place had quite a history, having been built back in the late

1800's as a home for the head of the U.S. Naval Observatory. They even had a big telescope there in the old days where former presidents would trek up the hill to look at comets and planets.

The large traditional home, built on a high point of rolling hills and lush acreage, became such a show piece that higher ranking officers kept trying to figure out a way to live there. Finally, in the 70's, Congress decided to make it the official residence of the vice president.

Cammy had driven by the place every time she had gone down to the White House. Now, she was anxious to see what the inside was like. When she rang the bell, it wasn't an agent or steward who opened the door, it was Jayson Keller himself, dressed in dark grey slacks, a blue and white striped button down shirt that was open at the neck, and a navy blue blazer.

"Good evening, Cammy, good of you to come," he said with a broad smile. "Here, let me take your coat. Guess it's still a bit misty out there."

She took off her trench coat, put her purse on a hall table and followed Jay along the hardwood floors into the nicely appointed living room. He motioned for her to sit down on one of the light green sofas behind a glass coffee table. She gazed at a series of paintings and realized that they must be on loan from a museum. They were all lovely landscapes and bore little brass plates with the name of the artist and date they had been painted. Impressive, she thought.

A steward then appeared and inquired about a drink before dinner. Cammy opted for a glass of Chardonnay while Jay asked for a Scotch neat.

"Now then," he said, sitting down across from her, "before we get to the heavy issues, why don't you tell me a little bit about yourself? All I know is that you are a brilliant scientist who invents breakthrough technologies for missile defense. And that's a pretty heavy topic all by itself. But what about you? Tell me where you're from. Seems that everybody in Washington is from somewhere else."

Cammy leaned back on the soft down cushions and thought about her reply. He certainly was playing the role of the gracious host. She had to wonder if all he really wanted tonight was an update on her work. It wasn't starting out that way.

"I'm from a lot of places, I guess. My dad was an Air Force pilot. We spent a lot of time at Travis Air Force Base out in California. I love that area. It's pretty close to San Francisco, you know."

"Yes, I know it well. I campaigned all over California the summer before the election. The only problem was that everywhere we went, it was nice and warm, but when we got to San Francisco, the fog was in and . . ."

Cammy smiled as she interrupted, "And you froze! Remember Mark Twain's line about the coldest winter he ever spent was a summer in San Francisco?"

"He got that one right. But you say your dad was a pilot? Where is he now?"

Cammy hesitated and her face clouded over as the fiery images once again invaded her mind's eye. "Uh, he died in a plane crash when I was in high school."

"Oh, Cammy, I'm sorry. I didn't know that. What happened?"

"He was testing a new Sidewinder missile. It miss-fired and his plane went down."

Jay got up and moved over to sit down next to her on the couch. He took her hand and said gently, "I can imagine how you felt when that happened. I went through a pretty tough time once too."

"You mean when your wife died?" Cammy said, looking up into his slate grey eyes. They reminded her of the sky outside. Dark and just as troubled.

"Yes, it was pretty rough. It happened during the campaign, you know." Cammy nodded. "I was on the road so much, I wasn't even there when the aneurysm hit. I raced home, but it was too late."

"I'm so sorry."

"I worked my way through it as I'm sure you had to do."

The steward brought their drinks on a sterling silver tray, handed Cammy her wine glass, along with a small square linen napkin, and gave the vice president his cocktail. "Will that be all, sir?"

"Yes, that's fine for now," Jayson said. Turning back to Cammy, he raised his glass, "Let's toast to the future with the hope that it's a better one, shall we?"

Cammy touched the tip of her glass to his and took a sip. "Yes, let's do that."

"Well, looking ahead, we're keeping a full plate of issues front and center that have nothing to do with airplanes."

"Really? I didn't know you had time for anything else these days. What's going on?"

"Let's see," Jayson said, leaning back against the cushions and stretched his legs underneath the coffee table. "We had an economic policy discussion today on more health care reforms. The trouble is, the doctors are complaining that if they order too many tests, the insurance companies complain. But if they don't order enough tests, their malpractice insurance rates go up."

"I've often thought that what we have now is a veterinary system of medicine."

"Veterinary system? What do you mean?"

Cammy took another sip of her wine and explained. "When you take your dog to the vet, the vet does what *you*, the person paying the bill, tells him to do. It's not necessarily what's best for the dog. He's got no say in the matter. And it's just like that with us. We go to the doctor, and the doctor does what the insurance company—the one paying the bill—says he can do."

Jay drank a bit of Scotch and nodded. "Good analysis. Can I use that in one of my speeches?"

"Be my guest. What else is going on?"

"Let's see. The animal rights people are all over us for a whole bunch of issues."

"Like what?"

"Well, for one thing, word got out that the president's grandchildren keep goldfish in a glass bowl."

"So? Everybody does."

"According to the Rights crowd, if you keep the fish in a small bowl, it can go blind."

"How can they tell?" Cammy asked, with a half smile.

Jayson laughed. "Beats me. Oh, but in the good news category, our science advisor said today that they think they've broken the genetic code of beets."

Cammy almost choked on her wine. "So now we can make biotech borscht?"

The steward walked back into the room and cleared his throat. "And on that note," the vice president said with a smile, "I believe dinner is ready." Jayson got up and offered Cammy a hand. He led the way into the dining room where they sat down at a large oval table that could have handled sixteen guests. Just two places were set at one end.

They began their dinner with a serving of Senegalese soup, followed by broiled salmon, brown rice with pecans and haricot verte. The steward served more wine and Cammy began to feel slightly light-headed. It was a pleasant feeling, though. Here she was, having a very private dinner with a handsome, charismatic man who was charming, humorous and quite attentive. The way his gaze seemed to follow her every move almost made her blush.

At one point, he reached over and touched her hand again. It was a warm touch. An inviting touch, and it made her speculate about what it would be like to have not just his hands, but his arms around her.

The last man she had been close to was Hunt Daniels and every time he had touched her, she felt herself melting. Was she melting now? Not exactly. Maybe the wine was dulling her senses a bit. After all, Jayson Keller was quite a catch. She took another drink of wine and tried to concentrate on what he was saying.

"And so I wanted to hear about your work on the laser and any other ideas you have about this situation."

"I've been thinking a lot about those missiles and trying to figure out exactly how they're targeting our planes."

"Yes?" Jay prompted.

"Remember in our other meeting, I told you about the work I had done with Wen Hu at M.I.T.?"

"Yes, of course, Tragic situation. I'm just glad you weren't inside," he said in a gentle voice.

"I know. But when we were collaborating on the whole project, we had this idea that the missiles might possibly be using a new high-resolution camera, an imaging seeker that uses a CCD array. It takes a picture of its target and then tracks the object."

"And you think somebody might have put this kind of camera on a missile?"

"Sure. Let's say it has a memory chip so that when it takes the photo, it follows that particular object. I call it bread-crumb technology."

"Cute," he said. "But what about deceiving our radar?"

"As I said before, I think the missile has stealth capability," Cammy declared.

"I thought I was up on a lot of military applications, but who do you think would have such technology?" he asked staring intently.

"Well, China." she replied. "Dr. Hu learned about the photo angle from a contact in Beijing."

"China!" He narrowed his eyes and thought for a long moment while he tasted the salmon. "Intriguing. They sure as hell have the capability."

"Absolutely," she agreed. "Of the top nine Chinese leaders, eight are engineers and one is a geologist, and their kids are way ahead of ours when it comes to studying science and math. Of course they can develop great technology."

"You're right. We know they're hacking into all of our systems, stealing industrial secrets right and left. We've had to spend beaucoup bucks upgrading our cyber security systems over at the Pentagon because of their penetration. Then again, you probably know that."

"Sure. I've read a lot about it," Cammy said. "And what are most of our universities producing these days?"

"Lawyers and investment bankers," Jay answered.

"And not enough scientists and engineers. See what I mean? I really think it's China."

Jayson finished his rice while mulling over Cammy's theory. He thought about a lot of other women on the staff who made presentations in meetings. Many of them often prefaced their remarks with an apology. *This may not be what you're looking for*, or *I hope I'm not over-stepping my bounds here but* . . . Cammy didn't use such preambles. She dove right into her subject like an Olympian swimmer executing a jack knife. He liked that.

The steward came in to offer seconds but Cammy said, "No thank you, it was lovely." Jay shook his head as well. The man took his silver serving tray back into the kitchen.

"China," Jay repeated. "But why? What the hell is their motive? I've been grappling with this ever since the first plane was shot down. I've gone through every possible scenario and each time I can only come up with al Qaeda or some similar group. The trouble is, that bunch always ends up taking credit for their killing sprees. Not this time. In fact, they're denying it on their websites and all over Twitter."

"I know what you mean," Cammy said, her eyes guarded. "I don't know about a motive. But let me ask you this. Can you direct some of our satellites to photograph areas in China where they might have built new missile factories? I mean, they have plenty of places they could make things, but I'm thinking that if this is a whole new generation of missiles, maybe there are brand new facilities of some kind that we can see. If we can figure out where to look, I mean."

"Cammy, that's a very good idea. I'll get on it first thing in the morning." The steward came into the dining room again. This time he placed a simple dish of chocolate ice cream at each place and then picked up a silver carafe from the side board and poured each of them a cup of steaming coffee.

"Hope you like chocolate," Jay said.

"Are you kidding? This is perfect. Thank you."

They finished their dinner, going over Cammy's latest theories once more. They moved back into the living room but before sitting down again, Cammy glanced at her watch. It was eleven o'clock. "Gosh, I didn't realize it was so late. I completely lost track of the time," she said.

"I did too."

She started toward the entry hall and he followed, pausing at the closet to retrieve her trench coat. "I think the rain has stopped. There won't be much traffic this time of night. I'm just sorry I can't escort you home."

"Oh, no problem. It won't take long to get back to Bethesda."

As he helped with her coat, he took hold of her shoulders and turned her around. His face was inches from hers. He nudged her chin up, leaned down and gently kissed her. She was so stunned, she hardly knew how to react. When he encircled her with his arms and deepened the kiss, she closed her eyes and felt herself being pulled into a very strong embrace. His tongue found hers and he cradled her head with one hand, his fingers twining through her long blond hair, the faint scent of vanilla lingering there.

"I've wanted to do that since the first time I laid eyes on you," he murmured.

She didn't know what to say or do. She stood there with her head resting against his chin and tried to breathe normally. But she couldn't. He kept holding her for a long moment, finally looked down at her and added. "Now I'd better let you go or else you're never going to get out of here. Then what would the reporters say?"

Cammy took a tentative step back and absently straightened her headband. "You're right," she muttered. "I've got to get home . . . I . . ."

He reached over and put one of his fingers on her lips. "Don't say anything else. Thanks for coming over. I'll call you tomorrow."

"Okay . . . uh . . . thanks for the dinner . . . and...everything."

He opened the door for her, walked with her to her car, and helped her inside. "Just one last thought, my lady," he said.

Cammy fished in her purse for her car keys and then looked up. "Yes?"

"Whatever you do, stay safe!"

CHAPTER TWENTY-THREE

THE WHITE HOUSE

"Talk to me about our network of satellites, Iggy," the vice president commanded as he turned the key to encrypt and shifted the blue secure phone closer to his ear.

"Sure thing, Jay. You know almost as much about 'em as I do. What do you need? Specifically?" the secretary of defense asked.

"I know we've got about four hundred and eighty of them up there, doing all sorts of things. But they're pretty well spaced out. So my question is, what have we got that's looking at China?"

"China? Why?"

"Just tell me what we've got."

"We've got a lot of 'em. Now, if you could tell me what you need, I can tell our people to move them around, home in on whatever you want to check on."

"Okay. What are we using to detect missile launches?" Jayson asked.

"Missile launches? Jesus! We've got a ton of equipment monitoring that sort of thing."

"I know, but I was thinking about special photography."

"Well, we've got SPIRS high and SPIRS low."

"You mean Space-based infra-red satellites?"

"That's them," the crusty secretary replied. "SPIRS high is about a thousand miles up. Or higher. Then there's SPIRS low which is only about a hundred, maybe a hundred twenty miles up there."

"Sounds like we want SPIRS low."

"For what? I'm not sure you need a SPIRS just for launch photos."

"No. Not just launches. Actually, I'm more interested in new factories. Facilities where a new type of missile might be produced and tested."

"What kind of missile?"

"Not sure. I just want to know if we can spot new activity. I need your people to take pictures in strategic areas and compare them to what we had some time ago. Maybe a few months, maybe a year. I'm not sure. I just want an update on what the hell they're doing."

"Wait a minute, Jay. Are you saying you think the Chicoms are building some new kind of missile that could be involved in our plane crashes?" he asked incredulously.

"They just might be."

"You got evidence? I mean, where did this come from? How could they be involved? I don't get it."

"You don't have to get it. Just get me those photos, can you do that?"

"Well, sure, but our people are going to wonder what the hell they're analyzing."

"Tell them not to think so much, just follow orders. I thought that's what they were good at."

"Well, yeah, most of them. But the analysts aren't all in the military, you know. They're a different breed of cat. But I'll get on it right away. I have to say though that this is pretty far-out."

"Maybe so, but I really need your help on this. If we can pinpoint some new facilities over there that look like they're building a new generation of missiles, especially in areas near ports, shipping or airport facilities, all hell is going to break loose around here."

"You mean more hell than is already breaking loose?"

"That's about it."

"Okay. I'm on it. By the way, what did you think about Winters' hearings? Did you see how just about every cable station and network news show led with that pretty widow crying at the witness table? And then the way he lambasted Janis and the others, you'd think we were all sitting around on our asses doing nothing. And how'd you like his parting shot?"

"You mean when he said that for this administration, the road to peace is always under construction?"

"Yeah. Sounds like a campaign ad for God's sake!"

"Par for the course, I guess," Jay said with a note of resignation in his voice. "Sounds like the guy is off and running for the primaries already."

"Yeah, and trying to leave you at the starting gate."

"Well, after that performance and all the lousy headlines this morning, we've decided we better get the committee heads up here for a special briefing on our whole program. We've got to tell them about the increased surveillance over at NSA and give them an update on the DHS contracts. I'm not going to talk about your satellites though. Not until we have something concrete to report."

"Are you gonna tell 'em about Dr. Talbot's project?"

"Sure. It'll be the usual classified briefing. We want them to know that we're on top of these issues and have something new in the hopper. But the last thing we need is for her name to be leaked. She's been through enough already."

"You mean her last go-around with that Q-3 thing?"

"Not just that. She almost got herself blown up in that explosion up at M.I.T."

"Oh yeah. Jesus! Well, good luck briefing the Hill boys. I assume Winters will be there."

"As chairman of the Senate Intelligence Committee, we can't ignore him," Jay said.

"Actually, one-on-one, I suppose the guy isn't a bad sort."

"I know. It's just that when there are cameras around, the word *preen* takes on a new dimension."

The defense secretary laughed out loud. "You sure got him pegged. Well, there won't be any cameras in the Roosevelt Room, so you just might be able to contain the egos this time. Your biggest problem is going to be briefing those guys and keeping it off the record."

CHAPTER TWENTY-FOUR

STERLING, VIRGINIA

"What the hell is this all about?" Nettar Kooner railed at his team gathered at the conference table in his spacious office. "This message from the Taiwan defense minister says that our whole system of missile defense components is ineffective. Ineffective? How could it be ineffective when it worked perfectly against a whole battery of missiles here in the Atlantic as well as our Pacific testing facilities?"

His chief of staff looked around the table at the young men Kooner had recruited and brought over from India, dubbed the I-Men, to head up his research and development, legal and communications operations. "I don't know, boss. This doesn't make any sense. We all worked on that system, it performed just fine before we shipped it over."

"Taipei is now saying that they're not going to make their payments on the contract. And if this gets out, it means our stock price will go through the floor. Even lower than the market in general these days. Now I want to know what's going wrong over there.

"We all know that Taiwan is scared shitless over China's increase in defense spending", he continued. "Hell, it's been going up in double digits for the last dozen years. Now the mainland is hiking their spending on everything from troops to anti-satellite weapons by over fifteen percent and everybody knows they've got close to a thousand missiles pointed at Taiwan right now."

He looked down at the report from the defense minister and added, "China's got a whole host of new missiles like the DF-31, the DF-31A long range nuclear missile. They've also got that JL-2 submarine-launched nuclear missile that came on line. Of course, Taiwan is scared, and we were supposed to be the white knights in this scenario. Instead, our reputation will be blackened, and Taiwan will be defenseless," he bellowed.

"I'll get going on a complete re-evaluation of the system," his chief replied. He went around the table, handing out new assignments and then pulled a clipping out of a folder. "You're absolutely right about the tensions over there. Here's a report from the New China News Agency about the exercises in the Taiwan Strait. The Chinese are evidently getting ready to practice a whole series of amphibious landings. And where would they land except on Taiwan?"

Kooner grabbed the article and read the headline. "This makes it all the more important that we get our act together here. We've got to figure out what's wrong with our system and give those people some help. How in the hell are 23 million people supposed to defend themselves against a billion Chinese bent on re-claiming their island?"

"But we don't know that China is going to invade," one young man said. "After all, Taiwan has been investing in China for years. Look at Pudong Province. That was done with a ton of money from Taiwan. And besides, if China did try to make a move on the island, they know that the United States would race over there to protect them."

"Are you mad?" Kooner barked? "This government can't even figure out who's shooting down a couple of airplanes. Besides that, their military is still bogged in Syria, Iraq and South Korea, along with providing more troops to bolster NATO. Sure, they've got a couple of carriers in the Pacific, but they'd need more than that to help Taiwan, especially if it means going up against all of China."

The young man sat silently chastised as Kooner made some notes and issued more orders. They had to move fast to find out what was wrong with their system. If they didn't, his profit margin, his potential deal with Bollinger, and the vibrant democracy on Taiwan could all be history.

CHAPTER TWENTY-FIVE

THE WHITE HOUSE

Tensions were rising as members of the House and Senate Intelligence Committees gathered in the Roosevelt Room for a top-level briefing.

"The whole travel industry is being destroyed," one congressman was saying to a colleague. "And with FedEx and UPS refusing to fly their planes, Amazon is on its ass."

"I know, my constituents are screaming that we're all a bunch of incompetents in Washington. I got one letter saying that now that the story is getting worse every week, there'll be nothing written that goes beyond a Chapter Eleven!"

"And you know all the aircraft our big boys bought at the Paris Air Show?"

"Yep. I'll bet they try to renege on all those contracts and save their money for re-fitting their existing fleet with missile defense technology."

"What technology?" The door opened, and the vice president and one of his aides walked in. "That's a question for Jay to answer."

"Yeah, fat chance he's got any good news," the other Member said.

"Gentlemen. Thank you for coming here today," Jayson Keller said, taking his place at the center of the large conference table. "We have a lot to talk about. The president wants you to know about the measures he is taking to find out who is attacking our airplanes and also where we are on the new technologies to protect our fleet."

Keller went on to outline the added surveillance being conducted by NSA involving wire taps, internet monitoring, currency movements and data mining. He explained a new system that was now able to analyze thousands of numbers and patterns a second. When he stopped to pour a glass of water from a silver pitcher in the center of the table, the senator from Vermont interrupted.

"Wait a minute, Jay. Are you saying that NSA is spying on law-abiding Americans again? I thought we went through all of this. Have you got FISA Court okays for all this new snooping?"

"The new laws are being followed, Derek. But let me remind you that we have lost four plane loads of innocent people and we *must* find out who's attacking us before it happens again. I dare say that Americans are much more concerned with nailing the terrorists than they are worried about whether some NSA analyst happens to overhear a conversation with their broker. I'm sure you've seen the latest polls."

"I don't give a rat's ass about polls, I'm concerned about law suits and basic human rights here," Derek Winters countered.

"Take it easy, senator," Jay replied. "I know we're all taking the heat for these developments. But right now, our top priority is the protection of the American people, and we're trying to do just that. In terms of our operations overseas, the president has signed a secret finding regarding a number of covert actions in a number of countries. As you all know, it is our duty to brief your committees whenever he signs them."

His aide handed him a memo, and he continued. "Now on the subject of new technology, you know we have programs underway with two of our top defense contractors."

"Yeah, and neither one is producing a damn thing," the chairman of the House Intelligence Committee said in a disgusted tone."

"That's not entirely true," Jay answered. "Sterling Dynamics is close to testing its airport protection system and DHS reports that the other contractor is on a fast-track to protect the planes."

"How fast?" another member asked.

"You know Franklin Thorne has been trying to get an added appropriation from the Hill for quite some time now to speed things up."

"Even if we vote them new money, who's going to pay to retro-fit the planes once their military technology is converted to commercial use? I hear it's gonna cost tens of billions. The airlines can't afford that, so it'll probably be up to us to pop for the conversion." There was a murmur of agreement around the table. "So the question is, what have they got that's worth that kind of money, and how do we know it'll work?"

The vice president cleared his throat, looked around the table and answered. "Gentlemen, at this point we're moving ahead on those contracts as best we can. But I wanted to announce today that we have another project coming on line that, hopefully, will not only work but be much more affordable."

Several voices erupted all at once. "What project?"

"New technology?"

"Who has it?"

"How soon?"

"My people can't wait."

Jayson raised his hands in an effort to quiet the members. "Look, this is new and quite frankly, I'm excited about the prospects because of the person in charge. You all remember Dr. Cameron Talbot."

"You mean the woman who saved New Delhi from that missile attack?" Derek asked.

"Yes, that one," Jay answered.

"I know the company well. Bandaq is a first-rate operation," the senator said. "But I didn't know they were developing some new technology."

"That's the first time he's admitted not knowing something," a congressman whispered off to the side. "And with him dating that French dish over at Bandaq who does their PR, you'd think he'd know everything." The man next to him gave a side long smirk and nodded.

"So let me fill you all in on this," Jay said. "Dr. Talbot is working on a new Top Secret laser that would be contained in a pod affixed of the underside of an airliner. If a missile were launched, even though it couldn't be seen on radar, it would give off an infra-red signal which would be recorded on a panel inside the cockpit just as it is on a military jet. At that point, a series of lasers would be deployed in a three-hundred-and sixty-degree arc that would blind the incoming missile and send it off course as the plane takes evasive action. And what's more, we have reason to believe that the missiles used to attack our airplanes are of a newer generation, something with stealth technology, and Dr. Talbot is on top of that issue as well."

There was silence in the room for several seconds before another round of questions erupted.

"How soon will she have it?"

"How much will it cost?"

"What if we're hit again before it's operational?"

"Wait a minute. Are you telling us that you're putting all of your cards on this one woman who has an idea just every once in a while?" the House Committee chairman scoffed.

"Not all of our cards," the vice president said. "I told you before, we're playing every technology hand we're dealt here. And we're also sending every agent we have available around the world to gather humint on this problem."

"And they've come up with zip," Derek said.

"Let me just say that we're following up on any number of leads and as soon as we have something tangible to report, we'll get back to you. But for now, I shouldn't have to remind you all that this is a classified briefing. We particularly do not want Dr. Talbot's name out there. She's been a target before, and we must ensure her safety to continue work on the laser."

"But shouldn't the American people be told that we have a possible new defense against these missiles?" a congressman asked. "Good God, Jay, the media is killing us, the market is down again, nobody is going anywhere, and industry after industry is going down the toilet. We've *got* to give our people some hope here and begin to turn this economy around."

"Let me assure you that no one is more anxious to restore our economy than the president of the United States. That goes for our entire administration. But right now we're engaged in a difficult and delicate balancing act. Give us another week to analyze NSA's results, gather intelligence, and test the new laser. Then we'll get you all back here to review the results."

With that, the vice president and his aide got up from the table, nodded to all of the attendees and went across the hall to brief the president.

CHAPTER TWENTY-SIX

BETHESDA, MARYLAND

ammy carried a load of groceries down the hall to her apartment, fumbled for her key, opened her door and flicked on the light. She was glad to be home after an awfully long day. The high point had been the call from Jayson Keller thanking her for coming over for dinner the night before. It was a gracious call although she felt she should be the one to thank him. After all, he had played the pleasant host.

He told her about the meeting that day with the Intelligence Committees. He didn't talk about the details of a classified briefing, but he did mention that he had told them about her laser project. Next he asked for an update. She told him she had made some progress and that her team might be ready to put it on a test plane in the next few days.

He was excited about that. He said he'd talk to some people about the best place to hold the tests and get back to her. When they ended the call, she had wondered where that relationship was going. The conversation had been mostly business, so maybe the goodnight kiss at his place had been just a spur of the moment thing. She wasn't sure.

The trouble was that on the drive home from that dinner, the whole experience brought back a flood of memories of other dinners, other kisses, other intimate scenes. All of them with Hunt Daniels. Every time Hunt had touched her, she'd felt that frisson of electricity. Every time Hunt had looked at her, she'd felt a tether, a connection that was hard to explain but wonderful to feel.

Now she felt nothing but exhaustion as she lugged the grocery bags inside and kicked the door shut. *Weird*, she thought. *Something's weird.* She glanced around the living room where the painting of the Golden Gate was hanging perfectly straight over the fireplace. Nothing appeared out of place on the coffee table. The two ficus trees, standing sentry in the corners looked the same.

So what was it? Ever since her encounter with an Islamic militant a few months before, her instincts had been honed, and she always had that watch your backside feeling. She couldn't shake it.

She walked around the room, still holding the bags, and finally went into the kitchen. Again, nothing seemed to have been moved and yet . . . she sniffed the air. That was it. Something in the air. Was it cologne? No. Something even worse than that. It was almost a dirty male smell. Sweat. The hint of a man who needed a shower. *Strange.*

She set the bags on the kitchen counter and then moved into her bedroom. The scent wasn't there. *Interesting.* She checked a box on the shelf of her closet where she always kept her grandmother's ruby necklace and earrings. They were still there. *If someone was in here, thank goodness he didn't find these.* She quickly changed into a pair of pull-on pants and a tee shirt and went back into the kitchen.

She started to put her groceries away and then remembered that she had promised Melanie that she'd go up and feed the new kitten since Mel had one of her Tae Kwon Do classes. Cammy reached inside one of the kitchen drawers and was relieved to see her set of sterling silver still lined up inside. *If someone has been in here, why wouldn't he take the sterling?* She grabbed the extra key to Mel's apartment that she kept there next to the forks, took along her own key and went upstairs to see little Domino.

Once inside, the kitten ran over and rubbed up against her leg with a plaintive meow. *Poor little thing must be awfully lonely. I'll just take him down with me for a while and feed him in my place.* She picked up the kitten, closed the door and took the elevator back down to her floor.

When she was in her kitchen again, she took out a carton of skim milk, poured a little bit of it into a small dish and set it on the floor. The kitten eagerly drank the milk while Cammy tried to decide what to fix for her own dinner. She thought about heating the oven and broiling a small steak she had bought. She was about to turn on the stove when she changed her mind and decided to just fix a salad instead.

She wasn't very hungry and she was still worried about who in the world could have been in her apartment. Maybe it was the supervisor trying to fix that leaky bathroom faucet she had complained about. *Yes, that's probably it.*

She went into the bathroom to check. But when she turned on the water and then turned it off again, sure enough, it just kept dripping. She stared at it and thought, *whoever tried to fix that thing certainly did a lousy job. Or maybe he hadn't shown up at all.*

Then she heard it. A strange little howl. *What the heck was that? Sounded like it came from the kitchen.* She raced in. Here, next to the saucer of milk, the kitten lay on the floor emitting a squeaky moan.

CHAPTER TWENTY-SEVEN

NORTH OF GUANGZHOU, CHINA

General Zhang Li marched quickly through the missile factory with Colonel Tsao in tow. "Amazing what a little money put into the right hands can build these days," the general remarked as they toured the new facility.

"Yes," the colonel replied. "Our network in the southeast region has provided us with plenty of yuan for new buildings and new machinery. The drug trade has been good for our military people, adding to our rather low salaries."

"True. Even though the Central Committee has authorized an increased defense budget, the money doesn't always get to our soldiers, our faithful warriors. We have to take steps to protect ourselves. And when we want to build a special factory like this one, we can do it with our separate revenues."

"Do you think Beijing will find out about this factory?"

"Of course not! With all the building going on, much of it involving foreign investors, it is impossible for our leaders to keep track of every project. No, we are quite safe using the drug money and our own ingenuity to produce these new weapons."

The general walked over to a worker in white coveralls who was polishing a long piece of tubing. The general picked it up. "These are our latest models. Easy to transport, simple to fit together with our new photo seeking device, difficult if not impossible to detect. Our scientists have come through for us once again."

"The only trouble is, after four attacks on their airplanes, I am afraid the Americans may figure out who is responsible," the colonel said.

"And how do you think they will find out," the general demanded.

"I don't know, but I have an idea."

"What is it?"

"Perhaps we should take a gambit and sacrifice one of our own planes. That way it would remove all suspicion."

"No! Our agents would refuse."

"But wasn't it Chairman Mao himself who always said, 'Wherever there is struggle, there is sacrifice. And death is a common occurrence'?"

"Yes, but he also said, 'We should do our best to avoid unnecessary sacrifices'."

The general started walking down the aisle of machinery again and waved his hand, "Don't spend your time thinking of ways to kill our people. We have to concentrate on killing their people."

"Which ones this time, general?"

"That scientist, for one. What's the latest from our Washington agent?"

"I don't have his report yet. I do know that he tracks her every move, so do not worry. He will dispose of her very soon, I am sure."

"And what about that vice president of theirs and that other colonel working with him that I've heard about?"

"The vice president of the United States is always surrounded by his Secret Service detail. Whenever he goes anywhere, he has at least ten agents with him. He is a very difficult target."

"And the colonel?"

"You mean Lieutenant Colonel Daniels, I believe."

"Yes, that one," the general said. "Our North Korean friends are particularly incensed at his meddling in their affairs. Our Russian allies mentioned his name as well. And now we hear that he may be working with that scientist again. He worked with her once before, so inform Washington that he is to be taken care of as well."

"Yes, sir. But if I may, as we move ahead with our plans for the military exercises, I have a question."

"You ask too many questions," the general snapped. Then he turned back to his aide and said, "What is it this time?"

"As we were discussing the wise observations of Chairman Mao a moment ago, I was remembering how he said that a frog in a well thinks the sky is no bigger than the mouth of the well."

"And what is your point?" the general interrupted.

"My point is that we must have a wider vision than just our attack on the island. We must plan the rest of the takeover, placating the people, and setting up the new government."

"Don't you think I know that?" the general replied with irritation. "I have a separate group working on the entire transition, putting a complete shadow government together that can quickly take over their capital."

"And you don't believe the Central Committee will learn of our plans?"

"When all they think about now is their precious economy?" the general scoffed.

"But what if our attacks on the Americans don't work to distract them enough, and they rush to Taiwan's aid?" the colonel asked.

"We have been over this a hundred times. You have been in the meetings. Why do you keep bringing up the same subjects?"

The colonel hung his head and kept walking silently as the general continued. "America has become incapacitated by our attacks. And when our agents inside that country finish their work, the White House and their Congress will be impotent to act.

"Besides, the general went on, "remember when the Russians took over Crimea in spite of the fact that they, the Brits and the U.S. all signed the Budapest Agreement to respect Ukraine's sovereignty if they'd give up their nuclear weapons? What did the stupid Americans do when the Russians moved in and not only *disrespected*—but attacked and acquired the whole Crimea region of Ukraine? Nothing! Oh wait. As I recall the feckless Americans did offer Ukraine meals for their soldiers. How do you think Ukraine could have fought Russian tanks with canteens? No. Once again, the Americans will do nothing.

"Even though they have a different administration now. I still don't believe they'd have the guts, or the voters' support or that matter, to go to war over our trying to reunite our country. In addition, the rest of the world doesn't give a damn about Taiwan. The only European entity that has recognized the island is the Vatican. And as they say, how many troops does the Pope have?"

The colonel again remained silent.

"The answer is none. No! The Americans won't be able to react, and the rest of the world will turn a blind eye."

CHAPTER TWENTY-EIGHT

BETHESDA, MARYLAND

ammy stared down at the kitten? *My God! What happened? Mel's only had the little thing a few days. Maybe it got sick at the shelter and nobody knew.* She looked at the almost empty saucer on the floor, reached down and picked it up. She sniffed it. Garlic. It smelled a little bit like garlic. *That means it could have been laced with arsenic!* Fear raced up her spine as she dropped the saucer in the sink and quickly washed her hands.

She picked up the kitten, still making the plaintiff mewing sounds, grabbed her purse and raced down to the garage. With the kitten on her lap, she drove as fast as she could to the Bradley Hills Animal Hospital. She had driven past it many time when she and Mel had gone to dinner in the area. She screeched to a halt, parked in front, ignoring the "No Parking" sign and ran inside.

"Please help me," she begged the woman at the counter who looked like she was getting ready to close for the day. "This kitten has been poisoned. Please!"

The receptionist took Domino saying, "Wait here," and rushed through a set of swinging doors.

Cammy kept looking at her watch, calculating when Mel would get out of her class. She paced up and down the waiting area, praying the vet could save the little kitten, the innocent victim of a bad guy's plan to dispose of her, if that's what happened.

She thought again about how her friend and colleague, Wen Ho, had been killed in the Boston explosion, an attack that might have been aimed at her as well.

What in the world was going on? She finally sat down, tried to check her email and texts on her cell, but couldn't concentrate. She'd do that later. What she wanted to do now was make sure that the kitten didn't die.

As the time wore on, she was becoming more scared just imagining what could happen next. Finally, a young man in a white coat with a plastic name tag that said, "Dr. Petrie" emerged into the waiting area.

"As you the one who brought in the kitten?" he asked.

"Yes. Is it going to live? Please tell me it will," Cammy said.

The veterinarian nodded his head. "Yes. You got him here just in time. We were able to pump his little stomach and give him a certain drug. We'd like to keep him overnight."

Cammy let out a huge breath and reached out to shake the doctor's hand. "Of course. I can't thank you enough, uh, Dr. Petrie. We'll call tomorrow and figure out the best time to pick him up. And thank you. Thank you so much!"

Back in her car, she called Mel, explained what had happened and heard Mel shout, "Oh my God! You said Domino was poisoned, but what about you? When you get back, leave everything. Don't touch a thing. Not in the kitchen anyway. Bring some clothes and come up to my place. You're going to stay with me until we find out what in God's name is doing on."

Back in her condo, Cammy immediately went to her bedroom closet, grabbed her overnight bag and shoved a couple pair of slacks, some sweaters and blouses, underwear, and an extra pair of shoes into the bag and carried it into the bathroom.

There she took her makeup, toothbrush, electric rollers, hair brush and a bottle of Tylenol and tossed it all into the bag. Her mind was racing. What else? Her computer, of course. She went back to the desk in her bedroom, unplugged the charger, shoved it along with the computer into another small travel bag.

Heading toward the door, she had one final thought. *Whoever was in here didn't need to take out my computer or any of my other things. They just needed to take me out.*

CHAPTER TWENTY-NINE

ROCKVILLE, MARYLAND

"I just got off the phone with the animal hospital," Melanie said, pushing into Cammy's lab the next morning. "Dr. Petrie says Domino is going to be fine. I'm picking him up after work. I can't thank you enough for getting him there so fast. Otherwise . . . well, I don't want to think about it. I've really gotten to love that little guy."

"Oh, Mel. I felt so awful when he was mewing and moaning. At least he'll be okay now. It's just that it looks like it's happening all over again," Cammy said in a forlorn voice.

"Melanie pulled up a chair and put her hand on Cammy's arm. "You mean you're a target again, right?"

"Yes. First there was that jogger that attacked me. But you saved the day."

"Just like you saved little Domino."

"Then there was the explosion in Cambridge. And now the poison in my fridge."

"I know. You should have called the police," Mel said.

"I didn't want to get them involved. I mean here I am, working on a Top Secret project. I can't afford to have some local investigation going on. I've been sitting here trying to figure out my next move. And thanks again for letting me stay at your place for a while."

"So what are you going to do? Have you told Bollinger?"

"Not yet. You know, last time I got in trouble with that crazy militant who was stalking me some time ago, I told Hunt, and he always came to help me out," she said wistfully.

"And you don't think he'd help you now? I'll bet he would. Why don't you just call him?"

"I can't. It would feel like I was begging. Besides, I might have a better idea. I was thinking I might ask Jay?"

"The vice president?"

"He tells me to let him know how I'm doing, what I'm working on, and all of that. In fact, the other night at his place, the last thing he said to me was, 'Stay safe.' Pretty ironic, huh?"

"Actually, that's a pretty good idea. Maybe he can get some people over to your place to really check it out. Maybe there's more poison around or something. You can't go back there until we know."

"You're right. I think I'll call him in a bit." She leaned over toward the side of her desk and grabbed a copy of the *Washington Post*. "And since I came in earlier this morning, I'll bet you haven't seen this." She pointed to a story on the front page where the headline read, "White House puts faith in new technology."

"Oh no!" Mel said, grabbing the paper and skimming the first paragraph. Then she read aloud. 'A high-level source with knowledge of the project disclosed that Dr. Cameron Talbot of Bandaq Technologies is developing a new laser as a defense against the recent attacks on our commercial aircraft. The administration is continuing to fund the original two contracts for missile defense at U.S. airports as well as for airplanes. However, they are banking on a quicker, more economical solution from the young scientist whose project should be ready for testing soon'."

Melanie slammed the paper down on the desk and stammered, "But how? Who in the world would leak that? This is dreadful."

"And I'm in the bull's-eye again," Cammy said softly.

The door to the lab flew open. Stan Bollinger barged in waving a copy of the newspaper. "There you are," he said, pointing to Melanie. "You're late, and you're in deep shit!"

"But I didn't . . ."

"I don't want to hear your excuses, Ms. Duvall. Everybody in this building knows you've been carrying on with Senator Winters. Everybody in this building knows that Winters is trying to tear down the administration and run against Jayson Keller in the next election. And everybody in this building wonders how you can put up with that piece of slime?"

"But I . . ."

"No buts," he declared, staring her down. "You are undoubtedly responsible for disclosing Dr. Talbot's name to Winters. You are responsible for our company's reputation being put on the line, and you just may be responsible for leaking classified information," he thundered.

Cammy got up from her desk chair and faced her boss. "Now wait just a minute, Stan. I'm sure that Mel did not leak any of this to Derek Winters. Okay, so she goes out with him once in a while. That doesn't mean she would dream of leaking classified information, especially when she's been told in no uncertain terms, that this project is to remain a secret."

She turned to Melanie who was practically shaking. "I know you didn't say anything to Derek about the laser, did you?"

Melanie shook her head. "Absolutely not. I swear!"

"Well, we'll see about that," Bollinger said. "You will report to our internal control officer immediately."

"Why?" Melanie asked.

"To take a lie detector test." Stan then turned and stomped out of the room.

Cammy's phone rang. As she reached to pick it up, Melanie started to leave the lab. Cammy motioned for her to wait, but Mel shook her head and mouthed, "Don't worry," and left Cammy alone.

"Cameron Talbot," she said into the receiver.

"Cammy, it's Jayson. I saw the Post story, and I called to apologize."

"Apologize for what?"

"Because I believe that leak came out of the briefing I told you about."

"Who all was there?"

"Members of both the House and Senate Intelligence Committees."

"But none of them would leak a story. I mean, especially not those members, unless you think Derek Winters . . ."

"I wouldn't have thought so, but to be honest, there was a lot of dissension in the room when I told them about your laser project."

"Dissension? Why?"

"A good number of them thought we should make it public to reassure the American people that we were onto a possible solution. You know, kick up the economy with some good news for once. But I emphasized that we needed more time to get it tested. And besides, I didn't want your name out there. You've been through enough already."

"Thanks for the thought, but I'm afraid I'm already a target, even without the cooperation of the Post."

"What do you mean? Has something happened? Tell me," he urged.

Cammy told him about the kitten getting so sick right after she gave him some of her skim milk. She explained about the strange smell in the apartment and how she had taken the kitten to the vet and then moved into Mel's apartment upstairs.

"Oh Lord! You can't go back to your place."

"I know."

"Not now. Maybe not for a while," the vice president warned. "I'm going to have the FBI go over there and examine the place. And for now, stay put at your office. You're safe there. Let me get Janis on this."

"Janis? You mean the director of the FBI?"

"One and the same. I'll ask her to send her people over to your apartment. Do you have an extra key they can use? I don't want them to have to break in."

"Of course. Here in my desk."

"All right. An agent will stop at your office to pick it up."

"Thanks. But when?"

"Leave it to me. I'll get back to you."

CHAPTER THIRTY

THE WHITE HOUSE

H unt Daniels pulled his suit jacket closed as he hurried across West Exec between the OEOB and the White House. A cold front had moved in, and the wind was kicking up. All rather unusual for this time of year in Washington.

He ducked into the basement entrance, nodded to the Secret Service agent and headed down the reception area past the Situation Room. He turned right and saw the ever-present Maitre d' of the White House mess.

"Good afternoon, Colonel Daniels, your table is ready. Ms. Del Sarto is waiting. This way please."

Hunt followed the man into one of the most exclusive lunch spots in the nation's capital. Exclusive, if you base that on how many people would like to eat there, but probably couldn't wangle an invitation. It was the place where most of the senior staff of the White House ate lunch every day. The service was quick, the food was good, and you didn't have to worry about a lobbyist or reporter overhearing your conversation.

He spotted Claudia, her dark hair pulled into a tight chignon at the base of her neck. She looked quite attractive in a dark red blazer with a red print scarf framing the neckline. She was studying the menu with its navy blue cover and piece of gold braid down the center when Hunt walked up.

"Hi there," she said with a broad smile. "Busy day already?"

"Always," Hunt said settling into the wooden chair. As he glanced over at his lunch partner, he reflected that she was truly a beautiful woman. Her dark eyes were usually flashing somebody a smile, and her figure would probably stop traffic. She had certainly been friendly toward him. Too friendly? He wasn't sure.

He figured she probably acted that way with most everyone. So why wasn't he paying more attention to her? The fact that he had decided a long time ago never to mess with anybody on the staff wouldn't have kept him from feeling some sort of attraction, if it were there. But, as he thought about it, it just wasn't.

There were times, years ago, when he would have been blown away by a woman who looked like Claudia Del Sarto. The combination of beauty and brains would have been almost overwhelming. But not now. Was he getting old or overworked or what?

No. None of the above. He knew damn well why he couldn't get excited about other women right now. He had to admit to himself that he still had the hots for Dr. Cameron Talbot. That gorgeous, brilliant but often maddening woman he had fallen for some months ago. He thought he could put his feelings for her aside. Just take a break. Come back later and pick up where he'd left off. But she had made it plain that she wasn't interested in an off-again on-again deal, hadn't she?

Or maybe she had simply moved on. Last time he noticed, the vice president was all over her like an umbrella. He realized it irritated him, but there wasn't much of anything he could do about it. Now, he was just biding his time until they had another meeting together. He knew there would be more meetings about her laser project. Maybe she'd warm up next time. Maybe.

He suddenly realized that Claudia was relaying some intelligence she had received from a contact in Nicaragua. He snapped to attention. "So you're saying that you don't think any of the missiles came from the old Sandinista stash down there?" he asked.

"That's right. I've been going over every angle I can with respect to South America. The conclusion is that they're not to blame for any of this. They don't have a lock on any new technology, at least not that we know of. Nothing with stealth capabilities that could be applied to the kinds of missiles that shot our planes down. So I'm afraid I'm at a dead end on that score."

A waiter appeared to take their order. "I'll have tuna on whole wheat with a side of fruit, please," Claudia said.

"Make mine the Manhattan clam chowder and the half sandwich. What is it today? Ham and cheese?"

"Yes sir. Or you may have any kind you wish, of course."

"No, that'll be fine. And just water. Thanks."

They continued their discussion of various terrorist groups, the latest DHS contracts and other technology that was in the works. Then they discussed the chances that a brand new off shoot of al Qaeda could be responsible for all the mayhem.

"I know it sounds strange, but these crashes just don't seem to fit the Islamic Fascist mold, not that those people wouldn't like to have the capability to pull off these kinds of attacks. Know what I mean?" Hunt asked.

Claudia thought for a long moment. "Yes, I think I do. In all the other major attacks here and abroad, some group has always come forward to take the credit. Even some pack of militants like ISIS. They all seem to want the world to know they have the power to bring us down. Or at least some of us," she added.

"Right. And that's what makes this whole thing so unnerving. Four attacks and absolutely no claims of responsibility. But now, let me tell you about a theory that's floating around the VP's office right now."

"What is it?"

"China," Hunt said.

"China? Why in the world . . ." her voice trailed off as she folded her arms and sat back in her chair.

"Turns out that Dr. Talbot came up with the idea after some work she did with that scientist at M.I.T."

"The one who was blown up?" Claudia asked.

"Yes, that one," Hunt said. "Evidently he had been corresponding with other scientists back in Beijing and heard about some new technologies they're working on. He had talked to Cammy about it. Then they figured out how a few of these things could have been applied to ground-to-air missiles, the kind that wouldn't appear on our radar."

"Fascinating. But what about a motive?"

"Nobody has a clue. What I do know is that Keller sent me a memo about how DOD was ordering SPIRS Low to make passes over China to look for new installations where some of these missiles might be manufactured. We're waiting for results right now."

The waiter brought their orders and quietly withdrew.

"So what do you think of her theory?" Claudia asked, taking a bite of her sandwich.

"Not sure," Hunt said. "But I have to say that when Cammy . . . uh . . . Dr. Talbot homes in on an idea of some sort, she doesn't give up. At first, I was pretty skeptical of some of her word, but now, the more I analyze all of this, I think she just may be on to something."

"But you don't know why this is happening," Claudia said.

"Not yet anyway." Hunt picked up his soup spoon and tasted the chowder. "This is good today."

After a few moments, he said, "By the way, there's a conference over at the Heritage Foundation later today on terrorism. They've asked me to sit on a panel, and they've got a bunch of scholars coming in for it. I'm going to head over there around six to make a few remarks and then see if there's anything new, anything they can shed some light on. Do you want to come along?"

Claudia checked her watch. "I've got a bunch of memos to get out this afternoon, I've got a press backgrounder at three, and then I have to review two sets of presidential remarks, but that shouldn't take long. Sure, let's go. Since it's toward the end of the day, we probably shouldn't take a staff car."

"Yeah, let's take mine. It's parked on West Exec. So I'll swing by your office at about twenty of six."

They finished their lunch and Claudia scurried off to handle her memos while Hunt went back to his office with another new plan.

CHAPTER THIRTY-ONE

ROCKVILLE, MARYLAND

"Okay folks, let's review the results of our latest simulations and see if we're all in agreement that we can put the laser on a test plane," Cammy said to her assembled staff in the company's conference room.

"I think we should use an F-16," her executive assistant suggested.

"Shouldn't we put the pod on a larger plane? Something closer to our commercial fleet?" another staff member suggested.

"The pod's not too large for the military plane. I think an F-16 would work pretty well," Cammy replied. She thought back to the time her father had flown F-16's at various Air Force bases. She had always been so excited to go out to the terminal with her mother and little brother and watch him land his plane. Then they'd let her run out onto the tarmac where he would scoop her up in his arms and say how glad he was to be back home again.

She had always loved those fighter jets. Until the day she learned that his had crashed. Now she had mixed emotions about the whole idea of even seeing one again. On the other hand, if she and her team could actually come up with a way to protect not only commercial airplanes but even the fighter jets from some new type of missile, wasn't that the whole point of her research? Yes, an F-16 would work just fine.

"I'm going to be talking to the White House about the best location for these tests, but let's move ahead on the supposition that we can use an F-16," Cammy said.

They went through their reports, analyzed the various angles that a missile could approach the plane, figured out how quickly the sensors in the cockpit and the pod could relay the information about an imminent attack to the pilot, and discussed how much time it would take to deploy the three-hundred-sixty-degree laser.

Next they talked about how soon it could blind the missile and throw it off target. They had the results of the NTSB investigations of the four crashes and figured out that all of the doomed planes were hit at a much higher elevation than other shoulder-fired missiles had flown in the past. They finally concluded that a pilot might have as much as two minutes warning after a missile was launched from the ground to deploy the laser and take evasive action.

Cammy was pleased with the dedication of her team. She had hired most of the people in the room. Most were fairly young, all were highly educated, all had been working their tails off late into the night to upgrade their previous laser project to her new specifications.

Her E.A., as she called her executive assistant, was an especially bright young guy she had first met at Stanford. The brainiest one in the group was Sarah McIntyre, a woman Cammy had recruited from Bell Labs. As she looked around the table, she thought she had done a pretty good job with this group. Now, if only Bollinger would give them some credit and dole out a few bonuses when the laser panned out, if it panned out, it would be even better.

As the meeting was winding down, her E.A. said, "By the way, I hear there's a panel over at Heritage tonight that some of you might want to check out."

"Oh?" Cammy said, "Which one is that?"

"It's on the whole terrorism issue. I hear they'll be going over the latest list of terrorist groups that could be responsible for these attacks. Could be interesting."

Cammy thought about that. She often dropped by the symposiums that were held all over town by various think tanks—the Heritage Foundation, American Enterprise Institute, Center for Strategic and International Studies, the Brookings Institution. They all put on pretty good forums because that's where a lot of former members of Congress or a previous administration hung out when the other party was in power. They also had a whole bevy of scholars who were constantly writing papers on every conceivable issue. She had been invited to several forums on defense policy, but now that she was enmeshed in this latest terrorist threat, maybe it would be a good idea to take in this one as well.

"Sure. Thanks. I think I may make that one," Cammy announced. "If anyone else wants to come along, let me know." With that, she closed her notebook, stood up and effectively ended the meeting.

CHAPTER THIRTY-TWO

THE WHITE HOUSE

"I want an investigation into who the hell leaked Dr. Cameron Talbot's name and details about the new laser," the president instructed his attorney general. He turned to Jayson Keller who was sitting on one of the sofas in the Oval Office along with other top advisors. "And you think it may have come out of your briefing of those committee members?"

The vice president nodded. "Could be. All of them have pledged not to reveal classified information. They all know the consequences. But right now, with the tensions in this town, anybody could be a suspect."

"What about Winters?" the chief of staff asked.

"Wouldn't surprise me," Jayson replied. Then he paused and added, "But somehow I really doubt it. I mean, the man is a pain in the ass. He's doing everything he can to bring us down while he revs up his own campaign. And yet, I can't imagine the chairman of the Senate Intelligence Committee leaking this. It just doesn't track."

"I'm not so sure. Did you see him on CNN this morning?" the A.G. asked.

"No, I missed that. What did he say?" Jay said.

"He said we were all incompetent, that we had no idea who was attacking our planes, and what the country needed was not only new technology, but a complete house cleaning."

"And he'd like to be the head janitor," the president said. "Well, see what your people can do. I want every single member who was in that briefing, along with their top aides, interviewed on this one."

"What about our own people?" the vice president said.

"I can't imagine any of our people leaking something like this. They know the stakes," the president replied. "Besides, there aren't that many who know about this project, are there?"

"Besides the top NSC staff, I'd say just the press secretary and maybe a few assistants," the chief speculated.

The president thought for a moment, sat back in his chair and shook his head. "No. Let's see if we can nail somebody on the Hill first. Then if that doesn't pan out we can look inside."

The president glanced down at his schedule and then at his watch. "I've got a meeting later this afternoon with the DNI and the SecDef to get an update on our surveillance programs and see if the Defense Intelligence Agency has turned up anything in the way of new satellite photos. Jay, you'll join us."

The vice president nodded as the president continued, "If there's anything new, I'll keep you all in the loop. And whatever you find out on that leak, I want a report ASAP."

"Yes, of course. Thank you, Mr. President," the attorney general said, got up and left the room.

Across West Exec in the OEOB, Hunt Daniels was pounding out a National Security Decision Directive for Jayson Keller, now his boss there at the NSC. Hunt wasn't sure if SPIRS Low had come up with anything definitive in its passes over the Chinese mainland, but he doubted it. The area was simply too vast and the capabilities of that particular satellite were best focused on single sites.

In addition to sending several ships equipped with the Aegis system to the Far East which would take some time, he was recommending the deployment of their brand new super-secret spy plane code-named "Borealis," the second generation to the earlier black program named "Aurora." It was based on the original "Blackstar system" whereby a large airplane, a mothership that looked a bit like the old XB-70 supersonic bomber, carried a special orbital component under its fuselage.

The plane would take off, get up to supersonic speed at a high altitude and launch or drop the smaller plane which then goes into orbit about one-hundred-twenty miles up and takes better pictures than anything else the U.S. currently has in its arsenal.

As Hunt typed up his proposal, he realized that it might be a hard sell because DOD probably wouldn't want their newest generation spy plane to be out there for others to see or even hear about. He knew that if word got out, there were a lot of people around the world who would accuse them of launching a vehicle in space that could be used as a first strike weapon-delivery system.

Who gives a damn? We're in a war against God knows who, and we have to use everything possible to figure out who the bad guys are, don't we?

He finished the memo by adding two lines at the bottom. AGREE_____ and DISAGREE_____, signed it and asked his secretary to expedite it to the vice president's desk.

CHAPTER THIRTY-THREE

ROCKVILLE, MARYLAND

t was getting late. As Cammy looked out of her office window, she saw the trees being whipped by a furious wind. Good thing she had brought her trench coat with her that morning. She didn't relish the thought of traipsing around the streets of Washington when it was so chilly and windy out there right now.

She still had a number of things to do before she left for the Heritage panel. She wondered whether she should plan to go back to Melanie's apartment after that or whether Jayson would come up with a better idea.

She hated the thought of being a gypsy again. She had gone through that routine once before when Hunt had secured FBI protection for her and had her move in with him at his home in Georgetown several months ago. Even though she was under a tremendous amount of stress at the time with some lunatic chasing her all over town, trying to steal her invention of the Q-3 missile defense system, she had felt safe at Hunt's place.

He had a wonderful house there on P Street with its homey western feel. She remembered that he had prints on the wall of the Tetons because he had gone to a ranch camp in Jackson Hole when he was a kid, and he liked to be reminded of the place. He had comfy leather couches in his living room and a few other western touches in the place. At least he hadn't gone in for the antler chandeliers or saddles made into bar stools that some westerners seemed to like. After all, it was Georgetown.

Yes, she had been scared at the time, but ultimately Hunt had taken care of her. Well, Hunt, along with the FBI. She wondered what she should do now.

She had a thought about possibly checking into a hotel in Chevy Chase. She could talk to the desk clerks, say she didn't expect *any* visitors and ask them to alert her if anyone asked about her. Yes, that might work.

As she was pondering her rather dire situation, the phone rang. It was Jayson Keller. She was continually amazed that the vice president of the United States could keep making personal phone calls on her behalf when he had the weight of the world on his shoulders right now. She was glad he had called, though.

"Cammy, I've got news," he said.

"About what?"

"About your apartment."

"I was just thinking about that and wondering if I should stay in a hotel for a while," she replied.

"My answer is absolutely not. I'll get back to that. First, let me tell you about a report I just received from Janis."

"The FBI director?"

"Yes. She sent a team over to your place this morning, right after we talked, and you were absolutely right."

"It was arsenic in the milk?" Cammy asked.

"Not just in the milk, in the orange juice, in the cranberry juice and just about everything else you had in that refrigerator."

"Oh no!"

"And that's not all."

"What?" Cammy asked as she felt herself cringing at the news.

"Your stove."

"What about my stove? I almost turned it on to broil a steak."

"My God! It was wired to explode if you as much as touched the controls."

Cammy closed her eyes and pictured the explosion that had rocked Wen Hu's lab. She shuddered. She couldn't speak.

"Cammy, you still there?" Jayson asked in a concerned tone. "Are you okay?"

She took a deep breath and finally uttered a sigh, "What can I say? Whoever did that must be some kind of explosives expert. Remember what happened to Wen Hu?"

"Yes, of course I do. Look, we've obviously got a cadre of killers on our hands. It looks like they've got cells or gangs or agents or whatever they are in a number of our cities. I doubt if one lone guy is traveling between Washington and Cambridge."

"Yes, I'm sure you're right. Did they find any fingerprints?"

"Unfortunately, no. But they figure it was a professional."

"What should I . . . ? Her voice trailed off.

"Janis and I have talked this over and here's our proposal. First, she's assigning a team to drive you to and from work every day. And wherever else you want to go. Okay?"

"Yes, that's good of her. I mean, I've been through this before. She probably told you that Hunt arranged . . . I mean, back when . . ."

"Yes, I know," he interrupted. "I know all about the previous attempts on your life. We're not going to put you in any more danger. So step one is that when you finish work today, you leave your car there in the company garage, and the agents will pick you up right outside the corporate entrance." He gave her a number to call to alert her new drivers when she wanted to leave.

"Okay. Tonight I had planned to go over to a seminar at Heritage. It starts at six."

"That's fine," Jay said. "Just give them an hour or so's notice so they can get to Rockville and pick you up."

"No problem. I'll do that. But after the seminar?"

"Tell the agents to take you back to Melanie's. Pick up your clothes or whatever you have there, but don't go back to your own apartment. When you exit the building, your driver is going to take you to the Indian Embassy."

"The Indian Embassy? But why?"

"Janis and I feel that you will be quite safe there."

"But why would you want me at a foreign embassy?" Cammy asked, rather bewildered by his suggestion.

"Janis and I talked about this and decided that it would be better than one of our safe houses right now. Besides they're all way out of town. I just got off the phone with the Indian ambassador. You know that their government has been eternally grateful to you for the way your Q-3 system worked to protect New Delhi from a cruise missile attack a few months ago."

"Yes, but . . ."

"No buts. They would be delighted to host you for a few days. I explained the situation. They've read the Post article. They can see how you are now a target of some terrorist group, just as you were before. They said that they have their own security that surrounds their residence 24/7. So with the embassy police along with the FBI, there's no way anyone is going to get near you. Besides, they have a pretty nice place over there on Macomb."

"You mean just above the Washington Cathedral?"

"Yes. The ambassador and his wife say they would be honored to have you as their guest for a while. Uh . . . hope you like curry," he added.

Cammy hesitated. Live in an embassy? Or rather an ambassador's residence? This would be unique and, as he said, she should feel perfectly safe there. She had a fleeting thought about whether she should bring them some sort of house gift. Maybe she could stop on the way and pick up a bottle of wine or something. Why she was cluttering up her mind with such trivialities was a question when she had so many other things to worry about right now. But this would be a new experience, and she wanted to be a good guest.

"I guess this could work out pretty well," she ventured. "And you said a few days would be okay?"

"Yes, of course. And that brings me to my next question. How soon do you think you could take your team to a base to test the laser?"

"The laser? We just had a meeting about that. It looks like we should be ready to go in a couple of days. We talked about using an F-16, so where do you think . . ."

"Travis."

"Travis Air Force Base?" she exclaimed. "That's where I used to live. It's a MATS base. But it's way across the country."

"Yes, I know. Military Air Transport. But we'll ferry over an F-16 for you to use. I had Iggy, uh, the secretary of defense, call the base commander to give him a heads-up that we may want to use his facilities out there. He was happy to oblige. He can send a cargo plane to take all of your equipment to California. So as soon as you give us the go-ahead, we'll arrange to transport you, your people and your supplies out there. We all realize it's a distance from here, but we feel it would be the best facility. Besides, you told me you had lived there, so we thought you might feel more comfortable working in such a familiar place."

Her mind was racing. First, she'd be staying with the Indian ambassador and his wife, then she'd be flying to California where she'd not only revisit her childhood haunts, but maybe she could see her mother who was teaching computer science at San Francisco State University.

The only problem was, she'd have to fly. The mere thought of getting on a plane again made her tense up. Even though she'd had to fly to India several months ago, she still hadn't gotten over her tremendous fear of strapping herself into an airplane seat and putting her confidence in a pilot and a machine. She could never erase from her memory the flip comment she once heard from a pilot who said that takeoffs were optional. Landings were mandatory.

She knew she had to do it. She had no choice. How else could they go test the laser and ensure that it could be mounted on a passenger plane and save a lot of innocent lives if they became the target of these crazy terrorists once again.

"All right," she said. "This sounds like a plan. I'll go through everything with my team again tomorrow and perform a few more simulations. Then, if everything's on track, maybe we can plan on leaving in about three days. But I'll let you know for sure."

"Sounds good. And in the meantime, remember, call that number I gave you. When you're not within the embassy grounds or inside your office, stay with the agents and don't let them out of your sight!"

CHAPTER THIRTY-FOUR

THE WHITE HOUSE

"That wind is really kicking up," Claudia said as she buttoned her trench coat and pulled the red silk scarf around her head. "No sense in getting my hair blown around before we get to the seminar."

"You're right," Hunt said, opening the door of his dark green Jaguar for her. He went around, slid onto the tan leather seat and started the car. He realized that Claudia wore the same type of trench coat that Cammy always wore—that Burberry look. She was about Cammy's height too.

Damn. There he was thinking about that woman again. But he couldn't help it. The littlest things seemed to invade his sense of self control and turn his thoughts to the pretty scientist who was acting like the nickname he'd heard about some time ago. She had told him that Stan Bollinger had once called her the "IQ." But it didn't have anything to do with her intelligence. It stood for "Ice Queen." Now he could understand why.

They drove out the Southwest Gate of the White House and headed toward the Hill. "Great car," Claudia said, examining the dashboard. "Where'd you pick this up?"

"Friend of mine from State got assigned to Nigeria. Got this for a song."

"Nice lyrics," she said with a wink.

They chatted about the background briefing she had given to a reporter from the Miami Herald that afternoon. She said that she had focused on her belief that the terrorist groups had not secured their missiles from Central or South America and that the administration was following up on a number of other promising leads.

"Promising?" Hunt asked.

"Well, we have to let people know that we have some decent leads, don't we?"

"Sure. Just don't mention China."

"Of course not. I've got the guidance."

When they pulled up to the Heritage Foundation building on Massachusetts Avenue just off Columbus Circle, Hunt said, "Why don't you get out here. I'll go park and meet you inside."

A dark blue sedan pulled up a block behind them and stopped in an opening to an alley. The driver watched as the woman in the trench coat and scarf got out of the Jaguar and rushed up the stairs of the building. Then he saw the Jaguar head around the corner to look for a parking place.

The man figured he had plenty of time. *Must be some sort of meeting going on in there. This should be easy.* He had been trailing this colonel for quite some time. They told him the colonel often worked with the scientist. He had his orders, and he intended to follow them. Tonight.

He sat quietly and stared at the entrance to the building where a number of other people darted inside out of the wind.   He waited a while and then glanced at his watch. Ten after six. Nobody had gone inside for over five minutes. The meeting, whatever it was, must have started at six.

He grabbed a small package, one he had been keeping for just such an opportunity, and held it carefully as he got out of the car and started to walk toward the building.

He looked around, but didn't see anyone on the sidewalk. Most of the traffic was headed down Massachusetts Avenue, workers heading home. No reason any of them should notice a man of medium height and medium build in jeans and a dark jacket and cap walking down the street carrying a small box.

This was perfect. He couldn't have asked for a better place. He walked nonchalantly up to a FedEx box right in front of the building, pulled open the deposit door and slowly slid his package inside. Then he turned and quickly walked back to his car. Once inside, he pulled out his cell phone, punched in a series of numbers and set it on the seat beside him.

He knew he could relax for a while. He turned on the radio, put his head back and listened to his favorite sports talk show. He planned to start watching the door again in about half an hour.

Then, all he had to do was to wait for the tall woman in the trench coat to come back outside. If the colonel was next to her, that would make his job just that much simpler. But whenever he saw *her*, he could hit the "Send" button.

CHAPTER THIRTY-FIVE

THE WHITE HOUSE

" T hanks for coming over so late," the president remarked as he, the
vice president and DNI leaned in to examine the sheaf of high
resolution photos the secretary of defense handed him.

"No problem," Iggy said. "We just got these in. I knew you'd want
to see them right away, so I thought it best to get them over here."

Jayson Keller looked over the president's shoulder and said, "I'm not
sure we're getting anything new here, are we?"

"I don't believe I see any changes either," the intelligence director
said. "Our people have been comparing photos like these to others DIA
took six months ago, and we can't identify any new installations. At least
not in those areas."

"Looks like another big flood in this section," Jay remarked, pointing to one picture.

"Oh yes, floods and polluted water. Big problems all the time over
there," the DNI said.

"Another spill in the Songhua River?" the president asked.

"Looks like it. They've had over seventy spills in just the last year. You know there are something like three hundred million Chinese with no decent water to drink. Well, out in the countryside, I mean. Though the cities are having more and more problems as they modernize. In fact, the top ten polluted cities in the world are all in China," the DNI said.

"Make a note that we could propose a massive water clean-up program with our latest technology when we head to those new trade talks next month," the president muttered, turning over another photo.

"Good idea," Jay said, writing in his ever present leather folder. "But if it turns out that China has anything to do with these attacks, there'll be no more trade talks or talks about anything else. Right?"

"God damned right," the president barked.

"I wonder if we have the right satellites looking at the right locations," the DNI ventured. "You know, the Chinese are experts in what they call strategic deception. Their word for it is moulue. They're very clever about it."

The vice president pulled a memo out of his folder and handed it to the president. "Take a look. I just got this NSDD from Hunt Daniels."

"Daniels?" the president said as he grabbed the memo. "Guy usually has some pretty good ideas. What's he got this time?"

"He's suggesting we deploy Borealis."

"Borealis?" Iggy blurted. "We haven't used that system. It's Top Secret! We can't let that out of the bag yet, it's our strategic ace in the hole. You know that."

The president leaned back in his leather chair behind the handsomely carved Resolute Desk, given to Rutherford B. Hayes by Queen Victoria and used by many U.S. presidents ever since. A panel had been added during FDR's time to hide the view of his wheelchair. Now this president took a moment to think about Daniel's recommendation and he could hardly hide his concern. "That system is the best thing we've developed since the space shuttle. But Iggy's got a point. If we deploy, how can we ensure that word doesn't get out that we've got it?"

"Everyone working on that system knows it's Top Secret, and I'm sure we can get that plane to take off from its base without arousing suspicion. After all, we test lots of different kinds of planes all the time. If we emphasize secrecy about its launch, I think we can pull it off," Jayson said.

"It might work," the DNI said. "I'm not sure we have the culprits here, but the more we analyze their capabilities, you have to admit that China's got the brain-power to come up with a new stealth missile. One that has some type of tracking device. Think about all the technology that's coming out of there these days. Motorola, Microsoft, IBM. They have research labs all over China. They're working on everything from voice-morphing to nanotechnology. Why wouldn't they develop a new stealthy missile?"

The secretary of defense looked from one man to the other and shook his head. "This could be a damn disaster as far as our relations with other countries are concerned."

"We can't worry about foreign relations right now," the president said. "As for China, the big question is, why in hell would they be shooting down our planes?"

"We don't know yet," the DNI said. "If we can get some proof of new facilities over there by using Borealis, I say we should go for it."

"This time, let's concentrate our efforts along the East coast where they're about to begin their military exercises in the Taiwan Straits," the vice president suggested.

"Good plan," the president agreed. "I want to know what those people are doing in that area anyway. How many missiles have they got aimed at Taiwan now?"

"Almost a thousand of various kinds. They've got the JL-2 submarine launched nuclear missile too. And in terms of these exercises, last time we checked, they were testing a whole load of new amphibious landing craft."

"Speaking of exercises, I see in this Decision Directive that Hunt Daniels is also recommending we send some Aegis systems to that same area. That might be a good move as well. I don't think we can ever have too many missile defense systems."

"I'll talk to the joint chiefs about that. As for testing those new landing craft, of course they do that all the time. I mean it's the whole exercise they've been going through every year or so," the SecDef said.

"Look, I know you're not supporting the use of Borealis," the president said, "But I think this is the one time we've got to use everything we have. See how quickly you can get it up and running. Then if we find evidence of new missile factories, I'll go to the chairman of the Central Committee and threaten World War Three!"

CHAPTER THIRTY-SIX

WASHINGTON, D.C.

The FBI agent driving Cammy apologized. "Sorry. Looks like we're fifteen or twenty minutes late for your seminar, ma'am. But you saw that traffic."

"No problem," Cammy said. "I'll catch most of the reports. Besides, I knew 270 would be a mess. It always is at the end of the day. I probably should have left sooner, but I was pretty busy. Anyway, thanks for the lift. I think I'll be about an hour."

"Okay, Dr. Talbot. We'll go pick up some coffee and be back soon."

Cammy held her trench coat closed as she rushed up the stairs and into the building. She went to the auditorium and found a seat in the back. The place was jammed. With the heightened alert, the press scrutiny and criticism from the Hill, terrorism was the topic du jour and she wasn't surprised to find a row of cameras and reporters off to the side recording the proceedings. C-Span was there too. They usually were.

As Cammy took off her coat and settled down in her seat, she looked up on the dais and saw Hunt sitting at the long table along with three other panelists and a moderator. *I didn't know he was going to be here. Maybe I shouldn't have come.* Then as he began to answer a question, she realized she couldn't wait to hear his voice and what he was going to say.

He gave a quick run down of possible terrorist organizations and their usual methods of operation. He also talked about the problem of nuclear proliferation, especially in Russia and how terrorist groups had such easy access to various kinds of weapons. He was careful, concise and a great communicator, and she was disappointed when the moderator then turned to a professor to ask his opinion.

She scanned the room and saw Claudia Del Sarto sitting off to one side. *So that's it now. Claudia must have come with Hunt. Didn't take him long to find another woman. Damn him!* With her dark hair and flashing smile, it was easy to see how Hunt could succumb to such beauty.

Suddenly, Cammy wanted to slink away before Hunt saw her. He'd probably think she had come here just to see him again. Well, she hadn't. But if she got up now, it would be too obvious. She crouched down in her seat and was glad she was in the back row. Maybe when it was over, she could slip out before he saw her.

The seminar went on for another hour. Then it was time for Q&A. When several people stood up to ask questions, Cammy figured she could head out and Hunt might not notice. She grabbed her shoulder bag and her coat and crept out to the hallway. She decided to stop in the Ladies Room before heading back outside to her waiting agents.

CHAPTER THIRTY-SEVEN

ROCKVILLE, MARYLAND

"You're on a very short leash, Ms. Duvall," Stan Bollinger bellowed as he waved a report in front of Melanie.

"What do you mean, Stan?"

"Your lie detector test."

"But I told you, I never leaked . . ."

"All I can say is that these results are," he stared down at the pages in his hand, "at best inconclusive."

Melanie folded her arms and took a defiant stance. "See. I told you I would never leak classified information, or any other kind of information out of this office. You have to know that . . . sir!"

"Maybe. Maybe not. All I know is that somebody leaked Talbot's name and *our* name. Since you're the one who talks to the press all the time, to say nothing about your little affair with that sleaze bag . . ."

"He's not a sleaze bag, Mr. Bollinger. He's a respected United States senator who often takes a middle-of-the-road position. And what's wrong with that?"

"When you stay in the middle of the road," Stan scoffed, "you get hit from both sides."

"Well, just because you don't agree with him all the time doesn't mean he's not a loyal American," she said defiantly.

"Not all the time? Not any of the time," Stan retorted.

Melanie looked down at her watch. "May I go home now?"

"Yes. I know it's getting late, but you're still not off the hook as far as I'm concerned."

"I don't know what else I can do to convince you," she said, reaching over to turn out her desk lamp.

"Just do your job and think twice about who you're sleeping with," he ordered as he turned and stomped out of her office.

CHAPTER THIRTY-EIGHT

WASHINGTON, D.C.

The moderator cut off the session after just a few questions, citing the need for the professors on the panel to get to a dinner in their honor. Hunt stepped off the dais, greeted a few former colleagues, gave Claudia the high sign, and the two of them headed out.

Cammy was about to step out of the Ladies Room when she caught a glimpse of Hunt and Claudia coming down the hallway, she ducked back inside to wait for a few minutes.

The wind was still blowing. Hunt turned to Claudia and said, "Why don't you give me a few minutes. I'll go get the car. Parking around here was a bitch. It's a couple of blocks away. No point in your walking around in this wind. I'll be right back."

"Okay, thanks."

Hunt sprinted off to get the car and Claudia donned her trench coat, put the scarf over her head again and waited by the front door for a few moments as others exited the building. Then she started to walk out as several reporters and cameramen followed her, carrying their equipment down the stairs.

Cammy had seen Hunt leave so she walked out behind the cameramen. She was pretty sure she could quickly find her FBI driver and get out of there before Hunt came back with his car.

Suddenly, an explosion blew out the sides of the FedEx box and practically knocked Cammy and the people in front of her to the ground. She grabbed the handrail to steady herself, started to cough, covered her mouth and closed her eyes as shards of metal came flying over the crowd. When she opened her eyes again, she saw that the blast and resulting fireball had engulfed a woman and one of the cameramen. Both of them were on the ground, their clothes encased in flames.

There were screams and shouts as reporters hit the ground, and two of the professors, now coming down the stairs, were shunted aside. The Heritage security officer burst through the door and raced to the scene.

Cammy's two FBI agents jumped out of the car they had parked just down from the entrance, took off their jackets and tried to beat out some of the flames. The two agents looked horrified to see the two bodies lying on the ground, mangled, covered with blood.

The security officer shouted, "What the hell?" and tried to help the agents. Hunt came racing back toward the bodies. He looked down and saw a scarf that had been singed. Then he saw part of the face. The burned and once beautiful face of Claudia Del Sarto.

CHAPTER THIRTY-NINE

EASTERN CHINA

General Zhang Li straightened one of the medals on his uniform and called across the make-shift office. "Any report from our agent in Washington?"

"Not yet, sir," Colonel Tsao answered. "But our people in Taiwan have sent a special message, one I'm sure you will be pleased to read," he said, pulling a page from the printer in the corner. "Here, you can see for yourself."

The general quickly read the report, and a broad smile lit up his usually stern face. "Ah this is good news indeed. The missile defense system that the incompetent Sterling Dynamics Company shipped over is not working. It will never work, and they'll never know why," he said triumphantly.

"A brilliant move, general," the colonel said with a slight bow. "They are now more helpless than ever when it comes to our missiles arrayed along the coast."

"The military exercises will be starting soon. Do you realize what this means?"

"Yes, I do," the colonel replied. "It means that all of your plans are about to become a reality."

"We have waited so many years, decades, for this moment. But before we let the world see our ultimate objective, we have a few more plans for the American government."

"Yes, I figured we would have to, as you say, 'distract' them further so they cannot retaliate or help Taiwan in a timely way."

"Once we have Washington's report," the general said, "we will analyze the next target."

CHAPTER FORTY

WASHINGTON, D.C.

"Oh my God!" Cammy exclaimed as she stared down at the smoldering remains. She put her hand at her mouth to stifle a cry.

One agent was now radioing for help, but the other one had moved protectively to Cammy's side as a large crowd gathered to stare at the macabre scene. The security officer had run back into the building and emerged carrying a couple of blankets that he now spread over the two bodies. "Okay folks. Stand back. Police and fire are on their way."

As Cammy moved away, Hunt saw her and rushed to her side. "What are you doing here? Are you okay?"

She nodded. "I heard about the seminar, but I didn't know you were on the panel," she said with tears in her eyes. "God, Hunt, this is just so awful, I can't imagine . . ."

Hunt raked his fingers through his hair. "I was just going for the car. If only I had taken her with me . . ." his voice trailed off.

"You can't blame yourself," Cammy said, putting her hand on his arm.

"I sure as hell can," he said curtly. "And as soon as the police get here, we're going to examine every inch of this place. See what kind of explosive that was, interview everybody, go over every possible . . . oh hell, I can't believe this happened. Why Claudia? She hasn't done anything? She was just standing. Just waiting . . . for me."

Cammy thought for a long moment and then said, "Seems like there's somebody in this town who's an explosives expert. Did you know somebody broke into my apartment and had my stove set to explode if I had touched it?"

"What?" he exclaimed. "When?"

"Yesterday."

"How did you find out? Without setting it off, I mean?"

"It's kind of complicated. They put arsenic in my food and the FBI went in and figured out the stove had been rigged. I had to move out. And that's why these agents are with me now," she said, motioning to the man standing off to her left.

"Jesus Christ! Did you call Janis yourself?"

"No." She hesitated and then added, "I told Jayson . . . uh . . . the vice president. He called the director, and she sent in the team and arranged for my protection. Again."

"So you're on a first name basis with the VP, I guess,"

"Uh, yes, I suppose you could say that."

Three police cars screeched to a halt at the edge of the curb, and six officers jumped out. They examined the bodies, conferred with the FBI agents and security guard and started talking on their cell phones. They then fanned out and began interrogating people in the crowd. The agent standing next to Cammy said, "Are you sure you're all right, ma'am?"

"Yes. A bit shaky, but I guess I'm okay." She glanced over at the bodies again. "This is all just so terrible. How . . . ?"

Hunt turned to her. "Looks like a bomb was placed in the FedEx box and was either timed to go off or set off remotely," he said.

The agent nodded and then grabbed Cammy's arm. "Look, the police are getting this thing under control. Let's get you outta here."

On the drive back to her building, Cammy sat still in the back of the car. She reviewed the terrible scene in her mind and remembered staring down at Claudia with her silk scarf on fire and her trench coat . . . Cammy looked down at her own coat and realized it was just like Claudia's. *Oh no! What if that bomb had been meant for me? And that poor woman, she wasn't involved at all, was she? Why would she have been a target? No, it was me they wanted. It had to be.* Her eyes welled up with more tears as she leaned forward and said in a halting voice, "Excuse me, Agent Larson. You said your name was Larson, right?"

One of the agents turned around to look at her, "Yes ma'am. Do you need something?"

"I think that bomb was meant for me," Cammy said.

"You? Why do you think that, ma'am? It looked like it was set to damage the building."

"No, don't you see? Somebody tried to blow up my apartment, that's why you're here."

"We know, but that was a breaking and entering," the agent said.

"But they had rigged my stove to blow up. And then there was that other explosion in Cambridge."

"What explosion in Cambridge," the agent asked. "We weren't told anything about another explosion."

"I was up in Cambridge last week working with a colleague at M.I.T. While I was out getting coffee, somebody blew up his lab, and he was killed. But I could just as easily have been inside. I was just a few minutes late getting the . . ."

"Hey, Tom, you hear that?" The first agent turned to his partner. "This lady really is in trouble." He shifted back to stare at Cammy who was wiping her eyes with a Kleenex. "We're going to get your things at your friend's place and then get you over to the Indian Embassy. After that we've got a report to file. But from now on, you don't go anywhere, not inside a building or outside a building, except for the Indian Embassy and your office, without one of our agents going with you. Got that?"

"Yes." She blew her nose and added, "Thank you."

CHAPTER FORTY-ONE

ROCKVILLE, MARYLAND

"Thank God you're all right," Melanie announced, jumping up from the chair in Cammy's lab and running over to give her friend a hug. "I was out last night when you came for your stuff, but I got your text, and then I heard the details on the news about the explosion over at Heritage. I didn't think I should bother you at the embassy, and I wanted to hear it all in person. So I came in early to wait for you. I've been sitting here practically holding my breath till you came in. Tell me what happened."

Cammy sighed, hung up her beige blazer and slumped down in her desk chair. "Oh, Mel, you can't believe how horrible it all was. That poor woman."

"Claudia Del Sarto?"

"Yes. She was young and really pretty. Well, we knew that. But, Mel, she was just an innocent bystander. I think the bomb was meant for me."

"You? How? How would anybody know you were there? That's just too strange."

"I know," Cammy said, leaning her elbows on the desk and putting her face in her hands."

"So how in the world could somebody try to kill you when you only decided to go to that seminar late yesterday? This just doesn't make any sense."

"I know it doesn't. It's just that she was wearing the same kind of trench coat as mine."

"So? Everybody wears khaki trench coats in this town. I still don't get it."

"I don't either. But she was there with Hunt. Unless . . ."

"Unless what?" Mel asked.

Cammy hesitated and thought for a long moment. "Unless they were trailing Hunt because they knew we used to work together," Cammy speculated.

"And then when they saw a woman with the same coat, they thought it was you? But Claudia had that long dark hair. I saw her picture on the internet, remember? And yours is blond. Nobody could make that kind of mistake."

"Yes, they could. Remember how windy it was last night?"

Melanie nodded.

"Well, Claudia was wearing a silk scarf. It seems she was about my same height, and she was with Hunt. So when she came out and was standing there . . ."

"Somebody set off the bomb?" Mel said.

"That's about it. I was right behind her. I mean, right behind a couple of cameramen. One of them was blown away too."

"Oh Cam. They just missed you then?"

Cammy looked up and slowly nodded her head. "By about a few seconds."

"What are you going to do now?"

"What can I do? I'm going to stay at the Indian Embassy again tonight and maybe tomorrow. Then we should be ready to head out of here with all the laser equipment. I've got to get word to Jayson so they can arrange a transport. We're going to Travis, you know."

"Yes, you said that. Back home again. Sort of."

"Sort of."

"Is Hunt going too?"

"I don't know. Nobody's told me who all would be on the plane."

"And speaking of Hunt, what happened to him last night?" Mel asked.

Cammy looked pensive as she remembered the look of devastation on his face and his cutting remark about her being on a first-name basis with the vice president. "He was pretty upset. I mean, he had gone to get the car. He said that if only he had taken Claudia with him, she'd be okay. Well, you can imagine."

"Yeah. Sure. Do you think there was something going on between the two of them?"

"It sure looked like it to me. I mean, the man was practically crying. Of course, I can't blame him. I mean it was awful, just awful with burned bodies and twisted metal and, oh I just don't think I want to talk about it."

"So he was having an affair with her, right?" Mel pressed.

"I don't know, but I wouldn't be surprised. Oh, and then I told him about the break-in at my apartment and how I had called Jayson. And he made a snide remark about my relationship with Jay."

"Guess that pretty much puts an end to things, doesn't it?"

"Looks that way," Cammy admitted. She leaned over, switched on her computer and stowed her shoulder bag in the bottom drawer of her desk. "Hey, Mel, thanks for being here this morning. It was a pretty tough night."

"I had to see you and be sure you were okay." She got up and moved toward the door. "One more thing."

"Yes?"

"I was here until after six last night because Bollinger told me to wait for the results of the lie detector test."

"And you passed, right?"

"Not exactly," Mel admitted.

"Not exactly? You sound like an old Hertz commercial. What happened, Mel?"

"I told Stan I would never leak anything improper, especially anything classified. And all he said was that the results were 'inconclusive,' and I'm on a short leash. Can you believe that?"

"Ignore him. That's what I usually do." She turned toward her computer. "And now I've got to get to work and iron out a few problems I found yesterday on this darn laser. We're down to the last tiny parts. Sometimes I ask myself how I'm going to finally thread this needle."

"You'll do it," Mel said, "But before you go to California, maybe you'd better stock up on thimbles."

CHAPTER FORTY-TWO

THE WHITE HOUSE

Hunt Daniels sat across from Jayson Keller in his West Wing office and recapped the events surrounding the explosion that killed Claudia and the cameraman. He said he was surprised to see Cammy there and then got to thinking about what she'd said about her apartment being rigged with an explosive device. "So it seems to me that the bomb last night might have been meant for Cammy, I mean, Dr. Talbot," Hunt said.

"I believe she only decided to go to that seminar at the last minute, so unless the killer was stalking her and followed her from her office and had the bomb with him, no, that doesn't quite track."

"Maybe he was following me," Hunt suggested. "I almost got nailed a couple of times when I was in Russia and who knows? Maybe somebody's still tailing me."

"But you weren't anywhere near that FedEx box when it blew up, right?"

"Well, no. I was getting the car. But back on the Cammy-as-the-target idea, Claudia was wearing a coat just like Cammy's, uh, Dr. Talbot's."

"It's okay, Hunt. We all know you and Cammy worked together. We know you're friends."

"Used to be," Hunt muttered under his breath.

"So where are we here?"

"Cammy's got protection. Thanks to you and Janis, I hear."

"Yes. And she's staying with the Indian ambassador until she takes her laser team out west."

"Out west?" Hunt asked.

"Yes, and that's what I wanted to talk to you about too. The president wants you to go along as a liaison with the base officers out at Travis. That's where they're going to install the laser. On an F-16. The president says you used to fly that plane and since you're on top of the whole issue, it would be best for you to go."

Jayson hadn't wanted to send Hunt across the country with Cammy. He'd always sensed that they had some sort of relationship, and he wasn't about to encourage it again. Whatever it was. But he could hardly argue with the president when he made such a cogent case. So he'd just have to send the two of them out there and hope that whatever was in the past stayed in the past.

"When do we leave?" Hunt asked.

"Day after tomorrow. I just talked to Cammy and she says she's working on some last minute fixes but hopes everything will be ready by then."

"But I think the funeral for Claudia is later this week," Hunt said.

"I know. Most of the NSC staff will be there, I'm sure. But we need you out at Travis. I'm sorry."

After Hunt left, Jayson worked on a number of briefing papers and then saw a light blinking on his desk phone. He grabbed it. "Yes?"

"Can you come to the president's office for a minute?" the secretary asked.

"Of course. Right away," Jay replied. He hung up, reached for his suit coat, and walked the few feet over to the Oval Office. The secretary, sitting in the ante room, nodded for him to go in.

"Just got a call from the president of Taiwan. You know that missile defense system that Sterling shipped over there?"

"Yes, of course," Jay said.

"Well, the whole thing isn't worth a damn. They've been testing it and it won't even track, let alone shoot down an incoming missile. The Taiwanese are scared shitless, and they're asking for help."

"What kind of help?" Jay asked, sitting down in a chair next to the president's desk."

"They've heard about Dr. Talbot's Q-3 system that she deployed in India. Of course, everybody's heard about that little stunt. Anyway, they're asking if they can purchase her system."

"Did you okay it?"

"Sure, why not? They can only use it for defensive purposes, and Lord knows they need something to go up against that array of missiles, some ballistic, some cruise, that the Chicoms have set up across the Straits. And with those military exercises set to begin any day now, well, you can imagine how they feel. They're so upset they're even sending the pandas back that the Chinese gave them."

"Doesn't sound very promising, does it?" Jay said.

"They need arms, not Pandas, because China is armed to the teeth right now. And by the way, he even quoted ole man Reagan."

"Really? Which quote?"

"He said that President Reagan used to say, 'Nations do not disagree because they are armed. They are armed because they disagree on important matters like human life and liberty.' It's still true today. And they're willing to pay. Anything. The only question is, how soon can they get it, and how soon can they learn how to use it? You know the Bandaq company. What do you think?"

Jayson stared out the trio of windows behind the president's desk for several moments. The wind had stopped, and the sun was out. But that seemed like the only bright spot in this otherwise difficult day. "Tell you what. I've got a couple of ideas. Let me put them together. I'll have something on your desk by Noon."

CHAPTER FORTY-THREE

ROCKVILLE, MARYLAND

"Hey, Cam, did you see this article in the *New York Times* about the attorney general's investigation of that leak?" Melanie said, poking her head into Cammy's office.

"No, not yet. Any suspects?"

"It says they're focusing on the Hill."

"Derek Winters?" Cammy asked raising her eyebrows and wondering what Melanie thought about his possible involvement.

"Not him specifically, thank God. It just says they're interviewing every member of the House and Senate Intelligence Committees." She shuffled the paper to the inside back page. "But the interesting thing is this editorial. It's got your name in it."

Cammy jumped up from her desk chair, "Where?"

"Right here," Mel said, pointing to the second paragraph. "It says your project never should have been classified, that the American people have a right to know what the government is doing to protect the airliners. Then it's got a blast here at the president for his various surveil-lance programs."

"How do they know what surveillance programs he's using?" Cammy asked.

"It doesn't say. It's just a general rant."

"The American people may have a right to know a lot of things. But all in due time," Cammy remarked. "Let me ask you something. If a newspaper editor had learned the details of the invasion on D-Day, would the American people have had a right to know that?"

"Touche," Mel said, putting the paper on the desk. "So are you crash-ing to get everything ready to leave for Travis? Oh, sorry. Bad terminology."

"Don't worry. I've said the same thing," Cammy said, sitting down and swiveling around in her chair. "I'm trying to get it all together. But I did take time to make a note for you about something I had at the embassy last night."

"Really what?"

Cammy reached into the bottom drawer of her desk, pulled out her shoulder bag and fished inside for a slip of paper. "Here it is. For your stupid recipe file. 'Sago Sabudana Khichdi.'"

"What the heck is that?"

"Some sort of Indian snack food made with sago, chili peppers, peanuts and ghee."

"So where do I get some ghee?"

"Hey, you're the chef. I'm just the observer."

"And speaking of observers, this is the first time all day that I've observed even a hint of a smile on your face," Mel said.

"I'm just trying to keep last night out of my mind and concentrate on the project," Cammy said with a sigh.

"What's Bollinger saying about all of this?"

"What could he say? Jay called him personally about sending my whole team to Travis."

"The vice president called Stan?"

"Yep. So Stan says to me that he still thinks the whole laser idea may not work, but he has to let us go try it out. And I have the distinct impression that if, for some god-awful reason, it really doesn't work, he's going to be madder than . . ."

"The pacifist who went to the ball game on Handgun Night?" Melanie said with a laugh. "Do you suppose we could nominate Stan for an anger management class or something?"

"Good luck," Cammy said turning back to her computer. "And now I'm going to need all the luck I can get to have this software ready to go."

Mel turned toward the door and said over her shoulder, "By the way, you told me Hunt is going to Travis too. How are you going to feel having him on that plane with you?"

Cammy shrugged. "Right now I'm playing Scarlett O'Hara. I won't think about today, I'll think about that tomorrow!"

CHAPTER FORTY-FOUR

THE WHITE HOUSE

"Did you ever see that cartoon of two guys in the dungeon, hanging from chains on the wall? And one guy looks over and says to the other guy, 'Now here's my plan'."

The president chuckled. "On a day like this I can use a cartoon or two." He looked up at Jayson Keller and asked, "So you've got a plan for me?"

"Yes, I've put together a strategy for your approval."

"Let me see," the president said, reaching for the memo. "Hmmm. So you want us to move two of our carriers closer to the Taiwan Straits along with two others with the Aegis systems. That'll work. We have several in the Pacific right now." He read the second bullet point. "And then you want to go to Japan to arrange a mutual defense agreement whereby the Japanese, along with us, of course, would come to Taiwan's defense in the unlikely event of an attack by China."

"Yes, sir. Now that Japan has amended Article 9 of its constitution, I believe we can convince them to use some of their defense forces to come in to help Taiwan."

"That article has stirred up controversy for years ever since McArthur and his boys had it added right after World War II."

"Well, sure. We didn't want them building another military machine, so that article precluded any of that. But over the years, they've created forces they say are for their own defense and now with the re-wording, they'll be able to help out when it comes to other problems overseas."

"Like committing peace-keeping troops once in a while," the president said.

"Yes. And as for deciding where to take a stand, well, you know how irritated the Japanese get with China all the time. They scramble their jets about a hundred times a year to intercept Chinese spy planes," Jay said.

"I know. And every time a Chinese submarine or any other kind of ship gets anywhere near them, Tokyo raises holy hell."

"Another thing is that we're in a pretty good position to ask them to help us out here. We're already working with their people on that big ballistic missile defense system over there."

"The one at Yokota Air Base?"

"Yes. Our guys are also upgrading some systems at Camp Zama in Central Japan, so obviously, we're improving our positioning in the area in a lot of different ways." The vice president pointed to the third bullet on the page and continued. "Besides, the Japanese are a hell of a lot closer to the Taiwan Straits than Guam where a lot of our people are stationed, although Guam has had its share of threats as we all know. But Japan really could be key in all of this."

"All right. I'll put in a call to their prime minister to tell him I'm sending you over there." He turned the page and perused the next section of the memo. "Now, what about Taiwan's request for Q-3?"

"I think we can cover that too. I suggest we get Bandaq to put a Q-3 team together along with their components, and we can send them over to Taiwan in a transport to set up the system and begin training the Taiwanese defense specialists."

"What about Dr. Talbot? It's her baby."

"She could go too. She's heading out to Travis Air Force Base tomorrow. She can get the technicians out there started on the installation of her laser on an F-16. While they're doing that, I would guess that her old Q-3 team will take a couple days to get everything together. Then they could stop at Travis . . . they'd need a fuel stop anyway . . . they pick her up and they'd all fly on to Taipei. She could work there for a few days, and I could pick her up and fly back to San Francisco when we could all rendezvous."

"Rendezvous?" The president asked. "With whom?"

"The way I see the timing on this thing, sometime after Dr. Talbot and the laser team fly to Travis, I'd head over to Japan. I'll be there for a while trying to hammer out this agreement. You know they like to take their time with these things."

The president replied, "They sure do. I sometimes feel that the only way we can speed things up with those people is if my mother knew the prime minister's mother. Well, you get the picture."

Jayson gave a half laugh and went on with his plan. "So Dr. Talbot spends a few days at Travis, then flies to Taiwan with her team. Her team stays here for a while to be sure everything works okay. I pick up Dr. Talbot on the way back from Japan. And when we land in San Francisco, Hunt could bring the test F-16 to SFO and give me a demonstration of the laser which, we hope, will be operational. And since the whole world now knows we're testing it, I figure you could make an announcement about how well it's working and at the same time, I can give that speech I've scheduled at the Commonwealth Club out there and include a whole section on our new laser that I will have just seen."

The president leaned back in his tall leather chair and put his hands behind his head. "This is the first decent plan of action I've seen in weeks around here. Good work, Jay." He started to make some notes in the margin of the memo and added, "You know, if this whole scenario pans out, I mean if that new laser actually works, Franklin Thorne is going to be in a bit of a quandary. In fact, he and those other two contractors will probably be the only people in the entire country who will be sorry to see a success here."

"I'm afraid you're right. He was still lobbying for money for those guys only yesterday. I mean, I can understand his trying to beef up those contracts. His office awarded them. But he's been a broken record on this thing. Seems kinda odd, know what I mean?"

"Yes. He's a regular Johnny One-Note for those guys. But when this is all over, I hope we can find other meaningful work for the secretary. To be honest, I've been trying to figure out a way to get rid of him for months now."

"I know. He's never been much of a team player and he hasn't turned out to be much of a manager either," Jay agreed.

The president nodded. "When this is all over, maybe we can find an ambassadorship for him someplace."

"How about the Seychelles?" Jay said with a wry smile.

"I'll take that under advisement." The president looked over at his schedule for the day, saw that he had a few minutes before his next meeting and said, "Now then, I'll make that call to Tokyo and I'll also call the Taiwanese president back to tell him to get ready for the Q-3 team to arrive. You call Bandaq and get that team organized, and I assume you'll let Dr. Talbot know all the details."

"Yes sir. I'm on it."

CHAPTER FORTY-FIVE

STERLING, VIRGINIA

D r. Nettar Kooner was furious. The defense minister of Taiwan had just called to cancel their missile defense contract, emphasizing that the entire shipment from Sterling Dynamics was faulty, and there would be no further payments made. Kooner had told him that his people had gone over every component, every piece of software, every test results and had not found any errors, so the problems must have occurred during installation of the system of Taiwan by their own engineers.

The whole discussion had almost deteriorated into a shouting match when the defense minister had informed him that they had made arrangements to use another company's system for their defense needs and he had finally ended the conversation with a simple, "Good day, sir."

Kooner swiveled his chair around and stared out the large picture window of his office. The trees off in the distance swayed in a gentle breeze, but he felt a cold chill creeping up his spine as he pondered how he would explain this fiasco to his board of directors next week. He

241

turned back to his desk and pulled up the calendar on his computer. He had a meeting scheduled shortly with the weasel from DHS. The man had been on the take for months now, and he wasn't exactly coming through with added money for their airport contract.

It was that contract that could make the difference between profit and their worst quarter ever. He called up his email, saw that he had at least forty unread messages. He sighed and got back to work.

An hour later, his secretary buzzed him to announce that Secretary Thorne had arrived. She showed the gaunt, slope shouldered man into Dr. Kooner's spacious office and came back with a tray of coffee, cream and sugar, cups and saucers, sterling silver spoons, napkins and a plate of croissants. Kooner nodded his thanks and moved over to the conference table for his chat with the DHS director.

"So what have you got for me today?" Kooner asked, hoping for at least one piece of good news.

The secretary poured some cream into his coffee, added three lumps of sugar and reached for a croissant. It looked like he was stalling for time as he carefully stirred his coffee and then broke off a piece of the roll.

"Well?" Kooner prompted.

Thorne took a sip of his coffee and cleared his throat. "I was up on the Hill again yesterday. The committees are all saying that they want to see some test results of your airport system before they vote any more money. Right now they're being hounded for more funds for National Guard troops and Coast Guard units to patrol the areas around the airports, and they're trying to figure out how to pay for the installation of new technology on the airplanes, once it proves out, because they know damn well that the airlines don't have any money to pay for it."

Kooner felt his pulse quicken as he stared at this sorry excuse for a Cabinet member. "Are you telling me that after all these months of . . . shall we say . . . supplementing your income to cover your gambling debts, you can't even push through one measly appropriation for our company?" he asked, his voice rising.

The secretary sat still, his eyes cast down as if he were searching for a bug on the plush gray carpet. "I've tried my best, Nettar. You know that."

"I don't think you've tried hard enough. In fact, you're trying my patience right about now. If this funding doesn't come through, I can see no reason to keep funding your bad little habit."

Thorne looked up at him with pleading eyes. "I've worked hard for you. I got you the contract in the first place. That should be worth something, you know."

"I think the payments we've made into your offshore account have more than compensated you for your initial efforts."

"But I still have debts."

"And if you don't shape up, by the time I'm through with you, you'll be so poor you won't be able to pay attention," Kooner scoffed. "Besides, you think your profligate spending in those casinos is somehow *our* fault?"

"I didn't say that."

"No, you didn't say that," Kooner echoed. "Well, I'm saying this, and I want you to listen carefully. Either I get word by next week that we're getting that appropriation or our agreement will be history. Do you understand me?"

The secretary devoured his croissant as if it were his last meal. He took one last gulp of coffee, wiped his mouth on the linen napkin, got up from the table and quickly walked out the door.

CHAPTER FORTY-SIX

GEORGETOWN

"**A**re you excited about flying out to Travis tomorrow?" Melanie asked as the hostess showed them to their booth in the Omelet Room of Clyde's restaurant in Georgetown. This was one of their favorites haunts. Lots of action, a good wine list, great location right there on M Street near Wisconsin and besides, they could always park downstairs in the huge underground lot below the Georgetown Park shopping mall.

The place felt like a fancy saloon with its long bar in the front room, paintings of horse races and fast cars on the walls and brass sconces at the edge of every booth. So many people hung out at Clyde's starting in the late afternoon, word was that the place had been the inspiration for the old song "Afternoon Delight."

Cammy sat down, stowed her shoulder bag and blazer next to her and grabbed a menu. "If I didn't have to actually get on an airplane, it would be better. You know I hate to fly. It's this phobia I can't seem to shake. I've just got to stop thinking about it." She picked up the menu and added, "But it'll be interesting to go back and see the place. I mean I haven't been there in years. I hope they've improved the housing. It's always pretty sparse on an Air Force base."

"Yeah. Speaking of housing, I've got an idea for that land over on the Eastern Shore."

"You mean the lot you inherited some time back?" Cammy asked.

"MmmHmm. Now don't laugh, but I'm thinking about building a yurt," Melanie said with a smile.

"A yurt?" Cammy blurted. "One of those little round things?"

"Sure. Why not? They're cheap, and I can't afford to build a real house."

"But a yurt? Where the heck did you get that idea?"

"With the president of Mongolia in town, there've been all these articles about life over there. I think maybe they invented them."

"Good grief! A yurt!" Cammy said, staring at her friend. "You come up with the darndest ideas sometimes."

"Hey, I was just thinking that it would be fun to have a weekend place. You know, get out of this town once in a while. And I've got the land, so why not have some fun with it?"

"Have they got a kit for those things? I mean, how are you going to build it?"

"I'm not sure, but I saw a program on HGTV where they put one together and it had a little kitchen, a bathroom, heating and everything. Of course, the rooms are sort of pie-shaped, but it was so cheap and quick, I'll bet I could get it done over the summer."

"You're amazing," Cammy said as she perused the menu.

"And I was thinking that if I had a place like that, you could come out there with me. I'll bet nobody could find you there."

Cammy looked up, suddenly serious. "Well, I sure hope I still don't have to have FBI protection by the time I get back from Travis. I mean, they've *got* to find the bad guys one of these days."

"You'd think," Mel agreed. "Where are your agents now?"

"Over there, in the bar," she said, motioning through an opening to the front room. "When I told them I was meeting you here, I think they were glad for the diversion. Sure beats parking outside of the Indian Embassy or our office building all the time."

The waiter came up, said his name was Ned, poured water into their tall glasses and asked if they'd made a decision.

"I'll have the Norwegian Salmon. And could you bring some extra lemon with that?" Cammy asked.

"Sure thing. Any wine with that? Or something to start?"

She scanned the wines-by-the-glass list and asked for a glass of the Kendall Jackson chardonnay and said the Heirloom tomatoes would be great too.

"And for you?" Ned asked Melanie.

"I'll go for a small Caesar and the New York strip, rare please. Oh, and a glass of the house pinot noir."

Ned made a note and sashayed off to the bar to fill their drink orders.

"Glad you could get out tonight," Mel said. "I thought it would be fun to have kind of a send-off, you know?"

"Thanks. I've been working so late the last couple of nights, I've missed dinner with the ambassador and his wife. They were nice enough to leave me something cold in the kitchen, but still . . ."

"That reminds me," Mel interjected, "since you're going to be traveling with Hunt again, are you still going to give him the cold shoulder?"

Cammy sighed and took a sip of water. "Oh, I don't know. I still feel terrible about Claudia, and I'm sure he's pretty devastated over that whole thing. I can't imagine he'd try to spend much time with me at Travis. I mean, we're going to be so busy, trying to fit our new pod onto that F-16, getting it all wired and then running our tests.

"Besides, when Jayson called to tell me about the schedule and said that they wanted to get my old Q-3 team to fly out just a few days after I get to Travis, I couldn't believe it. Talk about a tight time frame."

"I know. Bollinger is going crazy trying to get the Q-3 components together, get the radar and satellite systems and all the software programs ready to be shipped. When you moved over to do the laser research, there were a lot of changes in that division."

"I know. But at least it's up and running so they should be able to get it ready to go to Taiwan. Besides, Stan must be happy to be getting a fat contract from Taiwan for the system."

"Let's hope so."

The waiter brought their wine and Cammy raised her glass. "I'll tell you one thing though. I know it's not right to do the whole schadenfreude thing, but when Jay told me that the Taiwanese cancelled their contract with Sterling because their defense system didn't work, I really felt like celebrating."

They clinked glasses and Mel said, "I'll drink to that." Then she added, "Looks like you're going to beat Kooner at his own game."

Cammy took a sip of her wine and simply smiled.

CHAPTER FORTY-SEVEN

NORTH OF GUANGZHOU

"Collateral damage," The general declared, reading a report from his second-in-command.

"But, he killed the wrong woman."

"I'm not so sure," the general replied, pulling the goose neck lamp closer so he could read the report more carefully.

Colonel Tsao yanked a wobbly folding chair up to the table. "Her name was Claudia Del Sarto, not the scientist, Dr. Talbot. I tell you, they killed the wrong woman. I don't know how our Washington agent could be so stupid."

The general finished reading and put the memo down. "It turns out that she was spying on our friends in Venezuela. You know our country has completed a series of contracts with Venezuela for everything from oil exploration to lifting trade tariffs. They are proving to be most helpful. So when they tell us that someone is a nuisance, sometimes it pays to take care of the problem. Even if it's an accident."

"But she wasn't *our* problem," the colonel protested.

"True. But by getting her out of the way, we've enhanced our stature in South America, so I am not troubled by this development." He switched off the lamp, got up from the table and started to walk toward the door.

The colonel jumped up and followed as the general stalked out of the building and said, "What *does* trouble me, though, is the general incompetence of our agent in Washington. On the other hand, perhaps we won't be needing him for a while."

"What do you mean?" the colonel asked, trying to keep up with the general's fast pace.

"We have agents in many other places. I also received a report this morning from our man in Taipei."

"We have many providing information from Taiwan. Which one is reporting this time?"

"The man we have placed in the Defense Ministry."

"Ah, the most important spy in our network."

The general turned on his aide. "They are not spies! The other side spies on us. Our people gather information for the motherland. Information that should be forthcoming to us anyway. Do you understand?"

"Yes, sir. What did he say?"

"He told me of a most interesting development. Do you remember when we talked about that American company, Sterling Dynamics, that sold their missile defense system to Taiwan?"

"Of course. And then it never worked."

"Right. I knew that system would not work in Taiwan. The reasons do not matter. They have abrogated their contract with Sterling."

"But that is excellent news."

"Not quite."

"What is wrong?"

"Instead of Sterling's system, they have asked for Q-3, that original missile defense system developed by this Dr. Talbot, the one who should have been eliminated long ago."

"Taiwan is going to get Q-3? When?"

"Our agent reports that the American government is going to send it over in a matter of days."

The general hurried along the path from the hangar to a warehouse where jeeps and armaments were stored. When he yanked open the door, he saw dozens of soldiers preparing various vehicles and weapons for use in the upcoming military exercises. He surveyed the cavernous room and began to inspect the process.

The colonel followed him inside and shut the door. "Will Dr. Talbot be coming to Taiwan to set it up?"

"Our agent believes she will come, yes." The general stopped and turned around. "So do you realize what this means?"

"Certainly, sir. All we need to do is get their exact itinerary from our agent in Taipei."

CHAPTER FORTY-EIGHT

THE WHITE HOUSE

"You're delaying your trip by a couple of days, Jay?" The president said. They were having their usual weekly luncheon in a private study just off the Oval Office. The stewards maintain a small kitchen nearby and were used to serving lunch, coffee and snacks off and on during the day.

One time many years ago a president asked the stewards to rustle up a few bottles of champagne because he was so pleased that Congress had finally passed a major bill reducing tax rates by twenty-five percent. He had invited any members of the White House staff who happened to be nearby to come into the Oval Office to raise a glass and toast their victory. Photos of that celebration had ended up in newspapers and magazines all over the world. It was displayed on board an aircraft carrier, the USS Ronald Reagan, and even appeared in *Paris Match*. That had been especially welcomed by the White House press secretary. They didn't always get such great coverage in France. But no such champagne celebrations had taken place in the current Oval Office in quite some time.

The vice president ate some of his onion soup and said, "Yes. After some calls, we decided it would be best to send the advance team over to set things up. We all know what the Japanese are like when it comes to protocol. And this mutual defense pact is too important to leave to chance."

"You're right. When I made that first call to the prime minister, he was gracious and said that they would naturally welcome your entourage and all of that. But I got the distinct impression that he needed a bit of time to consider his options."

"The only thing is," Jay said, "I don't want to wait more than a couple of days. I'm worried about those military exercises the Chinese are about to start in the Taiwan Straits. Since I missed the intelligence briefing this morning, anything new there?"

"Just that they're moving more equipment into the area than they ever have in the past. It had to be the usual scare mongering though. I can't conceive of the Chinese trying to do anything to Taiwan right now. We've got trade agreements with that crowd, and foreign investment is at an all-time high."

"Of course, they keep putting in more regulations to screw up a lot of it," the vice president interjected.

"I suppose they have to do something to keep all those bureaucrats busy. Sure wish we had some results back from Borealis. But that's going to take another day or two."

"Yes. Iggy really got his back up over that order. But they finally rolled it out and took off. There's been no hint of it in the press, not even *Air Force Times*. I think they're doing a pretty good job keeping that whole operation Top Secret."

"Right. But I keep thinking, what's the use of having all this hardware if we can't use it?" the president said.

Jayson nodded and used his large spoon to cut through the thick layer of Gruyere cheese on top of his soup. "As long as we have a few minutes here, I wanted to see if there's anything else I should be doing for you before I leave?"

The president finished his first course and started on his chicken Caesar salad. "There are so many things on our agenda right now, but I'm farming them out. You've got enough to worry about with the Japanese, the Taiwanese and maybe even the Chinese acting up."

"I know. Just thought I'd check," Jay said.

"In addition to our whole terrorist issue, we're still trying to work out a few things with the Hill on that new Medicare benefit."

"Nobody understood the last one."

"I know. However, it turns out, I might veto it anyway. We can't afford what we've got now. Oh, and the New York delegation is pissed off, again, about the whole parking ticket game around the city."

"You mean all the UN delegates who park anywhere and ignore the tickets because they think they've got diplomatic immunity?"

"Sure. Comes up all the time, except that now the city is screaming for their share of the funds," the president said with a weary shake of his head.

"Who's the worst offender this time?" Jay asked as the steward replenished his iced tea.

"I think they said it was Egypt this time. They still get over a billion bucks in aid from us, and they've got almost eighteen-thousand parking tickets. Can you believe that?"

"What about Nigeria. They've always been on the list."

"I think I heard they owe close to a million dollars worth. Actually, the House did pass something to deal with the situation. It's in conference."

"Now that nobody is flying anywhere, they're all using cars to get around so I expect the problem is just going to get worse."

"Probably. And with the media still pounding us on the attacks, nobody wants to talk about anything else," the president said. "I pray we don't have any more situations where I have to go on television and explain that more innocent Americans slipped the surly bonds of earth to touch the face of God," to quote one of Peggy Noonan's most inspired lines. Of course, that was decades ago, and nothing like that challenger explosion has happened until now."

"I know what you mean."

"At least it's been a whole week without an attack, but the market is still sliding. So of course, I get nailed for every single loss in stock price. Did you see that editorial about how my predecessor had a great economy?"

"Oh for God's sake, Warren Harding had a great economy," the vice president scoffed.

The president shook his head and said, "By the way, I just had a report that NSA may be on to a new communication scheme."

"A new scheme? What is it this time?" Jay asked.

"It's called Steganography."

"Don't know that one. How does it work?"

"It's pretty damn clever. Term is Greek. Means hidden or covered or something like that. What they do is encrypt a message and then disguise it as something else. Like a photograph maybe."

"So how do the NSA types figure it out?"

"I was going to include you in the meeting on it this morning, but I knew you were tied up on the plans for Japan, so I let you off the hook."

"Thanks, but I'd still like to know how we deal with it, if that's what some of the terrorist groups are using to communicate."

The president leaned back an thought for a moment. "The way I understand it, with a photograph, they have to analyze all the pixels. If there's just one or two that are sort of *off*, too bright or not bright enough for example, they go on to take the whole damn thing apart. I don't know all the details, but they've got people on it because they're starting to pick up a few of these things. I just hope to God they can decipher some messages before we're attacked again."

"At least I guess that's good news," the vice president said. "In fact, if they've really got something new, it's the best news since the call I got from the National Zoo this morning," he said with a slight grin.

"Oh? What was that?"

Jay started to laugh. "The yaks are having a baby."

"Well," the president said, "At least we can expect something in this town besides disasters."

CHAPTER FORTY-NINE

TRAVIS AIR FORCE BASE

Cammy was nervous during the entire flight across the country to Travis Air Force Base, located half way between Sacramento and San Francisco. At least she had been surrounded by her laser team from Bandaq. All of their equipment had been packed on board the military cargo plane. Yet, she had never been able to shake her fear of flying. It had been a tense experience all the way.

Hunt had been seated up front with some of the crew. She and her former lover had been avoiding each other all during the boarding process. He didn't even bother to come back and chat with her at any time during the long flight. That was fine with her. This was a business trip. All business.

She was going to be racing to work with the crew chiefs to get her entire laser apparatus installed on an F-16 that they were ferrying over from Luke Air Force Base in Glendale, near Phoenix.

They didn't usually have F-16s at Travis these days. It was home to the 60th Air Mobility Wing and they had big transport planes like C-5

Galaxys and KC-10's that were used for in-flight refueling. The base handled more cargo and passengers than any other military terminal in the entire country, so it was logical that their planes would be used not only to transport her equipment, but also to take Bandaq's Q-3 components and staff all the way to Taiwan in a couple of days.

She didn't have much time to work on the laser before joining her former colleagues on the trip overseas. She'd never been to Taiwan. It could be quite an adventure. And it would be good to exercise her skills on the Q-3 software again where she had figured out how to identify, lock on and take control of a cruise missile, allowing her to redirect it back on the heads of the bad guys if she wanted to.

It was an incredible invention. At least that's what everybody said at the time. Now she just hoped they could get it deployed in Taiwan as a defense against some of those missiles that the Chinese had aimed at the island.

When they finally landed at Travis, Cammy and her top assistant, Sarah McIntyre, were shown to their suite of rooms at the DV quarters. She knew that stood for "Distinguished Visitors," and she was pleased that they were being allowed to stay on the base. Their place was actually a small house with two bedrooms.

Civilians usually had to stay in nearby Vacaville. But since this visit had been requested by the White House, the base personnel were scurrying around to treat her like a real VIP and make everyone comfortable.

The White House must have worked all of this out with the Travis Protocol Office, Cammy thought, because she saw that they did follow some of the other rules. They had put Hunt over in "Air Force Lodging" where visiting officers and enlisted men stayed.

For the DV quarters, either you were a special civilian like Cammy, or you were military at the rank of bird colonel or above. And since Hunt was just a Lieutenant Colonel, he was in the other building.

It was actually a rather large hotel, kind of like an on-base Marriott. But since it was some distance from her quarters, it meant she probably wouldn't see very much of him during their down time, if they had any at all. And that was fine with her. She doubted if he'd make a move to talk to her anyway. And she certainly wasn't about to break the ice on her own. No, she had work to do here. As for her feelings, she'd just have to put all of those on cruise control. For the time being anyway.

She knew it would take a while for the crews to unload all of their equipment and get it organized in the hangar housing the F-16. She took the time to call her mother in San Francisco. She hadn't seen her mom in months as both of them had full time jobs, and it was always hard to break away. But they often talked on the phone. Cammy explained her crazy schedule and said she didn't know if she could get to San Francisco on this trip, but she'd try.

When she hung up, she looked out the window and saw planes taking off and landing in the distance. It brought back such a flood of memories. Memories of growing up on bases. Memories of her dad, Captain Casey Talbot, coming home from a mission, picking her up and dancing around the living room while singing an old song. She even remembered some of the lyrics because she'd heard them so often. "Casey would waltz with the strawberry blond, and the band played on. He'd glide cross the floor with the girl he adored, and the band played on."

Her eyes began to mist over as she reflected on her childhood and how much her father had meant to her. She'd never found another man who could match his warmth, his encouragement, his dedication to duty until . . . she had met Hunt.

Damn it. There I go again with the nostalgia routine. She shook her head as if she were trying to clear away the old images. She turned around and unpacked her suitcase, hung up her clothes, put her make-up kit and hot rollers in the bathroom and finally walked across the hall to check in with Sarah.

The former Bell Labs scientist was sitting by the window glancing through a copy of *Popular Science* when Cammy knocked and came in. "Hi boss. All settled in?"

"Sure. Pretty nice place we've got here."

"Better than I expected," Sarah said. "Where do people eat around here? I'm starved."

"We could go over to the Officers' Club if you want."

Sarah jumped up, tucked her cotton blouse into her khaki slacks and said, "Am I dressed okay? I've never been to an Officer's Club."

"Oh yes. You're fine. Most of the guys there will be in uniform or even flight suits or BDU's."

"What's a BDU?" Sarah inquired.

"Battle dress uniform."

"You know, with all these pilots around here, I been thinking that someday I might take lessons. I've always wanted to fly."

"So did Icarus," Cammy said. "And look what happened to him."

Hunt swiveled on his bar stool in the Club when another officer came up and slapped him on the back. "Hunt? That you?"

"My God, Pete. Haven't seen you in ages. I didn't know you were stationed here."

"Yep. Been here for a year now. Jesus, it's good to see you, man. Last thing I heard you were at the Pentagon working on nuclear stuff or something pretty high level."

"Well, I was. Now I've been detailed to the National Security Council," Hunt said, taking a swig of his beer.

"At the White House?"

"Yeah. Pretty good assignment."

"Pretty damn good," Pete replied.

A bell rang and the officers began to hoot, laugh and point at a young Lieutenant who had just placed his hat on the end of the bar. "What the hell's going on?" Hunt asked as the bartender held up his hands and shouted, "Drinks all around."

"Poor bastard," Pete said with a big laugh. "There are two things you do not do in this club?"

"Yeah? What?"

"Number one. You do not take a call on your cell phone from a spouse. And number two, you do not put your hat on the bar."

"Why not?"

"Because if you do, you have to buy drinks for everybody in the house. Want another beer?"

Hunt burst out laughing. "Yeah. Sure. Crazy rules around here."

"That's why I always toss my hat on the table by the door over there. And as for a cell call, well, I'm okay with that because I haven't got a wife. How about you?"

"Nah. She left me a while ago. Didn't dig the military life, I guess. I was gone a lot, you know."

"Same here."

They got their second round and talked about old times when they had trained together as Air Force pilots. Hunt started joking about the time they had gone to what they thought was a strip club, and it turned out to be nothing but guys dancing on stage. The star had been called "Thunder Thighs."

Then Hunt glanced over Pete's shoulder and saw two women walk in and move toward the bar. Hunt stopped laughing, shifted on the barstool, and wondered if he really needed this encounter. But they were headed his way, so he knew he'd have to be polite.

"Hi Cammy," Hunt said as she approached. He turned to the other women. "And you're from Bandaq. I saw you on the plane." He motioned to his friend, "And this is Colonel Pete Feldman, an old buddy from training days."

Sarah looked up at Pete and gave him a broad smile. Cammy extended her hand but was much cooler in her approach. Pete offered them a drink and Sarah quickly accepted. Pete suggested they move to an area on the other side of the pool table where there were four available chairs. They trooped past historical pictures on the wall, photos of past commanders and old fighter planes and finally they sat down.

There she was, sitting so close to Hunt that he could feel her knees under the table. *What now?* He wondered. Pete kept on talking about their training exploits and then started to tell stories about some of his deployments overseas. Sarah gave him her rapt attention while Cammy sat fidgeting with the strap on her shoulder bag.

Maybe I could ask her to go for a walk or something, he thought. *No, she'd probably brush me off. Wrong move. Maybe if I just get her to talk quietly about the project. No, we shouldn't talk details in front of other people. Maybe if she has another drink she'll loosen up. After all, we're working together again, just like we were two months ago. Sure we had some ups and downs back then, but there's gotta be a way I can break through that ice shield of hers and get her to listen to some logic. After all, I had good reasons not to call her before. At least it seemed like I did at the time. Maybe she'll have dinner with me. Then I'll finally be able to explain.*

Cammy's cell phone rang. She fished in her purse and pulled it out. "Excuse me," she said to the others, as she turned her chair slightly away from the table and took the call. She chatted in a low voice for a few minutes, closed her cell, pushed it back into her bag and got up from the table.

"I've got to go. Sorry," she said.

Hunt jumped up. "Wait a minute, I was just going to ask if you'd like to join me for dinner."

Cammy pushed some stray blond hair back under her headband and said, "No, I can't really do that. There are a few things I have to do."

"Look, Cam," Hunt protested, "You've gotta eat. I mean what could be so important that . . ."

"I have to get a memo together."

"A memo?" Hunt said. "At this hour? Who could need a memo unless it was the president or something."

"No, not the president," Cammy said. "That was the vice . . ."

Hunt raked a hand through his hair, sat down and muttered. "I should have known."

CHAPTER FIFTY

THE WHITE HOUSE

Trenton LaSalle wiped his forehead with his handkerchief and shoved it back into his pocket. "The controllers are walking!" he declared, as he stood in front of the president's desk in the Oval Office, his shoulders in their perpetual slump.

"They can't do that," the president barked. "It's against the law."

"We've been through all of this," the transportation secretary said. "They know it. We know it. The courts know it. But they're out anyway. Okay, so they're calling it a 'work stoppage' or some such bullshit, but everybody knows it's the same as a strike. Nothing, absolutely nothing is moving right now. And I have no clue how long this is going to last. The trains are so jammed, you can't get a reservation to go anywhere for at least a week. It feels like the day after 9/11 around my shop."

"It's still about safety at the airports, right?" the president said, motioning to the secretary to pull up a chair and sit down.

"Yes. They say it has nothing to do with money."

"Good thing because we haven't got any."

"I know. And neither do the airlines. Three of their presidents came to town last night. They were in my office at seven this morning saying that if we don't find the terrorists, get new fail-safe technology, or give them a federal bail-out, they're all filing for bankruptcy."

"Isn't that a case of collusion?"

"Not technically. They all just have the same bitches. It has nothing to do with setting fares or anything."

"Back on the strike situation. Anybody else supporting this *illegal* action?" The president asked.

"On yeah. The flight attendants are taking a vote later this week to maybe join in. And the pilots are waiting to see how we handle the controllers. But, with nothing moving, they don't have anything else to do anyway."

The president's chief of staff came in through a side door. "Sorry to miss the start of this meeting, Mr. President, but our senior staff meeting ran long."

"Anything urgent?" the president asked.

The chief of staff glanced down at his notebook. "There's still a lot of fallout from Winters' hearings."

"Like what? Didn't he get enough headlines out of that charade to last him a while?"

"Something besides headlines. He got a bump in the polls. Everyone expects him to announce for the presidency pretty soon. Now that he's at about fifty-six percent, he's got all the other candidates cowed. He leads Jay by a wide margin."

"We've got plenty of time before the elections. Those polls are like network ratings. One week they like *Game of Thrones* and another week it's *House of Cards*, or maybe *The Bachelorette* or whatever they're touting these days," the president said with a wave of his hand.

"Speaking of a house of cards, ours has been falling down big time," the chief said. "Our numbers have never been lower."

"Nothing I can do about that now. As soon as we nail the bastards shooting down our airplanes, all will be forgiven."

"And if we don't nail them?" Trenton asked nervously.

The president ignored the question from his transportation secretary and asked one of his own. "Does anyone have anything new from NSA on the surveillance? Anything on the whole steganography process?"

"Nothing firm yet," the chief of staff said. "I just checked. It turns out they did find several emails that might contain some samples. They're analyzing them right now."

"Good. Let me know as soon as you hear anything." The president turned back to the transportation secretary. "Now then. I want you to get a hold of the head of the Air Traffic Controllers Union. Haul his ass into your office and remind him of what we do to striking controllers. I know they want safer airports. Hell, we all want safer airports, safer planes, safer everything. But he's not running the show here. I am. And I'd like a little cooperation from our government employees. You remind him about the agreements they've signed but then brief him on all the technology that's in the pipeline. While you're chewing him out, let him figure out that you're taking him into your confidence on what we're doing here. That ought to satisfy him for a while. And if he can't handle his troops, well, maybe they need a new leader."

"Yes, Mr. President. I'll do that." The secretary headed toward the door and the chief of staff stepped forward and checked his notes.

"What else have you got?" the president demanded.

"Dr. Talbot sent a memo to the vice president indicating that they're getting started on the retrofitting of the F-16 out at Travis."

"And?"

"And they're having a few problems. She's not sure the pod is going to fit right under the fuselage. They have to make it a bit smaller and lighter because they're working with a tactical aircraft, not a big airliner."

"Oh Christ!"

"But they're working on it." He looked down again. "And Jay also told me that the Japanese are taking their sweet old time agreeing to some preliminary language on the proposed mutual defense pact with Taiwan."

"But he's scheduled to leave in two days," the president said.

"I know. He says he's still going to fly out there on time and try to iron out the differences when he gets to Tokyo."

"And what about that Q-3 team from Bandaq? Is that at least on track?"

"Yes, sir. Their CEO reports that they have all the equipment ready to go. They load and take off first thing tomorrow, refuel at Travis, pick up Dr. Talbot and head over to Taiwan to deploy the Q-3 defensive system."

"How long will it take them to get it up and running?"

"Not sure. All I know is that the Chinese started their military exercises this morning."

"Already?"

"Yes. They've started to move their ships into the Taiwan Straits, and we just got word that they've got a whole slew of amphibious landing craft ready to go."

"Go where?" the president asked, raising his voice.

"That is the question of the day."

CHAPTER FIFTY-ONE

TRAVIS AIR FORCE BASE

"I hear the coffee's pretty decent at Rickenbacker's," Cammy said as she and Sarah pushed open the door to the Air Force Lodging Hotel.

"Hope it's Starbucks," his assistant said.

"And I hope I don't run into Hunt Daniels."

"What's with you two anyway?"

Cammy sighed. "It's a long story. Let's just say we were an item once."

"Once? Boy, if I ever had my hands on that hunk, I wouldn't let go," she said with a grin.

"I wasn't the one who let go," Cammy said, walking up to the counter and scanning the menu posted on the wall.

"Sorry about that," Sarah said. "Oh look, they've got rolls and crumb cake and a lot of good stuff here."

"Right. I could use something good before we head over to that hangar and get more bad news."

"You really think those crew chiefs won't be able to attach the pod and connect the systems?"

"As of yesterday, all they were saying was that the system was FUBAR."

"FUBAR?" Sarah asked raising her eyebrows.

"It's a military term. 'Fucked-up-beyond-all-recognition.'"

Sarah burst out laughing. "At least they sound like they've got a sense of humor."

"They'll need a lot more than that if we're going to get the test flights on track. I'm supposed to be leaving for Taiwan this afternoon with my old Q-3 team."

"I know. When do they land anyway?"

"Around five. They're not taking a long break here. Just enough time to refuel and get going. We want to get there first thing in the morning and get started."

"You never get a break, do you?"

Cammy straightened her headband and gave the clerk their order. "As things are going right now, I may not get a break at all."

"What do you mean?"

"If we can't get the pod on right and check the system before that first test flight tomorrow, I may have to stay, finish the job and figure out how to get to Taiwan later."

"But commercial planes aren't flying. Then again, I'm not sure about all the international flights," Sarah said.

"I know. It's a total mess."

At precisely 1705 hours, the C-5 Galaxy cargo jet made a smooth landing at Travis, taxied to a terminal and came to a stop. A sergeant driving her jeep turned to Cammy and said, "Those pilots have a pretty good on-time record."

"Yes, I can see that."

"Of course, they're about the only planes flying these days."

"I know. It's a complete catastrophe how our whole transportation system is down. That's why it's so important that we finish our job here."

"Yeah, I know." He steered through a gate onto the tarmac and drove up to the C-5. Several people were coming down the stairs. Cammy jumped out of the jeep and ran over to her colleagues.

"How was the flight? Everything get on board okay? Is everyone ready for this?"

The questions kept spilling out before anyone had a chance to answer. She hugged two of the women who got off first, then four men as several crew members also came off the plane.

"Hey Cam."

"Hi Dr. Talbot."

"Great to see you."

"How's it going with the laser?"

"Got it working yet?"

Everyone was talking at once. After a frustrating day when some of her simulations didn't seem to be working right, it was great to see these happy faces. Faces of young scientists and researchers now working on her invention, the Q-3 missile defense system. She had trained all of them. She was proud of the way they had taken over her division and expanded the production line so that the system could be deployed around the world to protect American troops stationed abroad.

She was proud that this new technology actually could neutralize a cruise missile and save lives. She was proud of the fact that ever since her invention had been incorporated into the president's system of layered defense, nobody had even fired a cruise missile near any of their forces. And the allies who had purchased Q-3 had remained safe from attack as well. What rogue state would shoot off a cruise missile if everyone knew it could be diverted and destroyed? What would be the point?

They all trooped into the terminal to take a break. The women headed to the Ladies Room, the men went off on their own to hit the snack bar and coffee machines.

"So, Cammy, where's your luggage? We're leaving in less than an hour," one young scientist said.

"Well, that's the problem. Now I can't go with you."

"What? But we need you. I mean, to set up, to get organized, to show the Taiwanese . . ."

"I know. I know. I thought I could be ready, but I can't. Not yet. The processor has been over-heating and going into a soft fail. It needs to cool down. It just isn't responding the way it did back in the lab. Right now I'm calling it a faith-based initiative, if there ever was one."

One of the woman laughed as Cammy continued. "Back in Rockville, I thought I had everything lined up right, but now I seem to be stuck. I feel kind of like a fly in amber."

Her colleague shook her head and grinned. "Aw c'mon, I'm sure you'll nail it."

"Sure hope so. Guess I just need a little more time."

"How much time?"

"Hopefully just one more day," Cammy said. "I figure if I can work on this thing all day tomorrow, I found out that there is a flight out of San Francisco tomorrow night. Direct to Taipei. At least some of the international flights are operating. I've got all the numbers of where you guys are staying, who your contacts are. So you go on ahead. Start getting set up. It'll take a while to get the satellite and radar functional anyway."

"Yes, but we thought . . ."

"I thought so too. It's just that I don't have any choice. But hey, it's only one day. This all just came up at the last minute. I had already packed a few things and was working on the F-16 this afternoon when I realized it was still screwed up. I can't leave. Not yet."

The scientist pushed into the ladies room with Cammy and another girl in tow. "Well, okay. I can see how you've probably got your hands full out here. By the way, it's really hot right now. Is it always like this?"

Cammy laughed. "At Travis? Oh yeah. The summers can be pretty brutal. It's almost like being in the desert. And with all of this open concrete around, I mean with the runways and all, they reflect the sun all the time."

"And it doesn't rain much, right?"

"Right. On the other hand, we're only about an hour away from San Francisco, when anybody can get away that is. And that city is blessedly cool this time of year."

"So I've heard. So you'll get to go there tomorrow and catch your flight, huh?"

"Yes. If I can wrap things up here, or at least get it all hooked up for others to test. I figure I'll leave a little early, stop and see my mom on the way . . . she lives in the city . . . and then catch that flight tomorrow night."

They all freshened up, washed their hands, brushed their hair and the scientist commented, "I don't know why I'm trying to look good right now. As soon as I'm back on board, I'm going to have to try and get some sleep. Once we get to Taiwan, it's going to be crazy."

Cammy put her brush back into her shoulder bag, swung the purse over her shoulder, and the women headed back out to the snack bar area. They sat and chatted with the other members of the Bandaq staff and told stories about how the company got its name. Cammy told the newest staff members the story about the two guys who were bare-boating down in the Caribbean and how they came up with ideas about some new technologies. They were drinking Banana Daquiris at the time. Voila. "Bandaq."

Then Cammy and her colleagues talked about how they had to deal with various foreign governments when they set up their system overseas, and speculated on how long it would take them to get Q-3 up and running over in Taiwan. One man said he heard the Chinese had started their military exercises, and he wondered if that's why the Taiwanese were so nervous all of a sudden.

"Yes," Cammy answered. "Jayson, uh, the vice president told me that China is going through their usual saber-rattling routine, but whenever they do this, Taiwan gets pretty upset. And it's especially bad now because there are several factions within Taiwan's government who are talking more openly about bringing up another vote on independence."

"Good luck on that idea," one man replied.

Cammy glanced at her watch and got up. "And good luck to you all on this mission. I'll call and let you know if I make that flight tomorrow night." She went around the group, gave each person a hug, and they all walked back out to the huge cargo plane.

"Looks like they're through refueling," one young man said. "Better get on board."

"Okay guys, do a great job. See you soon."

Cammy waved as she watched them board the plane. She turned and walked over to the Jeep that was parked nearby. As she got in she said to her driver, "What a great group. I loved working with them, and I'll have a chance to be with them again in Taiwan. There's one scientist who used to work for Sandia National Labs. She's got a lot of patents to her name. I'm really impressed with her."

"Brainy bunch, huh?" the sergeant said. "Say, do you wanna watch the big one take off? It's quite a sight. Sometimes when I see those babies on the runway, I wonder how they ever get enough lift, but they always do."

"Sure, let's do that."

The sergeant started the jeep and drove back toward the gate. He turned the steering wheel and lined up perpendicular to the runway. The sun was still pretty high in the sky, and her friends would be heading west. Cammy poked around in her bag for her sunglasses, put them on and watched as the huge jet taxied out.

She heard the roar of the engines as it headed down and gathered speed. Then she saw the plane gently lift off and soar toward the heavens. It kept going higher and higher. Cammy shielded her eyes and craned her neck. "You're right," she said to the sergeant. "It's quite a sight."

Just as the plane climbed to an altitude that made it seem like a tiny toy, it suddenly exploded in a fireball that rivaled the sun.

Cammy screamed. The sergeant jumped out of the jeep and dozens of enlisted men and officers poured out of the hangars and nearby terminal to stare at the horrible sight as the plane broke apart and separate pieces of flaming wreckage rained down in a hail of flares and twisted steel.

CHAPTER FIFTY-TWO

THE WHITE HOUSE

"Mr. President," the press secretary careened through the door to the Oval Office and without preamble almost shouted, "Another one. The C-5 Galaxy. Travis Air Force Base. The Bandaq team. The missile defense system . . ."

"What?" The president said, jumping up from his chair and coming around the edge of his desk to face the young man. "You mean the cargo plane on the way to Taiwan?"

"Yes sir, right now, shot down, right after take off."

"Oh my God!" He grabbed the phone that automatically rang on his secretary's desk when he lifted the hand set. "Get the vice president in here, and the chief of staff. No, wait, get the DNI on video conference in the Sit Room and the SecDef. Get the base commander at Travis on it too if you can. We'll head downstairs right now."

He turned back to his press secretary. "I can't believe this. A military plane shot out of the sky? They have certain systems on board that can detect an attack." He shook his head and pointed to the notebook the press secretary had in his hand. "Don't say anything. Not yet. We need a coordinated statement here. I've got to get the facts from that base commander. We've got to find out if the Tower saw or heard anything, anything on radar this time. I've got to have a complete list of all those on board and, God, I've got to make calls to their families. This was a mission that we ordered and now all those bright young scientists and engineers are . . . oh, what the hell!"

The press secretary made some notes and stared at his boss. "I'll try to hold off for a little while, sir, but you know how it is. Press is scream-ing. It's already a complete madhouse back there."

"I know. I'm sure. But it's very important that we handle this right. Taiwan was counting on those people to protect them if the Chinese decide to do something stupid. Now we've got to figure out how to calm them down and . . ."

"Calm down the nation?"

"Yes. That too. And the vice president is scheduled to head over to Japan but now with this . . . Look, I've got to get downstairs. Why don't you come down with us? Stay out of the press room for a while. We'll draft a statement in the Sit Room when we figure out what the hell hap-pened out there."

Jayson Keller raced down the carpeted steps to the basement level of the White House and headed toward the door to the Situation Room. When the agent sitting outside the door saw him coming, he swiveled around and punched the numerical code into the key box and held the door open so the vice president could head in without breaking stride.

As Jay got to the door of the conference room, he saw the president, the press secretary and chief of staff gathered inside. "I just heard," Jay said. "I can't believe this. Cammy was on board that plane," he announced to the small group in a forlorn voice.

"We know," the president said. "This is the worst God damn night-mare I could imagine. We send over the best and most dedicated work force, and they get blown out of the sky by these maniacs. And for what? For what, I want to know."

A technician came in and began the video conference. "Sir, I have the director of national intelligence and the secretary of defense, but we're still waiting on the Travis Base commander. I'm afraid he's not in a position to . . ."

"Well, stay on it," the president ordered. "If you can't get video, just get him on the damn telephone. Let us know as soon as he's in position. We need his take on this God damn disaster."

Jay's face was a ghostly grey as he sat down to the right of the president and put his head in his hands. "She's gone," he muttered. "I can't believe she's gone." He raised his eyes and he added in a halting voice, "And *I* sent her over there."

The chief of staff put his hand on Jayson's shoulder. "Look, Jay, it's not your fault. She volunteered for this assignment. She knew how important it was. Or rather, how important it could be."

Jay pulled his handkerchief out of his pocket and blew his nose. "Uh, sorry, Mr. President. It's just that . . ." his voice trailed off.

"Take it easy. We're all over wrought about this thing." He glanced up at the screen as images of the DNI and the SecDef focused in. The president addressed his defense secretary first. "So what do we know? Anything yet?"

Iggy looked down at some notes and then said, "First reports are that there was no indication on radar in the tower that a missile of any kind was heading toward that cargo plane. But the sensors on board the plane did sound an alarm. The pilots radioed that they believed they had been targeted. They tried to deploy decoys that had been installed on their fleet just recently, but they evidently had no effect."

"Obviously!" the president murmured. "Anything else? How high was the plane?"

"We're still getting details on that. But they believe it was pretty high. Much higher than any type of old shoulder-fired missile that we've seen in the past could reach."

"Then what the hell was it?"

"We still don't know, sir."

"Well, see what else you can find out," the president said. "Now what's the latest on China's military exercises and the situation in Taiwan."

"Taiwan is on full alert, sir. The exercises are underway and we're monitoring every missile launch site that we know of at this point."

The president eyed the DNI on the screen and asked, "Anything new on these bastards?"

"We may have a line on some communications to a group in San Francisco. They've been sending and receiving a series of encrypted messages embedded in photographs that we're working on."

"San Francisco? Jesus! That's close to Travis. So, do your people think this group, whoever they are, could have played a part in this? And how soon can you trace their location?"

"We're on it, sir. We haven't got a translation yet, but I'll let you know as soon as we do."

The president then turned to Jayson who had regained his composure and was quietly making some notes. "How about the Japanese? Are they ready to sign an agreement yet?"

"Our people over there say they're making progress. I can probably leave tomorrow or the next day at the latest."

"All right. At least we've got that ball rolling. Now then, we've got to draft a series of statements. We'll need a strong statement of support for Taiwan to put the Chinese on notice."

"Uh, just a minute, Mr. President," the defense secretary interrupted. "I know it's our policy to aid Taiwan, if need be. But how in the hell are we supposed to pull that off if the Chicoms really do attack that island? I mean, our forces are over-extended right now."

The president studied the screen and replied. "I know that. We all know that. But the Chinese may not know that. In any event, we've got to say something. Ever since it got out that Sterling's system was a complete boondoggle, Taiwan has looked like a sitting duck. And a very appetizing one at that."

He turned to his press secretary. "Just come up with some language about how we support Taiwan's government as democratically elected.

Throw in some words about their free enterprise system, their human rights record or whatever else you can dig up. Say that our policy has always supported a peaceful resolution to their differences with the mainland. But in general, we want to come to the aid of freedom loving people everywhere. Or something like that.

"Wait," he continued. "This is more important. We need to tell the American people about those young engineers on board that cargo plane." He motioned to his chief of staff who was poised to take notes. "I want a thoughtful statement praising those people to the sky. You look it over. I want every single name of every single person on board that plane. Bandaq people, military people. Everyone. I need to call their families first."

He addressed his press secretary again who had been scribbling furiously. "Then I want you to go out there and blast the attackers, whoever the hell they are, for this callous, inhumane act of terrorism and make it clear that we will not rest until those people are found and prosecuted to the greatest extent of the law."

The press secretary was adding to his notes when the president said, "And we need to say that this is a time to pull together as Americans, not break apart . . ."

"Like that cargo plane," Jayson interjected in a soft voice, his shoulders sagging as he sat slumped in his chair.

CHAPTER FIFTY-THREE

TRAVIS AIR FORCE BASE

Cammy was sobbing uncontrollably when Hunt's car screeched to a halt near the terminal. He saw her hunched over, leaning against the side of the jeep, her body shaking as her driver looked on helplessly. Hunt rushed over and gathered her in his arms. Her body sank next to his. He held her up with one arm while brushing strands of wet hair out of her eyes with the other.

"Cam, I'm so sorry. This is insane," he said in a low voice as she continued to cry. "I can't believe they were able to target a C-5 right here on an Air Force Base. Must have been launched some place away from here."

He scanned the horizon and saw plumes of smoke lingering where the wreckage had plummeted to the ground. "I came as soon as I heard. The whole base is in an uproar." He nudged her chin up so he could look into her eyes, filled with tears. "I know they were your friends."

"Uh huh," she said with a slight hiccup.

"And you were supposed to be on the plane," he added.

"Uh huh. But when we couldn't get the simulations going, I was planning to stay here another day and then take a commercial flight over to Taipei from San Francisco tomorrow night and hook up with them."

"Well, you couldn't do that anyway. Even if there were people over there to work with."

"Why not?"

"I just heard that the controllers went out on strike. Nothing's moving."

"Then I'm stuck here. Taiwan is defenseless and, oh God, what are we going to do?" she asked with a plaintive cry.

"I don't know, but the real question is how did the bastards know you would be on board that plane? I mean, if you somehow were the target again?"

"I don't know," she whispered. "But you think it's because of me, don't you?"

He pulled her closer and stroked her hair. "We don't know that. Maybe they found out the plane was headed to Taiwan. Maybe you were right all along about the Chinese being behind all of this. Maybe they didn't want Q-3 to be set up over there. Maybe . . ." his voice faltered as she clung to him.

She finally pulled away, leaned inside the jeep to retrieve her shoulder bag and pulled out a Kleenex. She wiped her eyes. "Oh Hunt. I don't know what to do. Those were the best people we had. I hired them. I trained them. They were such good friends too." Tears began to spill down her face again as she looked imploringly at Hunt. "Why? Who knew we were going to be on that plane? Who could possibly know everything we're doing?"

He raked his fingers through his hair and stood still for a moment. "I don't have a clue. I know it's nobody in our government. It's got to be somebody on the outside. Somebody with tentacles into a lot of places." He thought for a few more moments and added, "The only thing that makes sense is that there are spies, foreign agents who have penetrated somewhere."

"But where?" she groaned.

"I don't know, but we sure as hell are going to find out. Come with me to the tower. I want to talk to the base commander. And after all of this, I'm not letting you out of my sight."

CHAPTER FIFTY-FOUR

THE WHITE HOUSE

"There has been no official statement as yet from the White House on this latest attack on a C-5 Galaxy taking off from Travis Air Force Base in California," the CNN news anchor reported solemnly.

"Early reports indicate that the plane was heading overseas, but CNN has been unable to confirm the number of passengers and crew on board nor its destination. The base is home to the largest military transport wing in the country and ferries troops, equipment as well as civilian passengers to assignments around the world. We expect an announcement from the press secretary on this latest tragedy shortly, but we do have this initial reaction from Capitol Hill. We now switch to our congressional correspondent, Margarita Garcia."

Jayson Keller looked askance at the TV set in his West Wing office as he sat back in his desk chair and tried to make sense out of the quartet of problems facing him at that moment. First, the attack on the plane. Second, the problem of Taiwan's defenses. Third, the upcoming negotiations with the Japanese, but most important, the loss of Dr. Cameron Talbot. He rubbed his eyes and tried to focus on the TV screen, but a picture of the pretty blond scientist kept invading his mind's eye.

He could just see her perched on the sofa on his living room, chatting about growing up on Air Force Bases, offering her views on our screwed up system of healthcare and her observations on breaking the genetic code of beets. Then he remembered her suggestions about China and how her intuition told her that they were somehow responsible for all of this mayhem.

He glanced over at the TV once again and saw that Senator Derek Winters was being interviewed about the latest disaster. He turned up the volume.

"And all I can see from this administration is total incompetence," the senator said. "Here we have five separate attacks on American aircraft, a transportation industry that has been completely grounded, a stock market that has now fallen two thousand points and an entire nation paralyzed with fear. And what do get from this White House? Silence!"

"*Bastard!*" Jay said to himself. "*All we get from the Hill is constant criticism, but not one single shred of a suggestion or program to handle this new terrorist threat. Not one. They're like a pack of unruly puppies biting our ankles with no sense of discipline or plan for the future. And besides that, every time we come up with action to try and find the bad guys, they just bitch and moan that we're intruding on the privacy of law-abiding Americans. How the hell are we supposed to infiltrate these groups if we don't know who they are or where they're operating?*" He switched off the set, turned to his computer and started drafting a plan.

His cell phone vibrated in his pocket. He always kept it on vibrate mode inside the White House because he never knew when he'd be called into a meeting, and the president hated to be interrupted by cell phones. If anyone's cell went off when he was meeting with the president, he knew he'd probably be banned from the next encounter.

He pulled the cell out of his pocket and looked at the number on the tiny screen. *What? How can this be? She must have left her cell behind,* he thought as he punched the button. "Jay Keller here,"

"Jayson, it's me," Cammy said in a halting voice. She sounded as though she was trying to stifle a sob.

He practically bolted out of his chair. He couldn't believe it. It was her voice. "Cammy? Cammy is that you? We thought you were . . . dead."

He heard her take a deep breath and say, "I was supposed to be. I mean, yes, I was supposed to be on board that plane." With her voice still shaking she went on to explain how she had decided to stay back at the last minute to set up more simulations and monitor the first test flight so others could work them while she was gone.

She paused again. He could hear her rustling something and then made a sniffling sound. "Cam, I can't imagine what you must be going through. I mean, you were right there when the plane was hit. I hope you didn't see it happen though, did you?"

Instead of answering, she started to cry again. After another hesitation she was able to describe how she watched the huge transport taxi down the runway, take off and be blown out of the sky.

"My goodness, Cam. You watched all of that?"

"Yes," she answered softly. "It was so awful."

"Of course it was. I just can't believe, I mean, the fact that you're alive, this is incredible news. I'm so damned relieved about you. But about the others. Damn! It's devastating. I've got to talk to the president right away. He's about to issue a statement, but he's trying to get all the names and contact the families first."

"Tell him to talk to Stan Bollinger. He has the manifest."

"Oh, yes, of course. But what about you? Where are you?"

"Right now I'm up in the tower with the base commander. He didn't even know I had decided to stay back. I mean it was all so last minute."

"Must have been. We had the commander on the phone, but he didn't mention your name, just said that all were lost, what a horrible tragedy it was and how his people were out at the wreckage. But now, what about you? You shouldn't be alone at a time like this," Jay advised.

"Hunt is here," she said.

"Okay, I'll get a report from him later. The important thing right now is for you to try to try and stay safe."

"So, should I just stay here and work on the laser? I mean, what about Taiwan and a possible missile attack? Do you know anything more about those exercises in the Straits?"

"You shouldn't be worrying about things like that right now. Let me do the worrying. I'm scheduled to head over to Japan in another day or so to work on a defense pact. Let me think about this and get back to you."

"Okay. I just wanted you to know . . ."

"Thanks, Cammy. You have no idea how relieved I am just to hear your voice. Down in the Sit Room a little while ago, we were all in a state of shock over this. Well, you can imagine. And we all thought that you were on board. It was a pretty tense meeting."

"Uh, sure."

"I'm heading into the Oval Office right now to tell the president. And do you want me to call Bandaq and tell them? And what about your family? Did anybody else know you would be on that plane?"

"Actually, I had called my mom just before they took off to tell her I would try to take a commercial flight out of San Francisco, and I might be able to come see her for a little while before the flight."

"Call her back because there won't be any flight from San Francisco. Well, maybe you know that now. Anyway, I'm sure she'll be glad to hear from you. And if you want to call Bandaq, that would probably be a good move. Losing all of those other people has got to be a huge blow to that entire operation. You call them. We'll call Bollinger separately to get that list of names and numbers."

"Okay, I will." She started to choke up again, but finally added, "I still can't believe this happened. They were some of my best friends and now . . . now they're gone."

CHAPTER FIFTY-FIVE

ROCKVILLE, MARYLAND

Melanie sat stoically at the table in the company conference room where Stan Bollinger had called a meeting of all the top officers. She wiped tears from her eyes as she listened to a report on the crash of the C-5 Galaxy with so many of her colleagues on board. Worst of all, her best friend had been with them.

She had started to cry when she saw the first report on the TV set in her office. When the order was given for the staff to come to the conference room, she had tried to pull herself together. But she just couldn't. Cammy had been her rock, her confidante, her companion. Cammy, the brilliant scientist who didn't just hunker down in her lab all day long, she was a woman who befriended so many people, took time to hire and mentor the young college grads she brought on board, and even tutored some high school kids in math and science once in a while.

Why her? What in God's name did it have to be her?

Stan Bollinger was going over the list of employees on board the plane, lamenting the loss to the company. *What about the loss to their families?* Mel thought.

As she sat there listening to the man drone on, the cell phone in the pocket of her blazer rang. The CEO gave her an outraged look and said, "Turn that damned thing off!"

Mel reached into her pocket and pulled out the phone. She was about to switch it off when she saw the number on the read-out. She let out a cry.

"What is it, Ms. Duvall? Didn't you hear me? I asked you to turn that thing off." Bollinger demanded.

"But sir," Mel said, holding up the phone for everyone to see, "I've *got* to take this call. I don't believe this."

"You don't believe what?" he said, banging the table with the palm of his hand. "Don't we have enough problems around here without you . . ."

"My God it's you!" Melanie blurted out to the bewildered officers around the room.

"Who?"

"What's she talking about?"

"Who's on the phone?"

Melanie held up her hand and said into the phone, "Wait a minute. I've got to tell everyone. This is unbelievable." She wiped her eyes with the back of her hand, stood up and announced, "It's Cammy. She's alive."

"Alive?"

"How?"

"Wasn't she on board?"

"What the hell?"

"Amazing. Where is she?"

Bollinger folded his arms and stood mute at the head of the table as Melanie spoke into the phone again. The rest of the room went silent as everyone listened to her side of the conversation. Melanie knew she could have put her cell on speaker, but she wanted her friend, her surviving friend, to be able to talk freely just to her at this moment. She would translate the important points.

"You say you couldn't go at the last minute? You're still working on the laser? Oh my gosh! What? Oh, and the White House is going to call Stan? For the list? Well, we're all here right now. Yes, here in the conference room. Stan was just going over the names of everybody on board. Oh, Cam, we know how awful it is. But at least you're safe." She hesitated for a moment, listening to Cammy explain how the Travis crews were heading to the wreckage and how distraught she was.

"Sure, of course. How could you be anything but upset? I mean, we're all friends. But can you stay there and be safe now?" She listened again and nodded her head. "Okay, we'll hold off on any announcements. Thanks, Cam. Thanks for calling when I know you're in the middle of all of this. Thanks, and keep in touch."

Melanie sat down again and addressed her boss. "Cammy had to stay back and work on the laser. She's staying there until the White House decides what they want her to do next. Oh, and the president is about to make a statement, but he needs the names and numbers of next of kin to make all the calls first, so they're going to be calling you any minute."

Stan looked at his watch, gathered his papers and said, "I'd better get back to my office and take that call. We'll be talking to the families as well, and HR will be handling all the paperwork." With that, he hustled out of the room.

"Paperwork? He's thinking about paperwork at a time like this?" Melanie muttered to another company officer in the next chair. "Stan has no soul!"

CHAPTER FIFTY-SIX

SAN FRANCISCO

"Man, we should get a fat bonus for that one," Wai Yougping said as he steered the SUV into a garage in the middle of Chinatown. The drive from Fairfield, the town outside the gate of Travis Air Force Base had taken just over an hour. They had found a grove of trees down an old road, not far from the edge of the base and had set up their equipment. All had gone according to plan and even though they hadn't had much notice, they had been ready. They were always ready. That was their deal.

They had the missiles, the launchers, the special photo encased warhead. They had everything. They had been receiving regular messages from General Zhang Li. Now Wai was anxious to get back to his apartment and write up his report. The general would hear about it on the news, but Wai wanted to give his own version of how they had found their launch site, fired at the plane and then made their getaway completely undetected. Yes, it was a perfect mission, and now they were going to get a perfect pay check.

"How many more do you think we'll have to take down?" one of the gang members asked.

"We never know. We just wait for our orders. You know that."

"But with the military exercises going on right now, don't you think they'll attack the island pretty soon? And if they do, they won't need us any more."

"Maybe. Maybe not. We've got such a good network set up here, they would be fools not to use us."

"For what, if we're not shooting down airplanes?"

"Who knows? Maybe they'll decide to contract us out to others," Wei speculated. He turned off the engine, got out of the driver's seat, opened the back door and retrieved the long metal cases.

"Others? What others?"

"Do you think the general is the only one who wants to cause trouble for the United States? Don't you read the headlines?"

"Yes, but I thought . . ." the young man said, closing the garage door and hurrying after his leader.

"You think too much, Just like that piece of shit we got rid of a while ago."

The young man cowered behind Wai and stopped talking. This wasn't a time to ask questions. It was a time to simply comply with any order the man happened to give.

CHAPTER FIFTY-SEVEN

THE WHITE HOUSE

"Here's Plan B," Jayson Keller said, striding into the Oval Office and pulling up a chair.

The president grabbed the page and furrowed his brow. "I've been inundated with paper all day long. First I got the manifest and phone numbers of the people on that plane. I've called all the families." He looked up at the vice president. "When you take over this office, that'll be the hardest part of the job. Trust me."

"*If* I ever take over this office," Jay said, shifting in his chair.

"I know how you feel. At the rate we're going, they'll kick everybody in our party out of office next time around. But let's not talk about that right now. Tell me about this Plan B you've got here."

"After you talked to Stan Bollinger over at Bandaq about his employees, I called him myself to ask about his production line of Q-3 components. He said that they have several because they've had inquiries from a number of other governments. He's been ramping up production in case he gets the go-ahead to export them."

"And?"

"And so that means that he could still put a usable system together that we could ship to Taiwan."

"But what about the people to man those systems?" the president asked.

"There are still a few who know how to handle it, if they agree to go over there, that is. Stan is checking on that right now. Anyway, they could outline the process to the Taiwanese defense crowd. And I have another ace in the hole here," the president said.

"I can't imagine we have any aces right now. So what do you mean?"

"If we can get Bandaq to go through the whole drill all over again, and I think we can because Bollinger is anxious to sell that system anywhere he can, then we get them to load up the components on another military cargo plane. And since the only controllers working are military ones, they could leave from Andrews again, but refuel at Hickam, not Travis."

"Then when I leave here to go to Japan," Jason added, "I could stop at Travis since we'd keep a lid on my schedule. I'd want to refuel anyway. At Travis I could pick up Dr. Talbot and fly her to Taipei. That would give me a chance to reassure their president that we're standing with them right now. I'd leave Cammy there to supervise the situation. She could get their engineers and scientists squared away on the whole Q-3 system. I'd fly to Tokyo and after I've wrapped up the agreement with the Japanese, I could swing by Taiwan again, pick her up and fly her back to San Francisco. The other Bandaq people could stay as long as they're needed to finish training the Taiwan Defense Forces."

"I'm with you so far, but if the controllers are still out in San Francisco, you couldn't land there," the president said.

"Not unless we sent a few military controllers over from other bases. And we could do that. We did it the last time they walked."

"You're right. We did. Why not land at Travis?" the president asked. "No, wait a minute. Bad idea. They've already hit there once. So they've already scoped that out. No, you're right. It would be better to land at San Francisco."

"Yes, I could work. And remember I have that speech to the Commonwealth Club scheduled. I'm thinking that if I land at SFO, we can pick up on the original plan to have Col. Hunt fly the F-16 over, give me a demonstration of the laser . . ."

"Which better be working by then," the president said.

"Yes, it should be," Jay agreed. "Then, you make a major announcement that we now have a good defense against this terrorist threat, and right after that, I give the speech to try and reassure the business community. You know the Commonwealth Club is a base for the West Coast heavy hitters. It's a perfect venue to make the case."

"I know. I've always gotten a fairly decent reception when I've given a speech out there, in spite of the general nuttiness of the city government."

Jayson chuckled. "Last time I checked they were still giving government grants for sex change operations."

"Speaking of nuttiness," the president said, "have you seen those demonstrators over in the park?"

"How could I miss them? They were there early this morning when I came in."

"Did you read the signs and hear the chants?"

"I saw a couple that said, 'Controllers are right. We have to fight.'"

"And there's one that says, 'Don't be insane, protect our planes.'"

"Actually, there was one that wasn't so bad though," Jay ventured.

"What did it say?"

"Missile defense makes good sense."

"And that's exactly what we're trying to do for God's sake. By the way, even if Dr. Talbot's laser works, it'll take a while to get the pods produced and retrofit all our carriers. What's the latest on Sterling's airport protection system?"

"Thorne hasn't checked in lately?" Jay asked.

"No. In fact, come to think of it, I haven't seen him in days. Can you find that idiot?"

"I'll do my best. Now, about Plan B. What do you think?"

"I think it'll work," the president said. "Get things moving with Bollinger. I'll talk to the Travis Base commander again and see if he can send us another transport plane. Oh, and on this particular trip, I know your staff usually puts out an advisory on your travels. Well, not this time. Don't even tell the press pool. Just give 'em a few hours' notice to pack up and get out to Andrews. Don't tell them where you're going or where you're stopping. And for God's sake, don't mention Dr. Talbot's name to anybody. Got that?" the president asked.

"Absolutely. I was going to suggest the same approach. This mission is going to be so shrouded in secrecy, they'll end up calling me Nicolo."

"Nicolo?" the president asked, raising his eyebrows.

"That's Machiavelli's first name."

CHAPTER FIFTY-EIGHT

TRAVIS AIR FORCE BASE

"After all the tragedy here, I've been telling myself I have to stop replaying the scene of the C-5 exploding and try to concentrate on my job here. But it's so hard," Cammy said, shifting forward in the chair in her room to look directly at her principal assistant. They were comparing notes about next steps to take before the test flight took off.

"I hear you," Sarah said. "I've been doing the same thing. And now they're sending another shipment and more of our people on another flight. Let's just pray there aren't any crazies in Hawaii when they stop to refuel."

"Exactly. Maybe we can try to change the subject. At least for a few minutes," Cammy said. "Fr example I learned a few things about travel-ing to Taiwan. That is if I ever get there safely."

"Stop. You said we'd change the subject," Sarah said.

Cammy sighed and said, "You're right. Before we left Rockville to come out here, the White House sent over a briefing memo from somebody at the State Department. It was some sort of travel advisory with all sorts of things in it about customs, even clothes, like taking your shoes off whenever you go inside somebody's house."

"Do you take them off when you go to a restaurant?" Sarah asked.

No. Not usually. Oh, and it's not a good idea to wear sandals to a business meeting. They dress better than we do, I guess."

"Okay. No flip flops."

Cammy nodded. This was the first time she could even think about anything except the ghastly crash. She had spent the previous day crying her eyes out, thinking about her friends and trying to figure out why anybody would want to keep shooting down plane loads of innocent people. She'd had a fitful night and woke up with a headache. So she'd taken a slew of Tylenol and tried to concentrate on her laser project. Anything to get her mind off the explosion and fireball she'd seen in the sky.

Then tonight, she had made her mind up to try and concentrate on her upcoming trip to Taipei on Air Force Two. Even though she hated the thought of flying again, she was glad when Jayson had called her to ask if she would go over and supervise the installation of another shipment of the Q-3 missile defense system.

They'd had a long talk about security. He assured her that nobody would know she was on the plane. She would get to Taiwan quite safely, work there a couple of days, maybe have a chance to see a bit of the city and get her mind off the loss of her friends.

She had told him that the laser was ready to be tested in flight, and now it was up to Hunt and the crew chiefs to see that it worked, so yes, she'd be free to go over there with him. She was relieved that he was going to all the trouble to stop and pick her up at Travis, but then he had told her he had to refuel anyway. Still, she was getting a lot of attention from this man.

The trouble was, she was also getting attention from Hunt. Ever since the crash, he had been so nice to her. They didn't have much time together. They were both working hard with the crew chiefs and everyone else involved in the F-16 project. But still, he had acted very protective toward her, and now she was really conflicted about him, about Jay, about everything.

Ever since she had dinner at Jay's home when he had kissed her goodnight, he'd never made another move or even another suggestion, so maybe she should stop worrying about some sort of triangle developing here. The more she thought about it, the more ridiculous it seemed. The vice president of the United States was not going to be romantically involved with someone a good deal younger than he was. Besides, he had to concentrate on all the problems facing the country right now. He could hardly think about an affair.

Then again, he was coming to pick her up. Coming to take her overseas on a special mission. Then he'd be coming back for her. That meant they'd be flying together for hours and hours. What would they talk about? How would he act? What would happen on board Air Force Two? She wondered if there were any private compartments on board that plane or if it was all wide open like a regular airplane. She knew he'd have press people with him. No, he'd have to be pretty careful with all those probing reporters on board.

She realized that Sarah was asking her a question. "Oh, sorry," Cammy said, "I was just thinking about my trip again."

"I was asking what else they told you to do, or not to do, when you're over there," Sarah said.

"Well, let's see. After you finish your dinner, you never leave your chop sticks sticking up in the rice bowl."

"Why not?"

"Because that's what they do when they offer food to their ancestors, and if you did that in a restaurant or somebody's house, it would mean a curse on the owner, because maybe he should be dead too. Or something like that."

"That's weird," Sarah said with a shake of her head.

"Oh and you can't use red ink for anything."

"Why not? We use it all the time, to highlight important stuff."

"I know. But over there it means a protest or something."

"What about the whole honor-the-old-people thing they do in Asia?"

"I think you're supposed to address the oldest person in the group first. I'll have to try to remember that," Cammy said. "And one more thing, everybody says that they don't show their anger very easily. In fact, they laugh a lot."

"Guess Bollinger wouldn't exactly fit in," Sarah said with a slight grin.

"And the last thing I remember was something about presents," Cammy said. "First, if somebody gives you a present, you don't open it in front of them. And if you're going to give somebody a present, you never give them a clock."

"Why not? I like clocks."

"I don't know. You just don't." Cammy glanced down at her watch. "And on the subject of clocks, it's getting late, and I still have some work to do tonight. I need to send a bunch of emails to the staff back at Bandaq, the ones who've agreed to go to Taiwan."

"I can't imagine that there would be very many who would sign up to go after all the others . . ."

"I know," Cammy said. "There they are in the midst of organizing funerals, and they get asked to take the places of the ones who were killed. What a horrible exercise."

"But as you said, there's going to be no publicity on this trip. So everybody should be okay."

"God, I pray you're right. Anyway, thanks for letting me bend your ear tonight. It's just been so hard all day. Well, you know that I mean."

"Sure thing, Cam. Try to get some rest, okay?"

Sarah went to her own room and called over her shoulder, "Will do. Good night."

Once she was alone, Cammy turned on her computer and started to write a note to one of the Bandaq engineers. There were only a couple who could man the radar and satellite units now. Would it all come together? Would they be able to train the Taiwanese to use Q-3 the way it was supposed to be used? She pondered that for a long while. Then she suddenly had a brilliant idea. At least she thought it was brilliant. But would it work? Would the White House let her do it? It was too late to call Jay. The man was so busy getting ready for his own trip to Japan. And with all the other troubles in Washington, she didn't want to bother him with her crazy ideas.

She stared at the computer screen and thought about it some more. It could work. She just knew it could work. It could make the whole Taiwan project come together and be functional. Sure it would. Did she need permission? Probably? Could she get it? Maybe. Should she even ask? Or should she just try to pull it off all on her own? That was the question of the night.

CHAPTER FIFTY-NINE

STERLING, VIRGINIA

"**S**tan, good Lord, my man. I'm calling to add my condolences about the people you lost at Travis. Nasty business these attacks. I'm very sorry."

"Yes, well, I appreciate the call, but I'm pretty swamped right now. I can't really talk."

Nettar Kooner cradled the phone against his shoulder and pressed on. He desperately needed to keep Stan Bollinger on his good side since every other side of his business seemed to be caving in. "I'm sure. I'm sure. I just wanted you to know that we're all in a state of shock over here. I'm hoping that when you get a chance to come up for air, we can get together again and continue our former discussion."

"Former discussion? I'm afraid that's out of the question," Stan said.

"Out of the question? But that can't be. The synergy between our two firms is just so obvious, the dual contracting, the cost savings, the personnel." *Why is Bollinger snubbing me now when I thought I had this deal wired? He probably got cold feet when he heard about our*

Taiwan missile defense boondoggle. I'll just have to explain that away.
"Look, if you're worried about that problem with our system over in
Taiwan, I can explain that."

"How?"

"They wanted to deploy it on their own. Didn't even want my tech
reps on the scene. So we sent over all the specs but, well, you saw what
happened. They obviously didn't follow all the instructions and screwed
it up all on their own. I'm sure that's what happened. I mean, the entire
system checked out perfectly in our test sites."

"So I heard," Stan said. "I just can't talk right now. Sorry, but I've
got so much going on, I'm afraid that everything we talked about is off
the table."

"You can't mean that," Kooner said, his voice sounding agitated. He
rarely lost his cool, but now that his profits were heading south along
with the rest of the stock market, he was reaching for his last lifeline here,
and it looked like Bollinger was letting go of his end.

"Afraid so. Good luck with your other systems. I'm sure you'll be
pretty busy with your airport protection project. Now I have to run.
Goodbye Nettar."

Kooner hung up the phone and stared at it. *Damnation! Unless we
can figure out what went wrong with that hardware we sent to Taiwan,
we're toast. That stupid DHS Secretary Thorne has imploded now that
I've cut off his payments, and the Hill is screaming about deficits and
not having enough money to put new technology on the planes, to say
nothing about ramping up our contract for airport security, which is
nowhere near reliable.*

Kooner sat back in his sleek leather desk chair and looked over at
the wall. The framed diplomas from prestigious universities in India and
the photos of launch sites and missiles blasting off were now just so much
history. How could it have come to this?

He thought about the Taiwan situation again and decided to mount
an all-out examination of the system once more. He'd have his people

check and re-check every single component. Then they'd set up a whole series of new tests in both the Atlantic and Pacific areas.

Yes, that's what he'd do. And when it worked, he'd plaster the defense community with press releases and watch when other countries lined up to buy his systems. He'd show the world that Sterling Dynamics was still in the game, a game that it simply was not in his nature to lose.

CHAPTER SIXTY

TRAVIS AIR FORCE BASE

The sleek blue and white modified 757, tail number 80002, with the words "UNITED STATES OF AMERICA" emblazoned on the side rolled to a stop. A white truck drove up to extend the long stairway to the forward door.

Hunt watched as several Secret Service agents came down the stairs dressed in dark suits, their ear pieces firmly in place. Next, Vice President Jayson Keller, clad in grey slacks, white shirt and a blue blazer walked down the stairs to greet the base commander and a number of other officers standing in line to shake his hand.

A passel of press types streamed out the back exit, down a separate stairway and headed to the terminal for a short break during the refueling process. There were only a dozen of them representing the various news organizations. One wire service reporter, a couple of print reporters, a few covering the networks and cable outlets, along with a collection of cameramen. They would write a "Pool Report" which would be made available to every member of the press corps back in Washington before filing their own dispatches. They now knew they were going to Asia, but they didn't yet know why. The vice president's press secretary was continuing his news blackout until they safely dropped off Dr. Talbot in Taiwan.

Hunt went over to his boss and shook his hand. "Welcome to Travis, sir. A bit warmer here than DC this time of year."

"Hello, Hunt," Jayson Keller said. "Good to see you. I'm anxious to hear how you're doing retrofitting that F-16. Come on into the terminal. We have some time here before we have to take off for Taiwan." Jay looked around and asked, "Where's Dr. Talbot?"

I figured that would be the man's first concern. I'll bet he's relishing the thought of spending so many hours alone with her. Well, maybe not exactly alone, but with her all the same.

Hunt felt his stomach tense up when he thought about the vice president making a move on Cammy. Not that he didn't have a right to, but Hunt had been trying to win back her confidence, little by little, over the past couple of days. He thought he'd been making some progress. Now, with her agreeing to go to Taiwan with the second most powerful man in the world, well, what the hell was he supposed to do?

The entire group walked into the terminal where the base commander ushered them into the Visitors' Lounge. An Airman offered them coffee or cold drinks. They sat around a small conference table and reviewed their progress on the laser.

A few minutes later, Cammy walked in, pulling her carry-on bag. She had packed a few pair of slacks and cotton shirts to wear during the days when she would be working with the technical crews and also included a simple black dress and heels she always carried in case she was invited to a decent dinner. A second small bag held her computer, a sheaf of notes and a book to read on the plane.

She saw the group seated at the table, drinking coffee and having an animated discussion. There were several Secret Service agents sitting nearby. They nodded to her as she walked by. "Sorry I'm a bit late, gentlemen. Last minute packing and all."

"No problem, Dr. Talbot," Jayson Keller said formally. "Come sit down. We're just reviewing your progress here."

They went over the work of the last several days. Cammy and Hunt both explained how the crews were finally able to attach the pod to the underside of the F-16 fuselage, install the 360-degree laser mechanism inside and wire it to the panel in the cockpit. They were going to use the next several days for test runs while Cammy was away in Taiwan.

As she looked around the table, she couldn't help but compare the two attractive men sitting side by side. There was Jay, with his slate grey eyes, muscular build, and take charge attitude.

And there was Hunt, with his brilliant blue eyes, six foot two physique, straight-line grin and more quiet demeanor. Jay was interesting, brilliant in some ways, politically astute and probably calculating. You had to be if you were any kind of successful politician these days. Hunt was smart, dedicated to a fault, a bit rah-rah when it came to his military training, but then so was she.

Hunt was a pilot, just like her dad. Did it matter? Maybe not, but she felt she understood him better than the ambitious man asking the probing questions there at the table.

Hunt had certainly been solicitous of her the last few days during those moments when they had any time at all to chat. But he still hadn't told her why he hadn't called her or been in touch for months after their wild affair in India.

Cammy thought back to the nights they spent at the hotel overlooking the Taj Mahal. They had sat out on his balcony and stared at the incredibly beautiful building bathed in moonlight. Studded with precious stones, it was a place that took a thousand elephants and twenty-thousand men to build. At least that was the story in all the brochures.

They had been there as honored guests of the Indian government after they had worked together to deploy her original Q-3 system that was able to lock on to a cruise missile launched by a terrorist group. She had used her complicated algorithms to invade its guidance system like a virus in a computer and then redirect it safely over the mountains, thus saving the city of New Delhi from a devastating attack.

At that hotel in Agra, she and Hunt had made love over and over again while night breezes wafted through their open balcony doors. She could still feel the warmth of his embrace, the smell of the soap he used, the soft touch of his hands as they roamed over her body and sent shivers of anticipation to her core.

She had relived the moments when he had raised her to such a peak that she cried out his name and finally collapsed. It was so intense, so erotic that she had told him later she felt ethereal. And she described her feelings in terms of those "E words." He had just grinned at her, pulled her closer and held her throughout the night.

She had fallen so hard for the man. She had thought about a future with him, made plans about how they could combine their careers and be together from then on. But when they had returned to Washington, everything suddenly changed. He had been sent away. God knows where. He didn't call her, didn't send an email. He was just . . . gone.

Now what? Was he back in her life? Did she want to go through it all over again? Would he want to pick up where they had left off? He hadn't said so. Not in so many words. And in the meantime, Jayson Keller had roared into her life. Talk about attentive. The man found a reason to call her almost every day in spite of his grueling schedule.

She wondered if he was fascinated with her or with her work. After all, he had a lot riding on her technology right now. If it worked and could be deployed on our entire fleet of air carriers, he could proclaim it to the world and show that his administration really did have an answer for the crazed terrorists who were holding our economy hostage. And if he could do that, he'd be a shoe-in for the next election.

If he were elected president of the United States, what would he want from her then? The role of First Lady? The mere thought of such a thing was absolutely daunting. She didn't know if she could picture herself going through a long campaign or presiding at all those receptions and dinners, giving speeches, promoting causes and smiling at every available camera.

Hers was a life of research, technology, computers and challenges. She had decided years ago to concentrate on the whole subject of missile defense as a way to preclude attacks and save the lives of soldiers as well as innocent bystanders. A way to perhaps change the entire concept of war.

It wouldn't be mutual assured destruction or the MAD doctrine that had been U.S. policy throughout the Cold War days. No, now that the world had changed, their defenses had to change too, and she wanted to be a part of the process.

If she hooked up with Jay, maybe she would have more opportunities, more power. If she hooked up with Hunt, maybe she could still work on her projects, form a kind of partnership and . . . enjoy his other talents.

So how would all this play out? As Cammy studied the men at the table, she realized that at this point, she didn't have a clue.

CHAPTER SIXTY-ONE

GEORGETOWN

Senator Derek Winters slapped a man on the back as he passed a table at Café Milano in the heart of Georgetown. "Good to see you, Harry. Remember me to your lovely wife." He nodded to a couple across the room and continued to follow the hostess who led him to a table along the side where Melanie was perusing the menu.

"Hi gorgeous," he said as he sat down opposite her. "Sorry I'm late. Had a vote on the floor. You know how it is," he explained, waving at yet another woman who was smiling at him from a nearby table.

Melanie looked up and said, "I know. You're never really sure of your schedule when the Senate's in session." She glanced around the room, "But you're always sure to see your contacts whenever we eat out."

"All part of the game, my dear. And right now I feel like I'm at match point."

"Why?"

"What do you mean, why? You of all people are up on the news. Hell, you *make* the news."

"I know, but . . ."

"C'mon sweetheart. This whole administration is crashing and burning along with our airplanes. You can see that. I've taken in more donations in the last two weeks than I raised in the whole campaign for my Senate seat. We're riding high."

"You mean, riding high on the back of tragedy," she observed glumly.

"Look, Mel, that's the way it's played in this town. When you're in the White House, you take the blame, or the credit, for whatever the hell goes on in the country. The economy, foreign policy, terrorist attacks. Everything. You know that."

"Yes, but what if the president doesn't have anything to do with it? I mean if we're attacked, well, he didn't cause that," Mel said defiantly.

"Of course not. But he didn't prevent it either. And he hasn't done a damn thing to catch these guys, whoever they are. No, the man is a complete incompetent, and I'm the one who's going to point that out in every single speech from now on."

A waiter walked up and asked if they'd like to order a drink. Mel was glad for the interruption. This conversation was getting downright depressing. "I'll have a glass of your house cabernet please," she said.

"Red wine for the lady, and I'll have a Manhattan," Derek said. The waiter went to the bar in the other room while the senator resumed his observations. "Don't you see, sweetheart, this is a golden opportunity. Market's in the tank, controllers are out, flight attendants have joined in, protesters are crowding the parks, and the talk shows, well, did you see me on Tucker Carlson's show last night? I think I really nailed the bastard."

"Sorry, I missed that one. What happened? I can't imagine that Tucker gave you an easy ride. He's famous for taking on the other side. And to be honest, I like that show."

"Yeah, well, during our little exchange, it got kind of heated. Probably made his ratings go up though."

"Derek, do you mind if I change the subject here?" Mel asked.

"Of course not. What would you like to talk about?"

"Have you been interviewed by the attorney general's people yet about that leak situation?"

"Of course I have," Derek said, a serious expression covering his face. "Do you think I could be the one who leaked Talbot's name and information on her project? What do you take me for anyway?"

Melanie studied the man across from her. Yes, he was attractive in an angular sort of way. And he had that killer smile that he turned on like a faucet all the time. He had a high forehead and a shock of hair that often fell down, giving him an almost boyish look at times. She wondered if he used hair spray to get that effect. "I don't know. I've just been trying to figure out how her name got out there. And now after that explosion at Heritage and the attack on the cargo plane at Travis."

"Yes. Terrible situation., Really tragic. I am sorry about losing all those people, Mel. You have to believe me on that one."

Should she believe him? He was such a bullshit artist sometimes, it was hard to separate fact from fabrication. "Well, who then?"

"I don't have any idea. But I'm not losing any sleep over it. They can investigate all they want. Nobody cares. It's all out there now anyway. About her laser invention, which may or may not work," he said. "Do you think it'll work?"

"If I knew I couldn't tell you," Melanie said.

The waiter brought their drinks and asked if they were ready to order.

"Insalata Milano and the veal chop, medium rare, please," Mel said.

"Good choices, ma'am. And for you sir?"

"I'll have your tomato and avocado salad, and then how about the linguini and lobster?" Derek suggested.

"Always one of our best." The waiter left, walked past the other tables packed with lobbyists, House members and a few news reporters and slipped into the kitchen.

"Now then, Miss Melanie, I have to say you seem awfully preoccupied or upset or something tonight. You're not your usual bouncy self," Derek said, taking a sip of his cocktail. "Why don't we forget all of these weighty problems and drink to us, shall we?"

He raised his glass and Melanie picked up her wine. But as she clinked his glass she realized that she truly was preoccupied. With the terrorist attacks, the strikes, the market, the tension spreading through the entire city to say nothing of the rest of the country. But most of all, she was focused on thoughts of her friend, Cammy, and her flight to Taiwan to help that country stave off a possible attack.

Why couldn't Derek work on being part of the answer rather than always being part of the problem? It seemed he was constantly finding fault with everyone and everything. Always trying to figure out how to capitalize on others' misfortunes, especially if they happened to be in the other political party.

Maybe he was just playing the same role as most of the other politicians in positions of power in this town. But right now she was sick of it.

A lot of people she knew quoted Lord Acton all the time about how power corrupts. But she had another take on that. She realized that power amplifies character. As she gazed across the table at this man who had become her lover over the past few weeks, she started to feel ashamed of herself.

Was she only using him for a good time on a few Saturday nights, just as he was probably using her? She didn't really envision any sort of future with this guy. And the more she got to know him, the more they argued. So what was the point of all of this?

She picked up the conversation and turned it to other action on the Hill, the pending bills, the requests from his special groups back home. And as they finished their dinner, she finally made a decision. It had been a while in coming, but it was about time.

CHAPTER SIXTY-TWO

ON BOARD AIR FORCE TWO

"You did what?" Jayson Keller practically shouted at Cammy.

They were seated in two spacious leather chairs in the lounge of Air Force Two, a large compartment located just behind the communications center where classified memos were received and secure phone calls were made. Inside the lounge, there was a pull out couch, the two chairs, a table and a map of the world on the far wall. It was just large enough to hold small staff meetings or private tete-a-tetes like this one.

The vice president and Cammy were all alone in the lounge. The crew members were sitting in blue and silver leather seats in the next cabin. Farther back there was a conference area with eight navy leather chairs, tables with telephones and drink holders where the traveling staff sat.

Between that and another compartment for the doctor, the military aide, press secretary and official photographer, there was a door with the seal of the vice president affixed to the top. A blue carpet ran the whole length of the plane. It ended in the last section that had some two dozen seats. This was the only part of the configuration that looked like coach seating. This is where the press was stashed.

Cammy had been given a tour of the entire plane when she first came on board. Now she was comfortably ensconced in the lounge telling the vice president about the call she had made to the Indian ambassador, her former host in Washington. But she soon would be quite uncomfortable as her story unfolded.

"I wanted to call you first, but you were already on your way to Travis. Besides, I didn't want to bother you."

"I was on my way to Travis? Cammy, for Christ sake, we have the most sophisticated communication system in the world. WHCA can patch me through to anywhere."

"WHCA?"

"White House Communications. And what the hell is this about not bothering me? With an issue like this? You'd God damn well better bother me. You're not the secretary of state! At least not yet," he muttered under his breath.

"I just thought it was such a great idea. I mean, here we are going to Taiwan where I'll only have a couple of technical people to help me set up the entire defense perimeter. That's a Herculean task. It will take time to get the Taiwanese up to speed on the system. It's not just something where you can turn it on and walk away."

"I know, but asking another country to come in and help? Without authority? Jesus Christ!"

She didn't like his tone of voice one bit. Cammy thought her idea was positively brilliant. When she had first designed Q-3, there had been another scientist at Bandaq who had headed up their radar and satellite divisions. Then, when he had finished setting those up, he was assigned to her division, and he had been enormously helpful when she was nailing down the last tricky parts of the technology. His name was Raj Singh, and he was from New Delhi.

Unfortunately, when India was threatened by a bunch of Islamic militants from the Kashmir area a few months ago, everyone was afraid that the group would attack their capital city So Raj had spirited a copy of her Q-3 software out of the country in the diplomatic pouch of one of the Indian ministers assigned to their DC Embassy.

The FBI found out about it, arrested Raj, and he was immediately deported. When Cammy had been sent to New Delhi with Hunt right after that incident, she had requested that Raj be allowed to help them with Q-3, and the president reluctantly agreed. The Indian government, now chastised for stealing the program, was anxious to make amends. They sent Raj over to work with Cammy again, and together they had forestalled the attack.

Now Cammy figured that if she could just get Raj and some of his Indian technicians to come to Taiwan, they could all work together again and get the system up and running. Since she had gotten to know the Indian ambassador when she stayed at his embassy in DC, she had decided to call him and explain the situation.

He had said he would contact his government immediately to see if they would agree to help Taipei. She knew that India had been at odds with China recently over a whole host of issues from competing for energy contracts to filing complaints about copyright infringement. So she was hoping New Delhi would agree to her proposition.

On the other hand, she figured that if they did send over a team, and the Chinese found out about it, it might cause some complications. But she didn't want to think about that possibility. She had to concentrate on deploying Q-3.

She tried to explain all of this to Jayson who sat staring at her with unconcealed anger.

What the hell am I going to do with this woman? He thought. First, I think she's going to save the world with her technological brilliance. Next I'm afraid she's going to start World War III with her meddling. He tried to get a grip on himself, but he was seething.

"Cammy. This isn't the way we conduct our foreign policy. You can't just make random phone calls asking one nation to come to the aid of another nation. Especially when it's not your nation! Holy shit, this could blow up in our faces."

The vice president took a drink of water and turned to her, barely controlling his temper. "Listen here, young lady, we are enmeshed in a whole host of complicated relationships right now. We need China on our side in dealing with North Korea. In the Mid-East, China and Russia are constantly vetoing our proposals for dealing with Iran and Syria. In South America, it's China versus us when it comes to Venezuela, and, in a separate challenge, China and India have been having a feud over land and activities in the Himalayas.

"Then you've got China exchanging technology with Pakistan while Russia is befriending India," Jayson went on in an exasperated tone. "We're trying to keep Pakistan on our side in the war on terror while we sell military hardware to their arch rival, India. And in the middle of this mess, you've got Taiwan trying to become independent. Jesus Christ, Cam, we're involved in so many balancing acts I feel like a flying Wallenda while you're out there dropping the net."

Cammy leaned forward in her chair, undaunted, and pressed on. "But look, maybe this could work. I simply reminded the Indian ambassador about how our president had agreed a few months ago that Raj could help our team in New Delhi. And that was after we knew he was acting as a foreign agent and after we had deported him. He helped us once. Why couldn't he help us again? Besides, the Indians are geniuses when it comes to computer software, and I knew they could handle Q-3 in a heartbeat. They've had it for a couple of months, so undoubtedly they're all experts by now. Besides, what would be wrong if India offered some help to Taiwan? We wouldn't even be involved."

"But Q-3 is an *American* system, or had you forgotten?" Jay said with a wave of his hand. "And one other thing. A big thing. Since we put you into the Indian Embassy for protection, and since this little venture of your going to Taiwan is sanctioned by the White House, the ambassador probably thinks we're using you as a back channel."

"A back channel?" she asked, looking somewhat bewildered.

"Unofficial contact."

"Well it was."

"Not the right kind. Jesus! I've got to think about this."

He was silent for a long moment while Cammy sat still and wondered what she should do next. Okay, so maybe she over-stepped her bounds by making that phone call. But she was on a tight time-table now. And she could use all the help she could get. She looked over at Jayson who was sitting there, his arms folded, staring up at the ceiling.

Finally, Jay gave an audible sign and said, "I'm really afraid this whole cockamamie idea of yours could cause an international incident."

"But we don't know whether the Indian government did in fact contact Taiwan," Cammy said. "And we don't know whether they offered to send Raj or any of their other technicians. And even if they did make the offer, we don't know if anyone else knows about it." Cammy sat up straighter. "And if New Delhi does want to help, couldn't we ask them to keep it quiet? I mean, just make it a secret trip of a small delegation? Don't countries do that all the time?"

Jayson eyed her and wondered again how she could be such a brilliant scientist and such an impossible meddler all at the same time. He checked his watch and figured out that it was already the middle of the night in Washington. He had to talk to the president, but he'd better wait a few hours. In the meantime, what the hell was he going to do with this exasperating woman? The more he thought about it, the madder he got. How in the world was he going to dig out of this mess? He looked at Cammy again and when he saw what looked like a smug expression on her face, he bolted up from his chair and stormed out of the cabin.

CHAPTER SIXTY-THREE

TAIPEI, TAIWAN

The city was amazing. As Air Force Two came in for a landing, Cammy pressed her nose against the window to take in the sight of a huge city situated in a basin with two rivers running through it.

She spotted a towering building the color of an aquamarine spiraling above everything else against a backdrop of the nearby mountains and figured it must be "Taipei 101," one of the tallest buildings in the world.

She knew that Taipei was a busy city of some three million people, but she wasn't prepared for the panorama below. Hundreds of impressive structures were spread out before her eyes. Many were white. Some were the color of sandstone and several had roofs that looked like the skin of a tangerine. Wide boulevards were punctuated with rows of trees. There were also large bands of forests throughout the city.

The place was quite green, gigantic and gorgeous. As she thought about it, she mused about Melanie who often asked her if she wanted to write press releases filled with her alliterations. She wondered how Mel was doing with Derek Winters and whether there had been any more fallout from his noisy hearings. She'd been so busy at Travis that she hadn't had time to check the news very often. If she got a break here, maybe she could make a quick call to her best friend and get an update. She wanted more details than she could glean from an exchange of texts.

Cammy hadn't spent much time with the vice president after his outburst. She had gone out and sat down where the crew was gathered so she could have dinner with them. Jay had gone back to his lounge, and he'd basically ignored her for the rest of the trip.

She knew she'd screwed up by contacting the Indian ambassador and asking for Raj Singh's help. But after the crash at Travis, she was desperate to find extra advisers to set up the Q-3 system, and it did seem like a rather creative idea. Now, she wasn't going to dwell on it. As for Jay, she hoped that after he thought about how she was only trying to help Taiwan, he'd get over it.

When the plane came in for a smooth landing, the vice president, surrounded by his group of Secret Service agents, got off first. They were greeted by a line of diplomats and military brass. He was then whisked off in a long motorcade. She watched the scene out the window. Seeing the line of highly polished cars, she thought to herself that it looked like a Mercedes dealership out there.

She gathered her carry-on luggage, her laptop and shoulder bag and went down another stairway toward the back. She had her own welcoming party made up of several military officers and a couple of people from the American Institute in Taiwan, diplo-speak for a huge office that does everything an embassy does, but since the United States has to play the balancing game with China, they give it another name.

A colonel from the office of National Defense stepped forward to shake her hand. "Dr. Talbot. Welcome to Taiwan. We are honored by your visit and grateful that you would come to help us in the deployment of your amazing missile defense system."

Cammy took his hand, gave a slight bow and smiled. "I'm glad I can be of service. At least I hope I can be. There will be more team members from Bandaq arriving tomorrow with all of the equipment, but I'm looking forward to seeing your set-up here and getting to know your engineers and technicians."

"But, of course. I have arranged for you to come with us to Defense headquarters where you will meet our entire staff. Then we will go to the site where your Q-3 systems will be deployed."

He glanced down at her luggage and asked, "Did you have a good flight? Were you able to get any rest? We can delay our meeting if you would rather go immediately to your hotel."

"No, I'm fine," Cammy said, pushing some strands of hair back behind her headband. "I can rest later. Now, I'd like to get started. I hear that we may not have a lot of time."

The colonel frowned. "I pray that isn't so. However, everyone knows that the military exercises are proceeding on schedule, and we feel we must be ready for any eventuality." He pointed to a number of cars parked near by. "We have already taken care of the immigration papers, so if you will please follow me, we will be on our way."

"Raj! You're here," Cammy exclaimed as she walked into a conference room. A tall, thin man with hair the color of mahogany jumped up from the table and rushed to greet her.

"Yes. When we heard you needed help here, we put a team together and flew over as quickly as we could."

"We?"

"I mean our minister of defense and others high up in government circles in New Delhi. They called me in, and we all decided that I should come."

"Thank goodness," Cammy said, though she wondered if Jay knew about this. "Uh, was there any controversy about your coming?"

Raj gave her a broad smile. "Let's just say we didn't issue any press statements."

"Good move."

They all worked together for several hours going over the basic elements of the satellite and radar systems and the software programs Cammy had developed.

During a break for lunch, Cammy noticed a young Chinese man in what looked like an airman's uniform, wheeling in a cart with coffee, tea and dessert cakes. He took quite a bit of time clearing the dishes and straightening things up and then went around the table to take orders for coffee or tea.

During this process, the colonel asked Cammy, "How long will you be able to stay with us?"

"It all depends on when Jay . . . uh . . . Vice President Keller is finished with his mission to Japan."

"Ah yes, we know that is where he went after greeting our president. You have no idea how pleased we are that your vice president would go to Japan to put together a mutual defense pact. This means a great deal to us."

"Yes, I know," she said. "I hope it works out because Japan is so much closer than my country's forces could be in case China made a move."

"Of course we realize you are moving two of your carriers closer to the Straits, and that is a good thing. But they won't be able to stop missiles should there be an attack. On the other hand, we were notified about the additional deployment of two of your Navy vessels equipped with the Aegis missile defense system that will be arriving bit later. I can't tell you how much their presence in the area gives us additional confidence that any attack could be repelled. One by cruise missiles, at least. But back to the vice president's travel, you say that you can stay until Vice President Keller has achieved his goal in Japan?"

"Yes," Cammy said. "You see, when I'm finished working with the technicians here, he will pick me up, and we'll head back to the States." She stopped and glanced nervously around the table. "But my travel plans are not to be publicized. Will you please keep my itinerary just within this room?"

They all nodded, and the colonel added, "We all know too well that the first cargo plane carrying your Bandaq colleagues was attacked. Please be assured that we will do everything in our power to be certain that no one knows of your visit here, nor your return plans. You can count on us."

Cammy smiled at the colonel. "You see, I can only stay here a few days to help set up. But with Raj Singh here and the other Bandaq engineers arriving tomorrow, you'll have plenty of tech support. I have to get back to California pretty soon because I still have a lot of work to do there on my other project."

The young airman was just to Cammy's right. He leaned down as she finished talking and asked what she would like to drink with dessert. Cammy whispered that a cup of coffee would be fine. He nodded and moved back to his cart to pour it for her.

"And is your other project the one to protect your airliners from further attack?" the colonel asked. "We read about that."

"Yes. I guess everyone knows about that now," Cammy said, accepting the coffee and adding some cream and sugar. "We have high hopes that our new system will be effective against any type of missile that the terrorists are using."

"That would indeed be a blessing," the colonel said. "But you still don't know who is shooting down the planes, is that correct?"

Cammy sighed, "Not yet. No group has come forward, our markets are down again, nobody wants to travel and, well, you've read the headlines, I'm sure."

"Yes, we are used to bad news here as well. I suppose you saw that once again the People's Republic has managed to keep us from joining the United Nations. They've done it over a dozen times now. They just keep appointing committees to study the issue."

"But that's ridiculous," Cammy replied. "You've got, what, twenty or thirty million people on this island, don't you? And your products are sold all over the world."

"Correct. And when you consider that we have a population larger than sixty percent of the U.N. member states, you can see how frustrating it is to be stymied at each and every turn by the Central Committee on the mainland."

"Has China ever controlled Taiwan?"

"Not since we were founded in 1949. And yet they want to treat us like you treat Hawaii. A distant state, but nevertheless a part of the mainland."

"But Hawaii asked to be admitted to the United States. You want to be on your own because you're totally different," Cammy said.

"Ah yes. We are a democracy. We have regular elections, free speech, freedom of religion. All the things that your own country has. And yet we are not allowed to join the United Nations. But Nauru is a member."

"Nauru?" Cammy asked.

"It's basically a rock in Micronesia. But you see what I'm trying to say here."

"I most certainly do." Cammy glanced at her watch. "Colonel, I have another question for you."

"Yes?"

"Since we've gone over the materials on Q-3, and since we can't do much more until the cargo plane arrives tomorrow, I wonder if you would let me go see the system that Sterling Dynamics sent over here?"

"The one that doesn't work?" the colonel asked.

"Yes. I wanted to see if Raj and I could have a look at it. Maybe we could figure out what went wrong." Cammy didn't have any idea what was wrong with Sterling's system. And she didn't want to save that company from financial ruin. In fact, she had done everything in her power to compete with them ever since she had taken the job with Bandaq. But here she was in a country that was facing a possible attack, and they needed every possible arrow in their quiver right now.

The colonel looked around the table at the other officers. Some were shaking their heads. Others were avoiding his stare altogether. "I don't know. I'm sure there are proprietary considerations. After all, that system belongs to a different company and their patents . . ."

"I'm not trying to steal a patent, sir. I just want to see if we might be able to make it work. I can see that we're all under tremendous pressure, and since Sterling doesn't have any engineers over here, I just thought that we might be able to help. That's all. Besides, my system is a defense against cruise missiles. Sterling's is a defense against ballistic missiles, and China has both. Not that they would use them . . . but still . . ."

The colonel sat back in his chair and rubbed his chin. He was silent for several moments. Finally he said, "You are right about the pressure, and you are right about Sterling not having any of their people here. So I don't see why we couldn't show you the system. It is still set up at the missile defense site where Q-3 will be deployed. It is right along the coast. If there is any way you could figure out what went wrong during the test phase, I'm sure that Sterling would be grateful. In fact, my entire government would be grateful."

Cammy gathered her things and pushed back from the table. "Then let's go."

CHAPTER SIXTY-FOUR

NORTH OF GUANGZHOU

"Look at this!" Colonel Tsao exclaimed, shoving a print-out into his boss's hand. The general was seated at the long folding table in the hangar, going over maps and plans for a barrage of missile strikes followed by an amphibious landing at the end of the military exercises.

"She's on Taiwan?" the general said, his voice rising with excitement. "This is incredible news."

"Yes, but it could be bad news for us."

"Why do you say that?"

"It's obvious."

"What is obvious?" the general said with some irritation.

"Don't you see? The only reason she would be there would be to help them with their missile defense system. They must have decided to send more parts after the first shipment was . . . destroyed."

"Yes. Yes, I am sure that is what she is doing."

"That is bad news. She invented that Q-3 system that can take over a cruise missile and redirect it. We can't have some upstart taking control of our cruise missiles. It would be a disaster."

"Only if we use cruise missiles," the general said.

"Yes, but maybe she'll get that other system working."

"Sterling's system?" the general asked, raising his eyebrows. "Impossible."

"It seems that nothing is impossible with that woman." The colonel paused and added, "Why did you say that this was incredible news?"

"She is working to develop a defense against our stealth missiles. The ones we aim at the planes," the general said. "We have plenty of other forces to handle Taiwan, but we need to keep taking down their planes so the Americans won't be able to intervene here. You know that."

"I don't follow you, sir."

"If she is on Taiwan, that means she has taken a break from her other project."

"Which may mean that she's finished, and it's working."

"No. If it were working, we would have heard about it. Don't you think the Americans would shout on every network that they finally had a defense against the missile attacks on their airliners?"

The colonel nodded.

"And that means they do not have it working." the general said. "So we must ensure that she does not return to finish the job."

The colonel brightened and said, "The message today said she would be returning with the vice president on Air Force Two. However, we don't know when that day will be."

The general waved his hand as if he just didn't care. "No matter. Our agent in Taiwan will inform us of her departure and I'm certain he will be able to find out where they are going to land. It is a long flight. That will give us plenty of time to get our west coast agents in place. After all, we did not get her on the previous plane, but now we have a great opportunity. An opportunity not only to finish off this irritating scientist, but to change history and get rid of Jayson Keller as well."

CHAPTER SIXTY-FIVE

THE WEST COAST OF TAIWAN

"Raj, come check this out," Cammy said excitedly, motioning to an item she had just pulled out of the motherboard. "I've been studying Sterling's software, and I think the problem with the whole system is right here in the computer processing unit."

Raj navigated his way through rows of tables holding computers, screens and telephones in the large missile defense headquarters situated at a base along the west coast of Taiwan. He had been working with a team of radar specialists, but he stopped and rushed over to Cammy's side. "Do you think you've really found the problem?"

"I'm not sure, but something is really weird here."

"If it's new software, it's not uncommon to have infant mortality," Raj said, looking over her shoulder. "With new systems, you almost always have strange things. That's why they probably went through a low-rate of initial production. Maybe this was the first iteration."

"No. I think it's a basic flaw," Cammy countered. "Look. I've been reading the lines of code in the software. This whole defensive system involves a GPS. It has to know where it is so it can figure out the distance to an incoming missile."

"I can see that," Raj said, as he pulled up a chair.

"Okay. Now stick with me on this. Read the lines of code here, and you'll see that the output of a certain chip isn't working right."

"So you're saying the error is in the chip."

"Maybe it is. Maybe there's some sort of internal design error on the chip itself, so we need to check this card." She looked around the room and motioned to the colonel in charge.

He came over to her console and said, "Do you need something, Dr. Talbot?"

"Is there any way we can get a microscope?"

"A microscope?" he asked, furrowing his brow.

"Yes. I need one."

"Wait a minute." He pulled out his cell phone and punched in a series of numbers. He had a quick conversation, hit the end button and turned back to Cammy. "We're having one sent over immediately. But why is there a need for such a tool right now, if I may ask."

"I need to check something on this software. I have an idea, but I have to confirm it."

"All right. It should be here shortly. You all have been working hard. Why don't you take a break? There is coffee in the next room, and we have brought in other refreshments."

Cammy pushed her chair back and said, "Good idea. But first I'd like to make a call. Is there a phone I can use to call Maryland?" The colonel nodded and pointed to a private office in the back. She turned to Raj. "I'll meet you next door in a few minutes. I want to check in with Mel."

At the mention of Melanie's name, Raj looked startled. When he had worked at Bandaq, he and Melanie had become quite involved. In fact, they'd had a torrid affair. But when he'd been caught stealing the software for the Q-3 system and been deported, he knew he'd never see her again and it broke his heart. "Uh, Cammy, would you please tell her I miss her and still think about her? Please say that I wish her well."

"Will do."

Cammy closeted herself in the office and dialed Mel's private line. "Melanie Duvall here."

"Hey Mel, it's Cammy. I'm in Taiwan. I wanted to check in and see if everything's on track for that new team to fly over here tomorrow."

"Cam! Great to hear from you and yes, we're gearing up back here. Of course, nobody else knows about the flight. At least we pray that nobody knows except the base commander at Travis and the cargo pilots. And Bollinger, of course."

"How's he doing with all of this?"

"He's been his usual curt self, barking out orders all over the place."

"Maybe we can have some Bollinger fright masks made for Halloween," Cammy said. "I'll bet the whole staff would buy them."

"Now there's a thought. Oh, we did have one bit of good news. Our stock went up a couple of points."

"Are you sure that's not a dead-cat bounce?"

Melanie giggled. "No. There's a lot of speculation around town that you'll come up with a defense for our planes, so the analysts on CNBC are touting Bandaq's stock right now."

"Oh Lord! And I feel like I'm juggling book-ends here."

"Bookends?" Mel asked.

"I mean, I have two problems. First, protect our airliners and second, try to help Taiwan."

"And how's that coming?"

"You'll never believe who's here helping me," Cammy said.

"Who?"

"Raj!"

"Raj Singh?" Melanie exclaimed. "How in the world did that happen?"

"I asked for him?"

"How?"

Cammy explained how she had called the Indian ambassador and put in the request and then how the vice president had exploded when she told him about it.

"Oh boy," Mel said. "Does this mean you and Jay are history now?"

"I don't know, but after all the attention he's been giving me, let's just say he's executed an amazing pirouette."

"Well, give it time. Besides, you'll have the whole flight back to the States to get him to warm up again."

"If I want to warm him up," Cammy said.

"What now? More thoughts about Hunt?" Mel asked cautiously.

Cammy sighed. "Well, maybe. When we worked together the last few days at Travis, he was so . . . oh, I don't know . . . so nice to me."

"Did he ever explain why he hadn't called?"

"Not in so many words. But we weren't alone much, so maybe he will . . . later."

"Interesting. But Cam, now that we're talking about old loves, did Raj? I mean, did he say anything? Anything at all?"

"Of course he did," Cammy assured her." He said he still thinks about you and misses you. And I know he means it. He looked pretty sad when he said it."

There was a long pause. "Well, tell him I miss him too. But I don't know how I'll ever be able to see him again. He won't be admitted back into the states, and I'm not about to move to New Delhi."

"I know. By the way, what's the latest with Derek?"

"Oh, I meant to tell you. I dumped him," Mel said.

"Really? Why?"

"It just wasn't working. I mean that guy only seems to be happy when he's standing in a spotlight, and I decided I didn't want to spend my life shining in reflected glory."

Cammy chuckled. "Well, congratulations. That's the best decision you've made in ages."

"I guess. The only trouble is that now I spend my evenings alone. Last night I watched a program on the History Channel about ancient aliens."

Cammy burst out laughing. "Wish I had that kind of time on my hands. Look, I'd better get going. I have a lot of work to do here. But is there any other news I've missed lately?"

"Well, there is one really weird thing that people are talking about."

"What's that?" Cammy asked.

"Nobody's seen Franklin Thorne in ages."

"The secretary of Homeland Security?"

"Yeah. He hasn't been in his office. Hasn't been in any White House meetings. Nobody knows where he is. He's always been sort of an odd duck though, you know?"

"Well, he has no history of involuntary confinement," Cammy quipped, "but you're right, that does sound strange."

"Maybe he's resigned or been kicked out, and they haven't announced it yet."

"Is there any gossip about who a new director might be?"

"I haven't seen any white smoke yet," Melanie said.

"Well, keep watching the news, send me a text, and I'll try to check back with you later. Now, I've got to get back to work."

"Okay. Thanks for the call. But Cam . . ."

"Yes?"

"Nobody on this side of the Pacific knows you're there or how you're flying back. Just make sure that nobody on that side figures it out either."

Cammy shared a cup of coffee with Raj, grabbed a few cookies off a side table and headed back to the Sterling command center. A young man was standing next to the desk holding a box. "You requested this microscope, ma'am?"

"Oh yes. Let's set it up over here."

Cammy pried the chip loose from the card and peered at it under the scope. She studied the configurations and noticed a slight architectural difference. She had seen something similar in some of her research a while ago. She tried to remember where. She stared at the chip again. *This just doesn't look right. It's different from everything else in this system. It looks like an orphan.* She stared into the microscope again and called out to Raj. "Can you come over here again?"

"What is it?" Raj said, walking over to the scope. "What do you see?"

"Look here. Tell me if you've ever seen a chip that looks like that."

Raj leaned over and looked through the scope. "This is strange, but yes, I believe I've seen something like this, and it was made . . ."

"In China, right?" Cammy said.

Raj looked up, puzzled. "Yes. China could have produced it. I wonder why it's in there?"

"I don't know," Cammy said, "Let me think about that."

CHAPTER SIXTY-SIX

ON BOARD AIR FORCE TWO

"Welcome aboard," Jayson Keller said as Cammy climbed up the long stairway leading to the front cabin of Air Force Two. She noticed that he was wearing a crisp blue and white striped shirt with the sleeves rolled up, but he had discarded his tie and suit coat. He smiled and reached for her computer bag. An aide followed with her carry-on luggage.

He must have decided that I wasn't starting World War III after all, she mused as she saw Jay's wide smile. *Or maybe he's just happy he got the Japanese to sign onto that defense pact. That's probably it.*

"Hi Jay," she said. "Where would you like me to sit?"

"Come on into the conference room," he said, leading the way past the communications center where an Air Force major was studying his computer screen. "I'm anxious to hear all about Taiwan and whether your old system is up and running."

Cammy stowed her bags and sat down in one of the plush leather seats. She saw that a flight attendant had placed a glass of ice water at her chair. She took a sip. "You have no idea how relieved I was when that cargo plane landed with our engineers and all the equipment. I guess they really did keep a lid on all the travel plans."

"They had to after the orders we gave to your boss."

"I think they were all pretty nervous about flying over," Cammy said. *And I'm nervous again about this flight back.*

"I can't blame them. They were real troopers to volunteer for that assignment. So you got things working to set up the defense perimeter?"

"Well, with Raj's help . . ." she stopped and looked up at Jay with guarded eyes.

"Raj?" Jayson asked, arching his brows. "You mean that man from New Delhi you told me about? He was there?"

"Yes. I figured you knew. I mean, by now," she murmured.

He stared at her and shook his head. After a long pause, he started to smile. "What am I going to do with you?"

"You didn't know?" Cammy persisted.

"No. No one from India contacted our people. They must have just decided to send him over quietly when you asked. I must say you have a lot of pull for one American citizen."

"Only with India," she said. "And Raj told me that the people in the Defense Ministry in Delhi told him to go to Taiwan, but not to release any statements."

"Well, that was a smart move."

"That's what I thought."

Cammy went on to explain how they had worked together for several days setting up all of the components to sense, track, and take control of a cruise missile if one or more should ever be launched against the island.

They still would have trouble with a whole battery of ballistic missiles because Sterling's system was not working. She told him how she had received permission to examine Sterling's software because she thought she might be able to get the system up and running. But then she explained how she had found the strange chip inside the system.

"Strange?" Jay asked. What do you mean, strange?"

"It was the weirdest thing. I examined the chip under a microscope and studied the code, and I realized it was totally different. I sensed that it was configured to allow the system to work in one part of the world, but not in others. It all has to do with the GPS and the frequencies the system uses. It sounds wild, but I figured that it worked just fine in American testing areas. But if it's outside those areas, it transmits through a different frequency. So, of course, it wouldn't work overseas. It's like the system was sabotaged by a tiny chip."

Jay stared at her wide-eyed. "How could that be? Sterling manufactured that whole system, tested it and sold it to Taiwan in a huge contract. Why would they sabotage their own system?"

"Of course, they wouldn't, unless . . ."

"Unless what?"

"Unless they didn't know it was a bad chip."

"How in the world could they not know? They built it," Jay protested.

"Maybe not all of it. That chip looked like it was made in China."

"China?" Jay blurted. "But how? Wait a minute. You don't think . . ."

Cammy nodded. "Yes, I think that maybe they broke the law and had the chip manufactured by a foreign power. And that power, China, knowing that Sterling was selling to Taiwan, developed a chip that wouldn't allow frequencies to operate as expected if the GPS sensed that it was deployed outside the U.S, or anywhere near Taiwan."

"But that would be against our ITAR regulations."

"I know," Cammy said. "That's all part of the Arms Export Control Act, isn't it?"

"Exactly right! Jesus Christ! So we have an American company getting components for a sensitive missile defense system manufactured in another country that's proscribed from contributing to national security projects?"

"An American company run by an Indian named Nettar Kooner," Cammy replied.

All these years she had been trying to compete with Sterling. All these years, she had blamed that company for making a missile that she knew in her heart was defective, a missile that she believed caused the death of her father. And now, finally, she may have caught them breaking the law.

She had worked and waited for just such a moment. A moment when she would get revenge. Is that what she felt now? Was it a sense of revenge? No. It was a feeling of intense sadness. She was sad that Kooner had tried to skirt the law probably in an effort to lower his costs. She was sad that the man had built a system that should have worked perfectly to protect a thriving island from a possible attack by a well-armed communist regime.

She knew that once they got back to Washington, Jay would take steps to bring charges against Sterling. Would that make her happy? As she thought about it, she realized that the answer was: not especially.

"Cammy? What are you thinking? You seem miles away," Jay said.

"Oh, guess I'm just sorry that a company would do something that stupid, something that could sabotage an entire system and allow another country to be put in harm's way."

Jay reached over and took her hand. "Well, first of all, we'll take care of Sterling and the ITAR regs. But second, there's still a good chance that China has no intention of attacking Taiwan in an effort to reunify it with the mainland. We've discussed this over and over, and we just can't fathom that they would attempt such a thing."

"But that's why you went to Japan," Cammy said.

"Yes, and we were able to get them on board." A small bell sounded and Jay said, "Buckle up, we're about to take off."

She fastened her seat belt and grabbed the ice water. She took another drink to try and steady her nerves. She thought she'd get over her jitters about flying after the recent trips. But no. Her heart was beating faster now, almost in sync with the sound of the revved up engines. She tried to concentrate on what Jay was saying about his meeting in Tokyo.

"By the way, the lead negotiator was this really old Japanese general. Probably in his 90's. They brought him out of retirement to sit in on this one. I suppose they were honoring him in some way. Anyway, he told me that when he was only 18, he had been a kamikaze pilot in World War II."

"Then why was he still around?" Cammy asked with a grin.

Jay shook his head and laughed. "Actually, I wondered the same thing. But the negotiations went surprisingly well. You see, after they amended Article Nine of their constitution to allow for military actions abroad, especially if they are of a defensive nature, it was easy for them to agree to provide help, if needed. And you can be sure that we'll notify China of the agreement."

"So forewarned is forearmed and all of that," Cammy said.

"Precisely."

There was a light knock on the door, and the vice president's military aide walked in. "Excuse me sir, but you have a call from the White House."

Jay got up and left the conference room, calling over hto Cammy, "This is the president returning my call about the new treaty. Be back in a while."

Jay sat down in the small communications center a few feet from the cockpit and spoke to the president's secretary. "Jayson Keller here."

"Yes, thank you sir. I will put the president on."

"Jay, on your way back, are you?" the president said, sounding rather upbeat.

"Yes, Mr. President. It's been quite a trip." He briefed the chief executive on the new treaty, on Japan's plans to raise their own spending on various missile defense systems by almost sixty percent, Cammy's work on Q-3 and her discovery of the bad chip in Sterling's system. They decided to have the State Department investigate the situation since their Directorate of Defense Trade Controls was in charge of enforcing Title 22 of the Act.

"On the whole Chinese problem," the president said, "we got the report from Borealis."

"Did they find anything?" Jay asked.

"You bet! We have some high-resolution photos of what looks like fairly new installations in Eastern China, buildings that are undoubtedly factories of some sort along with a large hangar and docks where soldiers are seen loading long canisters that could hold new types of small missiles."

"Could those be the ones that have been shooting down our planes?" Jay asked.

"We're not sure yet. But we also have photos showing additional military units being dispatched to China's coast nearest Taiwan."

"You mean more troops than they normally use in those military exercises?"

"A damn sight more. So I just got off the phone with the Chinese president. I brought up the troop movements, and I asked him, point blank, about his intentions regarding Taiwan."

"And what did he say?"

"As you might imagine, he denied everything. He said that China has absolutely no plans to invade Taiwan."

"And you believed him?"

"He sounded pretty adamant about it, but I still sense a disconnect here."

"Did you ask him about the new missiles?" Jay said.

"No, not yet. I want to get another pass from Borealis as well as SPIRS Low, which we've now repositioned. And as soon as we can tell where those missiles are going, if that's what they are, I'll get him back on the phone and present the evidence. And I'll also tell him about the new pact with Japan," the president said.

"Sounds like a good plan."

"Oh, and a couple of other things. I'm expecting a report from NSA any time now on the latest analysis of their new intercepts. When I get it, I'll get back to you."

"Okay. I'm not going anywhere. Except to San Francisco, that is," Jay said.

"And the other thing. We can't seem to find Thorne," the president said.

"What do you mean you can't find him?"

"Exactly what I said. Nobody's seen the guy for several days now. He's not home. His wife has no idea where he is. But she did say that he often takes short trips and doesn't tell her where he's going. Guess they don't talk much. But seriously, this is very troubling. His office doesn't have a clue. There are no reports of accidents or anything."

"So who's looking for him?"

"I've got Janis on it."

"Well, let me know if you find out anything. And on those intercepts, I'll wait for your next call."

CHAPTER SIXTY-SEVEN

TRAVIS AIR FORCE BASE

"So you think this new contraption of yours will really work?" Pete asked Hunt as they walked across the tarmac toward the F-16. Hunt, dressed in his flight suit was carrying his helmet. Pete had come along to see him off.

"I sure as hell hope so. It checked out in those test runs we took yesterday. At least I think it did. It's a lot different running simulated tests than trying to take down an actual missile on your tail, so it might not be time for a victory lap just yet."

"I'll bet. At least you're only going on a short hop to San Francisco. And if it checks out, you can do your little show-and-tell for the vice president. That's pretty good duty. And the flight time will take about a nano-second in this baby."

"Well, not quite. But it'll be good to get off an Air Force base for a few days," Hunt said.

"After this drill, they should give you a bunch of days off to enjoy the city."

"I can take time if I want it," Hunt replied.

"That'd be nice, especially if your lady friend is along for the ride," Pete ventured with a grin.

"I'm not sure if that's in the cards," Hunt said thoughtfully. "But I'm going to give it a try."

The fact was, he had tried damn hard the whole time Cammy had been working with him. He had endeavored to pry through that ice shield she had erected, and there had been times when he saw flashes of the old Cammy. Times when he tossed her a compliment on her work and smiled at her off-hand remarks. She really did have wry sense of humor. He appreciated that, and he told her so.

They had been so busy with the crew chiefs that he didn't have a chance to get her off for a quiet dinner. There just wasn't time. By the end of the day, they were both so exhausted, they had grabbed a quick bite with the rest of the crew, called it a night and started off at dawn the next day. But still, he thought he sensed a thaw in her whole demeanor.

Maybe when they were both in San Francisco, he could talk her into going off for a little quiet time together. Maybe then he could sit her down and tell her the whole story of his assignments to all those bases in Russia, his search for nuclear weapons, his investigations of arms dealers and run-ins with all manner of characters.

He'd tell her about his time in South Korea, of debriefing defectors and trying to learn about new weapons systems being developed in North Korea and elsewhere. He'd explain that there had been times when he wasn't sure if he'd ever get home in one piece and how he hadn't wanted to burden her or ask her to wait in case he never made it.

He'd do all of that if she'd simply give him a chance. The only problem now was that Cammy would have spent a ton of hours on Air Force Two being charmed by the vice president. Could he compete with that?

Just before he climbed into the plane, Pete put a hand on his shoulder. "Listen, buddy, it's been great catching up with you the last few days.

I eally hope this laser thing pans out. We sure could use it, what with crazy terrorists, the strikes and shutdowns and all."

"I know. Say a prayer, will you?" Hunt said, strapping on his helmet.

"You got it. Oh, and remember, if and when that lady decides to give you the time of day, use the key I gave you. You have it with you, right?"

Hunt patted his zippered pocket. "Got it right here."

CHAPTER SIXTY-EIGHT

SAN FRANCISCO

"It's show time!" Wai Yongping announced to his two young Chinese roommates. The leader of the group pushed a knot of black hair off his sloping forehead and waved a print-out at his cohorts.

He had just deciphered the latest message from General Zhang Li about the arrival of Air Force Two at San Francisco International Airport. He knew that the air traffic controllers were on strike, and most activity at the airport had been shut down. But a few official flights were being handled by controllers from nearby military bases. That didn't bother him. He knew they'd never be able to figure out where his precious missile came from because they'd never be able to see it until it was too late.

Wai Yongping had lived in one of the new Chinatown areas that had sprung up in the Richmond district of the city. His apartment was on Clement Street near Park Presidio. After his father had been gunned down at the Golden Dragon restaurant on Washington Street back in 1977 in what the press called the "Golden Dragon Massacre," he and his mother had moved away from the old Chinatown. His father had been a member of one of the Chinese gangs, and a rival gang had started the shooting spree that killed a whole slew of people back then.

His mother had died in the 90's. Now, after all these years, he still carried resentment about the way his father had been murdered. He had created his own gang. And his group was smarter, stronger and more careful. Except for the weak one that he'd disposed of, the other members had lived and worked together on their various plots and schemes for years.

Their ancestors had been immigrants from the southern Guangdong province of China back in the early 1900's, men who came to build the Transcontinental Railroad. Since that time, a newer wave had come from Taiwan, but he wanted nothing to do with that crowd. No, he still had his loyalties to mainland China. He was going to prove those loyalties today in just about an hour.

"Get that case out to the SUV," he ordered as he gathered up his wallet, binoculars, sunglasses and keys. The two other men carried the case out and loaded it in the back of the car. They opened the garage door, jumped in the back seat and Wai got into the driver's seat. He started the car and headed out toward the Bayshore Freeway.

"How much time do we have?" one man asked.

"Enough," Wai replied. "The general said that this will be a shining moment for his grand plan."

"What did he mean?"

"Don't ask. Just be aware that this is the most important mission we have conducted so far. We will receive special pay for this."

"What if someone sees us this time?" a younger man asked anxiously.

Wai snapped his head around. "Don't be a fool. There's hardly anybody left at the airport, only a few military controllers."

"What about the police?"

"Why would they be patrolling the area when there are hardly any planes landing?"

The young man was silent for a few minutes. Then he asked, "What about this plane? Why is it so special?"

"Okay. Since you seem so interested, and since it will be the headlines around the world, I will tell you. This plane is Air Force Two."

"Air Force Two?" the two men exclaimed in unison. "We're going to shoot down the vice president of the United States? We can't do that!"

"Why not?"

"Because . . . because . . . there will be Secret Service agents all over the place. We'll get caught. And besides, the vice president . . ."

"Shut up you idiots. The general knows what he's doing. Besides, this vice president is on the side of Taiwan. The general says that he is returning from a trip to Japan where he was negotiating a mutual defense pact."

"What kind of pact?"

"The kind where Japan comes to the aid of Taiwan in case of an attack."

"Our attack? The general's attack, you mean?"

"Well, well, now you see the light," Wai said taking the turnoff toward San Bruno. "This vice president could be president next time. We can't afford to have his kind in the White House. So not only will we be taking down a man who stands in our way, we will be changing history with one single shot."

Wai Yongping pulled off the road into a grove of trees on a ridge overlooking the airport. It was a location he had scoped out several times in the past in order to be prepared if he was asked to stage any attacks there. He knew very few people drove through this particular area. He parked the car, set the hand brake, took out his binoculars and scanned the sky. The other young men got out, opened the back of the SUV and began assembling their newest missile with the special photo enhanced warhead. Wai opened the sunroof, took the missile, hoisted it onto his shoulder and waited.

CHAPTER SIXTY-NINE

ON BOARD AIR FORCE TWO

"The president just called again," Jay said, settling into the plush leather chair next to Cammy's in his private lounge.

"Anything new?" she asked, trying to suppress a yawn. It had been a long flight from Taipei. She hadn't been able to get much sleep. Every time she'd tried to doze off, the sound of the engines seemed to conjure up old dreams where she would see images of her father's plane crashing. Then the scene would morph into the F-16 that Hunt was flying right now.

She'd wake up with a start, try to erase the macabre thoughts and concentrate on the fact that Hunt was just fine, that he was in the air at this very moment, headed to San Francisco where they would work together to give the vice president a demonstration of her new laser.

She thought about seeing Hunt again. He certainly had been solicitous of her back at Travis though they never seemed to find the time for quiet conversations. Still, she had to admit that it was wonderful to be working with him again and be able to glance over to see his deep blue eyes, the sandy hair, the straight line grin when she said something even mildly amusing.

Now here she was with the vice president of the United States who also was being particularly kind to her on this trip. She figured he was completely over his initial snit about her contact with the Indian ambassador. He hadn't mentioned it again. She was grateful for that. She hated when somebody kept harboring an issue and bringing it up again and again. At least Jay wasn't like that.

Over the past several hours of the flight, he had suggested she sleep on his pull-out couch, and she had tried that for a while. But she felt rather guilty knowing that he had a big day coming up with a speech scheduled at the Commonwealth Club in downtown San Francisco. So she had spent some time in another cabin chatting with the crew to give Jay some privacy and a chance to rest himself.

A few minutes ago she had splashed cold water on her face in one of the small bathrooms and tried to hide the dark circles under her eyes with a bit of makeup. Her hair was always a bit unruly. As usual, she had brushed it back and simply replaced her headband.

Now she had returned to the conference room to share a hot breakfast with the vice president. They would be landing soon. She took a sip of her coffee and waited for him to report on his call with the president.

"There is incredible news, some interesting news and some bad news," he said, reaching for his own coffee mug.

"Tell me."

"First the best news of all. NSA has been able to decipher a set of messages sent from various places in China to an address in San Francisco."

"Oh no. The terrorists? They found them? It really was China?" Cammy asked excitedly.

"They haven't found them, but they've evidently got an address and other information. The FBI is swarming all over a neighborhood in the Richmond district."

"But that's fabulous. My goodness! How did they figure it out?"

"Steganography."

"You mean they embedded messages under other symbols?"

"You know about that?" Jay asked, cocking his head.

"Well, I know the term. I think it was named after a Russian named Steganos, although the idea goes way back. So how did they do it?"

"They evidently sent encrypted messages inside photographs."

"Photos," Cammy said. She thought for a moment. "Photos. That's what I think they also used on their missiles to shoot down our planes, remember?"

"Yes, I most certainly do. So, it now looks like you were right fingering China on these attacks."

"But why? We still don't know why the Chinese would do such a horrible thing and kill so many innocent people."

"It may not have been the Chinese government, though we don't know that yet. The messages came from some obscure locations, not from Beijing."

Cammy covered her mouth in surprise. "Obscure locations? You mean somebody could orchestrate attacks like this, and the central government wouldn't know about it?"

"That does sound preposterous, I admit. But we're checking out everything. They're looking for the contacts in San Francisco, and they're also trying to pinpoint the exact locations in China. It won't be long now until we know for sure." He took another sip of his coffee and grimaced. He touched a button for the flight attendant and continued. "Now let me tell you some other news. The leak. They figured out who leaked your name."

"Who? Was it Derek Winters?"

"No. Much as I'd like to nail him with something, I didn't really think he'd do it. It turns out it was the legislative aide to the chairman of the House Intelligence Committee. They had evidently discussed your program after my briefing, and they both felt that the public needed to be reassured that we had something new in the pipeline, you know, to reassure the folks and get them think about flying again. So they disregarded my order and leaked word of your project."

"So what'll happen to him?"

"Not sure just yet. We'll let the A.G. handle it."

After a slight knock on the door, a young woman walked in. "You rang, sir? Can I get you something?"

"Yes. Do you have any more really hot coffee back there? This is cold."

She gathered his and Cammy's coffee mugs and said, "I'll be right back. And would you like more croissants or anything else?"

Jay looked at Cammy who shook her head. "Just coffee would be great. With a little cream and sugar. Thanks."

The woman left, and the vice president resumed his report. "Now for the bad news."

"Do I want to hear this?" Cammy asked.

"It doesn't concern you, but it's certainly got Washington all riled up. Remember we talked about Franklin Thorne, the secretary of Homeland Security, and how he had the job of leaning on the other defense contractors to get their missile defense systems up and running?"

"Yes, but I heard he was out of town or something. I mean, nobody knew where he was for a while, right?"

"That's because he killed himself."

"What?" Cammy shrieked.

"At least it looks that way. They found his body over in Rock Creek Park near Pierce Mill."

"You mean where Tilden crosses Beach Drive? I know where that is. It's all forests in there. How did they ever find him?"

"Somebody was out with his dogs. Dogs found the body."

"Oh no! But why? Why did he do it?"

"Well, here's the incredible part. The president said they're now searching his files, his emails, phone records, bank records, everything."

"And?"

"And, by the way, keep this to yourself, we haven't released anything yet."

"No problem." Cammy said, leaning closer to Jay.

"The bank records show that at one point he was down so low they wondered how he made his house payment. But then he suddenly was getting infusions of cash."

"From where?"

"Not sure yet. Looks like regular payments may have been made into his local account from some offshore bank."

"That's weird."

"You better believe it's weird. They're talking to his wife now and a whole lot of other people, including Sterling Dynamics."

"Sterling? Why?" Cammy asked.

"It seems there were an awful lot of contacts, emails, calls. Now I know he was supposed to be on top of that airport contract Sterling was developing, but it looks like a much more complicated relationship than just one contract."

Cammy sat quietly mulling over a possible scenario. "Do you think he was on the take from Sterling? I mean, with more money coming into his account?"

"That's what we'd like to know."

"But why would they be paying him?"

"I can think of a whole host of reasons. If they figure out a connection, a bad connection that is, you marry that with what you discovered in Taiwan about their violating the law with their Chinese chips, if that's what they were, well, I can tell you that Nettar Kooner is going to be in deep shit."

The military aide suddenly burst through the door. "Sir. Emergency in the cockpit!"

Jay and Cammy both jumped up and raced to the front of the plane.

CHAPTER SEVENTY

ON BOARD THE F-16

"Missile. Imminent threat!"

Hunt heard the automated voice from Air Force Two on his radio. He had just been in contact with the tower in San Francisco and had asked to be left on approach frequency. He had wanted to time his arrival just after Air Force Two landed.

But what the hell was that? It sounded like someone had just fired a missile at the vice president's plane. The plane that also carried Cameron Talbot. He heard the warning again. *Holy shit! What the hell? How much time?*

Hunt knew that Air Force Two could detect the ultra violet energy of a launch even if the controller in the tower couldn't see it on radar. He heard the warning again, "Inbound imminent threat." Then he heard the pilot shouting, "Mayday Mayday."

Hunt gave his call sign, "Break break. Air Force Two, this is Phantom One. I am ten miles southeast of airport. Say your position."

The pilot tried to think. Beads of sweat poured down his forehead as he signaled his co-pilot to release the chaff with the hope that the missile might go off course and target the bits of hot metal rather than the fuselage. But from what he knew of the previous crashes, he doubted it would work.

Shouts of panic were heard from the back of the plane.

"What's happening?"

"Warning?"

"What warning?"

"Jeez? Are we under attack?"

"Hang on."

"We'll go down."

The officer in the communications center rushed toward the cockpit.

Jay was bracing himself against the cockpit door with his other arm around Cammy. He called to the officer. "Stay back. Order everyone to get down."

The pilot was about to bank right when he heard the voice from the F-16. The jet that was supposed to land right behind him in San Francisco. *Now, there won't be a landing, only a gigantic explosion. Get a grip, man, you've been in combat before. You've been painted before. You've used evasive moves before. Think, God damn it. Think!*

It was all happening at once. The automated voice sounded again, "Missile. Imminent threat."

He shouted over his shoulder to the vice president, "Sir, we're under attack. I must take evasive action. You must get down . . ."

Jay interrupted. "Who was on the radio?"

Cammy cried out, "That was Hunt's voice. He's in the F-16. He's supposed to meet us."

The pilot looked at his gauges again and tried to answer the question. "Air Force Two. Fifteen miles due west of airport with two minutes, maybe less, to impact."

"My God!" Jay said, pulling Cammy closer to him in a protective move.

"Phantom One. I'll be there in about a minute." Hunt lit his after burners and went super sonic.

"What?"

"What's he doing?"

"What's going on?"

"Mayday Mayday," the pilot repeated.

"Air Force Two, repeat your position," the tower called.

"Remain on course," Hunt shouted. "ETA one minute. Will perform E-DIRCM maneuver and deploy laser."

"What the hell?" the vice president said, trying to steady himself while he held Cammy in a tight grip. "What's that mean?" he demanded.

The pilot tried to keep his hands from shaking as he replied, "It means 'Escort-Directed Infra-Red Counter-Measure."

"In English," Jay demanded.

"He's going ballistic. I mean he's flying fast to get to our position. Then he's going to fly right underneath us, and it sounds like he's going to try some laser gimmick he's got on board."

"Oh no!" Cammy shouted. "He could be killed. We could all . . . Oh my God!"

"Can he do that?" Jay exclaimed as the automated voice repeated, "Missile. Imminent threat."

"I don't know," the pilot said in a shaky voice, "But look out there," he nodded toward the right cockpit window. Jay and Cammy leaned in to stare at a far away object that looked like it was closing in. Fast. "That's not a missile. That's an F-16."

As Hunt closed the distance to Air Force Two, he cut the burners and flew his fighter plane as close to the 757 as he possibly could. Matching its speed, he ducked just underneath the tail with the American flag and the numbers 80002 emblazoned on it. He figured he now had thirty seconds, maybe less. He reached over to release the laser.

Nothing happened.

CHAPTER SEVENTY-ONE

SAN FRANCISCO

"Where the hell are those bastards?" the FBI agent asked as his car careened down Arguello Street.

"Wish I knew," the other agent said. "At least the local police are helping us all over town. I hear they've sent units to every section of every Chinatown."

"Yeah. That report said they were questioning everybody from guys running restaurants on Grant Avenue to those old men who play chess in Portsmouth Square."

"Trouble is, that community can be pretty tight, you know?"

"Yeah, but in this case, they'd better cooperate. We've got every federal agent, policeman, Coast Guard patrol and God knows who else on this case right now."

"Can you believe that these guys just might be the ones shooting down our airplanes? I mean, can you believe this report?"

"It's phenomenal if it's true. I mean, if it's guys from here in our own country."

His cell phone rang. "Adelman here . . . What? . . . Under attack? . . . Air Force Two? . . . Holy mother of pearl! . . . But wait . . . They've got defensive measures . . . yeah . . . chaff . . . may not work? . . . Evasive maneuvers? . . . Can they do that with a big plane? . . . Jesus Christ!"

He slapped the phone shut and said to his partner, "Radio our other units. Looks like those boys have staged another attack."

"At Air Force Two?" the other agent almost shouted. "I can't believe this. The veep is about the land at SFO, and those guys are taking him down?"

"Yes. They could crash any minute," the first agent cried out in a shaky voice. "That call was from our contact in the tower."

"But if those missiles don't show up on radar, how would they know?"

"Air Force Two has a panel display that shows up if it's under attack in any way. It senses things even if you can't see 'em," He called to his partner as he raced down another roadway.

"What can they do?"

"Say a prayer."

CHAPTER SEVENTY-TWO

NORTH OF GUANGZHOU

"Ready the first ballistic missile launcher," General Zhang Li barked into the telephone. He turned to Colonel Tsao, "This is a great day for China. A day that will be remembered for generations to come. A day that will begin the reunification of our great country with all its people."

He pressed the phone tighter to his ear as he strained to hear the other party over background noise. "Say again? Yes, right after the missiles are launched, we will move in the amphibious assault. Are you ready?"

"Nobody is ready!" a voice boomed from across the hangar. "Put down that phone, and put your hands up!"

The general jerked his head around to see a dozen men in uniform with guns drawn advancing across the wide expanse of concrete flooring. Their boots kicked up a cloud of dust as they moved closer to his command center. He held onto the phone and called out, "What are you doing? Our attacks are about to begin."

"There will be no attacks," the man in charge said, rushing forward.

The general bellowed into the phone, "I said ready the first ballistic missile launcher."

Colonel Tsao began trembling as the first officer pushed him aside and grabbed the phone from the general's hand. Zhang Li tried to draw his gun, but four other officers were quicker. They surrounded him and the colonel as their leader stared at the phone and then listened as the party on the other end was repeating the last command.

"Stop! There will be no launch. Do you hear me? No launch. I have my orders from the Central Committee in Beijing. No launch. You will cease the military exercises at once. Is that clear?"

He waited a long moment. "I want your name and rank. Name and rank of every person in your division. Is that clear?" He waited again. Then he nodded. "You have been misled. You will not stage any further attacks. In fact, you will report to your commanding officer . . . no, not General Zhang Li. He is no longer in command of anything. You will report my orders to your commander on site, and he will report to me. Is that clear?" He gave further instructions and slammed the phone down on the makeshift desk.

His men handcuffed both General Zhang Li and Colonel Tsao and began to push them out of the building. The leader checked his watch and called after them, "Get them in the truck, we don't have much time."

CHAPTER SEVENTY-THREE

ON BOARD THE F-16

"It won't deploy!"

Hunt tried again. He was endeavoring to keep his jet flying right under and aft of Air Force Two with just enough space between them to avoid a collision. At least that's what he thought he was doing. But he could hardly focus on flying when he was trying so hard to get the damn laser to activate.

"Why won't it start?" Cammy cried out from the back of the cockpit. She leaned closer to the pilot and said, "Can he hear me?"

The pilot turned up the volume and nodded to her. She crouched down in the space between the two pilots and shouted into the radio. "Hunt. It's me. Tell me what you're doing."

He only said a few words when the automated voice interrupted, "Missile. Imminent threat."

"It's following us," the pilot exclaimed. "The chaff isn't working. I knew it wouldn't. We only have about twenty seconds."

"Please!" Cammy shouted. "Let me talk to him." She gave some instructions, and there were a few seconds of silence. She knew the missile was closing in. She wracked her brain and suddenly she shouted, "Double check the circuit breakers. Look for the one that's collared."

"I see it. I see it," Hunt exclaimed.

"It was disarmed for the actual test. Push it in. Push it in," she commanded and then she held her breath.

Hunt pulled off the collar and shoved in the breaker. Suddenly, a series of bright lights lit up the sky as the laser sent out short bursts in a wide 360-degree arc.

The missile was seconds away from impact when one of the laser beams blinded the photo cell. "Bank right," Cammy shouted. "Bank right."

The pilot took her advice. As the plane shifted sharply to the right, Cammy and Jay dropped to the floor and held on.

There were more shouts from the crew and other passengers in back. The communications officer once again ordered, "Down, everybody down and hold on."

The missile kept flying on its original course, sailing off just left of the plane as Cammy shouted, "It'll reach its end game and detonate on its own." The pilot and co-pilot stared, dumbfounded, into space. After another moment, the pilot turned on the intercom. "All clear. All clear. Threat has been neutralized. Sorry about that, folks. Prepare for landing."

The members of the press pool were quiet for only a few seconds as they raised from their crouched position, heaved collective breaths and suddenly all started jabbering at once."

"What the hell. We're alive!"

"Incredible!"

"Did you see those lights?"

"What were they?"

"Was that an F-16 with us?"

"Anyone get pictures?"

"I was shot at in Afghanistan, but never felt anything like this."

"My producer will go ape-shit over this lead."

"Hey guys," the female reporter from Fox News shouted, "I'm thanking God for this one."

"Him and that pilot, whatever the hell he did."

"No, I think it was that F-16. See, he's peeling off."

"What did he do?"

"He might have saved our lives along with the vice president of the United States."

Air Force Two circled the airport and finally made a smooth landing as adrenaline still coursed through the pilot's veins. When he applied the brakes and the plane came to a stop, he took a deep breath and called behind him, "You still there, Doctor Talbot?"

Cammy was now strapped into a jump seat just outside the cockpit. The vice president was seated in the communications center just behind her. "All here and accounted for, major. Great flying."

"Incredible save!" the pilot said, turning around and giving Cammy the thumbs up. "This'll be one for the record books. That was amazing. Absolutely amazing." He unstrapped his belt, got up and called out again, "Mr. Vice President? Are you all right, sir?"

Jay got up, came forward and said to the pilots, "Thanks to you two." He turned to Cammy, took her arm and eased her up out of the seat. "And as for you, young lady, he put his arm around her and nudged her chin up so he could look into her eyes. "You are unbelievable! You saved our lives. All of us."

"Hunt did it," she murmured. She still couldn't believe that Hunt Daniels had flown his F-16, maneuvered it, kept pace with them and managed to deploy the laser, all at the same time. But the most important thing in her mind was the fact that he had risked his life to save her. He didn't have to fly that close. He didn't have to rely on an untested counter measure, at least one untested in a live attack situation. No, he didn't have to do any of it. And yet he had come to their rescue.

Jay leaned down to brush her lips with his, but she pulled away. He looked into her eyes, those beautiful eyes the color of a robin's egg. There were questions there. What did she want? What was she feeling? Was she still tense and upset about their near death experience? Anyone would be, and yet she seemed strangely calm. "What is it, Cammy? What's wrong?"

"Nothing's wrong," she said with a smile. "In fact, I just figured out what would be exactly right." She gently pushed his arms down and turned toward the door where one of the flight attendants was beginning to open it. She saw the long white stairway being wheeled into position. She said to Jay, "After you. And thanks for everything. It's been quite a ride."

The vice president buttoned his jacket, hurried down the stairs and was greeted by the mayor, the police chief and the director of the FBI field office. After they shook hands, the FBI director said, "May I have a few words, Mr. Vice President?"

They moved to the side and the man said, "We got 'em, sir!"

Cammy stood at the top of the stairway and scanned the runway. There it was. Hunt's F-16 taxiing slowly into position as the ground crew signaled for him to park just to the side of Air Force Two.

She waited and watched as Hunt climbed down from the plane, took off his helmet and sauntered toward the 757. Other members of the vice president's staff along with the press pool were climbing down a second set of stairs at the back of the plane. She ignored them.

She also ignored the gaggle of reporters and cameramen who were bunched up taking pictures of the vice president and the FBI director. She ignored them all as she ran down the stairs and over toward the fighter jet.

With her blond hair was flying in the breeze, Camy threw herself into Hunt's embrace. He held her tight as she flung her arms around his neck, lifted her face to his and kissed him.

They stood there like actors on a stage, not caring about how many people were watching, who might be shooting film or what was happening nearby. She didn't care about any one or any thing. She only cared about Hunt. Hunt Daniels. The man who had saved her life. Hunt Daniels, the man she had fallen in love with so many months ago. Hunt Daniels, the man she knew she had never stopped loving.

They finally broke the kiss and stared at each other. "God I've missed you, Cam," Hunt said, trying to catch his breath. "I've waited a long time to do that again."

"Me too," Cammy murmured. "Thank you."

Hunt took her hand and started to walk toward the vice president and his entourage. "Don't thank me. You invented that gadget, you know," he said with a grin.

Jayson Keller saw them and excused himself from the coterie of officials. He walked over to Hunt and extended his hand. "God damn good flying, Hunt. I never thought I'd see anything like that. We're all in your debt."

Hunt laughed. "It was Cammy. She was the puppeteer. I was just the marionette."

"Yeah, right," Cammy said, "Let's just say you knew what strings to pull."

Jay looked at the two of them, standing hand in hand. "I think that all of this deserves a celebration, but as you know, I've got a big speech downtown. And since I've seen a rather graphic demonstration of this three-sixty laser of yours, I can report to the audience that we have a proven system to protect our fleet of airliners from missile attack. And," he leaned in to whisper to the two of them, "I'll be making another announcement today."

"What's that, sir?" Hunt asked.

"We got the bastards who shot that missile at us."

"Really?" Cammy said. "But that's fantastic!"

"I first have to talk to the president and see whether we got the bosses too. I expect we still have a bit of mopping up to do."

"If it really was the Chinese, do you think you can get them to make amends and restitution for all the other attacks?" Cammy asked.

"Either that or . . . well, I'll let the president handle that one." Jay looked at them again and said, "Well, it looks like you two could stand some down time after all of this. Hunt, why don't you take a few days? I'm sure the NSC will be able to function without you for a while. A short while, that is. And as for you, Dr. Talbot, you deserve not only a few days off, you deserve a God damn medal!"

Cammy didn't respond. She merely blushed.

"Thank you, sir," Hunt said as he gazed at Cammy and squeezed her hand. "I do have a few plans in mind."

Jay took one more look at Cammy and realized that it was probably the first time in his life that he had played a game and lost. He gave a mock salute to Hunt and said, "Take care of her."

CHAPTER SEVENTY-FOUR

EN ROUTE TO SAN FRANCISCO

The vice president's motorcade pulled out of the airport and made its way to the Bayshore Freeway. There were Secret Service vans in front and behind his car, followed by several staff cars and finally the press pool. Jayson sat in the back seat hurriedly jotting words on the margin of his upcoming speech. His chief of staff sat next to him. His press secretary was perched on the jump seat.

"Sir?" the press aide said, handing him a series of four by six cards.

"Yes?"

"You might want to incorporate these notes. They won't be on the prompter, but they should fit right in. The press pool that was on the plane is back there scrambling to get whatever they think they know, or saw, on the news feeds. Then they'll be showing up, along with the local boys, to record your speech in the city. Getting a first-hand account will be terrific coverage. So now, this first card would be your opening statement about your . . . our, I guess . . . miraculous escape with the help of Dr. Talbot's technology. You know, give her a big plug. The second card is about Col. Hunt Daniels and how he executed that maneuver and deployed the laser, the one the president should be announcing any minute now."

Jay nodded as his staffer continued. "Then the next card is a about catching the bad guys . . . uh . . . terrorists, although I'm not sure if you should use this until it's cleared."

"Right. I need to speak to speak to the president if I can get him now," Jay said, reaching for his cell phone. He dialed a number and hit the switch to encrypt the call. The president's secretary asked him to wait a moment. She had barely put him on hold when he heard the president's voice.

"Welcome to the world of the living! I was tied in to the tower and heard the whole exchange. Damn, Jay, what a story!"

Jay chuckled, "Yes. I suppose I could say 'you should have been there.' But it's best that you weren't."

"So tell me, you're okay? Dr. Talbot's okay? No injuries or anything?"

"As far as I know, everyone came through it. I can't speak to their blood pressure though."

The president chuckled as Jay continued. "I'm in the car heading to the Commonwealth Club. But I don't want to say too much until you make the announcement."

"We've got the technicians in here right now setting up for a short speech. I'm scheduled to go live in ten minutes. I'll thank Dr. Talbot and Hunt Daniels. Oh, by the way, where are they? I want to thank them personally."

"Actually, I don't know. After all they've been through, I told Hunt to take a few days off. Looked to me like they were going somewhere to unwind."

"That's exactly what they should be doing. What a feat though. I didn't know the boy could fly like that."

"I didn't either. Took a lot of guts to pull off that E-DIRCM maneuver, though. Looked like something you'd only see in a movie with special effects."

"I'll bet. Well, never mind. I'll get a hold of them later. Right now I've got my people writing a quick statement about how the laser saved Air Force Two and all on board. So you can incorporate that story into your speech. After all, a first person account will have that audience eating out of your hand. But I don't want to say anything about catching those three guys in San Francisco just yet. The agents had their license number and got them as they were leaving some place in San Bruno. That's where they launched that missile, right out of the sunroof of a God damned SUV. Can you believe that?"

"That must be how they did it all the other times too."

"I'm still waiting for a report from Janis about whether they've rounded up the other cells, especially the ones in Boston and right here in Washington. And then after I get off the air, I'm calling the president of China again because I see that those military exercises have been stopped, but I want to be damn sure that factory we saw on Borealis is leveled and the people who ordered the attacks have been arrested. We still have a lot of loose ends to tie up, so let's just concentrate on the laser, how we can now protect our planes and how our economy should recover soon."

"Got it! But you say you're going to call back about that missile factory? What if it turns out that the Central Committee knew about this whole thing all along? Or, if they didn't know, what if they won't take responsibility? Then what?"

"Well, I sure hope their president doesn't go through one of those, 'I was shocked . . . shocked . . .' routines."

"Yeah. I can just see a Claude Raines moment here."

The president chuckled and simply said. "Stay tuned."

CHAPTER SEVENTY-FIVE

SAUSALITO, CALIFORNIA

"I have a friend who told me once that 'Life is not measured by the number of breaths we take, but by the moments that take our breath away,' and that little stunt of yours sure took my breath away," Cammy said as she leaned over and squeezed Hunt's hand.

He was driving across the Golden Gate Bridge toward the first town on the right. He flicked on his blinker, took the turnoff to Sausalito and started down a winding road to the village.

"It was all your doing, my lady," Hunt said with a grin.

"Oh no! Listen, when I heard you say you were going to hook up with us, the first thought I had was that you were going to get yourself killed. Like Alexander Hamilton going to Weehawken."

"Not really. I knew I had the laser and besides, if Hamilton had the same kind of shield, Aaron Burr never would have nailed him."

Cammy laughed and shook her head.

Hunt went on. "Now think about it, Cam. You had the idea about missile defense."

"That was an idea I got from my father who heard it in President Reagan's speech. Dad told me about it when I was nine," she reminded him. "I just sort of expanded on the concept."

"Okay. So you had this idea, and you ran with it. Ideas do have consequences, you know. Your first idea, Q-3, means that nobody in his right mind is going to lob a cruise missile at our people, or our allies, because now it can be taken over and re-directed. And your second idea, the three-sixty laser, means that no terrorist group is going to be able to blow our planes out of the sky. No more crazy gambits by crazy gamblers."

"Because of my gadget," Cammy quipped. Then she gazed out the car window at the sight of San Francisco Bay where a group of small sailboats had hoisted their spinnakers and were heading toward Angel Island.

The wind was kicking up white caps, and she knew the sailors would have a challenging time as they hit the currents in Raccoon Strait that ran between the island and Tiburon. "I'm just so happy to be with you. And . . . I'm happy to be back here in the Bay area. You know we spent a lot of time here on weekends when my dad was posted at Travis."

"Yeah, I remember you talked about that. This really is a fabulous place. See that restaurant over there on that dock?"

"Sure. I know that one. It used to be called The Trident years ago. I think the Kingston Trio group was involved in it way back."

"Really? Sure has a great view right over the water. Maybe we'll go there for dinner tonight. What do you think?"

"I'd love that. There's another story I heard about the place. It happened a long time ago."

"What's that?" Hunt asked, continuing his drive down the main street of the colorful town.

"Well, I heard that late one Saturday night, the staff had closed the place. They were counting the money when all of a sudden these guys climbed out of the water over the deck and burst inside. They were wearing wet suits, goggles and they had swim fins, the whole get-up. They held up the place, took all the money, dove back into the Bay and evidently swam out to some boat. Nobody ever caught them."

Hunt laughed. "That's pretty clever."

"Not half as clever as you were in that F-16 today," Cammy said with a smile. "And when word gets around about that little maneuver you pulled off, I'll bet you get a promotion."

Hunt shrugged. "Well, maybe. But at least I don't think I'll ever be relegated to doing the elevator briefings at the Pentagon."

"Elevator briefings?"

"Yeah. They always have a guy on the staff of the joint chiefs. You know, the top officers who are too busy to read their briefing papers. So the staff guy has to read everything. Then when he's in the elevator with them, going to whatever event it is, he gives them a thirty-second briefing. He has to compress all the facts into whatever the general is supposed to know at the time."

Cammy burst out laughing. "I always wondered how they kept up with everything."

Hunt was reaching the north end of town. He turned to the right and headed toward the water.

"Where are we going?" Cammy asked. "You wouldn't tell me before."

"Remember Pete Feldman, at Travis?"

"Well, sure."

Hunt fished in his pocket and held up a key. "He gave me this key to his weekend place. Told me to take you there. Uh, I mean, if we worked it all out. He thought you'd like it." Hunt pulled the car into a parking space, hopped out and came around to open Cammy's door. "Let's grab the bags and see what this place is like."

Cammy took her shoulder bag and computer case while Hunt handled both of their carry-ons. He said, "Follow me." He led her out to a dock. They walked along until he found a number and pointed to a modern two-story houseboat painted blue and white.

Hunt walked with her down a small gang plank. They climbed on board, and he fit the key into a tall door. "Voila."

"Oh, wow, this is gorgeous," Cammy said stepping onto the polished wood floor and gazing out the tall windows. The light was almost violet as it glinted off the water. Along the walls, there were two couches covered in off white duck fabric and a large wooden coffee table in the shape of a wheel.

To the left was a wooden table and four chairs with blue and white striped cushions. A small modern kitchen was just beyond the dining table, and a small circular staircase led to the upper deck.

Hunt dropped the bags and took her hand. "First of all, let's turn off our cell phones for once. I think we deserve a little time away from . . . whatever there is."

She grinned, pulled hers out of her purse and switched it off."

He turned off his regular cell along with his blue secure phone and left them on the dining table. He took her hand and said, "C'mon. Let's see what upstairs."

They wound their way up the little stairway and found themselves in a large room with a king size bed covered with a navy blue comforter and a half dozen blue and white throw pillows with little anchors in the pattern. The down filled pillows were lined up next to the headboard.

"This is charming. The guy has great taste," Cammy said as she sat down on the bed and motioned Hunt to sit down beside her.

That's all the invitation he needed. He kicked off his shoes, sat down and pulled her into his arms. They lay back against the pillows. He pulled off her headband and tossed it on a bedside table. He smoothed a few wisps of strawberry blond hair away from her forehead, leaned down and kissed her.

She wound her arms around his neck as he deepened the kiss. He had waited so long to have her in his arms again. Too long. On the drive from the airport, he had told her his stories about being sent to Russia and South Korea, about meeting with arms dealers and all sorts of other thugs in his search for nuclear weapons on the black market.

He told her how he was afraid he might never get out of there and how he didn't want to make her wait for him in case the mob bosses decided to get rid of him altogether.

He told her about finally coming back to Washington and wanting to pick up where they left off, but then realized he should have figured out a way to explain the long absence. And he told her how he was afraid the vice president was making a play for her and how he wasn't sure he could compete with somebody like Jayson Keller.

She had listened intently and said it didn't matter now. She said that while Jayson was a good man, it never really went anywhere because all she could think about was Hunt. She admitted that she was devastated when he left and had decided that she didn't want to be hurt again, so she had put up a pretty strong wall between them. But then when he got into that F-16 and risked his life to save her, save all of them, she realized she had never stopped loving him and she was petrified he would be killed.

By the time they had crossed the Golden Gate Bridge, they were laughing and holding hands, and he was being very cagey about where they were going.

Now they were here in this gorgeous houseboat with nothing but time on their hands. Time to show her how much he had missed her, how much she meant to him, how much he loved her.

He leaned down, inhaled the scent of vanilla in her hair and once again kissed her deeply. He couldn't hold back any longer. Cameron Talbot was his once more.

CHAPTER SEVENTY-SIX

THE WHITE HOUSE

"Sir, I have the president of China on the line," the secretary said.

"Thank you. We'll take it in here. The president reached for one of the phones on the polished desk in the Oval Office and nodded to the interpreter sitting to his left. The chief of staff handed his boss another note, and the president glanced again at his talking points as he lifted the handset.

He greeted the Chinese leader formally and then began to outline the entire case they had built against the People's Republic of China. First, the president told him that FBI agents had arrested a nest of Chinese terrorists in San Francisco who had been given instructions by a general in China to shoot down several of our unarmed airplanes in U.S. territory, specifically the cargo plane carrying the Bandaq employees as well as Air Force Two earlier that very day.

He went on to say that the FBI was now in the process of rounding up additional Chinese agents in both Washington and Boston who had also committed acts of terrorism aimed at airplanes as well as civilian targets on the ground.

Next he demanded an apology and full restitution to the families of every innocent victim of their heinous crimes. Pausing just long enough for the interpreter to translate, but not giving the Chinese president a chance to interrupt, he went on to make his next demand.

"We now believe that the stealth missiles that were used to shoot down our airplanes were manufactured in Eastern China just north of Guangzhou and we want those factories destroyed immediately," the president said. "After we have those assurances, I will be sending a special envoy to Beijing to set up formal talks regarding several areas that need immediate attention such as cooperation on a host of national security issues including the handling North Korea and Iran, trade issues focusing on copyright infringement and currency manipulation, as well as several projects we need to pursue as partners for the development of additional energy resources

"Finally, we will pursue full membership for Taiwan in the United Nations." He sat back in his leather chair and waited for the reply while the translator quickly relayed the entire message.

"I understand, Mr. President," the Chinese leader began. "First I want to offer my profound apologies for the actions of these rogue agents and the actions of the completely unauthorized military group issuing those orders. They had been operating under the mistaken belief that all of China would rise and support their actions once it was learned that their aim was to distract, if I may use such a simple word, yes, distract the United States from responding when they staged an attack on Taiwan in an effort to reunite our country."

"We believe in peaceful measures only," the president interrupted.

"Yes, we know. And we too believe that peaceful dialogue is the best way to work with our brothers on the island. But I digress. I want you to know that I only learned of this entire matter a few hours ago, but I have taken immediate steps to rectify the situation. Military exercises have ceased, the entire military contingent near Guangzhou has been arrested. They will be brought to trial. As for your special envoy, we will welcome him and begin the process of negotiation and cooperation in areas we determine could be fruitful."

"And the missile factories?" the president pressed.

The Chinese leader paused for a moment, waiting once more for the translation and then said, "If you will simply examine the latest film from your *Borealis* aircraft, you will see that those factories have already been destroyed."

The president was dumb-founded. *Borealis* was a top secret black program. Most of the officers in the Pentagon didn't even know it existed.

He glanced over at his chief of staff with a questioning look. His aide held up both hands and shook his head. Finally, the president said, "I don't know what you mean."

"Please, Mr. President. It's all right. We are on the same side . . . at least for now."

CHAPTER SEVENTY-SEVEN

THE WHITE HOUSE

The following day the president's secretary walked into the Oval Office through her side entrance carrying a stack of papers. "Sir, here is your expanded schedule, along with the latest cleared version of your speech to the joint session of Congress tonight."

The president looked up, reached for the documents, and with a broad smile he said, "I assume you've seen that the market is up five-hundred points."

"Yes, sir. And still rising," she said. "I also saw that Bandaq's stock has hit an all-time high."

"As well it should," he replied. "Wish I could own some of it."

"Now, sir, you know that all of your assets are in a blind trust," she said with mock dismay.

"Of course they are," he said with a sigh. "Speaking of things I can't control, I haven't been able to find out where Colonel Daniels and Doctor Talbot are. I wanted to have them in the audience tonight. Up in the balcony. Then I could recognize them when I lay out our new program for national security. Well, you know the drill."

"Yes, Mr. President."

"So where are they? You'd think that the entire federal government along with our legendary White House operators would be able to find two people who are somewhere right here in the United States," he said with a note of frustration.

"Yes, sir. One would think so. In fact . . ."

"In fact, what?" he asked.

"In fact, I believe this is the first time our operators have not been able to find someone you had specifically asked them to find . . . uh . . . sir."

"I think you're right. Well, tell them to keep trying. We still have a few hours to get them into position.

"It's just that no one seems to know their position, sir," she said with the beginning of a smile.

"What are you grinning at?" the president said.

"After all they've been through, I just hope they're position is somewhere . . . well, some place where they're enjoying a little liberty right now."

"Liberty," the president repeated.

"Oh, and that reminds me," she said. "That's the name they gave the new baby."

"Who gave that name to what baby?"

"Don't you remember your gifts from the president of Mongolia? Liberty is the name of their new baby yak at the National Zoo."

######

What national security threat will the White House staff face next?

------------------------Turn the page for a preview of ------------------------

FINAL FINESSE

BY

KARNA SMALL BODMAN

REGNERY
FICTION

Finesse – v. "To handle with a deceptive or evasive strategy."

FINAL FINESSE

CHAPTER ONE

GEORGETOWN – MONDAY EARLY MORNING

"All non-essential White House employees remain home due to ice storm. Update in four hours."

Samantha Reid stared at the email and pushed a strand of her long brown hair back off her forehead. She knew that most everyone would try to show up for work today because nobody wanted to be thought of as "non-essential." At least she had a four-wheel drive jeep she'd been driving for years. Not the chicest car that regularly parked on West Exec., the driveway separating the West Wing from the Old Executive Office Building, or OEOB as they all called the big empire place that housed most of the staff. It was a car she'd bought near her parents' home in Texas where everybody drives jeeps.

She glanced out the picture window of her tiny Georgetown apartment overlooking the Whitehurst Freeway. Just beyond was a narrow park lining the Potomac River, its trees weighted down with icicles. To the right, the Key Bridge was silhouetted in the dim pre-dawn light where a lone taxi, trying to navigate the icy roadway, suddenly spun out and slammed into a guard rail.

Good Lord. It may look like a scene out of Swan Lake, but it really is treacherous out there. She had known a front was moving in, but an ice storm in early December didn't happen all that often, and nobody had predicted it would be this bad.

She looked down at her computer again. She always checked her personal and secure email accounts as well as texts when she first woke up, as she often got urgent messages from her boss, the head of the White House Office of Homeland Security. They had been working practically round the clock on a whole list of issues and new safety measures, coordinating with the agencies, following up on tips and executing presidential orders.

She had stayed late last night summarizing the fallout from a threat to a big shopping center made the day after Thanksgiving. Thankfully, that one turned out to be a hoax.

Today she knew they would be focusing on other problems including a new missile defense system they were trying to get deployed on a number of commercial airplanes. She checked her schedule and remembered that a group of airline executives was due for an 11:00 AM meeting in the Roosevelt Room. The mastermind of a new 360-degree laser defense, Dr. Cameron Talbot, was supposed to join the airline officers. But now, with the storm raging, she doubted if any of them would make it in.

She also had a meeting to follow up on an attack on the Metro. Transit cops had nailed a guy trying to leave a backpack filled with explosives on board a DC train headed for the Pentagon. When the Metro was built, some genius had designed a stop directly underneath the building. *What were they thinking?*

She shoved her computer aside and padded into the tiny galley kitchen. It looked like it could have fit into a train with its shallow cabinets on two walls, sparse counter space and a stove that was a relic from the eighties. Her whole condo was less than four hundred square feet, but she had gladly exchanged size for the convenience of a Georgetown address that put her within minutes of the White House, though this morning, inching along the icy Washington streets, she'd be lucky if she'd make it in an hour's time.

She flicked on the small TV set that took up way too much space on the kitchen counter and heard a commercial advertising a new drug. There were pictures of a kindly looking grandmother pushing a laughing child on a swing while the announcer said in the tone of an after-thought, "Side effects could include dizziness, nausea, muscle weakness, weight gain and in rare cases, temporary loss of vision, coma or stroke."

Samantha shook her head at the absurdity of it all, but then heard the news anchor come back on with the weather report. His map showed a wide swath of storms, snow and ice reaching from Oklahoma all the way up to Delaware, with D.C. on the leading edge.

She measured the coffee, stuck an English muffin into the toaster and checked her watch. She'd have to skip her morning workout in the basement fitness center. With the added commute time, maybe they'd delay their usual early morning staff meeting, but she couldn't take that chance.

As she reached for a coffee mug, she made a mental note to remind her boss about his appearance on CNN at noon to discuss the Metro train arrest and the shopping center situation. She knew she'd have to write his talking points, but wondered what other potential disaster would have to be added at the last minute.

CHAPTER TWO

OKLAHOMA – MONDAY EARLY MORNING

"**H**oney, wake up! Something's wrong."

Her husband rolled over and made a muffled groan.

"Really. Wake up. It's freezing in here. Furnace must have gone out or something."

"Uh huh," he mumbled and burrowed down inside the covers.

"Please, honey. I mean it." She reached over and tried to turn on the bedside lamp. "Oh great. Just great. The power's out."

The windows in the old farm house rattled as a strong gust of wind pushed sheets of ice and snow against the north wall. "It's gotta be forty degrees in here. We have to get the furnace going or something." She yanked open the drawer in the table and fumbled until she felt the flashlight. She flicked it on and shoved the man until he finally opened his eyes.

"What the . . . what do ya mean it's forty degrees?"

She pulled the heavy quilt to one side, and he snatched it back. "See what I mean?" she asked. "The furnace. Do something."

403

He slowly turned the covers back and ambled to the bathroom where his terry cloth robe was hanging on the door. "Okay. Okay. I'll check it out."

"Do you want me to go with you?"

"Nah. Stay warm. Gimme the flashlight. With this wind, it's probably just the pilot light. I figure we should get a new heater one of these days."

"You know we can't swing that now, not with the bills and all."

"I know," he sighed. "Just wish I didn't have to keep fixing the damn thing all the time."

The stairs creaked as he made his way down to the basement and headed to the back. He peered at the furnace and checked the pilot light. Sure enough. Out again. He held the flashlight with his teeth and tried to light the gas, but it wouldn't come on. He turned the valve on and off and tried again. Nothing. He grabbed the flashlight and muttered, "Damnation. Gas ain't getting' through. Must be a clog or somethin' in the line. Better check the fireplace."

He climbed the stairs, went into the living room and knelt down in front of the weathered brick hearth. He tried the switch that turned on the gas logs. Nothing. He shivered and pulled the belt on his robe tighter. "Never shoulda put in the damn gas logs," he whispered to himself, "regular ones burned fine. But no, she says they're too messy to clean up, so we get the gas logs. Fine mess we're in now."

"What's happening down there?" she called over the banister. There's still no heat coming on.

"I know, damn it. There's no gas gettin' into the house. No furnace, no fireplace. Nothin' works. Call your sister and see if we can come stay in town till we can get someone to fix the line."

"I can't call her now. It's five-thirty in the morning."

He got to his feet and started up the stairs to the bedroom. "So we wait an hour. Get back in bed. There's nothing we can do now but wait."

Several miles to the south, an underground bunker, covered by a golf course, had been built in the sixties with an elevator taking workers down to a ten thousand square foot facility. It currently is equipped with living quarters, a kitchen, bathrooms, and storage areas, all to support a massive control room where employees of GeoGlobal Oil & Gas monitor their maze of pipe lines.

The supervisor pointed to a large board covering an entire wall featuring a map with red, yellow and green flashing lights that indicate the status of the lines stretching over a multi-state area. Five computer screens have the capability of zooming in on a section of pipeline, checking diagnostics and analyzing their operation.

"Pressure drop on number twelve," he shouted. "What the hell!"

His assistant rushed over and stared at the map. "What the devil is that?"

"Gotta shut her down," he called as he hit a series of computer keys.

"Must be a break of some kind. Helluva storm out there, you know."

"Storms don't knock out our lines. Where the hell were you during Katrina, huh?"

"Yeah, I know, but . . . I just wondered . . ."

"Stop wondering and start acting," he ordered.

Suddenly several phone lines began ringing at once. The supervisor grabbed the one closest to his console. "Control room here."

"Hey Joe, that you? This is Sheriff Chapoton. Big fire west of town. My deputy just called it in, and now our phones won't stop. He says it looks like some gas line exploded. That's gotta be one of yours."

"Exploded? How the hell could that happen?"

"You're the gas guy. You tell me. I've got the fire chief on his way out there with his boys."

"We saw a pressure drop, so we closed down that line. Fire should burn off pretty quick."

"Fine. But what's going on out there?"

"Right now I can't say. But we'll get our crews over there pronto to check it out. We're on it."

The head nurse on the third floor of the small country hospital raced down the hall. "Blankets. We need more blankets," she called out, almost colliding with a doctor coming out of the neo-natal unit.

"It's way too cold in there" he exclaimed as he ran out the door.

"With that storm getting worse, we'll probably lose power now too" the nurse lamented.

"If that happens we're in deep trouble. No gas coming in, and the generator is being repaired," the doctor said as he raced toward a storage closet.

"We've been begging for a new one for ages."

"Fat chance," he said. "Generator, MRI, CT scan, you name it, we don't have it. Not in this town."

"Could you try to get some portable generators from Don over at the hardware?" the nurse suggested, hurrying along to help him.

"I'll try, but they won't open for a while."

She looked distraught as she followed the doctor into the unit where five tiny souls were wrapped in thin pink and blue blankets. "He's got to help us," she called over her shoulder as she picked up one of the babies and held her close. The newborn was whimpering. "Whatever happens in this storm, we've got to save the babies!"

CHAPTER THREE

THE WHITE HOUSE – MONDAY MORNING

amantha pulled up to the Southwest Gate of the White House and waved at the agent inside the guardhouse. He could see the sticker on the back of her rear-view mirror. He waved back when he also saw the badge she fished from inside her coat.

The massive black wrought iron gate opened to the driveway on West Exec. She headed toward her assigned parking space, giving a mental thank you to her boss for securing parking spaces for the six heads of his directorates. Gregory Barnes may have an inflated opinion of himself, but she had to admit he looked after his staff, especially the ones who made him look good to the powers that be.

After she had graduated from Princeton with majors in English literature and geology, Samantha had quickly figured out she couldn't make a living with the English part, but geology opened a whole raft of job offers. Her dad was in the oil and gas business, she had been raised near the Texas oil fields, and it was only natural that she would feel quite at home with a subject where she already knew the history as well as the lingo.

She had accepted a position with a consulting firm specializing in energy issues and when one of her op-ed pieces on energy independence was printed in the *Wall Street Journal*, Greg Barnes called to ask if she'd accept a position at the Department of Energy where he was assistant secretary. She had called her dad to ask his advice on whether to take a pay cut and go into government. She always remembered his reply, "You can either serve yourself or serve your country!" She took the job.

Secretary Barnes came to rely on her to do his research, write his speeches and statements when he had to testify before Congress and pull everything together when he appeared on television news shows. The man could speak in great sound bites and while others in the agency ridiculed his ego behind his back, the talk show hosts loved his act.

When the president asked Greg to be his White House chief of homeland security, figuring he would be a great mouthpiece for the administration, he took Samantha with him. Now, every time there was even the hint of a new threat to the country's national security, the television stations clamored for Greg Barnes' take on the situation which meant Samantha often felt like an adjunct to the White House speechwriters' office, except she wasn't writing for the president, which would have been a total head trip. No. She was writing sound bites for the biggest egomaniac on the staff. And she was sure that today would be no exception.

As she pulled into her spot, she saw the snow swirling against the wind shield. Suddenly, she was five years old and her dad had just brought home the little glass globe with a tiny house and the snow inside that swirled when she shook it. She thought about her father down in Houston and wondered if he had been affected by the storm. She'd have to remember to give him a call a bit later.

Grabbing her purse and black leather folder with some notes for the CNN interview she had drafted last night, she hurried to the door of the West Wing basement and pushed inside. A blast of warm air greeted her in the vestibule. "Good morning, sir," she said to the Secret Service agent as she again waved her White House pass hanging on a silver chain around her neck.

"Morning, ma'am. You made it."

"Took forever, but I'm glad to be here." She quickly walked across the blue carpet, past the door to the Situation Room and headed up the narrow stairway to her office on the second floor.

As deputy assistant to the president for Homeland Security, she was one of the lucky few who had an office in the West Wing. Greg had seen to that too. Hers was a tiny cubicle next to his, but she was grateful for desk space in this building.

Most of the staff had expansive offices in the OEOB with sixteen foot ceilings and tall windows. Some even had fire places and conference tables in their offices, complete with leather chairs and bookshelves. Her office didn't even have a window. But that was all right. She knew that if anyone were asked if he would prefer a conference room in the OEOB or a closet in the West Wing, the answer would be obvious. Proximity to power was the name of the game. At least that's what it was in Washington, D.C.

Tossing her folder on the desk and stashing her purse in the bottom drawer, she powered up her computer to double check the headlines. She scrolled through updates on the arrest of more opposition party members in Venezuela, trouble with the new virtual fence on the Texas border, the resignation of Congressman Davis Metcher who had been sued for additional child support by a former congressional page, the extent of the ice storm that now had knocked power out in a number of areas, and a gas line explosion in Oklahoma which killed one and left thousands of people in freezing conditions.

She clicked on the last headline and read the details. A local officer, Sheriff Chapoton was quoted as saying, "There was a huge gas fire that sent flames sky high. One firefighter has died and another one is in the hospital. GeoGlobal Oil & Gas sent their team to investigate, but they told me that so far they haven't figured out how it could have happened. We're in a real state of emergency around here. No gas, no electricity, no telling when the line can be repaired." The article went on to say that hospitals and nursing homes were scrambling to move their patients to other locations. Calls to GeoGlobal had not been returned.

That's odd. Gas lines don't just don't explode. And that poor fireman. This is awful. She remembered that a terrorist group in Mexico had sabotaged a number of gas lines some time ago. It had caused huge problems, but she couldn't fathom that a group like that would have a reason to do the same thing here in Oklahoma. She added the story to her notes for the morning staff meeting.

"Okay, folks, a lot on our plate today." Gregory Barnes shuffled some papers as he glanced around the small conference table at the heads of his six directorates. There was the man in charge of the executive secretariat who managed all the paperwork coming in and going out to the various agencies regarding threat levels and the efforts to coordinate policy, especially through the Department of Homeland Security with its some two-hundred and forty-thousand employees.

The deputy in charge of Borders and Transportation had her hands full working on security for the railroads and illegal immigration, especially the Mexican paramilitary groups who were teaming up with drug lords to smuggle people as human decoys to divert border agents from the billions of dollars of cocaine shipments coming across at different locations. Even though three had been arrests of several leaders of the Sinoloa drug cartel, the notorious group had still been able to consolidate most of the routes into Arizona, while its rival, the Gulf cartel was focusing on Texas.

Problems with the virtual fence just added to the challenge. At least the International Narcotics Enforcement Office at State was being cooperative on that one. Samantha had been somewhat amused to learn that this particular office was known as "Drugs and Thugs."

Next to her sat the head of Chemical and Biological Defense, then came deputies for preparedness, response and finally Samantha whose portfolio included Nuclear Defense and Energy, as well as keeping up to speed on all of their issues so she could write Greg's speeches and interview notes.

As he often did, Greg turned to Samantha first. "Are we set on the talking points for the CNN interview today?"

She nodded and pushed a two-page summary across the table. "I know they'll be asking you about the Thanksgiving threat and the great save on the Metro Pentagon stop. The guy is still being questioned, but it should be a good opportunity to highlight coordination between the agencies on that one."

Greg perused the points. "Coordination? Right. Good idea. Most of the time we can't announce plots that we stop because we can't compromise sources and methods. The press keeps hitting us for surveillance techniques, saying we might be infringing on somebody's rights somewhere. But when those contacts pan out and we actually prevent an attack, we can't take any credit. I mean when does this White House get accolades for things that don't happen?"

The deputies nodded as their boss went on. "Drives me crazy. At least with the nut job on the Metro, we got lucky. Can you imagine what could have happened if that back pack had been detonated right underneath the Pentagon?"

"There's an awful lot of concrete between the Metro and first floor of the building, so I'm not so sure . . ." one of the deputies remarked.

"Forget it. People *on* the train would have been killed, and we just don't know what could have happened to the building. Anyway, put that one down in the win column. Don't have too many these days."

"Uh, Greg," Samantha interrupted, "I wanted to mention something I saw in the headlines this morning that you might be asked about."

"What's that?"

"The gas line explosion in Oklahoma early this morning."

"I saw a headline about it too, but so what? It was probably some maintenance issue. That's the gas company's baby to fix, not ours."

"But there was a huge gas fire, one guy is dead, and it reminded me of the terrorist group in Mexico that blew up a whole series of lines down there. Remember?"

"Of course I remember. But that was EPR blowing up state-owned gas lines, Pemex lines and because those zanies . . ."

"The People's Revolutionary Army," Samantha supplied the name.

"Yeah, that group wanted the government to release some of their guys they've got in prison. Look, I can't imagine Mexican rebels coming up here and blowing up a gas line in Oklahoma for God's sake"

"But what if . . ."

"Forget it. We've got too many other issues right now. As I said, let the gas company handle their own problem. But now that you bring up Mexico, they announced in the senior staff meeting this morning that at least their government has those Bell 412 transport helicopters and CASA CN-235 surveillance planes up and running, the ones we gave them. Mexican police should be using them to track the drug dealers not only at our border, but the speedboats that are bringing the stuff from South America to some of the remote Mexican drop off points. Anyway, we all know it's a big god-damn problem."

"So they've got the planes, but what about tracking those submarines?" a deputy asked.

"That's another challenge," Greg said. "Ever since we found out they were building submarines in the jungles of Colombia, loading them up with as much as twelve tons of cocaine and dropping it off on the west coast to Mexico, it's just one more huge headache."

He turned to the deputy, "That reminds me. Get hold of that contact of yours over in the Pentagon and see what they're doing about those things, if anything. I heard they have a working group trying to figure out a strategy, so check on that. I don't want to elevate this to the SecDef's office at this point. But if they don't come up with some sort of solution, we may have to get some high-level attention for this one."

Greg then ticked off a number of other issues including an update on the 11:00 AM meeting with the airline executives. "That meeting isn't going to come off today. Dr. Talbot said she could make it in, but with the ice storm grounding so many planes, the airline group can't get here. I doubt that we'll get any cooperation from the airlines anyway. They pretty much stiffed the secretary of transportation over the idea of installing Talbot's anti-missile laser system on very many of their planes.

They're too broke to take that one on. At least that's their excuse. The thing is, her system would cost about a million dollars a plane."

"That's a hefty price when you consider most of the airlines are in deep shit right now," said one of the deputies.

"Get off it," Greg said. "A million bucks? That's about what their audio systems cost. And you tell me. Would you rather fly on a plane with a fancy music system or one you knew had protection from a possible attack?"

No one said anything.

"Point made," Greg said. He gathered up his papers and pushed back from the table.

Samantha closed her leather notebook but got up with a feeling of unease about the meeting. They went over national security issues every morning of every week, but something about the storm and the gas line explosion wasn't sitting right.

ABOUT THE AUTHOR

Photo by Didi Cutler

The Honorable Karna Small Bodman served on President Ronald Reagan's White House staff for six years, first as Deputy Press Secretary and later as Senior Director of the National Security Council. At the time of her departure she was the highest-ranking woman on the White House staff. She also spent fifteen years as a reporter, television news anchor and political commentator in San Francisco, Los Angeles, Washington, DC and New York City. Later she was Senior Vice President of a Public Affairs firm. Now the author of five novels, please visit her website: www.karnabodman.com